North Sea Mistress

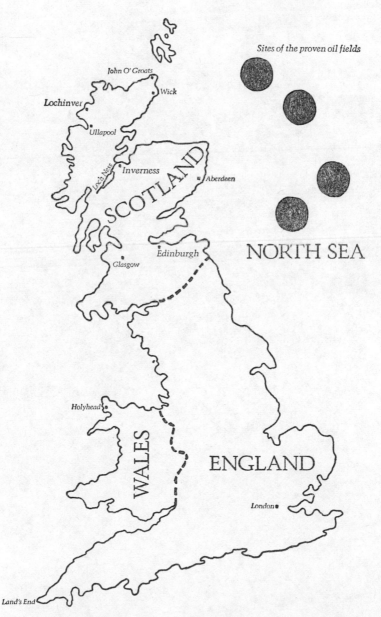

SHETLAND ISLANDS

Lerwick

Sites of the proven oil fields

John O'Groats

Wick

Lochinver

Ullapool

Loch Ness

Inverness

Aberdeen

SCOTLAND

NORTH SEA

Edinburgh

Glasgow

Holyhead

WALES

ENGLAND

London

Land's End

North Sea Mistress

Romance and Revolution
in Modern-day Scotland

By Katrinka Blickle

Doubleday & Company, Inc.
Garden City, New York
1977

ISBN 0-385-12749-9
Library of Congress Catalog Card Number 76–45262
Copyright © 1977 by Katrinka Blickle
Printed in the United States of America
First Edition

"It's Scotland's Oil!"

CONTENTS

BOOK I

I Loved Him

By yon bonnie banks, and by yon bonnie braes,
Where the sun shines bright on Loch Lomond;
Where me and my true love were ever wont to gae,
On the bonnie, bonnie banks o' Loch Lomond.

Songs of the North

ONE

The Widow Grimsby

It was in the Ness Cafe where I first met the eyes of Alastair MacLeod.

I should explain: The Ness Cafe—a small restaurant off Ness Walk, in Inverness, Scotland—was where I regularly took tea in the late afternoons. I favored it not for its ambiance of formica-topped tables and gay plastic curtains but for the generous view it offered of Inverness, the proud capital of the Highlands. I enjoyed a respite from the rude bustle of this now booming oil town seemingly grown overnight from a sleepy Highland community. Once, not long ago, Inverness' only visitors had been tourists in search of a glimpse of Nessie, the legendary sea serpent said to inhabit the black, unexplored depths of Loch Ness, a few miles to the south. Now a new search was on, in new black depths. The recent discoveries of oil in the North Sea, to the east of Scotland, had ended forever the quiet lives of the Highlanders, clogging the narrow, winding streets with rushing, dangerous traffic and bringing brash cowboys to crowd for space on the ancient slate sidewalks with diminutive, disconcerted Scots.

Yet, safe in my refuge, I could look across the River Ness, which divides the residential area from the main part of town,

3

across the squat, gray stone buildings of the city center, to the hilltop where once there had stood a castle, and dream of the way it had been. That castle (one of the many destroyed by retreating Hanoverian forces in the rebellion of 1745) recalled the last desperate effort of the doomed Stuarts to reclaim their Scotland from the hated English. Now that gallant revolt was marked only by a bronze plaque attached to the turreted walls of a refashioned pink structure. Castles seem unnecessary in present-day Inverness, and this new building was a functional police station watching over the city in the castle's stead. In my imagination, I pictured Bonnie Prince Charlie struggling to escape his grave and face this new invasion by the English some two hundred and thirty years later.

Unable to match the sudden growth of its population, Inverness had become an ugly city; its noisy, newly polluted streets were lined with garish tourist shops, pubs, and banks. It was no longer an austere and taciturn Highland city, but the headquarters for greedy oilmen. Unfortunately the Scots had turned just as greedy. Prices had skyrocketed in the past five years and there was a darker side: bonnie lassies on the High Street had discovered their own ways to turn a profit from the oil boom.

Yet I knew that I could not afford to feel too superior; the North Sea oil was also my reason for being in Inverness. Still, I could and did deplore the changes wrought in the name of progress. I sighed, and cradled the cup of strong tea between my hands, basking in the steamy warmth that took the chill from the dampness that spring brings to the east coast of Scotland. I drank deeply and gazed sleepily on the broad and shallow river hurrying past me to the Moray Firth and the sea beyond. Was it, too, joining in the race for the precious oil?

My musings about Inverness came to an abrupt end, for my view was blocked by intense masculine eyes that were startlingly blue, laughing eyes that promised life and love, eyes that begged I lift a glass with him in the pub next door. I gladly accepted his offer; I had been too long alone with my thoughts and painful memories.

Five meaningless, mournful years had passed since my husband of two months, Tobias Grimsby III, had died in a freakish

4

hit and run accident here in Inverness. A reckless motorcyclist gunning his way through town heading south had rounded a blind turn and taken Toby from me forever. The felon had never been found, for what that mattered, even though the motorcycle had been identified by witnesses as an unusual foreign make. The police had finally ascribed the accident to a passing tourist, perhaps some wild teen-ager too frightened to stop.

Toby and I had met and fallen in love at first sight in the shop of James Thin, on South Bridge, the largest bookstore in Edinburgh and the favorite haunt of booklovers and university students. I had been searching for the economics texts I needed for the fall term at the university; Toby had been browsing for a book that would clarify some minor legal matter. The result was a classic boy-meets-girl situation: turning down a narrow aisle, I crashed blindly into a squatting figure totally absorbed in a book. The volumes I had piled recklessly high in my arms tumbled to the floor. Of course, we bumped heads again in the confusion of retrieving the heavy tomes.

"Just stand there. Please. I'm perfectly capable of picking them up myself." I was annoyed with myself for being party to a stale vaudeville routine.

"Ah, an American. How charming! And, uh, what's a nice girl like you doing in a place like this?"

Uncharacteristically flustered at the silly question, and even more annoyed that I had no witty retort, I raised my gaze, intending to exit in stony silence with as much dignity as I could muster. I stopped short, however, for I had come face to face with the most sublimely perfect creature I had ever seen. He was a man in his late twenties, with his slim figure immaculately attired in a beautifully tailored three-piece suit complete with bowler hat and rolled black umbrella. Although he was only an inch or so taller than I, he seemed to tower above me as I reached awkwardly for the dropped books. All the while, he was appraising me with amused eyes that reflected the smoky color of his gray suit.

"Here, darling. Let me arrange for this mess to be sent round to wherever it is you live and come join me in a drink. I say, they are rather heavy; no wonder you couldn't hold on to them. Do you plan to actually read these dreary things or are they part of some colonial body-building program? Oh, by the way, have you a name?"

"Fiona Holden. The books are required for my course at university and I'm afraid I will have to read them sooner or later."

"I suggest later. Fiona? That's hardly the average American name. Was your mother given to reading romantic woman's fiction?"

By this time we were out on the street, and he was squiring me with a steady arm through the late-afternoon drizzle to the nearest pub. On the way he introduced himself as Tobias Grimsby. (That's hardly an unlikely name for you, my lad, I thought with some amusement.)

"You Americans, always looking the wrong way for traffic. Lucky for you I've decided to take you under my wing. You shouldn't survive long by yourself."

"You'd be looking the wrong way, too, if you were in Boston, you pompous popinjay." But my retort was swallowed up in the blare from the jukebox as I was ushered into the pub's lounge area.

"Now, tell me how you came by that unlikely name."

"It's really quite simple," I began sweetly. "My mother's father was the stationmaster at Lairg, a small village in the center of the Highlands. He and my grandmother emigrated around the turn of the century. Though Mother was born in America, she was raised to honor her Scots heritage and she named me after her mother. I've always wanted to come to Scotland. Spending my junior year here at the University of Edinburgh seemed a good time to do it."

"How touching! Discovering one's roots and all that." Toby (I had decided to call him that, Tobias was really too much) tried to sound blasé, but I sensed his interest.

"I suppose you English are above 'all that'?" I retorted.

"Darling Fiona," he replied haughtily. "I've so many roots I feel positively strangled at times."

We both amused and antagonized each other. Toby with his stuffy English public school manners and sophisticated charm seemed exotic to the New England college girl on her first trip out of Massachusetts. I, with my American mannerisms, equally appealed to the English lawyer bored with Edinburgh society.

We made a contrasting couple as we sat with our heads together in the cozy, smoky pub. My dark hair and green eyes were the perfect complement to Toby's blond handsomeness.

In the weeks that followed, Toby and I became inseparable. We took long hikes up to Arthur's Seat, the steep hillock at the edge of the city where sheep ruled and heather bloomed. We would stop to rest and munch chocolates among the ruins of St. Anthony's Chapel, above St. Margaret's Loch, with the romantic grandeur of Holyrood House displayed below us. Though I greatly admired the panorama, I found the palace itself uncomfortable, for the rooms still contained the treachery and intrigue of Mary Queen of Scots' tragic reign. I shivered as the tour guide gleefully showed us the very spot where Mary's trusted secretary, the Italian Rizzo, had fallen and bled four centuries before. The young and pregnant queen had been forced by her half-crazed husband, Lord Darnley, to watch the slaughter as the Scottish lords took their revenge on the hated foreigner.

Instead, I preferred the huge and romantic Edinburgh Castle, at the upper end of the Royal Mile, the cobblestone road that connects the two landmarks. The castle sits magnificently above the city on a basaltic plug that had once blocked the throat of a volcano active 300 million years ago. During the Ice Age, an eastward-moving glacier was forced to flow around this outcrop to form a "Crag and Tail," and that is why the Royal Mile slopes so gently from the castle down to Holyrood House.

For me, the castle *is* Edinburgh. Never taken by storm, it was once taken by stealth when the legendary Robert the Bruce and his men scaled the precipitous cliffs of the northeast wall. Today it is one of three Scottish castles that are permanently garrisoned with an army regiment. The oldest section of the castle is St. Margaret's Chapel; built in 1090, it is the oldest building in Edinburgh. The histories of the castle and the city have been intertwined ever since. Toby and I spent many fanciful hours strolling the parapets, repelling imaginary invaders approaching Edinburgh from the Firth of Forth to the north and arguing over how we would direct the fire of the enormous cannons spread about the castle.

There is another Edinburgh legend, though, that makes the city truly special to me: Greyfriars Bobby. As a child I had wept

7

over the story. After his beloved master had died, Bobby spent every night sleeping on the grave in Greyfriars' kirkyard off George III Bridge in central Edinburgh. One evening, the courageous little Highland terrier had inadvertently been trapped within the Edinburgh Castle walls, and had braved the treacherous rocky descent to the city to return exhausted and half-dead to his post. I was amazed at Toby's ignorance of the devoted dog that all Edinburgh had honored with a bronze memorial. I immediately set about correcting this gap in his education. I took great pleasure in the fact that I could teach Toby something about a city in his own Great Britain.

I loved Edinburgh. It was modern yet surrounded on all sides by tradition. It was at once city and country, where cars stopped so freely grazing sheep could cross the roads. I never tired of roaming its winding streets with such romantic names: Buccleuch Place, Randolph Crescent, Drumsheugh Gardens. I especially enjoyed poking around the antique shops throughout the city from Grassmarket to Henderson Row. Seeing the city through my eyes, Toby grew to love it also. Edinburgh became *our* city.

We traveled everywhere: twilight near Cramond's seashore; an afternoon at the Royal Botanic Garden; a Monday evening watching topless go-go dancing at the Tankard Lounge on Rose Street, Edinburgh's Amber Mile, where almost every building is a pub. When I rebelled against the Scottish diet of carbohydrates, Toby took me to Hanover Street for Henderson's "health food." Toby's favorite place was the Parthenon-like structure on Calton Hill—"Scotland's Pride and Poverty"—a memorial to the Napoleonic War left unfinished due to lack of funds. Toby said that it had been left standing as a reminder of the necessity of caution and thrift, traits dear to the Scots. I had discovered the warmth behind Toby's sarcastic façade and laughed at this statement as he laughed at so many of mine. Our days together were nonsensically eventful. We mimicked each other's accents, criticized the other's taste in clothes, food and books, gossiped continually about the White House and the Common Market, and groped for each other's hand under dinner tables.

We knew everything and nothing about each other, and I was not altogether surprised when Toby suggested a quiet wedding

8

with no guests but the witnesses present. It was too special a time to share with others.

However, I did share the news with my parents, phoning them collect the night before the ceremony. Though shocked by its suddenness, they were delighted by the announcement; their only regret was that my home would now be in Edinburgh. Mother was too overcome with emotion to ask many questions about Toby, but I gave her enough details to satisfy the neighbors.

"He's a lawyer, Mother, very good-looking and from a very old family . . . No . . . he doesn't talk about them . . . they live in London . . . Yes, yes, I'll finish school." And then my father broke in, saying that the transatlantic call was costing him a fortune and I could write them all about Toby.

Our honeymoon lasted a month. First, a trip through the splendid Highlands in their stark winter's beauty, to Lairg, my grandfather's birthplace. The town was as small as I had been told. Roosters pecked the ground near the train depot Grandfather had tended, scattering at the approach of our car. Lairg was a charming hamlet, but I could well understand my grandfather's desire to leave and seek a more prosperous life for his family. The promise of America's riches must have glittered irresistibly then. How odd that his granddaughter should find her happiness in the land he had left!

We drove directly from Lairg to Glasgow, then took the overnight train to London and a stilted interview with Toby's invalid mother, who resented a stranger (and an American one at that) in her family.

"So, Tobias, this is the girl. How nice! Though she's quite young, isn't she?" Lady Grimsby continued to speak of me in the third person, as though I weren't there perched before her on the sofa's slippery horsehair cushions. We declined her invitation to tea. It had been proffered out of form, not as an expression of genuine hospitality. We hastily departed, for Toby found the darkened rooms as oppressive as I did.

"I've always hated that house. It seems perpetually ready to depress me." Toby's usually confident voice quavered. "I was happier in our country home, but my mother sold it when Father died. Theirs was not a happy marriage. Mother was continually

9

being nursed back to health, and my father . . . there were always other women. I suppose there could be any number of Grimsbys scattered about the countryside, but I was their only child. I worshiped my father. He was so full of life, while Mother spent her days cloistered in that stuffy house. I was twelve when he died and terribly upset. From then on, I was always away at one school or another." Toby had seldom volunteered reminiscences of his childhood, and though I wanted to know more, I let it go—not wanting to upset him further.

Leaving London by boat train, we spent the remainder of our honeymoon gamboling through the fairy-tale-like Loire Valley. We pretended we were the count and countess of each romantic château we toured. Time stood still for us in that enchanted land.

Yet, as the month ended, we were both happy to fly back to our Edinburgh and to the luxurious eight-room flat Toby had arranged to be our first home together in the New Town section of the city. (Founded in 1767, it was hardly "New" to my American mind.)

One thing struck me about the apartment, and—when I paused long enough to think—about Toby in general. In our brief acquaintance, I had never thought about how wealthy he seemed. Our apartment was furnished opulently. He had given me a beautiful, four-carat white diamond. In fact, Toby always had more than enough money for everything he did, and we had never traveled anything less than first class. He was a lawyer, true, but with the kind of money he seemed to have, he either must have inherited a great deal or be involved in a very lucrative practice. I resolved to ask him about it; though, again, I didn't want to offend him by prying.

"Toby," I began one evening shortly after our return. "You are a wealthy man, aren't you?" I giggled nervously, for it seemed an odd thing to say to one's own husband.

"Yes, Mrs. Grimsby, I am. Do you want numbers?"

"No, Mr. Grimsby. It just occurred to me that we've never discussed finances, and my New England/Scots training steers me toward that sort of discussion. I didn't mean to be nosy," I added half apologetically.

Toby laughed and concluded the conversation with a giant

bear hug and his final word on the subject. "Dear Fiona, you shall never want again."

We had been playing house for three weeks (though a cook and a maid released me from its unromantic aspects) when Toby had to go on a two-day business trip north to Inverness. He left on a Thursday, one of those ambivalent Scottish March days—chillingly damp, yet daffodils and forsythia were in riotous yellow bloom. Toby was representing his family at a meeting. The Grimsby Corporation had invested in the first tentative explorations for oil in the North Sea in the late 1960s. Since then, it had been prominent in the financing of more and more explorations and discoveries. (I didn't know this at the time. My education came at a great cost.) Toby said he had to be present at this stockholders' meeting. I was unable to accompany him, as my last exam before Easter break was the next day, Friday the thirteenth of March. I saw him off, and Toby laughed as I wept bitterly over our first separation. He promised to call me immediately after the meeting.

It was a different sort of call that came that night.

I didn't take that exam on Friday, nor on any other day. Toby's business partner, Charles Haversham, went with me on that nightmarish ride to Inverness. Though strained and exhausted himself, he endured my ravings, shielded me from the reporters who wanted to question the "Widow Grimsby," identified the body when I could not look at the mangled remains of the man who had kissed me so cheerfully at Waverly Station the day before, and arranged for the body (I could not think of it as Toby) to be sent to London. He even bought me a black dress to wear at the funeral, where he was the one friendly face among the few stony relatives. And it was Charles who told me that as Toby's widow I was now sole heir to the Grimsby fortune and a very wealthy woman.

That I was rich seemed unimportant, indeed ludicrous. What had money to do with the life Toby and I would have shared? The money explained his mother's resentment, of course. She must have assumed I had married her only son for his wealth. And, indeed, one of the more blatant tabloids had referred to me as an "American adventuress." But money could not bring Toby back to me, and what was I without Toby? I left the Edinburgh

11

we had called our own and returned to the tranquil Massachusetts college town I had grown up in—no longer a place I scorned, but a blessed refuge.

For almost five years, I played the role of Fiona Holden, the dutiful daughter of adoring parents. I helped my mother organize her faculty teas and golfed with my father on weekends. They were concerned and tried to reawaken my zest for living, but I was content to re-enter the sheltered existence I had known —preferring to forget that a woman named Fiona Grimsby had ever existed. I was oblivious to the surrounding world. I was only dimly aware of the Watergate scandal and rising oil prices. My mother was the one who read and answered Charles Haversham's letters concerning the Grimsby Corporation, and she deposited the monthly checks to my account. I was barely interested. That part of my life seemed remote, and I hoped that it would remain buried with my husband. I filled my hours with needlepoint and with retyping the chapters of my father's new book. Yet, I cannot now remember what my father wrote about or how many unfinished canvases my mother discreetly threw away. At last, for no particular reason, I decided that I should travel. Perhaps I was picturing myself as a romantic, lonely figure wandering the face of the earth. (Why is that woman constantly dressing in black? people would ask each other when they saw me. The legend grew: they say she killed a man and now she must roam doing penance for her sin.)

Whatever my reasons, good or less so, I was determined to get away. My parents encouraged my plan. The romance of it appealed to my father, while my mother knew there were no prospects for her widowed daughter in Somerset.

I journeyed back to the Continent. It seemed the easiest place to begin my wandering—Asia too far, South America too obvious and Africa too dangerous for a woman alone. Avoiding Paris (a city for lovers) I followed no itinerary but drove through the European countryside aimlessly in the five-speed sports car I had rented, turning down whichever winding lane caught my fancy, retiring to whatever out-of-the-way inn beckoned me with charm. I was bored by the Alps, bored by the Black Forest, bored even by Italy's Renaissance. Then some power drew me back to the château country, to the Loire Valley, in France, where I had been so joyful five years before: to Chenonceaux, where I had played Diane de Poitiers to Toby's Henri II; and to Chaumont, where Diane had suffered her years in exile after Henri's death.

It was sometime during the night that I spent at the Hostellerie du Château, nestling at Chaumont's feet, that I dreamt that I should, no, must return to Scotland. I dreamt furthermore that I had to put some meaning to my life and that I had to make Toby's short life worthwhile. I dreamt that I had to go back to the scene of my marriage and face what I had fled.

The next morning was so beautiful that I decided to make my dream come true.

A tersely polite Charles Haversham met me with a dozen long-stemmed roses in the foyer of the small but newly modernized Edinburgh airport, then drove me the few miles into the city to the suite he had reserved for me at the George Hotel (Edinburgh's version of a Grand Hotel). Toby's (our) flat on Drummond Place had long since been sold to others. It was just as well, I knew, for I was beginning a new life.

My first few weeks back in Her Majesty's realm were frenetic as Charles tried to brief me on the family business as thoroughly as he could, along with the incredible changes that had taken place during my absence. After Toby's death, Lady Grimsby had tried to rid Grimsby of its involvement in the North Sea oil, perhaps blaming that whole venture for Toby's untimely death. However, in the legal battle that had ensued, Charles had refused. Acting as my proxy and my lawyer, he had insisted (correctly, I could now see) that Toby's wife, whom Toby had named his sole heir in a will made the day after our marriage, wanted Grimsby to continue with the North Sea enterprise. He, like Toby, had foreseen the possibilities of large oil strikes there and had shared Toby's dream of an energy-self-sufficient Great Britain perhaps in time becoming a major oil and gas exporter in her own right.

Toby and Charles had been proved 100 per cent clairvoyant. Energy had become big business after the most recent Arab-Israeli war had precipitated an international energy crisis. The first tentative explorations in the North Sea had become absolutely imperative ventures. The Grimsby fortune was now totally committed to the energy future of Great Britain and the Free World, as Charles so grandiosely put it. Britain could be energy-self-sufficient by 1980.

The immediate result of all this was that an oil boom was on in Scotland reminiscent of the California Gold Rush years. And through Charles's faith and expert management, the Grimsby Corporation had increased the size and number of its franchises in the North Sea and its profits had skyrocketed (as I would have realized if I had bothered to watch the quick growth of my checks over the years). Charles had even begun building an oil refinery on the outskirts of Inverness. As he put it, Scotland had become Texas, and we were the lucky people who happened to be in the right place at the right time with the right notions.

My old interest in international economics was rekindled the more I read and heard. I looked forward eagerly to helping Charles make this lucrative oil aspect of the Grimsby Corporation grow and prosper, and I felt sure Charles was equally glad I had returned. Grimsby's financial future looked rosy, yet Charles hinted one day at lunch about troublesome political clouds.

"These Scots," he muttered over *escargots* at L'Étoile, the best French restaurant in Edinburgh. "They just don't understand world economy at all, they're so . . . so provincial! They don't seem to care that it's British oil, that Grimsby is a British corporation, that the profits from the oil are British profits, and that Great Britain now has the opportunity to become a major oil nation. Oh, no. All one hears nowadays are flowery speeches about the rape of the grand and glorious Scottish coastline. No sense at all. Heaven defend us from these mad Scots!"

"But aren't Scotland and Britain the same thing?" I was having trouble maintaining a straight face, for this outburst was so like some of Toby's more outrageous statements. In fact, Charles's appearance also reminded me a great deal of Toby. They were the same height. They were both natty, with impeccable manners. Yet Charles's dark brown eyes, oddly out of place with his fairness, shone with a lean and hungry look, where there had been compassion in Toby's gray eyes.

"Of course they are the same country." Charles paused to wipe an errant crumb from his thick blond mustache. "But tell that to

14

some of these Scottish Nationalists. They are all for having Scotland be a separate country. Oh, they have themselves a great time, holding meetings at the West End Hotel, wearing Buttons with the legend 'It's Scotland's Oil.' I say, do you really take your tea without sugar or milk? How quaintly colonial."

"Hmmmm." I ignored his remark about my tea. "Like all those people who want to give America back to the Indians. I thought that sort of thing died down when the English and Scottish parliaments signed some sort of treaty in 1707."

"Don't believe it for a moment, my dear. Never did and never will. And the recent successes of the IRA have inspired these Scottish Nationalist fellows to threaten violence. 'Rich Scots or Poor Britons' is their battlecry. Why, there is even one self-styled Scottish lord and savior who fancies himself a resurrected Charles Stuart with a white cockade in his bonnet and who—oh, enough of that. I'll be at it all day. Nobody takes these fellows very seriously. It's just another excuse to sit for hours in a pub, as if the Scots have ever needed an excuse for that! It's certainly nothing for you to worry about, Fiona."

Though Charles had professed his pleasure at my awakened interest in my late husband's affairs, I soon discovered that he tended to patronize me, as if he were twenty-five—not ten—years older than I. It was as though he found the idea of a woman in business as ludicrous as he found the Scots' notion of controlling the North Sea oil. I sometimes felt he resented my presence. (I had anticipated this to some degree, and had purposely insisted on functioning as Charles's assistant even though I was the major stockholder.) I remembered that he hadn't discouraged my return to the States after Toby's death. In fact, he had avidly encouraged my departure. But I told myself that it was unkind to think so little of him. It was my inexperience that he mistrusted; or possibly he feared my new interest was a passing fancy grown out of boredom. Once I had proven that interest was permanent, I knew that Charles would be glad that a Grimsby, if only by marriage, was once more taking part in the operation of the company.

I learned quickly, and it wasn't too long before I was winning Charles's respect, along with what seemed a brotherly admiration.

It was Charles's suggestion that I add to my business experience, then, that had brought me, twenty-five years old and a widow, to Inverness, the capital of the Highlands, where I was now working at the main office of the newly incorporated Grimsby Petroleum, Ltd.

TWO

Alastair MacLeod, Laird of Lochinver Castle

"I hope ye dinna think me forward, lass, I canna he'p thinkin' yer hare a-loon. Wad ye be so gude to jann me i' a friendly pint a' yon tavern?"

"Uh . . . that is, yes. How nice . . . I'd be glad to." I stuttered the words as I stared at him. A clan hero from Scotland's history books had come to life before me. He was tall, dark, blue-eyed, and, of all things, gloriously attired in romantic tartan dress. He was not what could have been called cinema handsome—his features were too overdrawn for that—but he was a self-possessed figure who demanded a viewer's full attention. On his large head perched a cocky blue bonnet to which was pinned a silver crest engraved with a bull's-head design. His kilt was a tartan of a bold yellow and black pattern, overlaid with thin red grids. A matching wide sash was slung over his black velvet jacket, knotted at his left shoulder with the ends swinging long and free. A magnificent seal's-fur purse hung from his belt. His knee stockings were knitted in the same tartan and were supported by decorative red garters elaborately knitted. The silver buckles on his black-buffed moccasins reflected the last dull rays of the setting afternoon sun. I had seen the occasional man in kilts since my arrival in Scotland, but never an outfit as grand as this. My curiosity was aroused and overcame any shyness I might have normally felt when accepting a strange man's invitation.

"Weel, noo. I'm glad to see ye can drink yer beer lake a normal person, I was marvelin' a' the ungodly way ye tak' yer tea."

"Why is it that drinking one's tea plain seems to be an offense in this country?"

"Och. An American lassie. Noo, what wad ye be doin' i' wild Inverness? It's a wee early i' the year to be playin' the gran' tourist an' ye look the saft type wha prafers the shops of Loondun Town." He had nearly finished his second pint in one gulp, causing me to marvel once again at the Scots' capacity for spirits.

"Oh, I'm just a country girl at heart. Besides, I work here. But who are you? Why that outfit? Are you in a play or something? Is that accent real?"

"All right. As a matter of fact, it's not real. My natural accents are as bland as any BBC announcer's. But, my darlin' gurrl," he paused and drew himself erect in his seat. "This outfit, as you callowly refer to the harness of my ancestors, happens to be the dress tartan of the grand clan of MacLeod. And I, my laughing lassie, am Alastair MacLeod of the MacLeods of Assynt, laird of Lochinver, a direct descendant of Torquil, son of Leod!"

I had indeed started to chuckle, but there was something in his manner that stopped me. I was awed. No longer a ridiculously costumed clown, he had become a bold Highland chieftain.

"I really am sorry if I have offended you. I'm Fiona Grimsby and I've only been in Scotland a few months, and in Inverness a week. I'm afraid I don't know very much about the clans and such."

"What marvelous green eyes . . . dark forest green. And black, black lashes. Are the lashes real, or do you darken them artificially?"

"Huh?" This abrupt change in tone and conversation had caught me by surprise. "Uh—no, I don't use makeup."

"Good. They're MacKenzie eyes. You're a MacKenzie."

"As a matter of fact my grandfather was a MacKenzie. He grew up not too far north of here."

"I knew it!" Alastair drained his pint and waved for another, eying my still half-filled mug with disapproval. "Now, tell me, why are you masquerading as a Grimsby . . . hateful southern name that it is. Fiona MacKenzie. *That's* a name to be proud of."

"But it's not my name, now, is it? There's nothing the matter with Grimsby," I said, more than a little defensively.

"It's English!" Alastair banged his fist on the table and heads turned toward us. "It's English," he repeated, hissing through his teeth.

Apparently I had come face to face with a genuine Scottish Nationalist, one of those patriots whose ideals Charles had ridiculed. Alastair MacLeod was the first one I had met, and I hoped he would not become too drunk for rational conversation. I needn't have worried. I would soon discover that Alastair could drink almost any number of pints and still think faster than those around him.

"I'm *not* English." I hastened to assure him on this point. "My mother is a full-blooded Scot and my father is of German descent. There, does that satisfy you?" I realized as I spoke that Grimsby was hardly a common German name, but apparently he was either bored with the subject of my nationality or had made up his mind that I was Scots.

"So, what are you doing here?" he repeated his original question.

I hesitated. I somehow felt the truth might be offensive; yet, how could I lie to that level gaze?

"Oh, I've got a job here with an oil company. That's where the money is." It was a stilted explanation, but I wanted to be evasive about my true identity. Something warned me not to tell this exciting but violent man the truth about this green-eyed mistress of the North Sea oil. Alastair MacLeod, I thought to myself, you're a dangerous man. But I successfully fended him off this time, not by being clever or convincing, but because I had used a magic word that steered him completely away from me: *oil.*

"Aye. That's where the money is, all right." There was more than a trace of bitterness in his voice. "Scotland's money, Scotland's oil, stolen from her seas by English pirates . . .

> *These fertile plains, that soften'd vale,*
> *Were once the birthright of the Gael;*
> *The stranger came with iron hand,*
> *And from our fathers reft the land.*

Sir Walter Scott," he added as I looked at him questioningly. "But that will change. We'll win in the end . . .

> *To spoil the spoiler as we may*
> *And from the robber rend his prey.*"

"I'm afraid that I don't know much about politics, nor poetry. It just seems . . ."

"It just seems," he mimicked. "It's not your fault. Spending your days among the robber barons, it's to be expected." I flushed guiltily, but he seemed not to notice. "Stay in Scotland long enough and you'll learn the truth. Aye, you'll learn."

That afternoon was the first of many "learnings" with Alastair MacLeod. In the weeks that followed, there were many such late-afternoon meetings. They were always the same, a casual, as if by chance, meeting at the Ness Cafe, then the invitation for a drink or for dinner. Alastair was not always there to meet me, nor could I always get away from the office in time; however, I eagerly looked forward to our "dates" and missed the romantic Scot if I didn't see him for several days in a row. He never suggested that we meet at my office and rarely asked about my work. He seemed to have accepted the half-truth of my needing employment to prolong my stay in Scotland. Alastair considered my wanting to live in the land of my ancestors as natural. Since he lived for his native Highlands, he did not question my presence further, and I assumed he had forgotten about the real reason that had brought me to Inverness.

Whenever I saw Alastair he was wearing a kilt, though it was usually the more subdued blue and green MacLeod tartan meant for daily wear. The dress tartan was saved for special occasions. Alastair was quite active in local politics and appeared in full dress when he had to make a speech at some meeting. He said it inspired him.

We talked mainly of our childhoods and homes, for they had been radically different. Alastair's home was in the northern Highlands, in Sutherland County, on the west coast. Both of his parents were dead now, and he lived with his sister and her husband in their ancestral castle built in the fifteenth century on the banks of Loch Assynt.

"It's a splendid place. The best view of Lochinver is the first as you're driving along the one-lane road. You follow the curve of the loch and just when you've given up hope of ever seeing anything but fields and sheep, the road suddenly turns and there is the watchtower standing tall and proud. All of a sudden it's there. A magic castle in the midst of the low, rolling heather. We've completely restored that tower. It's the same as in the days of the clan's glory. And we've been working on the rest of the castle, but it goes slow. Proper restoration takes a lot of silver and my little sister, Mhari, was most stubborn about marrying a poor man." Alastair had explained that though Mhari was spelled with an Mh, it was pronounced "Var-rē." "But, then, there's little money in the Highlands, though there's other riches. Ian Nicolson, that's my brother-in-law, loves Lochinver as much as we do. His clan, the MacNicols, ruled Assynt until the fifteenth century, when Torquil married the daughter of the last MacNicol chief, so Ian's roots run as deep as ours. Beyond the castle, a mile or so on, is Lochinver, a small fishing village, for which the castle is named. Or, as we prefer it, the town got its name from our castle." Alastair could talk for hours about Lochinver Castle and seldom repeat himself. He knew the complete history of his family and that of most of the other clans.

"Now, the MacKenzies, they're a scrappy lot. They were always ones for feuding with the MacDonnells of Glengarry. That went on for two centuries and wasted a lot of good men. In spite of that, the MacKenzies managed to do all right for themselves, having more than their share of lords and earls. One of them was even made a British peer." Alastair grinned at me mischievously. "Perhaps that's where you got your love of the English."

Alastair's childhood, by my American and Spock standards, had been lonely and secluded, but it was far from being an unhappy one. The swashbuckling tales of legendary Scottish chieftains filled his days. At night he dreamed of his own glory in the never-never land of small boys' ambitions. His favorite pastime had been playing Bonnie Prince Charlie driving the English forces out of the Highlands at the battle of Culloden. He had forced his younger sister into the undesirable role of the Duke of Cumberland.

"But, this time, *I* won."

"Naturally; you were bigger," I couldn't keep myself from teasing him.

"I'll overlook that disrespectful remark," he sniffed.

Alastair had taken his degree at St. Andrew's ("my family has always gone there and, besides, the university is far more Scottish than Edinburgh's"), where his chosen field of study had been, of course, history. Anxious for the fate of his Highlands, he had committed himself to national politics after graduation and hoped someday to stand for Parliament.

"It will be hard to spend that time away from Lochinver, especially down in London, but I can't sit by and watch Scotland be ripped apart by the wolves. I'm not sure of the answer. Scotland's always been poor, but now there's a way to save her. I cannot tolerate the English and the Americans turning the North Sea oil to their own advantage, plucking Scotland's wealth from her helpless hands— Sorry, I do get on my platform at every opportunity. But surely you can understand the situation now that you've been here awhile."

"Of course I understand your need to help your country, but I'm not sure I agree with the group you're working with. They're separatists, aren't they? They want to make Scotland a separate state and not part of Great Britain."

"In a way, though it's much, much more complex than that. Some want a completely separate state, some want equal power with England, Wales, and Northern Ireland . . . as your constitution provides for your individual state governments. Then, some prefer other arrangements. It's quite complicated."

"You still haven't denied *you* want separation."

"Oh, Fiona, when you've come to love Scotland as I do, as all Scots do, you'll see that almost any method is the right one. If the only way we can have some control over the oil is to become a truly separate country, then we *should* be separate and not remain an insignificant part of 'Great' Britain. After all, to—uh— coin a phrase, we'd much prefer to become rich Scots than to remain as we are: poor Britons. When I think of the time that has been spent and will be spent and *still* nothing accomplished,

I can begin to understand my countrymen who admire the tactics of the IRA. The Irish have done more with their bombs than we have with our rhetoric."

"Surely you don't, you can't believe violence accomplishes anything!"

"No. No, lass, I don't. Well, not yet anyway. But there are times when I get so frustrated I could run down anything or anyone who gets in my way. Don't worry, Fiona. So far, when I've felt that way I've done no more than get on my motorcycle and scare the sheep by the loch." Our conversation then turned to the fabled Loch Ness monster, or, as Alastair called it, *each uisge—* water horse—the ancient Gaelic name for a sea serpent.

From then on, I was ever conscious of the shadowy side of Alastair's nature. In a way, it represented a part of his life that he kept well hidden, buried deep lest it should spring up and claim him totally. That was why I continued to keep the whole truth of who I really was a secret. I couldn't be sure he hadn't guessed, but still felt a sense of security in Alastair's not knowing for certain that his Fiona Grimsby and the Grimsby of Grimsby Petroleum, Ltd., were one and the same person. These secretive thoughts would disappear when Alastair and I were together, though, for we had too much fun and talked of too many things. It was only when I was alone that I would fret about my holding back. I wanted to tell him everything about my past, but continually stopped short of mentioning Toby or my real motives for living in Inverness.

And I kept more than one secret that spring. I kept my close friendship with Alastair from Charles Haversham. I knew that Charles would not approve of my spending so much time with someone irretrievably opposed to the oil business. The few times that I had suggested hiring Scots for management positions, Charles made sneering remarks about my pro-Scottish tendencies.

"Fiona, don't tell me you've been spending your idle hours in Sinclair's," he demanded. Sinclair's was well known as a meeting place for Inverness's Scottish Nationalists. I knew that Alastair spent many hours there drinking pint after pint with his friends, but I had never been invited.

"I've never set foot in the place," I answered truthfully, only to blush when Charles next mockingly guessed I had a Highland "correspondent" (his stuffy term for "lover").

"Don't be ridiculous, there's no such person," I replied. That much was also true, for as of then Alastair and I were friends only. Though sometimes, when I felt Alastair's eyes watching me intently, I fancied his gaze held more than friendship.

"Don't forget, Fiona," Charles continued, "you are a wealthy and beautiful young widow. Half the countryside must be pursuing you. I shall have to guard you very carefully, I don't want to lose you. That is," he added hastily, "I don't want Grimsby Petroleum to lose you."

"You flatter me, Charles. I'm just a simple working girl. Besides, how could I find the time for a love affair with all this?" waving at the phone-ringing, typewriter-clacking office. Another true statement, for whenever Charles came up to Inverness he kept me literally chained to my desk. We would pore endlessly over the accounts, checking the latest figures, devising more efficient means of production. Charles's ambition was overwhelming. He invariably insisted we continue our discussions over dinner. Needless to say, I saw little of Alastair during Charles's visits. I knew Charles worked as hard when he was in Edinburgh, and though I was grateful for his loyalty to the company, I sometimes thought he fancied himself in charge. But that was only natural, for he had been in total control the five years since Toby's death. And at least he did seem willing to listen.

Once, when an advertising campaign I had encouraged resulted in an increase in business, Charles was baldly ecstatic. He had insisted we celebrate with dinner in Inverness' best restaurant. Though I had planned to go to the Ness Cafe, I accepted and wore Charles's favorite dress to please him.

We toasted each other with French champagne, and I laughingly remarked, "You're spending the profits we worked so hard to bring into the company."

"I prefer to regard this as an investment," Charles assured me gravely. "A happy worker is a good worker. And, we should do this more often. It does you good to relax. You should see your eyes. They've caught the color of your dress and are sparkling like two emeralds."

"Well, you're certainly doing a good job of making me happy and relaxed. One more glass and I shall be flying!"

"Have I, Fiona? I'm glad." And Charles smiled slowly.

Spring turned into summer and the days lengthened quickly. Since Inverness is in the far North, the sun seemed to be up forever. Some days, I would not leave the office until after ten o'clock at night, and yet it would be twilight as I walked back to my apartment.

I had said good-by to Alastair for the summer, as he had had to return to Lochinver. It was a working estate, and his hands and back were needed. The MacLeods could not afford to hire many workers. I pictured him working on the grounds, tending the newly planted Sitka spruce, Norway spruce and, of course, Scots pine trees. (No trees grow naturally that far north.) I envied him, for he seemed to derive satisfaction from working the land his father and his father before him had loved. He sent no letters, yet I knew I would see him in the fall. I had to see him! As the long days passed, I found myself thinking frequently of my wild Scot.

Fortunately, that summer I made friends with Rosemary Beaton, whose father was one of my new business associates. A pretty young woman, of the type usually referred to as "pleasingly plump," Rosemary was in her final year of university in London and had come up to spend the summer holidays with her parents in Scotland. The Beatons gave a party in honor of her arrival, and I was delighted to talk with someone near my age. Up to this time, my only acquaintances in Inverness (excluding Charles and Alastair) were middle-aged businessmen and their wives. Rosemary was at first awed by my position, but soon we chatted as gaily as any two girls sharing interests in fashion and gossip.

This was Rosemary's first trip to Scotland, and she was eager to tour the countryside. We quickly ran through Inverness' tourist attractions, so that by July Rosemary and I began to take longer excursions, out of the city. I was delighted with this opportunity to tour northern Scotland, for, except for one swift overnight stay on an oil rig with Charles which I had made at his insistence to—as he had put it—"get a feel of the ropes," I had not been out of Inverness since my arrival. The brief visit to

Lairg that Toby and I had made five years before had been my only journey through the Highlands. I was unable to get away every weekend, but we managed a fair amount of what Rosemary termed "gadding about."

One of the loveliest trips was our drive along the east coast to the spectacularly sheer cliffs of John O' Groats, the northeasternmost point of Britain. On the way, we stopped at Wick, where our map had indicated a castle. We were eager to see everything of interest, so we turned off the main road and drove for quite a while along a dirt road that quickly narrowed to two tire tracks.

"Rosemary, you're quite sure you saw a sign that pointed this way?" I was becoming exhausted trying to maneuver our rented Volkswagen around the gaping potholes.

"Of course I did. Maybe around that curve. Oh, look! There's a sign . . . 'danger . . . target practice'? Fiona, I think we're at the edge of a rifle range. Do you suppose they use the castle as a target?"

"That's not all the 'castle' is used for. Look over there." I was laughing, for there were the ancient, barely recognizable ruins of Wick Castle standing guard over a public dump.

"Fiona, that's just too marvelous!"

"I'm glad *you* think so. *I've* got to get us out of here without getting stuck."

"Or shot!"

From then on, Wick Castle became our pet joke. We used it to describe anything or anyone that was phony. If either one of us mentioned its name, we would burst into laughter and guffaw even harder when we were asked what we found so hysterical. Rosemary started to privately refer to Charles Haversham as "Wick." She couldn't explain why, it was just a feeling she had. "He's too smooth and Wick-ed," she said, laughing heartily.

My favorite trip of all was our visit to St. Andrews. During our stay, we rented golf clubs, for I wanted to be able to write my father that I had played on the world's first golf course, The Royal and Ancient. Neither of us were very good—I was sadly out of practice—but we enjoyed playing by the sea. "It's terribly good for the figure," Rosemary kept reminding herself as we tramped about the course.

I was especially interested in strolling the grounds of the university (founded in 1411), where Alastair had taken his degree. It was as pastorally breathtaking as the rest of the granite Scottish village by St. Andrews's Bay, and I pictured him there as a gangly eager student some ten years before reading Scotland's grand and bloody history far into the windswept night as the North Sea pounded against the sea wall beneath his dormitory windows. It was certainly a brooding, melancholy and unforgettable place, and I could now understand why Alastair had preferred it to the urbanized and "modern" University of Edinburgh (founded in 1583).

I had mentioned Alastair only briefly to Rosemary, for I didn't want her to innocently mention him to her father. Mr. Beaton would certainly know who Alastair was, and then it would certainly get back to Charles that I was friendly with one of the more outspoken Scottish Nationalists. Yet Rosemary had confided to me that she was in love with a fellow student of whom her father disapproved strongly—hence her summer in Scotland—so I was eventually moved to confide that I, too, was separated from "someone" for the summer. I then turned the conversation back to her young man.

August turned into September, and, as the summer days shortened, my thoughts lengthened about Alastair. I decided he would be trim and tanned from his working outdoors. Frequently I would fall to daydreaming at my desk rather than attend to my paperwork. And Charles—who had moved his office to Inverness because of the rapid changes in the oil business—began to notice that my thoughts ran in a direction far from the North Sea.

One unusually warm day, thinking that what I needed was a rest, Charles had insisted we take the afternoon off. We were enjoying a picnic lunch on the shores of Loch Ness not far from Urquhart Castle (another ruin that was a crumbling reminder of the violence of the '45). As usual, I was wearing my favorite color, green, a new suit bought on a shopping expedition Rosemary and I had made to Edinburgh, and I was taking care not to spill any wine.

"Fiona, I sometimes have the feeling that you haven't been listening to half of what I've said."

27

"Hmmm? Oh, that's not entirely true, Charles, I was just enjoying the view. It's so peaceful here, so far away from everything." I sneakily threw a stone into the water. "Oh, Charles! Did you hear that splash? Just think, it might be the sea monster!"

Charles refused to play the game. "Don't be ridiculous, Fiona. You know there's no such creature." Unlike Alastair, Charles dismissed Nessie as an elaborate but sloppy fairy tale invented by Scots for Scots . . . and tourists.

I sighed and thought of the spring before, when Alastair and I had gone to Woolworth's one afternoon and bought a yellow rubber ducky for twenty-five pence. How we had laughed when we had set our Nessie afloat on the waters that gently lapped the sandy shore at the base of Urquhart Castle.

"Ye shouldna make fun o' the beastie."

The quietly spoken words had cut through our silly laughter. Alastair and I had whirled around to see an old man, an ancient plaid about his shoulders, puffing calmly on an equally ancient briar as he perched precariously upon a rock. Where he had come from I could only guess, for the shore below the castle had been quite deserted when we had arrived only minutes before.

"Oh . . . I'm sure . . . we meant no harm, sir," I began, flustered, feeling the slow burn of embarrassment creep up my neck. I felt guilty, as though we had been caught at a schoolboy prank.

"American, are ye? Aweel, the Yanks hae nae respect. If ye hae seen the beastie, ye nae wude be . . ." the old man paused, his gaze going beyond us to the loch itself, his alert blue eyes scanning the calm, inky waters as if he expected Nessie to rise from the unplumbed depths to punish us for our sacrilegious behavior.

"Excuse me, sir, but you've seen Ne—the monster?" Alastair asked respectfully.

"An' ye a Scot!" The man shook his head over the waywardness of brash youth. "Aye, I've seen the beastie." He made himself comfortable as he settled into his story. It was one that he had obviously told many times before and, equally obviously, one that he never tired of embellishing.

"Aye," he repeated. "It was when I was a wee lad, but I remember as if it was yesterday. I was oot wi' my father fishin' i' our boat. The sun hae just rose, the loch as smooth as a lassie's reflectin' glass, when I saw it. At first, it was nae muir tha' a hump movin' down the loch, too fast for a fish. Then it sank, leavin' a string of bubbles a mile long. Then it rose agin, an' made straight for our boat. Its heid come oot o' the water a full six feet. A thin, long neck it had, wi' twa horns atop its heid. It was sair ugly, like a gargoyle I seen i' a picture book once. Its mouth was open an' I cude see its long teeth. I thought sure it was goin' to eat us i' one gulp. When all o' a sudden . . . it sank not twenty yards frae our boat. I thought sure we wude capsize frae the waves. We sat, scarce darin' to move. There was a giant splash, an' when we looked aboot, we saw the creature some 250 yards down the loch. It seemed to turn an' look a' us; then it vanished i' the waters. I didna ken wha' it was, but my father told me, for his father hae seen it when he was a lad an' he hae heard the tale. An' as much as I look, I've niver seen it since."

I was dumb struck. Was the Loch Ness monster real? Even if his tale had improved with countless repetition, the old man had seen something that spring morning. The existence of the monster was one of Alastair's pet hobbies (as a May Day present, he had given me a book on the continuing search for the monster), and he, too, was delighted at meeting an eyewitness. Alastair pumped him for more details and recounted, in his turn, other, more recent sightings.

"Many others have seen it. There was Alex Campbell, and the 'Surgeon's Photograph' in the thirties and then, just a few years ago, Dr. Rines's 'Flipper' photograph."

"Aye, I've seen 'em all," the crofter replied. "They come wi' their fancy getup and fancy cameras an' radar. Aye, an' the fuss they made wi' tha' yellow submarine six years ago. An' the movie people! They built a fake beastie tha' sank when they put it i' the waters!" He laughed gleefully at the foolishness Nessie has generated through the years. "Eh, it's a wonder they hae na scared the beastie away wi' their antics. An' they'll be back this summer. They're comin' up i' June, wi' their underwater cameras tae get color snaps o' it swimmin'." He shook his head and spat. "All these fine gentlemen wi' their money an' it's the townspeople tha' seen the beastie best. The wife o' the postmaster in Inverfarigaig, she saw it layin' i' the bracken. Then the schoolchildren, they saw it layin' i' the marsh na twa hundred yards frae here. Aye, it kens who its friends are."

"What do you mean?" I asked.

"It ain't fittin'. The beastie hae been here since time began, it shouldna be studied an' poked at. It isna proper. It was St. Columba hisself who gave the beastie its freedom for all time for pullin' his boat across the loch. But," the old man's gaze shifted to the loch again, "I'm hopin' tae see it once muir afore I die. 'Tis a gran' sight. It was seventy years ago tha' I seen it, an' it's as clear as yesterday."

We talked with the old man for a little while longer; then, after I had shyly retrieved our plastic Nessie, we went up the hill to the castle, leaving him nodding in the fading sunshine as he waited for another glimpse of Scotland's "beastie."

"Nessie II" now lived happily in my bathtub, one of my most prized possessions. I sighed again, for the man beside me now would never indulge in such whimsy. And Alastair seemed so far away.

As I awaited Alastair's return, I was unsure of my feelings. Would we continue to be the friends who met for talk and a casual drink? Or would our relationship deepen into love? Were we already in love? A third possibility crossed my mind and heart occasionally: would our friendship cease altogether? I dreaded that last alternative, for I knew that I had begun to love Alastair. That old, trite saying might just be true, I told myself: wind is to fire as absence is to love, it extinguishes the small and enflames the great. Which was to be our fate?

I resolved to tell Alastair the whole truth about myself. I wanted him to know that my life and work represented all that he hated. I prayed this would make no difference and that Alastair could accept Fiona Grimsby the North Sea Mistress (Charles had nicknamed me that in a rare moment of levity) as readily as he had accepted Fiona Grimsby the American in Scotland. The two Fionas are the same, I argued to myself. Or would they be to a man who loved his country as much as Alastair? Could a man determined to protect Scotland forgive me that my company was one of those pirating Scotland's greatest national treasure?

When he looks at me, he'll see his enemy, I thought miserably.

Yet I must tell him the truth. He'll despise me if I continue hiding it, for eventually he'll find out. It's better that *I* be the one to tell him. Oh, but can I bear to lose him? No! But, I reassured myself, if he loves me it won't matter. Does he love me? He must, I answered. My mind was going around and around. Yes, no, yes, no, yes. In the end I knew there was only one thing to do. To love someone means to love all of that someone, good and bad. Alastair would either love me or hate me, but he would know the truth.

I knew that if Alastair and I did fall in love, I would have to tell Charles, though I dreaded his response as much as if not more than Alastair's. Charles would believe only that I was betraying Grimsby Petroleum, betraying Toby's dreams, going against all that we had struggled to create. In his mind it would be a treasonable act. Also, I suspected that Charles would argue from more than a business point of view. Several times that summer, Charles had worked to turn our conversation to more personal matters, and each time I had gently rebuffed his advances. I liked Charles, but there could never be more. I wondered why. Perhaps it was that he reminded me too much of Toby. Yes, those late-summer days were full of worry.

The October day that Alastair returned was the loveliest of the many bright fall days Inverness enjoyed that year. The crisp sea breeze cleared my mind as it swept the industrial smog out to Moray Firth. I had hurried to the Ness Cafe for a relaxing cup of tea after work. As usual, Charles had asked me to dinner but I had begged off, pleading a headache—that age-old excuse—and ever the gallant, Charles had kindly pretended to believe me. But regrets about Charles soon left me. As I sipped my orange pekoe, I was happily reliving the first time Alastair and I met, when there he was—blue eyes glittering, grinning broadly through a newly grown, reddish-brown beard.

"Ta' Fiona. Still drinkin' yer infernal brew?"

"Alastair!" I was so delighted to see him that I nearly spilled my tea on his brown slip-ons. "How long have you been back? How have you been? You look so healthy. I love your beard. Was your summer successful? Tell me all about Lochinver. Will you be in Inverness long?"

31

"Long enough, lass. Just long enough." Alastair laughed and held up his hands to defend himself from my quizzing. "I got in this morning and I've been tied up with meetings all day, getting caught up on the summer. I rushed over here as soon as I could. I knew you'd be here . . ." he lowered his voice, ". . . just like the first time."

I was overjoyed and blushed uncontrollably. He, too, thought of the Ness Cafe as our special rendezvous. It brought us closer together. We sat calmly for a few moments, looking at each other. Then I noticed something out of order. "Why on earth are you dressed that way?" I asked, in amazement. Alastair sat stiffly before me in an obviously just-bought tweedy brown suit. It was the first time I had seen him dressed in anything but a kilt. "You shouldn't hide your knees, you know; they're by far your best feature."

Alastair shrugged awkwardly. "Oh, this. I had to see some of the oil-corporation leaders. They're all English, and I thought it best not to overemphasize my Scottishness. The English frighten easily, you know, and I was out to woo them, not slay them." Alastair shook his head. "Fiona, it sometimes seems so hopeless. They just won't listen, not even to our compromises. They just sit there in club chairs, pulling at their pipes. And the fool who runs Grimsby, that ass Haversham . . ."

Now, I told myself. *Now* is the time to tell him. Now you should say: Alastair, there's something you must know. Instead, I stared silently into my now-cold tea and felt weak. At the same time, I thanked God that I had decided not to attend that meeting. Charles had called it a "public relations" session, saying there was no need for me to attend. Well, now his surly mood that afternoon was explained.

". . . but what am I doing? Here it is, our first evening together in months. We've more important things to talk about than a bunch of no-accounts. See? I didn't even change out of this confounded suit. I was that eager to be with you."

I smiled. "I must say, Alastair, I do prefer the kilt. It's more dashing. It's you far more than *that*."

"Fiona, you'll be a true Scotswoman yet!" He reached over, and his strong, tanned hands held mine firmly. "I do so wish you could have been with me at Lochinver Castle. The summers are so beautiful there, warm, not damp like here. Mhari does wonders with the garden. You'd enjoy helping her, and she you, especially now that she and Ian are expecting their first child."

"How wonderful, you must all be so happy." I envied their closeness, for a soft look had come into Alastair's eyes as he mentioned his sister.

"You must miss your family, Fiona." Alastair guessed at my thoughts.

"Yes, at times I do, though I'm glad I'm in Scotland. Somehow, I feel as though this is where I belong." Then I told Alastair of my arrival in Edinburgh as a student, my brief marriage to Toby —I said he was a lawyer—and my last five years at home. Of how I had become restless and returned to Scotland, hoping to find some adventure. Alastair listened sympathetically, and I told him everything except the most important: who I really was. Something still held me back. I told myself it was not the right time; but why? When would the right time be?

"That must have been hard on you. You were so young. I'd guessed that something happened to you long ago, at times you're so quiet—as if you had all the world's troubles to bear." Alastair leaned across the table and kissed me as if to tell me not to worry, he was here to take care of me. "Well, now. We've sat here long enough telling sad stories. What would you say to some dinner?"

By mutual consent, dinner was our favorite dish: fish and chips "taken away" from the little restaurant. Just at sundown, with a reddish peace settling over Inverness, we ambled up the riverbank to the Ness Islands—two thickly wooded areas in the middle of the river, attached to each other and then to the shore by suspension footbridges—licking the salty vinegar sauce from our fingers and enjoying the mess we had made of ourselves. We were crossing the bridge that connected the two islands when suddenly Alastair stopped and kissed me hard, greasy face and all. We stood there a long time, each holding tightly to the other, murmuring nonsensical syllables. Then, as he cradled me, Alastair started to hum an old Scottish tune, singing the words in his slightly off-key baritone.

The love that I have chosen, I'll therewith be content,
The saut sea shall be frozen, before that I repent
Repent it shall I never, until the day I dee
For the highlands of Scotland have twined my love and me.

"Fiona. My darlin'. Come with me to the Highlands. Come with me to Lochinver Castle."

"Right this minute? I look a sight."

"Ye've niver looked sae bonnie. Oh, my Fiona, come to Lochinver as my wife."

Oh, my God, I thought, now tell him who you are! Tell him! No, this was the wrong moment. Instead I managed the only word I could whisper among those whispering pines: "Yes."

"I canna hear ye, lassie."

"Yes!" I shouted into the night. "Yes, yes, oh, yes, you mad Scot. I'll marry you."

Both in a state of ecstatic shock, we ran back to the Ness Cafe. Entwined as we were, it was difficult going about the narrow walkway, but we stubbornly refused to let go of each other. The restaurant's one waitress congratulated us warmly when we told her our news.

"Och, sae ye've finally gone an' done it. An' haven't I been waitin' these many months fer ye tae ask her tha' verry question. An' her waitin' sae patient, day after day a' this table, niver touchin' my fresh scones." She clucked over us, a mother hen satisfied that two wayward chicks were growing up.

That night, we were two carefree children making plans. Alastair wanted to return to Lochinver in a week's time, and he insisted we be married before then.

"But my trousseau!" I exclaimed in mock despair.

"No arguments. I've been too long without you and I'll not be letting you out of my sight again. You'll come to Lochinver, married or not. And you'll have to admit that it would be less of a scandal if we were man and wife. You'll find I'm a bit traditional when it comes to things such as that, my dear."

"I wouldn't have you any other way. But, seriously, there are a few things I must take care of before we leave." Charles, I was thinking. What would Charles say? I tried to hide my trembling hands.

34

"There, there, darlin', don't be nervous. I admit I've been a bit hasty, rushing you into this, but I thought all girls enjoyed being swept off their feet by the man they loved."

"We dream of it all our lives. However . . ."—I groped for the words—". . . you don't know all that much about me. There is some—"

"Hush. I know everything I need to know to love you. As for things such as how you came by that fetching scar on your chin, well—I'll wait till we're wed before I ask after the gruesome details. Now, no more. Or I'll think you don't really love me. Face it, lassie; you've been snared. Once a MacLeod's set his sights, he hits the mark."

I snuggled deeper into his embrace, feeling sure in my heart that nothing would ever come between us. We loved each other and nothing else mattered. It was only when I was alone, after Alastair had kissed me a "gude nicht," that I began to worry. To calm myself, I wrote the news to my parents, hoping that thoughts of their happiness at the news would ease my mind. But I spent a sleepless night anyway, trying to decide what was the best way to break the news to Charles. I couldn't understand why I dreaded telling him, but I did. Dear God in Heaven, what should I say?

The next morning, I awoke with a start. I had somehow fallen soundly asleep and had slept through the alarm. As I rushed to dress, the anxiety that had kept me awake the night before seemed groundless and foolish. Of course there would be no problem in telling Charles, I told myself. There was no reason for him not to wish me happiness. He could hardly claim I was forgetting Toby. He would be glad I had found love again. Nothing would change. Marriage wouldn't interfere with Grimsby Petroleum. Indeed, Charles might very well be delighted to have the office to himself again. Tying a scarf around my hair, I whistled as I ran through the crowded streets. Just a few short hours, and I would see Alastair again.

I had barely settled behind my desk when Charles burst unannounced into my small office waving a sheaf of papers.

"Fiona! Look at these figures! They're . . ."

"Charles, sit down. I have something to tell you."

35

"Not now. You've got to look at this chart and explain to me how . . ."

"Charles, it's important!"

"Nothing could be more important than this mess. How . . ."

"Charles!"

"Well, Fiona, what *is* it?"

"I'm getting married on Saturday." In my exasperation, I had blurted the words out. The carefully prepared speeches of the previous night, designed to soften the blow, went completely out of my head. I waited. There was silence. Something had to be said, and apparently Charles was too stunned to talk. I repeated my announcement.

"I am getting married on Saturday. Really, Charles. Don't you think you should offer your congratulations? Oh, Charles, you really should see yourself. One would think the Last Trump has been sounded."

"Married! To whom? Did some old American beau show up and propose?"

"No, nothing like that. It's someone I've met here in Inverness."

"Who?!" Charles must be shocked, I thought, to lose control this way. "There's hardly a suitable bachelor in Inverness. Most of our English friends are married and the ones who aren't, well . . ."

"He's Scottish, Charles." I was not pleased by the way this conversation was going.

"Who *is* it, Fiona?" Charles had recovered his aplomb, and his narrowed brown eyes fixed on my mouth.

"Alastair MacLeod. I believe you've met him. He's quite eligible."

Charles visibly stiffened. "You can't mean it," he said softly. "Not that Scottish madman. How could you do this to Grimsby Petroleum? How could you do this to *me?* He's against everything we stand for. He wants to destroy Grimsby. You should have heard him yesterday afternoon; he—Fiona," he stopped abruptly. His voice almost hissed his next words. "Have you discussed Grimsby Petroleum with him?"

"No," I replied. "But it doesn't make any difference. We love each other. *That's* what matters."

"Doesn't matter? Ha! In love with you? Ha! *Grimsby's* the reason he wants to marry you. He thinks that, through you, he'll control Grimsby Petroleum. He and his Scottish Nationalist friends. He doesn't love you, Fiona, he's using you. He wants your wealth and power."

"Charles!" I trembled with rage. "You forget yourself. I can understand your surprise, but this outburst is completely irresponsible. You're talking of the man I'm going to marry. I swear to you he doesn't know who I am, so he can't possibly be marrying me for anything but me! He thinks I'm a secretary or something. You're wrong, totally wrong." I couldn't be sure I was right, but I had to convince Charles.

"Am I?" Charles's tone was honeyed. "Fiona, be sensible. How could anyone as politically aware as MacLeod not know who you are? Your name!"

"There are lots of Grimsbys," I said lamely.

"Are there? Even if there were, hasn't he ever asked you?" I shook my head. "Why not?" Charles didn't wait for my answer. "That in itself proves my point. Take my word for it; he knows all about you. You're being deceived, Fiona. I suggest you reconsider this matter and don't rush ignorantly into a marriage. Trust me. I'm only thinking of you. I don't want you to get hurt. Oh, I can understand a passing infatuation. You're lonely here in Inverness, and all I ever talk is business. But that can change; you must know how I feel toward you."

"Charles . . ."

"No, Fiona; let me finish. At first I liked you because you were the widow of my friend. Then I grew to like you as someone with whom I worked. But now I've also grown to love you, Fiona, and have begun to hope that we would always be and work together."

"Charles, don't do this." I wasn't used to this sort of talk from him, and I felt as uncomfortable and awkward as he sounded. "Charles, you're my friend, but that's all. You know, just then you looked the way Toby would have."

"Why do you say that?" Charles tensed and glared at me.

"Oh, uh—no reason. Just your, uh, pique. Toby looked just like that when he didn't get his way." I was puzzled by his overreaction. "Please, don't let's say anything we'll regret later. I do know what I'm doing: I'm going to marry someone I love and who loves me. Don't worry about Grimsby. I'll be spending most of my time away from Inverness, but you've managed well without me before. Can't we forget what's been said and still be friends?"

Charles looked at me pityingly. "I don't want to hurt you, but I cannot, will not approve this . . . this misadventure! I urge you to reconsider. At least delay your wedding, if you won't call it off. Surely you can see the sense of that. You need time to think. You're far too emotionally wrought just now to see clearly, and there is much to reconsider. There's any number of details to be worked out."

"Please, Charles, believe me. I have thought a lot about what I should do. And I hope that you will continue things the way they always have been. Once I'm settled, then the details can be arranged. But for now . . ." The words trailed off. I was suddenly very tired and wanted Charles to leave me alone. He sensed this and, apparently having nothing further to say on the subject of my marriage, left, suggesting we discuss the latest statistics on the oil drillings later.

I nodded weakly and, as soon as he had left, buried my face in my hands. I didn't weep. There was too much on my mind to indulge in that emotional release. Charles's words had unsettled me, though I would have died rather than admit so to him.

Suppose he's right? I thought. No, he can't be. Alastair isn't like that. He's honest. If he knows who I am, he would tell me. Did you tell him? I asked myself. No, but I couldn't; I had good reasons. I sat up straight in my chair. Suppose Alastair had had good reasons, the very reasons Charles had suggested. Was he marrying me for money? His proposal had been sudden. Had he found out who I was? Was he only pretending to love me? He had admitted that he would do anything to ensure Scotland's control of the North Sea oil. Could that include a cold-blooded, loveless marriage? But he thinks Charles is in complete control of Grimsby. He said so yesterday. Was he lying? No! He *is* in love with me, I know it. I paced back and forth in my office, following the pattern on the oriental rug. How do you know he's in love with you—from just one romantic night by the river? I just know it, I answered myself. I wished I had someone to talk to. I longed to confide in Rosemary, but she had gone back to London, and besides, I knew she wouldn't be able to help me. No one could. I sighed and tried to put myself in order for the rest of the working day.

Saturday approached to the beat of my heart. I worked madly to organize my affairs, for I wanted things to run smoothly while I was away. From now on, Charles would make most of the decisions on his own and could contact me when he needed my approval on major matters. But, then, I wouldn't be totally cut off. Alastair would be coming to Inverness frequently, and I would accompany him. Lochinver Castle was only sixty miles to the north. I tried not to think of how our business trips would be at odds with each other.

After our confrontation, Charles had remained remote, and we only spoke of business matters. I accepted that he had accepted the inevitable, and that we were both determined to make the best of it, or, more to the point, to ignore it completely. Grimsby Petroleum was the only thing really important to Charles, and I knew he would let no personal matter interfere with its machinations. It was Grimsby he loved, not me, and it had been because of his desire to save the company from a Scot that he had said he loved me. I had assured him that my marriage was to have little to do with the company. One need not interfere with the other, I had said, and I was sure he believed me. At any rate, I heard no more lectures on my folly.

Several times that week, I tried to talk to Alastair about my work, but our moments together were filled with wedding talk. We were not inviting anyone to the ceremony, but there were many things to do: arrange for a church; attend the two required marriage conferences with the minister, Parson Wylie; hire an organist and, of course, buy the rings. We spent several days looking at all that the Inverness jewelers had to offer before finally deciding on matching plain gold bands. I had looked longingly at the more elaborately designed rings, but Alastair had flatly refused to allow any "fancy overpriced gee-gaws" to adorn his finger and I had acceded to his wishes. I was allowed one bit of extravagance: the rings were being engraved with our initials and the date of our wedding.

There was a freak but violent thunderstorm that Saturday

39

morning, and, though I had hoped for weather as cheerful as my heart, Alastair didn't seem to mind.

"It's said to be good luck if it rains on a bride and groom. Besides, any day that I marry you must be lucky. Your smile is the only sunshine I need." And for the hundredth time I thought how lucky I was to have found Alastair.

Getting us to the church on time but slowly, Alastair carefully drove through the downpour, muttering to himself that there was sure not to be a dry eye in the house on our wedding day. And sure enough, although we had raced from the car to the small kirk we had chosen, we were drenched to the skin as we presented ourselves to the Presbyterian parson. He didn't mind; we didn't mind; and we recited our vows as a wet Highland chief resplendent in tartan dress and a wet American career woman resplendent in a brand-new green dress (an old ivory locket of my grandmother's, a borrowed-from-my-secretary handkerchief and, of course, the obligatory ruffled blue garter).

It was over too too quickly for me. Our only witnesses were the pastor's plump wife and the dapper little church organist, named MacKenzie. Once the ceremony ended, as I had requested, James MacKenzie filled the otherwise empty chapel with the gentle strains of Bach's "Jesu, Joy of Man's Desiring."

Alastair gave me the traditional kiss, and then another, and then one more, crushing my already sodden bouquet of lilies of the valley beyond repair. Then Parson Wylie claimed his right to a kiss, and then, since I was feeling lighthearted, I bounded over to a blushing Mr. MacKenzie and kissed him on the cheek while Alastair heartily bussed a flustered Mrs. Wylie. We all trooped across the neatly manicured green to the small, cozy rectory and raised a glass of Drambuie to Marriage, to Presbyterianism, to the Highlands, to all the Clans, to the '45, to Marriage again, and finally to me, which for some reason made me start to cry.

I was in such an emotional state that I hardly recall just how long we stayed there chatting with the Wylies and Mr. MacKenzie (who told me that I was the prettiest MacKenzie ever to kiss him save his sainted mother). But soon we were on our drenched way back to Alastair's apartment on Union Street. Once inside, Alastair insisted on showing me my wedding present.

I dutifully shut my eyes, then opened them upon his command, gasping in admiration at what I saw. On the bed was spread a beautiful long silk tartan skirt. The colorful yellow and black MacLeod pattern was perfectly set off by the deep red of the bedspread. Beside the skirt lay a matching sash.

"Aye, Fiona, put it on, for you're a MacLeod now. It belonged to my grandmother; I brought it back with me from Lochinver."

"Oh, were you so sure I'd accept?" I teased.

"Aye. And if you hadn't . . . well, there's plenty of lasses who would have." At that statement, I pulled his beard, and the next few minutes were spent in some wrestling.

"Enough, enough! I surrender! I'm no match for such a strong lass. And heavy, too. Now put on your new clothes, I'm anxious to see how you'll look.

I changed quickly and slipped the long skirt on. I had always thought of myself as being tall for a girl and was surprised when the hem brushed the floor.

"Grandmother was a tall one, all right, and I take after her." Alastair adjusted the sash, knotting it at my waist. "Unfortunately, Mhari takes after our mother. She's a wee bit of a thing for a MacLeod. Och, how we used to tease her! Here, you pin it with this." Alastair fastened the sash to my left shoulder with a silver brooch engraved with the MacLeod crest. It was a bull's head, its horns affixed to two staves. Around the head were inscribed the words: HOLD FAST.

"That's the family motto. So beware, Fiona; once we MacLeods get what we want, we never let go." He held me tightly, proving his words.

"Well, it does explain why you're so bull-headed!" I teased.

"Enough, wench! Or I'll beat you!" I went down on my knees cringing in mock terror. "That's better. Now, how about some dinner? Can ye cook? Or have I married some useless lass, fit only for decoration?"

I was finally able to concoct a passable soufflé, and our first meal as husband and wife was an intimate one, complete with champagne and candlelight. We talked quietly and Alastair joked about my cooking. After dinner, Alastair built a fire and we sat before it, sipping brandy and foretelling our future in the dancing flames.

"Aye, Fiona, there you are, twenty years from now, grown fat from eating haggis." I was too sleepy to retort that if I ever should get fat, it wouldn't be on account of too much haggis. The thought of eating that famed Scottish dish made from sheep's innards appalled me. When the fire finally died down, Alastair gathered me up in his arms and with a tenderness that belied his size, undressed me and tucked me into bed. I was happier than I ever had been before. Alastair was gentle, yet demanding and passionate, and I knew he loved me deeply. I slept contentedly, and knew I always would with Alastair beside me.

The next morning, the sun shone brightly. Alastair said that was a good omen (everything is an omen for a Scot), and we happily finished packing and loaded Alastair's ancient car. I felt some regret at leaving our little apartment, but Alastair was eager to be off. I soon forgot my regrets in my excitement at the prospect of seeing Lochinver Castle.

The first thing we did was to drive a few miles east of Inverness, to Culloden Moor, where on a snowy 16 April, 1746, the bedraggled, half-starved Scottish Jacobites were disastrously defeated by William III's English army. As we tramped over the now peaceful fields, Alastair recited the verses of the "Skye Boat Song."

> Many's the lad fought on that day
> Well the claymore could wield
> When the night came silently lay
> Dead on Culloden's field.

> Burned are our homes, exile and death
> Scatter the loyal men;
> Yet, ere the sword cool in the sheath,
> Charlie will come again.

"It was on that bloody afternoon that the clan system ended," Alastair said after he had turned over a clod of soil as if looking for blood. "The English considered them a threat and even went so far as to pass an Act of Parliament disarming the Highlanders and making the wearing of the tartan a hanging offense. That act was repealed in 1782, but it wasn't until the early 1800s that the plaids came back. Aye, the English tried hard to strip our pride from us."

As I listened to Alastair's bitterness, I shivered slightly, wondering if the centuries-old struggle between the Scots and the English would ever end. In August 1745 the clans had risen when the Young Pretender, Prince Charles Edward Stuart, raised his father's standard at Loch Sheil. Now "It's Scotland's Oil" was the cry that rallied the Scots.

We drove quickly out of the Inverness area and were soon on the only highway that led to the Northwest of Scotland. It was a big enough road, with two well-kept lanes, but Alastair said that would change after we passed Ullapool, the small fishing village where we planned to spend the night. We saw only an occasional farmhouse in the countryside, and there were few cars now that the tourist season was over. I had prepared a picnic lunch, and we stopped by the waterfall at Loch Garve and feasted on the wine and cheese I had packed. Afterward, we walked down to the gorge framed by a spectacular fault and then onto the narrow suspension bridge over the chasm. The swaying of the bridge made Alastair nervous, so we didn't linger, but he was impressed by my bravado.

"Now I know you'll like Lochinver Castle, for there are all sorts of places you can climb to. I'll have to watch you very carefully. I don't want my wife tumbling over some cliff."

I laughed and assured him that would never happen.

We continued on past glistening blue lochs and white and black-faced sheep. The countryside turned hilly. In addition to the sheep, I noticed small herds of cattle. They were Herefords for the most part, but occasionally I would see an unfamiliar, long-horned, shaggy-haired beast I couldn't identify. Alastair informed me these creatures were Highland cattle or, as he pronounced it "Hē-lăn' kōōz." They were a sturdy breed and well suited to the harsh Highland winters. They also had a longer life span than other cattle; however, they did have one odd drawback. Some years, for some inexplicable reason, they would not calve. As a result, farmers who wanted to increase their herds quickly were obliged to keep other breeds; recently many cattlemen had begun to breed beef cattle with some success, thus bringing a new source of income to the impoverished Highlands.

The Highlands' general austerity was offset somewhat by the

43

rich purple heather and cheery yellow gorse, both blooming spectacularly between the strips of mountain ridges. Every so often, I'd see a newly planted forest of pine trees, looking out of place and artificial, the trees aligned in neat rows. Alastair explained that the rows would disappear when the forests were fully grown and the weaker trees were thinned out. These manmade forests were part of a government-sponsored program to cultivate the Highlands. As usual, Alastair's voice swelled with pride when he spoke of the plans to revitalize his Highlands.

We didn't reach Ullapool until sundown, for we had taken many detours along our way through Ross and Cromarty County and, to be truthful, poked along, keeping what Alastair called "newlywed time." And Ullapool is a village by the sea for newlyweds at any time, but especially when the setting sun romanticizes its charming and for the most part nineteenth-century cottages and inns. In summer, at the peak of the tourist season, Ullapool's cottages are filled with vacationing British families, and the nearby fields are covered with caravans; but in early fall the village was sparsely populated and peaceful. We were practically its only visitors. After securing rooms in the large, whitewashed hotel at the edge of the sea wall, we dined on seafood and white wine in one of the few hotel dining rooms that was kept open year round. Then, snuggling arm in arm, we wandered down the harbor road to watch the fishing fleet bob with the high tide. With a half moon overhead outlining the ridges surrounding the loch to the south, and Alastair in my arms, I couldn't have been happier.

The next morning, a cool, crisp one, we set out to explore the town and environs before driving on. Our map indicated a small loch to the east of the village, and we hiked up the rough gravel path from the main road. Along the way, our view was marred by a noisy concrete factory sending out truckload after truckload to the north, where a more modern highway was under construction. The earth was overturned, and the mountainsides were scarred by blasting and excavation. Even in this remote spot, the price of progress was ugly and sad.

After profusely thanking the innkeeper, yet another plump and motherly Scotswoman, we were once more on our way. Within half an hour the highway narrowed to one lane, a turnout provided every twenty yards or so in the unlikely event that another car should pass. We met no other cars, but we did have to stop frequently to yield the right of way to herds of sheep that grazed near the road. Alastair was a careful driver and was always on the lookout for the stray sheep who trotted on the road. But, once, he was taken by surprise when the leader of a herd spooked suddenly and cut across the narrow road directly in our path. The others, being sheep, followed suit, and we narrowly missed a serious accident, for Alastair in swerving to avoid the sheep had had to turn the car sharply to the left. Only his quick wits saved the car from plummeting down a precipice gouged out of the mountains by the construction crews at work on the highway. Once we were safely on our way again, Alastair tossed the whole affair off as a joke.

"Aye, those sheep, they think they rule the Highlands and they do. It's mostly our fault, letting them run wild most of the year, but there's hardly a man in these parts who would hurt a sheep; they're that precious. Did you see that blue mark on the haunches of the big ram? That's how we identify them. Those would be part of MacPherson's herd. Ours are marked with red. Aye, we've the devil's own time gathering them up, for they wander far and wide. Wait till you see the lambs in the spring, Fiona, you'll be wanting one for a pet."

Usually I would have asked a thousand questions to learn all I could about the Highland way of life. But I merely nodded and lay my head back on the seat. I didn't like sheep. They seemed dumb brutes, only interested in filling their large stomachs. And yet they had a cunning look, and were always watching. When we were on our way back from our hike to Loch Achall, near Ullapool, I had felt sure that someone was watching me. I had turned around suddenly and met the eyes of a sheep, who had merely smiled in a silly, self-satisfied way and pretended to graze again. I told myself I was being foolish. Sheep couldn't really smile, and they were certainly too stupid to think. Yet, the ram who had almost run us off the road had turned to look at us, and I had sensed a malevolent gleam in his eye. Nonsense, I told myself, you're just shaken up after a scare. But I couldn't shake the feeling that the sheep had wanted to harm us. And though I had never seen a newborn lamb, I knew I could never, never make a pet of one, no matter what Alastair might say. The rest of our journey passed without incident, and I soon felt from Alastair's growing excitement that we were nearing Lochinver Castle.

Alastair was now driving quite slowly, as if to prolong the pleasure of his anticipation. I found to my surprise that I was nervously straining for my first glimpse of the castle. The land-scape was lovely; to our right was Ben More Assynt, one of the highest mountains in the Highlands, its barren slopes snow-covered all year round. Deep-blue and cold Loch Assynt was to our left. We followed the road as it ran alongside the motionless, glass-like waters. Now the mountain was behind us—seemingly cutting us off from the rest of Scotland. I could understand why Alastair loved his home so dearly, for truly it was a separate world. Alastair savored my eagerness and happily pointed out many landmarks of his childhood. Though I was interested, I scarcely took my eyes from the road ahead. I didn't want to miss my first look at his home, which was now to be my home.

Suddenly, Alastair turned off the road and stopped the car, bounding out and striding around to open my door.

"Is anything wrong? Why are we stopping? Oh, Alastair, stop teasing me with this delay!"

"No, Fiona, there's nothing wrong. I just want to show you Lochinver properly. The best view of all is through these spruce trees. It's my favorite spot, and I want it to be the place where you first see Lochinver."

Laughing, hand in hand, we scampered up the slope and through the man-raised forest. Then Alastair became quiet, al-most solemn, and said gently, "There, Fiona; there is Lochinver, our home."

"Our home!" The words themselves were enough to thrill me, but that joy was small compared to my feelings as I turned to look where he pointed.

There, with pine trees thick all about us, was an opening, and through that opening was Lochinver Castle. I gasped, for I had never seen a more dramatic sight. The watchtower stood straight and tall against the early-evening sky. The setting sun gave the stones a rosy glow that contrasted pleasantly with the pale blue sky. The slowly lengthening shadow cast by the tower seemed to stretch forever, and I felt seduced by it. Indeed, I thought, that shadow must stretch past the majestic heights of Ben More Assynt and reach to the North Sea—it seemed that powerful. We were too far away, and it was already twilight, but I could still see some detail: the small windows spotted around the tower walls, the outbuildings on the castle grounds, the winding steps that disappeared among the cliffs above the loch. The spirit of Lochinver moved me. I felt its nobility. Yet it was not a foreboding place, and I knew I could feel at home there. Now I knew also why Alastair had brought me to this place and why it was his favorite, for I had been swept away by the spell of Lochinver as he had swept me away in Inverness. As I looked, Alastair's eyes never left mine. He read my thoughts and caught me up in an embrace as mighty and dominating as Lochinver's. We were one being as we watched the grays darken and the tower disappear against the sky. We turned and made our way back to the car. It was only when we had come out of the undergrowth that I was able to speak.

"Oh, Alastair, it's . . . it's . . ."

"Sae ye approve o' my humble home." His words teased, but his tone revealed his happiness.

"I see why you love it so. I love it already. But I don't understand how you could ever leave it. It must break your heart to go away."

"Aweel, I can see that it will take the devil himsel' tae git ye away frae here. Maybe noo ye'll decide tha' Charles Haversham can run things by himsel'."

Though he spoke casually, my heart skipped a beat and then pounded wildly. I stumbled over a twig and stopped. I could not believe what I had heard. My worst fears were confirmed. Those teasing words, they could only mean . . . Oh, my God, I thought, panicking. Alastair does know! He has married me, knowing all the time that . . . that . . .

"Alastair!" My voice rang harsh. I didn't want to sound shocked, so I cleared my throat and tried again. "Alastair, what did you say?"

"Only that I hope you'll become so attached to this place that you'll never want to leave. Is that so strange?"

47

"No. But you said something else . . ."

"Well, why else would you want to go back to Inverness if not for that company of yours? Or are Haversham's charms more appealing than I thought?" Alastair's words were so offhand, his voice so unconcerned. Could I be imagining that steeliness in his glance?

"You . . . you know about Grimsby? That . . . that . . . but I never said anything."

"Fiona, my love, do you imagine that anyone could exist ten minutes in Inverness and not know who you are?" Alastair was unwittingly using Charles's very words. "A woman in business is unusual. It was the talk of Inverness when you came back to work for Grimsby Petroleum. Put Haversham's nose a bit out of joint, it did. We all had a good laugh over that one at Sinclair's."

I couldn't resist a smile at that, but I pressed on. "You mean, you did know all the time?"

"Oh, no, not when I first saw you, but when you said your name and that you had just come to Scotland, I guessed then. I must admit that I was tempted to leave you at that pub and have nothing more to do with you, but you . . . you . . . I guess you could say that you bewitched me. So I stayed. And it's glad I am that I did."

"Yes, . . . but"—I struggled out of his embrace—"Why didn't you say anything?"

"Why didn't *you*, my love? Besides, what does it matter? Your money's no matter to me. Would you expect anything different? I married you because I love you."

"I was scared that, well, apprehensive . . . that you wouldn't want to see me any more. I've wanted to talk it out, I've started to many times, but I couldn't. I was afraid it would ruin everything."

"Aha! So that was the deep, dark secret you hinted at. Well, there's nothing to worry about. Once I fell in love with you, even the fact that you had killed a man wouldn't have stopped me from marrying you. (And it would be polite if you said the same about me, my dear.) Fiona, you're not like Haversham and the rest. You care about Scotland almost as much as I do. So you see, we're not against each other at all. Now, come along. We've dawdled here long enough. Mhari will have tea waiting. Just

48

wait till you taste the scones laden with our homemade strawberry preserves!"

I let Alastair lead me back to the car and I sat silently while he started the engine. Night had fallen, and the tree grove, which only moments before had seemed full of welcome, seemed menacing. The conversation I had just had with Alastair had astounded me, and I went over and over it in my mind. I wanted to believe him when he said that my connections with Grimsby Petroleum made no difference, that he loved me for myself alone. But I kept recalling what Charles had said in my office. "He wants to ruin Grimsby . . . he doesn't love you, Fiona . . . he wants your money." Was Charles right? No, he couldn't be. Alastair noticed my clenched fists.

"Relax, darlin', we'll be there soon enough. I know it's hard on you, getting a new house and family all in one day, but you'll soon feel to home. I promise."

I watched Alastair's expression as he talked. It was as calm as it always was, his steady gaze fixed ahead on the winding road. I usually found comfort in his silent strength, but now I wondered —could it be a mask? Was he cleverly concealing his true thoughts behind this placidity? With a start, I realized I hardly knew Alastair, that my feelings for him were the most part based upon my pinings for him during our summer separation. I knew details of his childhood and what his favorite foods were, but what did I know of Alastair as a person? Infatuated as I was, I had been only too eager to believe his professions of love. I tried to tell myself that I was letting Charles's hate-filled words poison my mind, but I could not shake my doubts.

Now we were entering the main drive of the castle, a well-maintained gravel road. I was once again enjoying myself when suddenly I spotted some sheep grazing by the roadside. Their hindquarters were stained with large red blotches, so I knew they were MacLeod sheep. As we drove past, the leader of the flock, an oversized ram, turned his head and seemed to smile knowingly. I recalled the sheep we had seen earlier. Could that incident have been a warning? Were the sheep trying to tell me to turn back, to go no further? If so, then it was too late, for Alastair raced the car through the massive stone gates and with a

49

grand flourish spun us to an abrupt standstill, complete with protesting squeal of tires and flying stone.

I had come to Lochinver Castle.

We had parked in a courtyard formed by the three wings of the castle and dominated in one corner by the tower I had admired earlier. The wings had been added to the basic structure at a later date, providing comfort and more room. The gray tower itself was austere: there were only a few windows on the lower levels; more appeared farther up. Gothic turrets had been placed atop the looming structure at some perhaps battle-scarred point in the castle's history, giving it all a romantic appearance. The courtyard was quite large, and someone, I guessed Mhari, obviously spent many hours there, for there was a large, well-tended garden that I could imagine blooming magnificently in the spring and summer. There were even palm trees growing against one wall. When I laughed aloud at this strangeness, Alastair explained that because the west coast of Scotland was warmed by the Gulf Stream, tropical plants grew quite well if they were sheltered adequately from the whipping winter winds. I had no further opportunity to study or ask about my new home. Mhari and her husband, Ian Nicolson, burst from the main doors and enveloped us in a surfeit of welcoming embraces.

"Och, Alastair! She's so pretty, how ever did you persuade her to marry you! You're much too good for him, Fiona, you know that of course! I'm so glad he's brought you to enliven our dreary lives. It'll be such fun. Oh, la! You must be tired and starving after your drive, let's all go in and have tea."

Mhari MacLeod Nicolson was a whirlwind of energy as she gathered us up and swept us before her into the castle. She was dark, like Alastair, but small. She barely reached to my shoulder. Her childlike appearance was heightened further by her face, which with its pointed chin and overlarge eyes reminded me of a little girl who has yet to lose her baby fat. Ian was a handsome man, the same age as Alastair. His dark-framed glasses lent a serious appearance to his thin face, and his calm manner contrasted sharply with his young wife's eagerness. Although she was almost six months pregnant, Mhari scurried about lightly,

50

taking our coats. I suspected that she would have even carried our luggage upstairs had not Ian taken a firm hand and restrained her. Mhari obviously adored her elder brother and would have done anything to make him comfortable and happy. All the while, Alastair was regarding her with a bemused tolerance, the sort with which one watches an overactive puppy. But, once we were inside the great hall, he swept her off her feet in a giant bear hug that revealed his great affection for his sister. Alastair swung her around and around till she protested laughingly.

"Och! Alastair, put me down. Whatever will Fiona think of us, and me with my big stomach! How ever can I be the sedate matron with you around?"

"You'll always be my baby sister, no matter how large you get yourself. Remember how I used to toss you up—thus?" And they dissolved in gales of laughter. Then, seeing that Ian had brought the last of our luggage, Mhari suggested that she take me upstairs.

"Come, Fiona. I'm sure you want to see your rooms. You and Alastair are in the tower. It's ever so cozy. Ian and I stay in the west wing, the one we're in now. We'll leave them to themselves; I can see Alastair's dying to talk to Ian. Tea in a bit?" This last was directed to the men, and Ian nodded absently, as he and Alastair were already in conference.

I grabbed my small bag as Mhari led me through the great hall and turned up the large, sweeping staircase to the right of the main entrance.

"The hall is the same as it's been since the first MacLeods lived here. Alastair has had these portraits cleaned. There! That ferocious fellow is Torquil. He lost the estate in 1506, but it was restored to his brother Malcolm a few years later, and we've been here ever since. Don't you think Alastair resembles the portrait? Whenever he gets in one of those black moods, I mean. I've always teased him about it."

I studied the portrait, and Torquil's intense blue eyes glared back at me. It was a brooding figure, and though the artist had not been highly skilled, the power and energy of Torquil was apparent in spite of the crude brush strokes. I felt that he had been a man of purpose and determination and that he never would have let anything interfere with his plans. Yes, Alastair did resemble this ferocious man to whom I was now related.

We had left the main part of the castle and were now climbing the winding staircase in the tower. The stairs ran within the thick tower walls and opened out onto each floor. In order to climb to the next level, we had to cross the width of the floor to the opposite side of the tower to enter the next flight of stairs. Mhari explained that the stairs had been structured this way for purposes of defense. An unwelcome intruder would be delayed, thus giving the defenders ample time to surprise him from above. From the outside, a casual observer would not guess that so many levels were contained in the tower. The rooms that Alastair and I would share were on the fourth floor. I was thankful when Mhari gaily announced we had finally arrived at our rooms. I found the narrow passageways confining, and the dim electric lights on each level cast eerie shadows on the stone walls. However, I told myself I should soon be used to them and be running up and down as effortlessly as Mhari.

"Here we are at last, Fiona. I do hope you'll think it worth the climb. I'm afraid you'll have to get used to stairs at Lochinver— they're a way of life here!" And she flipped on the light switch.

The rooms we were entering were, indeed, well worth the climb. I would have gladly mounted twice the amount of narrow stone steps to reach this haven. The floors below had been barren and somewhat dreary. They had left me totally unprepared for the warmth and coziness I now found as I looked about me. The stone floors were covered with richly colored carpets, and several interestingly designed tapestries hung on the walls. The bedroom was high-ceilinged and large. It seemed even larger after the closeness of the passage. Aside from the huge four-poster bed, there was little furniture, but the pieces that composed the room were handsomely carved and looked inviting. A fire had been laid, and the snapping flames were casting a rosy glow, romanticizing the room's appeal.

"I do so hope you like it, Fiona. I had this fire started to take the chill away. These stone walls can be so cold. We have electric fires in some of the other rooms, but Alastair wouldn't hear of one up here. You know how he is." I nodded, laughing at Alastair's insistence on rugged authenticity. Mhari went on.

"Alastair spent the whole summer fixing and repairing these rooms. He and Ian moved some of the smaller pieces from other parts of the castle." She winked at me and said, "He didn't tell us why he was moving here, but now I understand the reason. And a very good one it is, too. There's a bath and a dressing room through that door, and through here is a small sitting room. We haven't done much with that; perhaps you'd prefer to fix it up the way you like. Here, I'll show you."

Mhari crossed the bedroom floor and opened a door next to the fireplace, flipping on another light. It revealed a room much smaller than the bedroom. Despite its severity, I loved it at first sight. Encircling the room were tall, narrow windows cut into the thick walls. When Mhari drew back the plain muslin curtains, I saw that the room commanded a breath-taking view of the loch. The moon shone strong and clear between the clouds, and its reflection turned the still waters of the loch below to silver. The pine trees I had earlier imagined to be so menacing were peaceful again, black sentinels against the gray sky embracing and guarding the castle. I could have gazed all night upon that scene, but Mhari's happy chatter drew me back into the bedroom.

". . . and you'll find there's plenty of closet space, though you don't seem to have brought too much. Now, I expect, you'll be wanting to freshen up a bit after your drive. I'll go down and see if all's ready. Do you think you can find your way back down?" I nodded and she hurried off toward the stairs; then suddenly she rushed back and reached up to give me a quick, enthusiastic hug. "Fiona, I'm so glad you've come and I do hope you'll be happy here with us." I kissed her warmly and assured her it could not be otherwise. Then she turned and ran quickly down the steps, light as a feather despite her pregnancy. I shook my head in amazement at her seemingly limitless energy. I proceeded to unpack and organize the few belongings I had brought with me.

After a hot and luxurious bath in the modern bathroom, which, I supposed, Alastair had put in for me, I changed into a pair of green slacks. Throwing a sweater over my shoulders, I proceeded to pick my way down the stairs. I went slowly, for the ancient stone steps were worn in some places. The lighting was barely adequate unless one knew what one was doing. When I arrived in the main hall, I followed the sound of voices down a hallway and found myself in a large and comfortable though plainly furnished room. Alastair and Ian were talking before a blazing fire, while Mhari poured out steaming cups of tea.

Alastair came over and, kissing me lightly, led me to the over-stuffed, floral-patterned sofa in front of the fire. "You look wonderfully recovered from the trip. Darlin', I do hope you're ravenous. Mhari has enough food for twenty starving people. She does so like to show off."

"Oh, fie. If I know your and Ian's appetites, all this will disappear in two minutes. Now, Fiona, how do you like your tea?"

It was, indeed, a lordly buffet that awaited us. There were ham and cucumber sandwiches made with crustless brown bread; there was a rich, dark cake laden with fruits and nuts; and, finally, there were the freshly baked scones Alastair had told me about, thickly spread with homemade strawberry jam and thick, fresh cream. It was a wonderful meal, and we all ate greedily, talking between bites. Mhari and Ian told me about the castle and the surrounding countryside, and Mhari was full of gossipy tidbits about the neighbors. By necessity, Ian was much quieter. But when he did speak, his words were well chosen, and I noticed how Mhari would listen attentively. She always took careful note of his opinions. The evening passed pleasantly and quickly. I knew I should soon feel at home with Alastair's family, and I looked forward to many more such evenings.

When Alastair and I retired to our tower, I went back to my window and looked for the moon I had admired earlier. But the howling wind had come up, and dark clouds were now rushing overhead. I felt the power and energy that was Lochinver's, a power and energy that was matched by the Scotsman who stood behind me, holding me close in his arms. I felt quite secure, and I reveled in Laird Alastair's embrace as I reveled in the embrace of Lochinver Castle.

THREE

Lochinver Castle

I soon settled into the easy routine of life at Lochinver. Mhari ran the small household with a bustling efficiency that I openly admired and secretly envied. Even though as Alastair's wife I was technically mistress of the estate, I was more than content to let Mhari continue in charge. Besides, I had been slightly worried that Mhari, born and raised at Lochinver Castle, might resent a stranger taking over her home. I had hesitantly mentioned my apprehensions to Alastair.

"Mhari resent you? Don't be ridiculous," he had replied. "She's more than happy to have you here. If there's anyone she resents, it's her big brother, for I've told her little about you. So be prepared to answer her many questions! She's bursting with curiosity. She loves Lochinver, and she'll be wanting to involve you in every aspect of the place and to share everything. Or," his voice becoming playful and a devilishness gleaming in his eye, "is it that you're not so worried about Mhari as your own domestic capabilities?"

I blushed. That had been part of my worrying. "Well, I've never had to do much along those lines . . . though you've got to admit I make a great omelette!" We both laughed heartily at that. On the first morning of our marriage, I had arisen early to surprise Alastair with breakfast in bed and had presented him instead with a mess of burnt eggs.

"Well, never fear, there's no chance of our starving here. We've a jewel in the kitchen: Mrs. Ross, who's been here practically forever. Och, the scoldings I would get for snitching cookies behind her back. I was convinced she had an extra set of eyes in the back of her head! She's the one responsible for those scones you've been feasting on, and once she's seen you, she'll be cooking twice the amount so as to put a bit of meat on your bones. But I like you just the way you are." A moment of most enjoyable silence followed. "And so, me darlin', do however much or however little you desire an' dinna worry yersel' aboot Mhari. She loves you like a sister already and only waits the first opportunity to know you better."

I soon found that Alastair had been right; Mhari was bursting to find out all she could about my life before my marriage to her brother. She was equally curious about life in America, and we spent many happy hours comparing our different childhoods. Most of our discussions took place as we lingered over breakfast. Ian and Alastair usually breakfasted early and were busy on the estate overseeing the remodeling of the barns by the time I arrived in the large dining room. Mhari also rose early, but she was always ready to share a second cup of tea with me and cluck disapprovingly over my lack of a morning appetite.

"Oh, la, Fiona. Only that one piece of toast? Here, at least put this fresh honey on it. I must say, I'm ravenous in the mornings. It's been such a long time since dinner, but, then, I suppose I am eating for two these days." Mhari laughed and patted her stomach. "We've always been a family for large breakfasts. I suppose it's the cold. We burn up calories just staying warm! Not even a bit of porridge? Mrs. Ross will be most upset. One of her main pleasures in life is to feed us."

"Alastair told me about her. I gather she's been at Lochinver a long time."

"Aye. It's hard to imagine the place without her. She was here before my parents were married. Her husband, Thomas, grew up on the estate. He's sort of a handyman. He helps with the gar-

56

dening and can fix almost anything. Whenever we have a large party, he's our butler. We always have to coax him, saying we couldn't possibly do it without him, but he gives in readily enough. It's sort of a game we play, for he adores us and would do anything for the MacLeods. And he loves when we entertain, says it reminds him of the grand old days when my grandparents feted the Highland gentry. Thomas's father was butler then."

"So he carries on in the family tradition?"

"With a vengeance," Mhari replied. "There have been Rosses at Lochinver almost as long as there have been MacLeods. But I'm afraid we'll soon see the end of that tradition. Their only son was killed in France during the war. He was quite a hero and saved many people. They're very proud of his memory."

"How sad. It must have been hard on them."

"Aye, it was. Fortunately Alastair was born soon after, and Mrs. Ross focused her maternal energies on him. Our mother died when I was two and Alastair ten, so Mrs. Ross has always been nursing and mothering us. She wouldn't let me wear lipstick until I was fifteen! But Alastair is the one she really adores. The 'young master' can do no wrong in her eyes. How mad that used to make me! She's so delighted that Alastair's finally married."

"Finally? But Alastair's just turned thirty."

"Mrs. Ross firmly believes in marrying young. She was married at eighteen, and she used to warn me of the dangers of being an old maid. She was greatly relieved when Ian proposed, though I was barely twenty years old when we married. She literally cried buckets of tears at the ceremony, and I'm sure she's disappointed not to have done the same with Alastair. She's eager to meet you, and I've promised to bring you to the kitchens before lunch."

"I can only hope that I'll live up to her expectations." I was beginning to feel slightly nervous.

"Och! She'll love you as much as we do, and be scolding and mothering you as if she'd done it all your life. Nothing will be too good for the wife of the young master."

We both laughed, and Mhari turned the conversation to the details of my life. I told her of growing up in a small New England college town; of how I had first come to Edinburgh as a student; and of my brief marriage with Tobias Grimsby. Her large blue eyes filled with sympathy as I related the story of Toby's death.

"How awful it must have been for you. You were so young and all alone in a strange country with no one to help you."

"I did find one good friend, a business partner of my husband's, Charles Haversham. He managed everything and was really wonderful to me, even though we had never met before. It was he who suggested I go home to my parents."

"Aye, I suppose that was the best thing for you to do. Haversham. That name sounds familiar, I suppose it's a common enough name in England. And they never found the person who killed Toby?"

"No, the driver was going too fast. All they could find out from the few witnesses was that it was a youngish man and that the motorcycle he was riding was quite large and German, I don't recall the name . . . something with initials . . . B . . . B something. I don't know anything about motorcycles, so the name meant nothing."

"BMW? Was that it?"

"It could be, it sounds right."

"Alastair has one of those. There are different kinds. His is quite large. He says it's just the thing for getting around on our narrow Highland roads. It's really marvelous. Has he ever taken you for a ride?"

"No!" My voice cracked on the word and my hands trembled.

A stricken look came into Mhari's eyes. "Oh, Fiona, of course not! How thoughtless of me! I'm so sorry; whatever was I thinking? Here, never mind that spill. I've got a napkin."

"No, Mhari, I'm all right; you didn't do anything wrong, really. It's just that I was back in the past for a minute and was thinking of the motorcycle that . . ."

"Don't say any more, Fiona. It's my fault, asking you all those questions. Ian always scolds me; he says I pry too much, that I always have to know everything. Curiosity killed the cat, they always say. Are you sure you're all right? Do you want to go lie down for a while?"

"Don't be silly, Mhari. Of course I'm all right. Now, why don't we tidy up and then go see this famous Mrs. Ross of yours before Ian and Alastair return and want lunch."

I had reassured Mhari, but I was far from reassuring myself. I still felt shaky, as shaky as I had so long before, when I was told about Toby's death. I had known that Alastair owned a motorcycle, but I had never known what kind it was. He had once suggested we go for a ride, but when I refused and had told him the reason for my refusal the bike was never mentioned again. There was no reason why the fact that it was the same type of motorcycle that killed Toby should bother me; after all, there must be many of them in Britain. But it did bother me. Don't be foolish, I told myself; there is not the slightest chance of its being the same motorcycle. You're being morbid and melodramatic. But I did feel an idle curiosity as to how long Alastair had owned the BMW. I took hold of myself and forced those unpleasant thoughts from my mind as I helped Mhari put the last of the dishes on the sideboard trays and followed her from the dining room.

A wood-paneled passageway led from the dining room to a room that could only be the kitchen, judging from the wonderful smells that were beckoning us to enter. The kitchen was a large room with tall windows that admitted generous amounts of sunshine. The room was warm from the oven's heat, and there was evidence of great activity. And at the center of that activity was a short, round woman, swathed in an overlarge blue checked apron, who was pushing an errant strand of gray hair from her forehead as she bent to peer into the oven.

"Noo, Margaret. Juist a few mair meenutes, an' it'll be ready tae tak' frae the oven. Mind it doesna burn, ye know the master doesna lake it burnt."

I smiled to myself. The woman could only be Mrs. Ross, and the person whose tastes she was catering to was Alastair, her favorite person, according to Mhari. Now he was no longer "young master," but the master.

At the sound of our approaching steps, Mrs. Ross turned and straightened up slowly. Her scowl at the interruption turned to a smile of pure and honest pleasure.

"Weel, noo, Mhari. Ye've finally brought the new young lady tae see me. An' it's aboot time. Weel, let us hae a look at ye. Fiona, is it not? Aye, a fine name it is, too. Mr. Alastair's new bride. An' yer a bonnie lass, tho' a bit on the scrawny side. Niver ye mind, I'll soon see tae tha'. This here's Margaret Stewart. She comes i' frae the village tae give us a hand. There's some tha' calls her Maggie, but I niver did hold wit' nicknames . . . whatever yer name is, that's what ye should be called."

Margaret was a girl of about fifteen, with a cropped head of bright, red curls and an unbelievable amount of freckles scattered about her face. She smiled shyly and made a small curtsey. I smiled at the bashful girl and turned back to Mrs. Ross.

"I'm so pleased to know you, Mrs. Ross. Mhari and Alastair have told me so many wonderful things about you." I hoped that hadn't sounded too formal, but my words had the proper effect, for Mrs. Ross's face turned even redder. Obviously the fact that Alastair had spoken well of her pleased her no end. But she soon recovered her brisk, no-nonsense manner.

"Aye, an' that's only richt. Me that's raised them after their mother died an' their father away on business mair often tha' not. Raised the twa puir motherless bairns as if they were mine ain."

Mhari was growing impatient with this speech, and she went over to Mrs. Ross, putting her arms around her, and said, "You were wonderful and soon there'll be a new baby for you to scold and bake cookies for."

"Aye, thare's nothin' lake a hoose wit' bairns i' it. An' this hoose has been overlong wit'oot 'em. But we'll soon hae a hoose full, eh?" This last was directed at me, and I promptly blushed— once again the proper response, for Mrs. Ross beamed. "I imagine the master will be wantin' an heir soon eno', seein' tha' he waited sae lang tae marry. Time an' time agin I'd tell him tae find hissel' a bride an' settle doon, but he'd just smile an' say he'd hae none but me. Och, he's a braw tease." She shook her head, chuckling. "By the way ye talk, are ye . . . Canadian?"

"No, I'm from the United States."

"Och, American. Aweel, tha' will cause some talk i' the village, Mr. Alastair bringin' home a furriner tae Lochinver. Hee, hee, that'll be puttin' some noses oot o' joint, an' I'm thinkin' of one tha' . . ."

"Now, now." Mhari was embarrassed. "Fiona's not really a foreigner: her grandparents were born and raised in the Highlands; so, you see, she's really come home. Now, we mustn't keep you any longer, for Ian and Alastair will be ravenous after their morning's work and they'll be wanting a large lunch."

After saying good-by to the tongue-tied Margaret, we left Mrs. Ross still chuckling as she inspected her freshly baked loaves of bread.

"Mrs. Ross does tend to gossip and say anything that comes into her mind. Though I'm afraid there will be a tendency in the village to consider you a foreigner. Anyone not born in the Highlands is an outsider. It's really nothing to worry about. Alastair is highly regarded, and you'll be warmly welcomed as his wife. An', of course, once ye've pradooced an heir . . ." Mhari mimicked Mrs. Ross's burr perfectly, and we both laughed.

"Oh, it's not that different from where I grew up. In New England, it can take three or four generations before one is considered a native."

The rest of the morning was spent pleasantly in the gardens about the castle. The day was sunny, and in the courtyard we were comfortably sheltered from the brisk October winds. Alastair and Ian joined us, and we went in to lunch, where the conversation centered on the home farm, a subject Ian talked of enthusiastically, even dominating the conversation—no mean feat in the face of Mhari's and Alastair's usual loquaciousness.

After lunch, Alastair decided it was time I had a thorough tour of the castle, and we spent hours that day exploring the many passages and rooms. I despaired of ever learning my way, for even though Alastair would tell me where we were, I felt hopelessly lost. Alastair told me that, as children, he and Mhari would spend hours playing hide-and-go-seek in the dark, narrow hallways.

"Ian would play, too. We were at school together and Ian came here for many holidays. He was never as good as Mhari and I were; he used to get so mad—he'd search forever and never find us. Then Mhari would relent and come out and apologize; even as a little girl, she was a charmer. Ian's always been like a member of the family, and it seemed only natural when he and Mhari married. We were all very pleased." Was it my imagination, or was Alastair speaking these words as though he were reciting from memory, words he had learned by rote?

"The southern wing, where we are now, was the best for

our games. The hallways are arranged in a more complicated fashion. This wing was added after the others, in the early 1600s, when the French style of architecture was predominant. Some castles built in that period resemble the Loire châteaux, though, of course, on a less sophisticated and smaller scale," he added, laughing as he continued his history lesson. "As a matter of fact, the French influence is seen in all aspects of Scottish life; even our national dish has its origins in French cooking. Haggis was derived from *hachis*, which is the French word for minced meat."

"All very interesting, Professor, but that bit of information won't enhance its flavor. Besides, all that proves is that the Scots couldn't pronounce the word correctly."

We toured the entire castle, from the tower's heights to the dank and musty rooms carved from the bedrock that supported the castle's foundations. I wondered if prisoners had ever stayed there, but Alastair said no, they had been used only for storing supplies.

"Some of these rooms were built for that purpose, but the castle is remote and most battles were fought far from here. I suppose the occasional errant servant or rebellious clansman might have spent a night or two as a disciplinary measure, but nothing drastic."

I was glad, for I preferred to think of Lochinver as a place of joy, with no dark side to mar its wind-swept beauty. The fact that the castle was desperately in need of renovation was evident as we continued to tour. Many of the rooms were completely bare, and some of the northern wing was in a state of actual disrepair: parts of the walls had crumbled, exposing the interiors to the elements.

"Aye, it's a long, slow process to rebuild this place. And it takes money," Alastair added bitterly. "My grandfather and father maintained the west wing and the ground floor of the southern wing. I've managed to make part of the tower comfortable, but as I've been unable to spend all my time here, the work has proceeded slowly. Unfortunately, Ian does not share my enthusiasm for restoring the castle to its original state. He prefers to first develop the estate as a self-sufficient and profitable farm. I do have a bit of the romantic in me, I fear. We've had many discussions and disagreements over how to spend our meager income, and he resents every penny I've spent on renovation—above and beyond necessary maintenance."

"Have there been serious fights?" I wondered about the possibility of a feud, and how Mhari reacted to this clash of opinions between her husband and her brother.

"Och, no, darlin'. Nothing serious. Actually, it probably works out for the best. Ian's practicality restrains my flights of fancy. We balance each other, and I'm sure Lochinver is the better for it. At any rate," he added, smiling, "I hope you'll share my desire to rebuild the castle. I'm looking forward to sharing the work with you."

"Of course, I *want* to help." The prospect of resurrecting Lochinver was an exciting one and I longed to begin. The house I had lived in as a child had been a charming New England frame house built around the time of the Revolutionary War (practically brand-new when compared to Lochinver). My parents loved the house and spent many of their leisure hours working on it. At first, I had only been able to toddle after my father holding his bag of nails. I proudly "helped," and I would pound as diligently with my rubber hammer as my father did with his real one. As I grew older, I shared my parents' enthusiasm, and some of my happiest memories are of Sunday afternoons spent driving about the Massachusetts countryside "antiquing." We were able to discover real bargains that these days would cost a small fortune. The thought of working to restore Lochinver was intoxicating, and I began to imagine the fun ahead. I knew I would have a lot to learn. My knowledge of Scottish castles was slight. But I should be a more than willing pupil, especially as it would bring so much happiness to Alastair. I pictured to myself the looks of pleasure on his face as I surprised him with a newly repapered room or a beautiful chair found after long hours of searching in some obscure antique shop. I began to plan trips to Edinburgh and London, shopping expeditions to find the treasures that would enhance the beauty of my new home. I would have the free time Alastair could not afford, and I had the money the lack of which had been hindering his dreams of a refurbished Lochinver. Work could now begin in earnest! I would hire experts, I would . . . my head swam from the excitement of these plans and I gave a bounce from the sheer joy of it all.

"Hold on, Fiona. Ye canna do it all in one day!" As usual, Alastair had read my thoughts. "There's plenty of time. You'll be spending the rest of your life at Lochinver. Now . . . I want to show you the portrait gallery before it gets too dark."

As we had talked, it had grown darker outside. A light rain was falling, hitting the small windows in a soft staccato pattern. A gray, gentle nightfall closed upon the castle. As I gazed through the narrow window panes into the darkening courtyard below, I realized with a shock how cold I was. The part of the castle we were in now was unheated, and the stone floors and walls gave off a damp chilliness that penetrated my thick pullover.

"Aye, Fiona, these rooms get mighty cold without the sun to warm them." Alastair had noticed my shivering shoulders, and he put his arm around me as we walked down the hall. "'Tis a blessing in summer, for these stone walls cool the castle, but a curse in winter. And winter comes quickly to the Highlands. We'll cut through the gallery and then we'll have a nice cup of tea—that will warm you, especially if there's a wee glass of whiskey alongside."

We quickly passed more halls and descended several sets of stairs. As I clutched my sweater around me, I idly wondered how much it would cost to equip the entire castle with a central heating system. The idea amused me, for even if Alastair would allow such blatant modernism, it would take all the oil in the North Sea to heat the castle for just one year. I would just have to get used to it.

The portrait gallery was a high-ceilinged, wood-paneled hallway that overlooked the great hall. The high walls were filled with many pictures, all depicting MacLeod ancestors. There were an equal number of men and women, the latter in formal Highland dress similiar to the one Alastair had given me as a wedding present. As I studied the paintings I recognized the largest as being the same man whose picture I had noticed in the great hall downstairs. Torquil MacLeod, who had lost Lochinver as punishment for taking part in a minor clan rebellion. The artist of this portrait was highly skilled—probably one of the many

Flemish painters who had traveled through Scotland—and his Torquil was an elegant, gracious chieftain. Yet he could do nothing to soften the angry glare of the hooded blue eyes. Alastair joined me in front of the picture.

"Och, Torquil was a fierce fellow, all right. And none too pleasant, judging from the stories I've heard. If you were a friend, he was unswervingly loyal, but to his enemies . . . he's the chap who installed our dungeons, but the castle was taken from him before he could put them to use. The succeeding lairds were more peaceful and everyone tried to forget about Torquil, the skeleton in the closet that every old family has. But I've always been fascinated by him and had his portraits reinstated. I prefer the one downstairs; I think it shows his character more clearly, but this one seemed more appropriate for the gallery, more in keeping with the others. Here, these two over here, these are of my parents."

We went over to the paintings he indicated, and I looked at them with interest. Alastair's father had been a man of goodly height and large in build. His hair was as dark as his son's and his large eyes were the same strong blue, but they had none of the intensity of Alastair's. His mother had been a beautiful woman, quite small and delicate, with curling blond hair that caressed her shoulders. There was a sadness in her eyes that I found strangely appealing.

"I've always loved this picture of my mother. She died when I was young, and I never got to know her well. To me, mother was a goddess, floating through the halls of Lochinver. You know, it's queer, but sometimes I still feel as though she were here, watching over me. But that's left over from a childish fancy. I wanted her to be alive so desperately that I made myself believe she was. She was never well after Mhari was born, and I remember visiting her in her room, showing her my schoolwork or something I had made. Her approval meant more to me than anyone else's. That last year was hard, for I had to be quiet when I was near her, and toward the end I couldn't visit her at all."

Alastair's eyes were clouded and his face took on a child's bewildered look, as though he were reliving those painful days when he couldn't understand why he was not to play with his mother.

I said gently, "She looks as though there had been a great sorrow in her life. Was this painted when she was ill?"

"No, just a year or two after I was born. I don't think my father was an easy man to live with." This last was said with a finality that closed the subject. I turned my glance again to the man with the placid blue eyes that were so like and yet so unlike those of the man I had married. There was no clue there.

"You know, we'll have to have your portrait painted. It's the tradition." Alastair's voice had recovered its usual energy. "All the lairds have had their ladies immortalized, and you deserve no less."

"Oh, Alastair, don't be silly. A color snapshot would do fine for me. How about something wallet-sized? Then you could always take me with you." Somehow the thought of sitting for a portrait did not appeal to me. I have never been able to sit for any length of time, and the idea of remaining still and maintaining a pleasant expression for more than five minutes seemed impossible, if not downright ludicrous. I was suspicious of the artist's mastery, his perception. What expression would he see, what would my face tell future generations of MacLeods? A photograph captures a moment's thought, but a painting reveals what you are. Silly, I thought, you have nothing to hide. But I felt a slight resentment all the same.

"Nonsense, Fiona. My mind's made up; it's a wonderful idea. You'll wear the gown I gave you and you'll look beautiful. A true mistress of Lochinver."

"I don't see your portrait hanging anywhere."

"No, I haven't wanted it done." Then, stifling my satisfied exclamation, he added, "There hasn't been any point. It's silly to have the laird without his lady. Mine will be done at the same time. That's the way it should be."

I sighed and resigned myself to the inevitable. The romantic in Alastair had taken hold, and he would be deeply hurt if I refused. He loved the traditions of Lochinver and wanted to maintain them.

"All right, you win. But I hope you won't regret it when you

66

see the final result. Do you think we could bribe the artist to make my nose thinner?"

"No. I love your nose just the way it is, and I shall give explicit instructions as to having those two freckles included. Ah, here we are; now you'll warm up."

We were back in the living room, and Ian and Mhari were seated before the fire, already enjoying the tea I was longing for. I joined them and gladly accepted the cup Mhari had poured for me. I sipped it slowly, luxuriating in the warmth the fire emitted.

"Fiona and I have decided to have our portraits painted," Alastair announced gaily.

"You mean, *you* have decided that you and Fiona will have your portraits painted," Ian corrected. We all laughed at this correct portrayal of the facts, but I wondered if there could be a double meaning to Ian's witticism.

"Whatever," Alastair acknowledged. "I admit it was my idea and that Fiona had to be coaxed into it. She protests from a sense of modesty, but I'll wager she can't wait for the sittings to begin." This sally again produced laughter, as did my embarrassed denial, and we teased each other back and forth for some time.

"Fiona, think how exciting it will be. What will you wear?" Mhari, as usual, was highly interested in details.

"She'll wear the Highland gown I gave her, of course. It's the only proper dress."

"Wonderful! Och, you'll look such a picture." Mhari giggled at her own pun. "I am sorry, but really, that's such a lovely dress. It was our grandmother's, you know, that is, our father's mother. She was tall and dark, just as you are. Mama was too small to wear it, so it's been packed away all these years, waiting for a new bride to come to Lochinver."

"Mhari, really, sometimes you talk like one of those romantic novels you're always reading."

"She can't help it, Ian; it's the setting. Sometimes I feel as though it's all slightly unreal: coming to live in a beautiful castle, having my portrait painted—"

"For heaven's sake, Fiona, don't encourage her!" Ian threw up his hands in mock despair. "Whom were you thinking of getting to do the work, Alastair?"

67

"I was thinking of that Demerest, Lewis Demerest. His father painted our parents, Fiona. Lewis has lived in Paris for the past several years, and I heard that he recently returned to the village and now plans to make it his permanent home. He had a show last spring in Inverness. You remember, Fiona; I took you to see it."

"Oh, yes. He's quite good. I especially liked that one . . . what was it called? . . . something about young girl and flowers. The colors were so subtle."

"Hmmm. I remember that one, too. He certainly has talent, more than his father had, though old Colin had the knack of capturing likenesses. I don't know if portraits are Lewis's specialty, but I'd like to ask him to do it. I'd prefer to have someone local rather than hire some stranger from Edinburgh. Besides, I'm sure that Lewis could use the money. Highlanders don't have much money to spend on art."

"Aye, Alastair; how much do you intend to spend on these paintings?" Ian's voice had taken on a slight edge and he had started to snap his fingers together soundlessly. I had noticed that Ian frequently did that when he was agitated.

"Och, I don't know. I'm sure that we can settle on a fair price. It's not really important . . ."

"Not important? Oh, no. *You* never worry about such mundane things as mere money. Not when it comes to your precious traditions. You'd spend every penny we coax out of this place on your whims. Well, all I can say is that it is a very lucky thing that you . . ."

"Ian!" Mhari's usually sweet voice held a sharp note of warning, and Ian stopped. Whatever he had been about to say was left unspoken.

After a slight pause, conversation resumed, and soon we were chatting away as if nothing had happened. However, I noticed that Mhari was quieter than normal. Occasionally I would catch her looking at me; her thin, dark eyebrows knitted, accenting her worried expression. I wondered what had caused her to look so concerned. Was it that Ian and Alastair had come close to arguing? Was this snapping over money a continuing one, with Mhari being constantly caught in the middle? What would Ian have said, and why did she stop him? Was it something she didn't want me to hear? What? Surely there could be no deep secrets I wasn't aware of. Both Ian and Mhari had gone out of their way to make me feel at home and a member of the family. So what was it that I couldn't know? These thoughts preoccupied me the rest of the evening.

Later, when Alastair and I were alone in our room, I asked him what he thought Ian had been about to say.

"What? About to say when?"

"Oh, Alastair, you know. When he was talking about you spending too much money on whims." I kept my voice disinterested, as I didn't want Alastair to think I had attached too much importance to the incident.

"Hmmm? Och, Ian's always saying I spend too much money. It's nothing to worry about."

"But Mhari seemed upset and made him stop."

"She's probably tired of hearing us argue. You really are concerned, aren't you, love?"

"Well, I like Ian and I don't like to think that you two . . . well, that you don't—"

"Aye, Fiona, you are a darling." Alastair came over and took me in his arms. "It's sweet of you to worry about us, but it's nothing. Ian and I may disagree occasionally, but it's friendly. We both only want what's best for Lochinver. I've known Ian for most of my life, and we've been friends since, well, since we were twelve and discovered we both hated Latin."

"I wish I had known you then."

"No you don't. I was a horrid little monster."

Alastair had reassured me about Ian, so I thought no more of the incident. Relations between them continued to be amicable, and I accepted Alastair's explanations. The next morning, I had an opportunity to chat at greater length with Mhari, but at no time did I catch her looking at me with that worried expression. When I mentioned the portraits again, she said she was as eager for them to begin as Alastair.

"I do hope Lewis lets me watch. It'll be such fun."

"We'll have to have you painted, too."

"La, Fiona. What a giggle that would be! Me sitting there with my large stomach. I'd be too ugly."

69

"Nonsense. They say the Mona Lisa was pregnant, you know. That's one of the loveliest paintings in the world."

"Och, no. Besides, it should be the mistress of the castle who has her portrait made."

"Well, then, it's Mrs. Ross that should be painted, for if any-one's mistress here, she is," I replied. Even though Alastair had assured me that Mhari felt no resentment at my arrival, I still felt somewhat of an intruder. However, I thought no more of the previous evening's incident, and life and Lochinver Castle assumed a workaday calm that I soon came to love.

It would be some time before I had cause to remember that argument between Ian and Alastair and to ponder its deeper significance.

One rainy, windy afternoon soon after, Mhari and I were sitting before the living room fire. Mhari had taught me to knit, and we were working on things for the baby she would have in February. My contribution, a blanket, was not progressing rapidly, for it seemed that for every row I knitted, Mhari would rip out two.

"Mhari, I'm afraid your child will be full-grown before I've finished this thing."

"Well, then, he'll use it for a scarf!" Mhari laughed, her needles clicking along busily. "You'll get the hang of it soon enough, your fingers have to catch the rhythm . . . La! What's this? Alastair, what on earth have you got there?"

Alastair had come into the room carrying a squirming bundle in his arms which he set down on the rug in front of us. First, a shiny black nose emerged and then a tousled puppy wriggled free of the sodden blue blanket that wrapped it. It was a chubby mite of a dog, and it immediately began to investigate its surroundings, obviously enjoying the fire's warmth. Soon it came over to me and promptly set about ruining my afternoon's labor —it had decided my blanket was more suited for a lively tug of war than for covering a baby. I could not help but agree.

"Oh, Alastair, he's precious. Look how it fights the yarn. Whose is it?" The puppy was now established in my lap.

"He's yours, if you'll have him."

"Have him? Of course I'll have him. I love him already." Indeed, who could not love such a puppy, now proceeding to lap my face from ear to ear?

"Ian and I were over to Stewarts'—the parents of Maggie, who helps in the kitchen. Their terrier had a litter about two months ago, and they had found homes for all but this wee fellow here. He was such a bold tyke, climbing all over my shoes, that . . . well, here he is."

"Alastair, thank you, thank you! He's wonderful. Listen, you little monster, if you're going to be mine, you'll show some respect. Stop chewing my hair!" Amazingly enough, the puppy stopped and settled down happily in my arms. "Look, he obeys me already. Now, do you have a name?"

"The Stewarts just called him 'Lad.'"

"Well, that's hardly a proper name. I could call him Bobby, he looks just like Greyfriars Bobby."

"Fiona, I've never cared for names that end in -y, they're not dignified, and since this dog is partly mine and I'm responsible for his being here, I insist he have a decent name."

"Dignified? This rapscallion?"

"He'll thank us for it when he's a staid old dog with a long gray mustache. I had thought, if you don't mind a suggestion, that 'Bruce' would be a good name for such a frisky one as this. The most honorable name in Scottish history."

"Bruce?" I asked in mock puzzlement.

"The Bruce!" Alastair started, eyes glowing as he drew himself up as would an eager student reciting his lessons to his master. "The Bruce, lass of mine, was the finest man who ever took the field against the English! Grandson of Robert the Bruce who subdued foul Baliol with no more than your ordinary Christian ferocity. All the Bruces descended from a Norman conqueror named Robert de Brus, who had the good sense to leave the South and the Saxons to William and the lesser Norman dukes and come North to where men are men and the Picts are, well, the Picts are considerably more than men. Aye, and it was Robert the Bruce who pounded Edward II and the bloody English in Stirlingshire that wonderful summer of 1314, at Bannockburn. Sent them back to Northumberland like the whipped dogs they are. They made him Robert I of Scotland for that. Crowned him at Stirling Castle, they did. And his brother Edward became King of Ireland two years later. The Irish are a good lot . . . they recognize quality when they see it. The Bruce's grandson became Robert II, the first Stuart king, and so it was until the '45, when the English stole . . ."

"Yes, yes, Alastair . . . I do know, I do!" I smiled broadly, for he was impressive when he forgot where he was and started making Hyde Park-like speeches about the kingdom of Scotland that was no more. "And Bruce is a wonderful name. But let's leave this important decision to him, okay? Do you like 'Bruce,' puppy? Were you listening to Alastair?" The little dog had been watching our faces with a curious expression, his head cocked to one side; now he started barking joyously and rolled around in my lap. "That settles it. He approves of your choice, Alastair. Bruce it is! Oh, Bruce, we're going to have such fun together."

Mhari stood up and carefully folded her knitting out of Bruce's reach. "Well, after all this speechifying, I think I'll go ask Mrs. Ross for some scraps to feed him. I doubt if she'll want him eating in her kitchen. She'll grumble, but I wager she'll soon be saving choice morsels for the 'wee beastie!' "

Within a few short days Bruce had made himself king of the castle (as his namesake had been king of Scotland). Everyone made a great fuss over him, even old Mrs. Ross. Mhari's prediction had proved correct, for even though she disapproved publicly ("I dinna hol' wi' animals livin' i' the hoose, thinkin' they're human; the place for the beastie is i' the barns, whaur 'e can do same gude an' earn 'is keep catchin' meece"), I noticed that in one corner of her spotless kitchen there was always a dish laid down with scraps of meat in it. On more than one occasion, I came upon her talking to Bruce as if he could understand her. And indeed he did appear to understand, as he sat there head cocked to one side.

Everyone loved Bruce, and while he responded equally to all, it was obvious from the start that he was my dog. He followed me wherever I went, even if I just left the room for a few minutes. If I went out and left him behind, the welcome I received upon my return was as joyous as if the separation had been two years rather than two minutes. He was happiest when he was curled up beside me, either on my lap or resting his head on my feet. At night, he slept on an old rug I had put beside the bed, and I knew that if Alastair and I had given him any encouragement, he would have slept in the bed between us.

Any fears that I had of Bruce's growing fat with Mrs. Ross's feedings were dispelled by the amount of daily exercise he had. He seldom sat still and was always prying into this thing or that. Alastair tried to teach him tricks, but without much success. Bruce would cock his head to one side and look at Alastair with a puzzled expression as if to say: "Noo, why wude I be wantin' tae roll over? I'm too canny for tha'!" I had always loved to take long walks, and now with Bruce for company I resumed doing so. Almost every afternoon, we would set off and explore the areas around the castle.

My favorite spot, the one I frequented most, was what Alastair and Mhari called "the Hundred Steps to Nowhere." They started at the grassy edge of the loch and wound their way through the cliffs, ending on a plateau high above the loch. It was a secluded spot, and I loved the quiet, protected feeling I had when I was there. The pine trees grew thickly, and their long, swaying boughs added to the serenity. From my perch I could look down on the jutting rocks and the icy and deep-blue waters of the loch. The castle was barely visible from there, and I could catch only glimpses of the tower as the trees leaned before the wind. The steps themselves intrigued me, for they started suddenly on a grassy knoll and then stopped on another grassy knoll. Nothing else was around them. There was no apparent reason for their existence. They were worthy of the nickname Alastair had given them. When I asked how they came there, Alastair could shed little light on the subject.

"I suppose there was once some sort of military structure at the top of the steps, perhaps a lookout post. They're very old, probably fifteenth century. If there was something else there, the stones were likely taken away and used for building a part of the castle."

"Typically thrifty Scots," I laughed.

"Aweel, it makes sense," Alastair replied. "No reason to let perfectly good cut granite go to waste. And do be careful while you're climbing around there, Fiona. They're steep and well worn in places. If you slipped, you could take a nasty spill."

"I'll be careful," I promised. "And don't forget, I always have my faithful watchdog with me."

"Aye, he is your wee guardian." Alastair bent down and scratched Bruce's ear. "Well, enjoy your walks, love, and soon you'll be knowing Lochinver as well as the wind does."

I heeded Alastair's sensible warning about the Hundred Steps. They were worn, and several tended to move slightly as I put my weight on them. However, I soon knew the path well: where to place my foot; what steps to avoid; which way to bend into the gusts near the top. In a few weeks, I was scampering up and down as lightheartedly as Bruce.

Bruce and I roamed over the entire estate. It often seemed to go on forever. There were several small stone cottages near the western perimeter, occupied by the families of the men who worked for us. At first, I was shy about imposing and hesitated to visit, but whenever I strolled by I was asked in for a cup of tea. Soon I mustered enough courage to accept.

I became comfortable first with the Stewarts, Maggie's parents and the original owners of Bruce. Maggie's grandfather was invariably sitting by the door of their cottage (or croft, as that type of small dwelling is called in the Highlands), a plaid lap blanket over his knees, warming himself in the late-afternoon sun and puffing away on a hand-carved briar. I had noticed him on several occasions and had made a point of asking Maggie what brand of tobacco her grandfather smoked. I arranged to make a gift of a tin of the stuff the reason for my first visit. As I chatted with the ancient, Mrs. Stewart bustled out and welcomed me, saying it was an honor to have the mistress of the castle visiting. Terribly embarrassed, I asked her to think of me as a new neighbor who had just dropped in for an afternoon visit.

"Weel, noo. Maggie said the new lady was a bonnie lass. American, are ye? We dinna hae mony i' these parts. Most folk here was born an' raised i' the Hielands. Aye, it caused a fair bit o' talk when we heard Master Alastair ha' brought hame a American bride."

I laughed and accepted her proffered cup of tea, saying that I hoped I wouldn't be considered a foreigner too much longer, and that I already felt completely at home.

"Aye, it's a canny lass ye are. The master knew wha' he was

aboot, marryin' ye. An' it's aboot time, too. Folk roun' here was sure Master Alastair wude end 'is days a bachelor, for he's always runnin' after causes an' niver ha' the time tae settle doon. Tho' there's some roun' here tha' tried hard eno'." She paused to sip her tea and beamed at me. "Noo he's brought a bride an' soon there'll be a new young master." She studied me carefully, trying to detect signs of pregnancy in my face. "It'll be gude tae hae wee ones up a' the big hoose agin."

"There will be a baby soon; Mhari is expecting in February," I hastily reminded her.

"Nae, it's no' the same a Master Alastair's bairn, i' it? For he'll be the new laird o' the castle. Noo, tell me aboot yersel'."

I spent the rest of the afternoon chatting pleasantly with Mrs. Stewart. She had grown up on MacLeod lands. Her father had worked on the farm all his life, and she had married Will Stewart, one of the other farmers. She had been pleased when Maggie, her youngest child, had started to work with Mrs. Ross in the kitchen.

"She'll get gude trainin', tha's for sure. There i' nothin' tha' Mrs. Ross doesna ken aboot runnin' a hoose. Aye, it's gude trainin' she'll get, better tha' wha' she'd get a some school. A' these new-fangled ideas o' educatin' women a same a men, I dinna hol' wi' it. But my Maggie, she thinks different an' is savin' 'er siller tae gang off a soon a she's old eno'. I canna stop 'er, for she's a stubborn a I am, but I'll make sure she can cook an' clean, for tha's wha' a husband wants i' a wife."

I nodded my head as if in tacit agreement. Yet I thought inwardly that I made a sorry wife, according to Mrs. Stewart's standards. I made a mental note to talk with Maggie and encourage her dreams of an education.

Since Mrs. Stewart had spent all her life in Lochinver, she had known Alastair and Mhari as children and had known their parents. Nothing fascinated me more than to talk about what I had missed: Alastair's mother; Alastair as a little boy; Ian and Alastair playing with little Mhari. I encouraged her reminiscences. I derived double pleasure from our conversation. Mrs. Stewart spoke in the rhythmical cadences of the northern Highlands, so that I loved the sounds of what she said as much as what she said.

75

"Aye, Master Alastair was such a lad, always one for gettin' i' mischief. He was a wild tyke, playin' pranks, but wi' such a sense o' fun it was hard tae be angry. He changed after 'is mother died. He worshiped Ceit lake the saint she was. He was a serious bairn after tha'. 'Is father sent 'im off tae school soon after, an' he'd be roun' the place durin' the holidays, but niver a carefree a before. He seemed tae grow up a' o' a sudden, he did, an' was mair o' a father tae wee Mhari tha' a brother, watchin' oot for her, takin' care o' her, which is mair tha' their ain father did. Tha' Jamie MacLeod, how he cude hae twa o' the bonniest bairns an' no' take a interest . . . weel, I dinna ken. There's some wha' say he drove 'is wife tae a early grave wi' 'is ways. Time an' time agin, I'd say tae Mrs. Ross . . . there, noo, I've gaun an' gossiped the day away. I'm sure ye've better tae do tha' spend yer time listenin' tae me gab!"

I suddenly realized that the sun was setting behind the trees that marked the edge of the estate, taking the afternoon's warmth with it. The Stewarts' home was cozy and warmed by the large fireplace that took up one wall of the building—a far cry from the medieval huts that had had only a hole in the roof for ventilation—but I knew that it was chilly outside. I now wished that I had worn a heavier sweater, for, as the croft was near the village, I had a long walk ahead of me. I stood up, buttoning my sweater around my neck, and thanked Mrs. Stewart profusely for a pleasant afternoon, saying I hoped I could visit again. She assured me that I was always more than welcome and thanked me for bringing her father his favorite tobacco.

"It's one o' Father's few pleasures, 'is pipe. 'Is eyesight's almost gaun, so he canna do wha' he used tae, tho' he still putters wi' the posies. But on a nice day he enjoys nothin' mair tha' tae sit i' the sun an' smoke 'is pipe. Tha's the best present ye cude hae gien 'im, Mrs. MacLeod, he's tha' pleased."

I said good-by to Mrs. Stewart and to her father, who had come in to sit by the fire now that the sun had gone. I whistled for Bruce, who had spent the afternoon reacquainting himself with his old home, and started walking back to the castle. I took the path that ran near the loch and past the Hundred Steps to Nowhere. Any other time, I would have climbed to my favorite spot, but with twilight's spookiness, all I wanted was to get home. I paused, though, by the loch and watched the pine trees dance in time to the wind. The trees around Lochinver continued to fascinate me, and I could watch them for hours, mesmerized by the changing images their attenuated boughs created. Tonight, however, I did not find the patterns peaceful, but faintly disturbing, as if the trees were waving their long arms in warning. I waited, but I couldn't decipher what they were trying to tell me. Finally, Bruce's anxious barking drew me on. I decided that I was just being girlishly fanciful. It was shadowy now, and familiar objects always appear odd to me in the evening, as though the dimness lends them an extra dimension impossible in the sunlight. It was an idea I had had since childhood, and I was just reliving some childish fear.

Bruce was now barking impatiently. He was eager to return to the warmth of the castle and to the scraps Mrs. Ross was sure to have waiting for him. I hurried after him, for I suddenly wanted very much to be within the strong stone walls, to sit by the fire and to sip tea, to listen to Mhari and to feel secure.

As we came out into the clearing, Bruce and I began to run toward the castle. Though it was now quite dark, the moon of little use now in its last quarter, we were overfamiliar with the path and raced each other pell-mell to the entrance to the west wing. As usual, Bruce won the race handily, running the course several times over as he came back and encouraged me with his sharp barks to hurry. We were a disheveled pair as we arrived on the stone steps of the door. I was panting with the exertion of the short race, and my hair was tangled and caught in the buttons of my sweater. Bruce's silky brown coat was matted and muddy from his explorations by the loch. I decided we both could do with a thorough scrubbing before high tea, and I gathered Bruce up in my arms. He squirmed and protested. He wanted to dash off to his supper; yet I imagined the look of horror on Mrs. Ross's face should Bruce bound into her spotless kitchen in this condition.

It was not easy to open the heavy oak door laden as I was with my wriggling, wet bundle, but I somehow managed and shut the door firmly behind me. Knowing he would scamper away, I continued to hold Bruce as I made my way up the back stairs to the first floor of the west wing. I had discovered this shortcut to the

77

tower while exploring the castle, and had grown to use it almost exclusively. The second floor of the west wing was connected to the third floor of the tower. By using this route I had only one flight of the narrow, winding tower steps to climb—steps I still found unpleasant. I could avoid using the main entrance and the great hall, which I considered a little too grand for my ordinary comings and goings. In addition, the west-wing entrance was more convenient for my walks to the Hundred Steps.

I ran lightly and soundlessly up the stairs in my rubber-soled shoes. Resigned to his fate, Bruce had settled into my arms and stopped his little growls. My way led past Mhari and Ian's rooms, and I thought I would stop for a minute to say I would be down after a quick bath. I paused by their door, shifting Bruce to free my right hand, but the sound of angry voices made me hesitate. The door was slightly ajar, and I could hear their conversation quite clearly, the more so as Mhari's and Ian's voices were raised in anger. I was surprised, for Ian's voice was always controlled, even when he was disturbed. I had never heard Mhari speak in sharp tones, especially to her husband, to whom she had always shyly deferred.

Embarrassed at being a witness to their quarrel—and almost never being one to eavesdrop—I turned away silently toward the tower. If it was something serious, Mhari would confide in me. I would know soon enough what was wrong. However, as I turned I caught a snatch of conversation that made me stop and listen. I tried to force myself to leave, but the words that I was hearing were so shocking that I literally froze.

"Ian! I won't have you say such things about my brother!" Mhari's voice was shaking with intensity.

"Well, I'm fed up. Totally. I'm the one who does the real work around here. I'm the one who breaks his back trying to make the farm realize a profit—a profit he blithely runs through. Alastair spends half his time running about Scotland on that motorcycle of his, stirring up God knows what trouble, and he expects to come back to Lochinver and play the grand lord of the castle and tell me what to do with the money I've worked so hard to earn. I struggle while he's off playing the grand Highland chieftain with those Nationalist cronies of his—those, those rabble-rousing revolutionaries. If he's so eager to save Scotland, he should put more effort into working its land!"

"Ian, that's not fair. He knows how much work you've put into Lochinver and he truly appreciates all that you've done. He's told us both over and over. And he always listens to you, he welcomes your opinions."

"Aye, you always take his side, Mhari. You always have, since we were children. You're still putting Alastair before me. Me, your own husband!"

"Ian! Don't! It's cruel and stupid, what you're saying." Mhari was nearly hysterical.

"All right. All right. I'm sorry. Mhari, I know you love me. It's just that you always defend him so vehemently. I begin to wonder sometimes where your loyalties lie."

"Ian, you can't mean that you would want me to go against Alastair?"

"No. He's your brother. But all the same, Mhari, I get so angry at times. Sometimes I feel as though I'm the faithful servant who bows to the lord of the castle. And I have to jump to attention and go along with all his expensive whims. Especially now that he's married and seems to want to spend all his time here, spending money on the castle. It's hard to know where one stands."

"I like having Alastair and Fiona here, it's less lonely. Fiona and I are getting to be good friends—"

"But don't you feel any resentment? Here Alastair has gone and brought a stranger, a stranger who is now the lady of the house. Whose child will inherit Lochinver."

"Ian! What *are* you saying?"

"Mhari, can't you see? Och, never mind, you're too sweet. Well, all I can say is that it's a good thing he's found himself a rich wife, someone to foot the bills for these projects he's planned. Portraits, indeed!"

"Fiona has money?"

"Mhari, Fiona more than 'has money.' She's one of the wealthiest women in Scotland. Does the name 'Grimsby Petroleum' mean anything to you? Tobias Grimsby, who initiated the company's ventures into the North Sea oil explorations was her husband—that fellow who was killed in the motorcycle accident about six years ago. You remember, it was in all the papers. He

was in Inverness for some important meetings. Grimsby Petroleum hadn't been formed then. His death brought things to a
halt for a while, but the company got going again and it's been
raking in the profits ever since. *That's* who Fiona is."

"I do remember reading about it. Alastair was in Inverness at
the time. Fiona told me about Toby, her first husband, but I
never made the connection. I was just concentrating on the
awful thing that had happened to her. The name didn't register.
But Fiona never said anything."

"No. Of course, she wouldn't. She's a sensible girl and
wouldn't want to put anyone off. The North Sea oil is hardly a
popular topic right now, and the fact that she's the major stockholder in a bloody English company wouldn't win her many
friends in the northern Highlands."

"But Alastair feels so strongly about the English taking control
of the oil. How could he, I mean—"

"Och, I don't know. *Alastair* says he fell in love with her before he knew who she was. *My* guess is that he knew a good
thing when he saw it."

"You can't mean that he married Fiona because she was Fiona
Grimsby?"

"What better way to save his precious Scottish oil? He's
infiltrated the enemy camp, so to speak. Or, to put it another
way, if you can't fight them—"

"Ian, you can't think that Alastair—"

"Married Fiona for her money? Does the possibility that Alastair might have feet of clay upset you? Why shouldn't he?
Money doesn't hurt, and Fiona's a beautiful woman in the bar-
gain. Almost too good to be true. Well, I hope we start seeing
some of that money around here."

"Oh, Ian, I just can't believe that . . ."

I was finally able to turn and stumble toward the tower. I had
remained tense and immobile throughout the conversation, and
Bruce was beginning to squirm in protest at his confinement. I
realized how tightly I had been clutching him, as a drowning
sailor clutches a life preserver to his chest. Bruce had started to
whimper softly, and I was afraid Mhari and Ian would hear him
and discover that I had overheard everything. I couldn't have

borne that; their conversation itself was already too much to bear.

Oh, why did I listen? I chastised myself as I ran up the steps to my room. Why, why, why? I threw myself face down on the bed, too dazed to think or even cry.

It seemed as though I had lain there forever when Bruce started licking my face and jumping around on the pillows to attract my attention, so I was surprised to look at the clock and see that only a few minutes had passed. Bruce was now barking excitedly, and I pulled him to me and held him close.

"Oh, Bruce, you're sweet to try and cheer me up. But I don't know if even your antics could help me now." Bruce's head was cocked to one side and there was a questioning look in his soft brown eyes. I suddenly thought of Toby, for his eyes had once watched me as adoringly. I sighed deeply, and Bruce's whiskered face took on an even more concerned look. "Bruce, I really do think you understand everything I say. You may well be my only friend. Well, we can't sit here like two bedraggled ragamuffins. Come on, let's get cleaned up. We'll both feel better after a bath and something to eat."

In spite of my brave words, I doubted that I would feel better. *Could* I ever feel better? I went through the mechanics of undressing and running the hot water for a bath, but my mind was on the conversation I had overheard. All my old doubts and fears had been reawakened.

Ian obviously thought that Alastair had married me for my money, an idea I had stoutly denied when Charles Haversham had suggested it. Charles's angry words came back to me as I lay in the tub: "He doesn't love you, Fiona, he wants your money." And I had protested that Alastair didn't know who I was, that he was marrying me because he loved me. But Alastair had known who I was, and he had known when we married. Did that mean that Charles and Ian were right? No. They were arguing from their own motives. Charles because he wanted to control Grimsby Petroleum, Ian because he was jealous of Alastair. Ian had told Mhari that Alastair had said he had fallen in love with me before he knew who I was. Alastair had told me that, too. But Ian didn't believe that, saying that Alastair had taken advantage of a good thing. Did that mean that Alastair had decided to marry me only after he realized who I was? Is he pretending to love me? No man could be that good an actor. Or could he? And what of the tensions within Lochinver itself? How much longer could the façade of a happy family be maintained with Ian feeling as he did about Alastair? Alastair had reassured me that their arguments about money were something that neither took seriously. But Ian had sounded serious to me. Could Alastair's offhand remarks to me be another example of play-acting? These thoughts kept going around in my head, and I felt overwhelmed by them. I didn't have the slightest idea of what I should do, and that was the most disturbing of all.

I tried to put the matter out of my mind and pay attention to what I was doing. I had finished my bath, and it was time to do something about Bruce's condition. Bruce hated to be washed and always made a fierce game of it, splashing water all over me and most of the bathroom. I recovered my spirits in spite of myself and soon was laughing at his carrying on and the way he was barking at the soap bubbles. We were both having a wonderful time, and I wondered why I had bothered to take a bath, as I was now getting a second drenching.

"Here you are. I might have known you two would be up to no good. Fiona, you should see yourself!"

I hadn't heard Alastair enter, and the sound of his voice startled me so much that my grip on Bruce slipped and he sprang from the tub and raced out of the room. Alastair managed to grab him and bring him back into the bathroom and set him down on the fluffy rug I had bought in the village. We both laughed at the sorry sight Bruce presented, a sodden woebegone figure all the smaller, for his usually fluffy coat was matted to his body.

"That's all right. He can come out now; he just needs to be toweled dry."

"I'll do that while you attend to yourself. You look as bad as he does. I've been looking for you and finally I heard barks and all sorts of noise coming from up here. And what do I find? A disaster area!"

"You know how Bruce hates being bathed. It's a major accomplishment just getting him in the tub. We were out all afternoon; I dropped in to see the Stewarts and stayed longer than I intended. She loves to talk and has some wonderful stories about your boyish escapades."

"I'll bet she does; I used to get into all sorts of trouble when I was little."

"Anyway, we came home by the loch and Bruce got muddy and we raced each other home and generally made a mess of ourselves. So here we are, getting all beautiful for tea."

"Aye, we've been waiting for you. There, you look fine now and so does Bruce. Let's go down; we're a pretty dreary bunch tonight and could do with some cheering up. Maybe Bruce will finally roll over when I tell him. What do you say to that?"

Bruce's impatient barks seemed to convey that he was only interested in eating and would have no part in performing for an audience. He raced out of the room and Alastair followed. I hesitated, not wanting to join the "dreary bunch" and yet not knowing how not to. Alastair came back into the room.

"Fiona, is anything wrong?"

"I was just looking for my sweater," I said quickly. "Alastair," I began and then stopped.

"Yes, what is it?"

"Alastair, do you love me? Truly love me?"

"Fiona." There was concern in Alastair's voice as he rushed over. "What a question! Did something happen to you today? Why, what's this?" I was clinging to him, holding the cloth of his jacket tight between my fingers.

"I just wanted to hear you say it."

"Darlin', of course I love you and I'll say it a thousand times if that will make you happy."

We held each other close, and as I clutched Alastair to me all I could think was: Let it be true. Dear God in Heaven, let it be true!

BOOK II

I Loved Him Not

'Twas there that we parted in yon shady glen,
On the steep, steep side o' Ben Lomond,
Where in purple hue the Hieland hills we view,
An' the moon coming out in the gloamin'.

Songs of the North

FOUR

The Scottish Party

The early fall passed quickly at Lochinver Castle. The days grew shorter. Sometimes they seemed to be over as soon as they had begun. The large fireplaces were continually aflame, but the high-ceilinged rooms were drafty and the stone walls gave them a permanent chill. The others hardly seemed to notice the cold, so I dressed warmly and did my best to ignore my shivers. Fortunately, I had become too busy to sit still for long. Lewis Demerest had been engaged to paint Alastair's and my portraits, and he had already begun the preliminary sketches for mine, which was to be done first.

Charles regularly sent large envelopes containing the latest information on Grimsby Petroleum's progress. Although I was no longer able to go in to the office every day, I still wanted to feel as though I was actively involved with the company. I had turned the small room next to our bedroom into an office of sorts, and it was there that I spent most of my mornings conscientiously going over those weekly reports in detail. There were several reasons why I had chosen to work there. As it was one of the smallest rooms in the castle, it was easy to heat with an electric heater, and I felt cozy and comfortable hunched over the table I used as a desk. Moreover, through the circular little room's diamond-paned windows I saw that same view of Loch Assynt below that had thrilled me my first night at Lochinver. I had removed the muslin curtains Mrs. Ross had hung, so that during the brief day the room was bathed in sharp-angled light. I also valued the privacy in my little office. I felt removed from the rest of the castle; I could work there undisturbed and at the same time keep the others from being too aware of what I was doing. It wasn't that I was hiding from my new family, not really, but ever since I had overheard that conversation between Ian and Mhari I felt that the less they knew of Grimsby Petroleum the happier we all would be.

In addition to my oil business, there were the preparations for Mhari's party that was to be the official celebration of Alastair's and my wedding and my welcome to Lochinver. Mhari had wanted to have the party as soon as we arrived, but as grand an affair as she was planning took time to arrange properly. She had finally decided on the first weekend in November, and the whole household was working toward that date. Since many of the guests would be coming from farther away than a day's drive, we were to have several as house guests for the entire weekend. Rooms that had not been used in years were being rid of their dust, and beds that had not been slept in within Mhari's memory were made up with fresh sheets. Some of the village girls were hired to help, and Mrs. Ross had her hands full with the "extras" as she called them. There were wonderful things happening in the kitchen. Many dishes were being prepared in advance, including a special cake that Mrs. Ross had said needed a month in which to age properly. She saw to that herself, not wanting to let anyone else see the recipe. It was a secret she closely guarded, because it had been in her family for generations. Mhari said I should be impressed, since Mrs. Ross made this cake only for those occasions she deemed worthy.

"Let's see, we had it when Alastair turned twenty-one and when I was married . . . we've not had it since. There are other cakes for birthdays, and at Christmas we have the traditional puddings, so this will be a real treat."

"It's one I'm certainly looking forward to."

"Och, it's grand. Though it's been over two years since I've eaten it, I can still remember the taste of it exactly. It's that good!"

"Does no one else know the recipe?"

"No, not a soul. Mrs. Ross says she remembers the day her mother gave her the recipe; apparently it was quite a solemn ceremony. Since Mrs. Ross doesn't have a daughter, she may take her secret to the grave, but I've always hoped I could coax it from her. Maybe she'll give it to you, Fiona."

"Me?"

"Aye, as the lady of the house. Then we'll be able to carry on the tradition of the Lochinver Cake; that's what we've always called it."

"Well, let's hope she gives it to us both." Since I had overheard that argument between Mhari and Ian, I was very careful to play down any references to my being the "lady of the house." I had watched carefully, but Mhari's behavior toward me was as friendly and open as ever. We had had fewer chances to chat these days, due to Mhari's constant rushing about. She seldom had time to sit still for more than a few minutes, and when she did find the time we were invariably interrupted by one of the "extras." I worried that Mhari was doing too much, but she seemed to thrive on the happy chaos. At any rate, she refused to let me do anything to help.

"No, Fiona. Absolutely not. This party is for you. One can't have the guest of honor working on her own party. No, I don't want to hear any more about it; this is your and Alastair's wedding present. A little late, perhaps, but that couldn't be helped. Now, you know I love doing this, so you just go ahead and let me. I want you to relax and enjoy everything."

I tried to follow Mhari's instructions, but I was too nervous about everything to relax completely. The majority of the invited guests were complete strangers to me. I have always been shy and uncomfortable in crowds, and I began to dread the ordeal of meeting so many new people at once. Yet, at the same time, I looked forward to the excitement a large party generates. I dared not reveal my ambivalent attitude to Mhari, for she was anxious that everything be perfect for me. I needn't have feared, however; Mhari was too busy to notice anything. Alastair was another matter, and he soon commented on my preoccupied state.

"A penny for your thoughts, Fiona," he said one evening as we were sitting alone by the fire. "You look as though you are trying to solve the world's problems. Out with it, lass."

I flushed, for I had been thinking, as I did so often, of Ian's words concerning Alastair. I decided to seize this opportunity to put into words my fears about meeting so many strangers.

"Oh, I'm just a little nervous about this party of Mhari's. There will be so many people there I don't know, and I'm not very good in large groups. I'm a little afraid of making a fool of myself in front of all your friends."

"Is that all? Och, from your expression I thought it was something serious. Darlin', it's only natural you should be somewhat jittery, but once the party's underway it'll be all right. You'll charm everyone, just as you've charmed me."

"Well, I just want everything to be right, Mhari's working so hard to make it perfect."

"I know she is, and everything will be perfect. The MacDonnells are coming; you'll like Flora—she's traveled in the States and you can chat about your 'old country'; the Duncans—Andrew was one of my lecturers at St. Andrews; the Grahams—Colin's a writer, and Sarah is an authority on antiques; she'll be full of advice on how to furnish Lochinver. You'll have lots to talk about with everybody, so there's no need to feel awkward. And some of the local families will be here; even if you don't know them well, you've met them in the village."

"You're right; it won't be so bad. If only I can keep everyone's name straight!"

As usual, Alastair had reassured me, and I ceased to fret about the party and began once more to anticipate happily the approaching weekend.

I spent several afternoons a week with Lewis Demerest, the young artist Alastair had commissioned to do our portraits. He was quite pleasant and boyishly attractive; his best feature was his constant smile, which lighted his whole face. Lewis looked more like an athlete than an artist; his broad shoulders and large hands seemed incapable of producing the delicate brush strokes that were characteristic of his work. Though he was the same height as I was, I felt quite small beside him.

It was decided he should work in one of the rooms in the

north wing, for we did not use it and he could leave his easel set up without fear of its being disturbed. The light was excellent for painting: the ground-floor room had large windows, and there were no trees outside to obstruct the daylight.

Though I had feared I would be self-conscious about posing, Lewis put me at my ease immediately with his warm and natural charm. He loved to talk, and I soon felt we were two friends spending the afternoon chatting instead of being artist and subject. As a result, I had to be constantly reminded to maintain my pose; yet Lewis was never impatient.

There was great discussion as to whether I should sit or stand, and so we tried both. I was secretly relieved when it was decided that the long, silk tartan skirt was displayed to greater advantage when I sat. Bruce preferred this pose also and made quite a game of hide-and-seek among the folds. I tried to bar him from the room, but he would not be separated from me and whined and scratched on the door so hard that I feared he would do it serious damage.

"That's all right, Mrs. MacLeod. You can let the little tyke in. I'll just put him in the painting. He's one of the Stewart pups?"

"Yes, my husband gave him to me several weeks ago."

"Aye, I thought I had seen him. I've got one of the litter myself, a female I've named Ellen, after Scott's *The Lady of the Lake*. Do you know it?"

"Not very well. It's one of my husband's favorites; he likes to quote from it and we've started to read it aloud."

"One of these days, I shall bring Ellen with me, then she and Bruce can run each other ragged instead of us."

Sometimes Alastair would join us and stay to comment on the work in progress, and Mhari would occasionally poke her head in, but, for the most part, Lewis and I were left alone. I knew he preferred it that way; he didn't like people looking at his work while he was painting. Lewis never said anything to that effect—he was too polite—but I could tell from the way his face clouded and his eyes changed from light blue to hazel. I was surprised to discover that I also preferred it when we were left to ourselves. The time I spent with Lewis came to be sort of a vacation, and I could forget any problems I had while we were talking. I came to look forward to the two afternoons a week that Lewis came and to hope (but not without some feelings of guilt) that the painting would take a while to complete.

Lewis had been born in the small fishing village of Lochinver, and after studying at the University of Edinburgh for a year he had gone to London and then to Paris, where he had lived until his return six months before. Although I had never been there, Paris was a city that fascinated me and I plied him with questions about the Bohemian life I imagined he had led.

"Och, it wasn't as picturesque as all that, for all that Paris is a lovely city. I shared a flat with some friends I had made in London. We were an odd lot: John was a poet, Stuart and I were painters, and Nick was constantly banging at our rickety piano. He said that he was working on the symphony that would make the world forget Beethoven, but I never liked any of his things. He was great fun, though. To earn money he played in a rock group that had some measure of success, and he was always bringing the strangest people home."

"It sounds like *La Bohème* come to life."

"Unfortunately, I never met my Mimi. And we were hardly starving. I managed to sell a respectable amount of my work, and John's parents sent him large checks regularly."

"Why did you come back to Lochinver?" I couldn't imagine wanting to give up that idyllic life.

"I had been thinking of it for quite a while when—Mrs. MacLeod, do keep your head tilted toward the door, good; hold it—when my father became quite ill. I came home to be with him, and after he died I decided to stay on. I live with my mother and Joan, that's my sister—she's the schoolteacher in the village. My father had converted part of the house into a large studio, so I couldn't be more comfortable."

"It was your father who painted Alastair's parents."

"Aye, he had quite a reputation as a portrait painter; he traveled all over Britain fulfilling commissions. I do mostly landscapes, but I was pleased when your husband asked me to paint the both of you; it makes a pleasant change and it's a bit of a challenge."

"Why is that?"

"It's easy enough to capture a likeness, but if that's all you want, you're better off having a photograph taken. The challenge comes in capturing the person's soul, their very being. That's where genius comes in. So, you might say I regard this as a test, to see if I have the genius to capture you in my painting. To get beyond the Highland costume to the real Fiona MacLeod."

"I hope you don't find anything bad." I strove to keep my voice carefree, but the uneasiness I had felt when Alastair first suggested the portraits returned. I had been relieved when I met Lewis, for I thought him too young, too ingenuous, to do more than reproduce a likeness. And now he was saying he hoped to reveal my soul. I told myself I was being silly, I had nothing to hide, yet the idea of Lewis capturing my thoughts was a disturbing one. Would the anxiety I had felt since overhearing Ian's remarks show in my face? I thought of the portrait of Alastair's mother; that painting had caught the sadness in her life; her brooding eyes haunted the gallery above the great hall. I tried to shake her image from my mind and told myself sternly: Fiona, the solution is for you to keep your mind on happy things. Now, let's have no more nonsense about haunting eyes!

"There! That's what I mean. If I could capture that expression in my painting I would be hailed as a genius!" Lewis's excited voice scattered my thoughts.

"I'm sorry; what?"

"The look on your face just then. A curious blend of sadness, wonderment. You seemed quite vulnerable and fragile—yet there is a strength, a certain lift to your chin that reveals your determination. Fragile, yet strong. Aye, you're a contradictory woman, Fiona MacLeod."

"Oh, Lewis, I was just deciding what to tell Mrs. Ross to order from the grocer's."

"Then, why so sad?"

"Have you seen what the Star is charging for meat these days? Well, then, mystery solved. Now, enough about my facial expressions; I'm self-conscious as it is. Tell me, how did you decide to go to Paris?"

"My father encouraged me to go. He had a love for all things French; he had spent a great deal of time in Paris and lived for a while in the South of France. I was named for one of his good friends: Louis de Cheyne. He was godfather at my christening and visited us every couple of years. Och, the stories he and my father would tell of their youth; they made prewar Paris sound wicked and exciting. De Cheyne never married, so he thought of me as a son and brought me wonderful presents. My mother didn't quite approve; being a true Scotswoman, she was suspicious of foreigners and my father would consume great quantities of wine when De Cheyne visited—they drank far into the night. She didn't want me to be named for him, either, but my father insisted. She was equally stubborn and made him change the spelling. They had the same argument when my sister was born. He wanted Jeanne and they compromised on Joan. I must say, I've always been grateful to Mother, you can imagine how our school chums would have teased us."

"Oh, yes, children can be quite cruel about odd names. I underwent a bit of hazing. Fiona is hardly a common name in America, especially in New England—romantic names jar the Puritan sensibilities. I remember, in the fourth grade, there was one little monster who christened me Telephone and the name stuck through grade school. *That* wasn't so bad, but it got shortened to Phony. *That* I didn't like at all!"

"Did the name stick?"

"No. I beat up Billy Walker, the little monster, after school one day and no one dared call me Phony after that!"

"I was right. You do have strength and determination!"

"Well, I've changed my tactics," I laughed.

Lewis and I talked about many things during our sessions; he was interested and involved in many activities. He loved sports and owned a small boat in which he had spent many hours that summer sailing and fishing along the coast. Lewis offered to take me sailing when the weather grew warmer, and I immediately accepted, for I had done quite a bit of sailing with my parents. It occurred to me that Lewis was probably lonely in Lochinver; he hadn't been back long enough to make many friends. In a way, I was in the same position; outside of Mhari and Alastair and Ian, I knew no one on more than a casual basis. My good friend, Rosemary Beaton, was far away in London, and her busy schedule didn't allow her much time for letter writing. My correspondence included answering my parents' weekly letter and the occasional note Charles Haversham included in the envelopes he sent concerning Grimsby Petroleum. I had hardly felt bored since my arrival at Lochinver, but I was glad of this opportunity to make a new friend.

Lewis talked frequently of his sister, Joan, and said on several occasions how eager she was to meet me and that I should visit when I was in the village. I replied I would, and then on sudden impulse I invited Lewis to the party Mhari was planning, saying he should bring Joan with him.

"There will be so many people I don't know, it'll be nice to see a familiar face," I added.

"If you're sure it will be all right."

"Certainly. The party's in my honor, so I should be able to invite at least two guests. I'll ask Mhari to send you a formal invitation in the morning."

"That's awfully nice of you; Joan will be thrilled. She's always wanted to see the castle and constantly plies me with questions. And of course," he added shyly, "I will be pleased to attend also. Thank you very much, Mrs. MacLeod."

"Good. Then, it's all settled. And I do think you should stop calling me Mrs. MacLeod; it makes me feel positively ancient. Please call me Fiona."

"All right, and thank you again. I think we've done enough for today, so I'll see you on Thursday, Mrs. M—excuse me . . . Fiona."

I noticed that, as he said my name, he blushed furiously. His face matched the tangle of reddish-blond curls on his head. To hide his embarrassment, he kept his head down and busied himself with cleaning his brushes as I left the room. Really, I thought to myself, he is such a little boy, though he's only a few years younger than I am. I found myself hoping he wouldn't change, for it would be a shame if he lost his enthusiasm. I smiled to myself as I went quickly upstairs to change out of my tartan costume into warmer clothes. If I hurried, there would be time to take Bruce for a walk before tea. I met Mhari on the stairs and told her that I had invited Lewis and his sister to the party and that I hoped she wouldn't mind two additional guests. Mhari was as delighted as I hoped she would be.

"Fiona, what a nice idea! Lewis Demerest seems such a nice boy and . . ."

"Mhari, he's a year older than you are," I reminded her.

"You know what I mean, he's so eager about everything. I'm sure his sister is just as nice; I've heard she's a very good teacher. I'll go and address the invitation right away. I'm glad to have more people from the village; we don't have large parties often, so it's nice to include as many as we can."

We parted, and I continued up to the tower. I changed quickly, spurred on by Bruce's eager barking. He could always tell when I was getting ready to take him for a walk.

The week before the party sped by. Since I had invited Lewis and Joan, I felt less nervous; I was now sure of another familiar face. We had postponed the portrait sittings until after the party; the room we had been using had to be cleaned and made ready. Most of the evening's activities—the buffet dinner and the dancing—would take place in the great hall, but the smaller rooms on the ground floor would be available for those who wanted to escape for quiet conversation.

There was no question of what I was to wear; I would be dressed in the tartan outfit Alastair had given me, so I was concentrating on helping Mhari. She also had a formal dress similiar to mine, but since she was entering her sixth month of pregnancy she was unable to wear it. My mother had taught me to sew, and I had always made most of my own clothes, so I decided to make a dress for Mhari. It was the one thing I could do for her when she was spending so much time on Alastair's and my behalf. Mhari remembered a sewing machine that Mrs. Ross had used to sew their clothes when Mhari and Alastair were small, and after a short search we located it in one of the bedrooms in the south wing. It needed some minor repairs, but Ian was soon able to get it into working order and I set it up in a room adjoining their bedroom, a room that would soon be a nursery. The machine was a veritable antique and had to be operated manually, but I soon became used to it and began to prefer it to the electric machines I had learned on, as I had more control over its speed.

On a trip into the village, Mhari and I had chosen the material, a wine-red velvet that enhanced the red highlights in her soft brown hair. The small dressmaking shop had offered little in the way of patterns, but I was able to make one using one of Mhari's dresses. The dress was to be fashioned in a simple Empire style, one that would flatter Mhari's shape and that I could alter so she could wear it after her baby was born.

The work had gone slowly at first: It was hard to get Mhari to spare the occasional half hours needed for fittings. I practically had to resort to locking her in the room, but I finally finished the preparations and soon was working on the dress itself. I have always sewed quickly and the majority of the work was done in less than a week. The hand sewing took longer, and every night after dinner I hemmed the dress as we sat and talked in front of a four-log fire.

The day of the party finally came, and miraculously everything was ready. The time for the gathering was set for seven o'clock, but those guests who would be staying over would start arriving in the afternoon, making Saturday morning the last opportunity for last-minute preparations. Mrs. Ross had been up before dawn working in the kitchen, but I had persuaded Mhari that she should sleep late and have breakfast in bed. I was worried that she would overdo and then be too exhausted to fully enjoy the evening. It wasn't hard to persuade Mhari; she readily admitted she was tired and could do with some extra sleep. She seemed to enjoy the prospect of being pampered a little.

Around three o'clock that afternoon, the first guests—the Duncans—arrived. Andrew Duncan was a lecturer in modern European history at St. Andrews, and Alastair had done research for him as a graduate student. Dr. Duncan had been so impressed with Alastair's work that he had listed him as coauthor on several papers and they had become good friends in the process. I immediately liked Andrew's wife, Morag, a pleasant woman whose lisp added a charming touch to her soft-spoken burr. Mhari and I showed her their room in the south wing, while Alastair and Andrew discussed the latest political news in the living room. Morag was tired from the drive, so Mhari and I left her to rest and went downstairs. Our guests had started to arrive.

Mhari and I greeted the guests together, with Mhari playing the role of hostess and then introducing me. A routine was developed: the men would join Alastair and Ian for a whiskey while we escorted the women upstairs to "freshen up." As dinner was

97

not to be served until nine, we had planned to have a light tea at five, thus leaving plenty of time for our house guests to change before the party. I was feeling slightly overwhelmed from the barrage of new faces and names, but it was less of an ordeal than I had feared. Everyone was pleasant and genuinely pleased to meet Alastair's "bride." There were the MacDonnells, Flora and Stuart; the Grahams, Colin and Sarah; the Campbells, Charles and Mary; the Scotts, the MacDonalds, the MacKenzies. My head was swimming; I had never heard so many Scottish names at one time, and I despaired of trying to keep all the Macs straight. At one point I whispered to Mhari that perhaps everyone should be required to wear a name tag with the legend "Hi, my name is _____" inscribed on it; Mhari laughed and squeezed my hand reassuringly and said I would know them all soon enough. It was easier than I had thought, for Alastair had briefed me on our guests, telling me a little about each one, and now I had the faces to attach to the names.

Most of the guests had been at Lochinver before, on the occasion of Mhari and Ian's wedding, two years past. Some were old family friends who had known Mhari and Alastair as children, and Mhari had to endure many comments along the lines of "Imagine! our little Mhari all grown up and having a baby of her own!" There were school friends of Ian and Alastair, some university friends of Alastair's and some new friends Alastair had made since his involvement in Scottish Nationalist Party politics. They were a diverse and interesting group, and since many seemed to be meeting each other for the first time, I wasn't alone in having to cope with new names.

I had noticed something unusual about many of the men. On their jacket lapels, near the heart, was a small stickpin fashioned in the shape of a red lion. At first I thought nothing of it, but as more men greeted me I studied that pin. It seemed to be made of pewter, with the lion painted in red, its eye marked by a small piece of glass or, in some cases, a gem. The lions appeared to be identical: each one clawed the air hungrily. Much later that evening, I was to be surprised by one particular lion, which seemed more desperate than its fellows; when I raised eyes to see whose plaid it adorned, I stopped short. It was Alastair. Where had he gotten that red pin? I resolved to ask him at the first opportunity, but then I thought again and decided I would instead ask Mhari what those red lions signified.

We served in the large dining room, and afterward everyone went upstairs to change. I dressed quickly, for I knew Mhari would already be downstairs supervising the last-minute preparations and I wanted to help her. I had finished putting up my hair, hoping it would behave for once and not fall down while I was dancing, and was pinning the tartan sash to my shoulder, when Alastair came into the room. He had dressed earlier and was resplendent in the MacLeod full-dress tartan, complete with sword buckled to his belt. The dashing costume made him appear larger than he actually was, and with his full beard and swashbuckling manner, I was struck anew at how he resembled the proud chieftains from Scotland's proud past. Alastair bounded into the dressing room and picked me up, swinging me around till I protested laughingly that I should be mussed.

"Disheveled or immaculate, you'll be the loveliest lady in the hall tonight. Here, lovely, I wanted to give you this." Alastair produced a small box from his jacket and presented it with a flourish. "To the Lady of Lochinver," he announced, his twinkling eyes belying the solemn tones of his deep voice.

I took the box and pressed the gold clasp. The lid flew back, revealing a silver bracelet engraved with the bull's head that was the MacLeod crest. On both sides of the emblem, in an old-fashioned script, was their motto: Hold fast. It was an exquisite piece of jewelry and very old. I was silent for a few moments, trying to think of the appropriate words; as I raised my head, Alastair saw the tears of happiness in my eyes and held me tightly. We remained close for several minutes, enjoying the intimacy of that special moment. Finally, Alastair broke the spell and, taking the bracelet from me, he put it around my wrist, his strong, thick fingers manipulating the delicate clasp expertly. The bracelet fit perfectly, almost as if it had been made for me.

"There, that's it. This bracelet has been in our family for many generations, Fiona. It's traditionally given to the bride of the laird upon their betrothal. But, since we dispensed with that formality, I decided tonight was the proper time."

"Alastair, it's the most beautiful thing I've ever seen. How can I ever thank you?"

99

"By staying just the way you are and loving me as much as you do now."

"Well, that's simple enough," I said.

"Good. Now let's go down and greet our guests."

We found Mhari already downstairs, bustling about the great hall, rearranging flowers, inspecting the tables where dinner would be served and giving last-minute instructions to the "extras" hired for the evening. She looked lovely, her curly hair tied with a velvet ribbon that matched the dress I had made; around her shoulders was a shawl in the MacLeod tartan, its strong yellow and black colors calmed by the burgundy dress.

"Och, here you are already, what a handsome couple you make. Fiona, you look so striking, I do so envy you your height. And your slimness." Mhari cast a rueful glance at her stomach and added, "though I must say, this dress does a remarkable job of camouflage. Do I look all right, not too matronly?"

"Little sister, you'll never look matronly," Alastair laughed, giving her hair ribbons a playful tweak.

The small orchestra imported from Inverness for the evening had started to warm up, and the strains of a waltz filtered softly through the great hall. Alastair seized Mhari around her waist and they began to dance, their staccato steps echoing in the large, empty room. I stood enjoying the lovely picture they made: Alastair, tall and magnificent in his Highland costume; Mhari, dainty and feminine and, despite her gown, looking younger than her twenty-two years. Though they were different in appearance, it was obvious they were brother and sister, and it was a joy to watch them. A noise behind me made me turn, and I found Ian standing behind me, watching the dancers intently. He, too, was in Highland dress, in a muted green and red plaid I supposed to be the Nicolson tartan. Although he looked quite handsome, the outfit did not suit him as Alastair's did him; Ian was obviously costumed for a single evening, while Alastair seemed to be naturally attired. I smiled at him, but Ian was oblivious to my presence, concentrating on the dancers. I tried once more to get his attention and commented on how nice the room looked.

"What? Oh, Fiona, I didn't see you. How lovely you look!"

The words were automatic; Ian's attention was still on Mhari and Alastair.

"Thank you, and you look equally nice. I've never seen you wear your tartan before."

"Hmmm? You must forgive me, Fiona, I'm afraid I feel rather silly in this and a little self-conscious."

"I know, but it's only for one night and I appreciate your sacrifice. Ah, here are the dancers—bravo! You looked lovely out there."

"Aye, it's pleasant to have the floor all to oneself. Though, really, Alastair, you should have had your first dance of the evening with Fiona."

"And so I shall. When the formal dancing starts. This was just for old times' sake, just us two—like the old days."

Any further conversation was halted as our guests started coming into the hall. They, too, were all dressed in Highland costume as we were, the men in the full-dress uniform of their clan, the women in either long white dresses worn with a plaid sash or dressed as I was in a long tartan skirt and sash. As we moved about the room, the various plaids created colorful and changing patterns; it was a glamorous and exciting scene, and I felt that we modern-day MacLeods were doing justice to Lochinver Castle. I even fancied that the ancestral portraits were smiling down from their perches on the gallery walls, beaming in full approval.

Soon Mr. Ross, who was our butler for the evening, was announcing the first arrivals—those who lived close enough to come for the party itself. A receiving line was formed; Mhari and Ian were first, then myself and Alastair. Our guests went through this formality quickly; they were all friends of the family and I knew many of them by sight. Lewis Demerest was one of the first to arrive, with his sister, Joan, whom he introduced a little stiffly, as though he felt shy before so many people. Joan also seemed a little awed and thrilled to be inside Lochinver Castle at last, but as she shook my hand she flashed a smile as warm and sunny as her brother's. I promised I would chat with them later.

Most of the people passed by in an endless blur of smiling faces and handshaking, but there was one guest that caught my attention immediately. There had been a pause in the arrivals and I was whispering to Alastair when Mhari touched my arm and said, still holding my hand, "Fiona, I want to introduce Ailis Campbell." There was something in Mhari's voice—a quality I couldn't identify—and I glanced at her quickly before turning to the girl who stood before me. Mhari's face was arranged in a polite and gracious smile, but there was an unspoken question in her eyes. I presumed she was silently asking if I had met Ailis Campbell before, so I turned to greet her.

Before me stood the loveliest woman I had ever seen. She was several inches shorter than I, with luxuriant, dark red hair that set off her pale, creamy complexion to perfection. She was dressed simply in a dark blue dress, with a tartan sash in the blue and green Campbell pattern her only ornament. The simplicity of her dress heightened her beauty. Her dark blue eyes were staring at me with frank curiosity, as though she were appraising my qualities. I couldn't know what she thought, but she appeared satisfied as she said in a low, well-modulated voice:

"I'm so pleased to meet you, Mrs. MacLeod; we've been hearing so much about you. I've known Alastair such a long time and we were at university together. I've been dying to meet his bride." Her slow drawl emphasized the word as if it were capitalized. "You were quite a surprise to us all, wasn't she, Graham?" Ailis turned to a thin, dark man standing behind her for confirmation, but he didn't respond. "Fiona, may I call you Fiona? Such a lovely name. Fiona, may I present Graham MacKenzie?" Graham MacKenzie shook my hand politely but gravely; there was no expression on his face. He nodded briefly, almost curtly, at Alastair before stepping back. He seemed anxious to be off and tried to take Ailis's arm, but she ignored his none-too-subtle hint as her eyes fell on my wrist.

"Why, Fiona, I see you're wearing the Lochinver bracelet. It's not as glamorous as having some family emeralds, but I'm sure the sentimental value more than makes up for that. 'Hold fast.' You must find our Scottish mottos so quaint. The Campbells' is 'Forget Not,'" she added, smiling at Alastair. "Well, now that we've met, I know we'll be good friends." She stood on tiptoe to give Alastair a quick, but warm, kiss on the cheek. "Alastair, it's good to see you; we must all get together soon." Ailis turned back to me. "Fiona, how ever do you stand this beard? I should find it so prickly." She and Graham spun away.

I was taken aback by this encounter and I didn't know quite what to make of Ailis Campbell. I had the feeling she was aware of and pleased by my discomfiture. I looked at Alastair to see if he would offer any comment, but a stern, almost angry expression had settled on his face. He turned toward me and must have read my thoughts, for he said, "I don't know about you, Fiona, but I've stood here long enough. I think everyone has arrived, so why don't we have a drink? I certainly need one after being polite for so long." As we walked away he added gently, "Fiona, don't mind Ailis; she loves to put on airs and be the center of attention. She and Graham and I were history students at university. Ailis and I had sort of a college romance, but that's been over for years. They're both very active in the nationalism movement, you see, though Graham goes along with it just to be with Ailis. He's carried a torch for her for years. I don't know why she just doesn't marry him, the little fool." These last words were more muttered than spoken, and again I looked at Alastair questioningly, but he obviously wished to speak no more of Graham and Ailis.

The party seemed a great success. Alastair and I were kept very busy circulating among our many guests, and for several hours the only glimpses I had of him were as we passed on the dance in the arms of other partners. At one point I saw him dancing with Ailis, they were on the other side of the room and his back was to me, yet I could observe clearly the way she raised her delicate face to his, her large eyes glowing, her lips parted in a smile. Then they were lost in the crowd of dancers. I wondered what they were talking about. Was Ailis recalling their past? Was she asking him to "forget not"? It was with difficulty that I returned my concentration to my own partner, Dr. Duncan, who was reminiscing about Alastair's student days and what an excellent scholar he had been. Ordinarily I would have been quite attentive, for I loved to hear stories of Alastair's past, but my eyes darted about the room searching for a glimpse of that dark head held so close to that red one, and I wondered about a different aspect of Alastair's past.

The waltz came to an end and I stood talking with Andrew Duncan when Alastair appeared beside us.

"I think you'll forgive me if I claim my wife for a dance, Andrew. This is the last waltz before dinner and I've barely seen her all evening!"

Andrew murmured something to the effect of "you young people run along," and Alastair whirled me onto the floor.

"Fiona, you're the belle of the ball," Alastair teased. "Why, even now I'm afraid someone will want to cut in."

"Well, Laird MacLeod, you've not done too badly. You've managed to dance with every attractive woman here."

"Aye, duty calls. It wouldn't do to have wallflowers; I have to make sure everyone has a good time."

"Is that why you danced twice with fair Ailis? Somehow, I don't see her as a wallflower. She doesn't seem the type."

"Hark! Do I detect a note of jealousy? I've always suspected those green eyes of yours, Fiona."

"Well, she is an old friend, as you said."

"Precisely. And, if you look yonder, you'll see my old friend dancing romantically with Graham MacKenzie." I looked and, indeed, there were Graham and Ailis dancing close together, as any two people in love would dance, as we were dancing. Alastair continued, "and while we're on the subject, my love, I noticed you in the arms of Lewis Demerest more than once."

"Oh, Alastair. Lewis doesn't know very many people here. I have my duty, too."

"He seemed quite attentive. Could it be the artist is falling in love with his model?"

"Alastair, he's just a boy. Don't be ridiculous."

"No more ridiculous than you were being. But I'm glad you're jealous; it proves how much you love me."

"I do love you, very much."

"And I you." Alastair kissed me lightly on my nose. The music had stopped, and the dancers were moving off the floor. "Well, Fiona, let's head for the dinner table. Our guests won't eat unless we do, so once again we must do our duty—one that I'm glad to comply with; all this exercise has made me hungry!"

The serving table was set up at one end of the hall, and Mrs. Ross had outdone herself in preparing a bountiful buffet. At either end of the table was a large roast, and in between were salads, meat pies, large loaves of bread, more food than I could have ever imagined. Tables were being set up, and Alastair sat me at the largest while he went to get our dinner. I was joined immediately by Mhari.

"Oh, la. It's nice to sit down and let the men wait on us for a change. I've not danced this much since, well, since my wedding."

"It's a wonderful party, Mhari; everyone's having such a good time."

"I'm so glad you're pleased. I wanted so much to make this a success, a proper celebration for you and Alastair. Fiona," she added in a low voice. "I hope you weren't upset by anything Ailis Campbell said in the receiving line."

"No, though I did wonder. Alastair said something about a college romance."

"Aye, they were together at university. It broke off, and then, a couple of years ago, they started seeing each other again. Ailis is very nice and quite intelligent, but I've never really liked her. I was so afraid that Alastair would marry her, they were even engaged for a while, but he suddenly stopped seeing her. And then he married you and brought you here to live happily ever after." Mhari laughed gaily and hugged me warmly.

"By the way, Mhari, maybe you can tell me—what is this red pin I've been seeing on so many men's jackets?"

"You mean the Red Lion?" she asked, and I nodded. "Well, the Red Lion is the national emblem of Scotland, as the Red Dragon is of Wales. It's on our flag, too, but, of course, it's illegal to fly that flag. The Scottish Nationalists have seized on the Lion as their symbol and they display it everywhere. I think the fact it's prohibited makes it all the more exciting. The SNP—I'm sorry, the Scottish Nationalist Party—sells these pins for a pound apiece to raise money for their cause."

The dinner was delicious, and we all ate heartily. The inevitable toasts to Alastair's and my health were proposed frequently. Finally, a general silence was called, and Alastair rose, glass in hand. He made a flowery speech, thanking everyone for coming and saying how grateful he was to Mhari and Ian for hosting the affair. Then, turning to me, he continued:

"And I want to propose a very special toast, to a very special person. My wife, Fiona MacLeod!"

Alastair drained his glass quickly and bent to kiss me. I smiled and half rose to accept the boisterous cheers and quickly sat down again, embarrassed by the commotion. Someone spoke to me, and as I turned to answer, my eyes met those of Ailis, who was sitting at the far end of the table. She smiled and raised her glass, but I fancied there was something mocking in her salute. I forced myself to smile politely in return. I was annoyed with myself for feeling an antagonism for someone I didn't know. Really, Fiona, I scolded myself, a party in honor of your marriage is no place to think such thoughts.

At this point the dessert was brought in. It was a spectacular sight, greeted with the appropriate "oohs" and "ahs." There were various tarts and pastries arranged on the table that was being wheeled toward us, but the center of attention was a huge, four-layered cake. It was obviously Mrs. Ross's famed specialty, the Lochinver Cake, as Mhari had called it. It was a dark cake, covered with a thin, cream-colored frosting and decorated with candied fruits. As the pieces were cut, I could see that it was studded with more fruits and nuts, yet the texture was not that of a fruitcake. As guest of honor I was served the first piece, and it was all I could do to restrain myself from tasting it until the others were served. Finally I took a bite, and it was as wonderful as Mhari had said—more wonderful, and I said as much to Mhari.

"Aye, it's pure ambrosia. The only problem is that it's so rich, one can only eat a small piece. I really shouldn't be having any at all; my baby will definitely be born with a sweet tooth!"

Coffee was served, and the party broke up into smaller groups. I was amused to see the age-old traditions maintained; the men retired to the living rooms to discuss politics over their cigars and brandy, while the women formed their own groups. In an hour or so, the dancing would resume and go on till everyone was exhausted. But now the hall was peaceful; the only sounds were the gentle murmurs of conversation and the clinking of dishes being cleared. I felt relaxed and was glad of this lull in the evening's activities. The conversation at our table turned to the subject of Mhari's baby, and soon the other women were talking of

106

their childbirth experiences. I glanced about and noticed Lewis and Joan sitting by themselves sipping coffee. I excused myself and went to join them.

"Fiona, it's been a lovely party, thank you so much for inviting Lewis and me. I've always wanted to see the castle, and now to be here as a guest—it's absolutely thrilling. Lewis had described it to me, but that's not the same as seeing it for oneself, is it?" Joan talked in the same eager manner as her brother. They were similar in appearance, but Joan's hair was quite straight and unbelievably blond. I said I hoped she would come again in the daylight, when I could give her a proper tour.

"Thank you so much, Fiona, and you must come for tea some afternoon. You know, Lewis had talked so much about you I feel as though I know you already!"

As Joan talked, I looked at Lewis, who proceeded to study his coffee cup with great interest, and noticed that the tips of his ears were bright red. I stayed with them a little longer and then decided to go in search of Alastair. The musicians had had their dinner and were now starting to warm up; soon it would be time for more dancing. I wandered around the hall, stopping to talk with several of our guests, until the sound of angry voices drew me to the door of one of the living rooms.

". . . an' I say the time *is* richt! Look a wha' the Irish hae done; they've got the English by the throat. Alastair, we've got tae do somethin' before we've nothin' left. The English an' the Yanks are rakin' i' the profits frae our oil. Are we tae sit an' watch? I say nae! An' the others agree wit' me." There was a chorus of assenting murmurs and shouts of "Aye, we mauna let 'em do it!" The speaker, whom I didn't recognize, continued. "We've gone wit' ye an' listened tae ye long eno', MacLeod. Ye've said tha' violence will be it' i' the end; why do ye hesitate now? Bombs will show British Petroleum an' Grimsby Petroleum an' the rest tha' we mean business; they'll be forced to negotiate. If I didna ken ye, I'd say yer bein' swayed by tha'—"

The speaker was silenced by a warning cough, and I heard Ian say, "Alastair!" Alastair had been looking out the windows, but now he turned and saw me standing at the door. Everyone in the room stared at me. The group was composed of Alastair's friends from university and from his work in politics. Ian was there, and

Graham MacKenzie, but there was only one woman in the room besides myself: Ailis, who was watching me speculatively. Alastair had an ashen look on his face, but he quickly recovered his composure and came over to me.

"Fiona," he said, putting an arm about my shoulders. "You must forgive me for neglecting you. When a group of Scots get together, they'll talk all night!"

"I didn't mean to interrupt." My voice sounded as unsure as I felt. "But the dancing is about to start again, and I thought . . . but do keep on talking if you want."

"Nae; we've said all that can be said. Politics and partying don't mix; one detracts from the other. Let's join our other guests."

Alastair and I walked back into the great hall, and I thought about what I had heard. I wondered what that man had been about to say. Was he aware of my connection with Grimsby Petroleum? Was he accusing Alastair of siding with the English oil companies because of me . . . because he was married to Fiona Grimsby? But that wasn't true. Alastair deplored violence and preferred to use other methods to help Scotland. But could his friends realize that, or would Alastair have to condone violence, perhaps bombings, to prove his loyalty? No wonder Alastair had looked so stricken when he turned from the window. Was Alastair having to choose between his wife and his friends, his country? No, it would never come to that. Alastair would make them realize that revolution was not the answer to the question of ownership of the North Sea oil.

The dancing progressed from formal waltzing to the more boisterous Highland fling, and the lively strains of "MacLeod's Praise," the traditional pipe music of Alastair's clan, were now heard. With Lewis and Alastair as my teachers, I endeavored to keep up for a while, but I quickly became exhausted by the strange steps and retired to the side to watch the colorful dance. The orchestra had stopped playing, and someone was playing the bagpipes, the strange, crying tones filling the hall. Although I had not yet grown comfortable with the sounds the bagpipes produce, that night I found it haunting and lovely for the first time. I looked for Alastair among the dancers, for he loved the traditional dances of the Highlands, but I could not find him. I looked around the hall, but he was not among the watchers either. I decided he had resumed the political discussion with his friends and didn't go in search of him. I wanted him to have time to settle the argument.

Midnight came all too quickly; the strains of "Oh, this is my departing time, for here nae longer maun I stay" faded away softly, and our guests began to take their leave. As I stood with Mhari and Ian by the door, I began to wonder where Alastair was. Much as he disliked formality, it was very unlike him not to be present to say good-by to our guests; the discussion he was involved in must be very important indeed. Then I noticed Graham wandering about the hall aimlessly, as if he were waiting for someone. As I watched, I saw him stiffen suddenly, and I followed his gaze to the other end of the hall. A door opened and Alastair appeared and stood to hold the door for someone who was behind him. And that someone was . . . Ailis! They didn't speak a word to each other. Ailis went over to where Graham was waiting, and Alastair joined us at the door. He didn't offer any explanation, though I looked at him inquiringly, but settled into the role of host and chatted pleasantly with our guests. Soon Ailis and Graham came over to offer their good-bys, but though Graham shook my hand warmly and thanked us all for the party, he pointedly ignored Alastair. Ailis smiled sweetly as she spoke to me, but was there or was there not a gleam of triumph in her eyes?

Soon the only people left were those who were staying the night. Mhari said she was exhausted and wanted to go straight to bed. I felt equally drained from the evening's activities and joined her as she turned to go up the stairs. Alastair and Ian were joining some of the other men for a last brandy. I was slightly disappointed, for I wanted to talk to Alastair, but I was tired and feared I might make a scene if I insisted he accompany me. At the top of the grand staircase Mhari and I hugged each other, and I continued the climb up the tower steps. As always, I felt uncomfortable in the close stairway, tonight more than ever. The shadows on the uneven stone walls flickered ominously, and my own attenuated shadow loomed ahead as if daring me to follow.

I sighed with relief as I reached my bedroom. It seemed a

haven, both warm and inviting, for someone had thoughtfully slipped up there sometime earlier and lit a blaze in the fireplace, which gave the room its homey glow.

Then I noticed that someone had forgotten to turn off the spotlight that lit the courtyard below. Fingering my sash, I moved to the window and, peeking through the curtains, I saw something that disturbed me more than it surprised me—for, like the Scottish Nationalist Party's lapel pins, no one had mentioned it to me before. On the flagpole over the main entrance, flapping in the sharp east wind, was a large white flag with that same red lion emblazoned on its field. The Scottish Red Lion, a sign of defiance, since technically it was against the law, or "not done," as Mhari had said. The spotlight caught the lion squarely, and as the gusts swept over the cloth I saw that same angry and hungry look, that same desperate clawing. I forced myself to touch the cold panes, to remind myself that I was tired and seeing too much in what, after all, was a decoration.

Quickly, I undressed, pulled on my warmest flannel night-gown, and climbed into the oversized four-poster bed, pushing a sleepy Bruce aside to snuggle into the warm spot he had made. Bruce licked my hand, but his company could not compensate for how the vastness of the bed emphasized the loneliness I was feeling. I pulled the quilt around my chin and hoped I would fall asleep quickly, but that proved a vain thought. Though my body was exhausted, my mind refused to sleep. The events of the evening replayed themselves in half-heard conversations, half-seen glances, and half-remembered movements. There were many unanswered questions.

Ailis was the central figure in my thoughts. What did she mean to Alastair? Did he think of her as a friend, or was he still in love with her? Although he had said theirs was only a university romance, they must have been deeply in love. Mhari said they had been engaged. Had it been a formal betrothal? Had Alastair once placed on her dainty wrist the bracelet that now lay on my bedside table? Ailis had recognized it; she might have worn it. If so, how long ago? Was Alastair sorry he had left her? Was he sorry he had married me? Could he have still loved her when he met and married Fiona Grimsby of Grimsby Petroleum, Ltd.? If that was true, then he *had* married me for my money, as

Charles and Ian maintained. Graham was clearly in love with Ailis; he had been furious at seeing them together, so furious that he had not spoken to Alastair afterward. Graham suspected that Alastair and Ailis were more to each other than just old friends. Where had Ailis and Alastair been all that time? Was he reassuring her that he still loved her—even though he was now married to another woman?

And the Red Lion! What did that mean? Was it a coincidence that the men who had come to Mhari's party for me were wearing that pin in their lapels? Why hadn't the Red Lion been flown before at Lochinver Castle? Had Alastair seized on this supposedly festive evening as a way of gathering all his political friends together to discuss violence and revolution? Had he hoped to keep that meeting a secret from me? That explained Alastair's stricken look when I had walked into that room where Ailis had been the only woman among the men—men who all had that stickpin affixed to their jackets. Had that been a casual gathering or one that had been planned in advance? Who came first in his thoughts—me, or Ailis and the Red Lion, the Scottish Nationalist Party? What kind of party had this been tonight?

These thoughts and more whirled through my head. They merged as I became drowsy, and all I saw was Ailis's lovely mouth curving into a satisfied smile. Her laughter echoed in my ears as I fell into a fitful sleep.

FIVE

The Hundred Steps

The party had been over for more than a week and events at Lochinver had resumed their normal pace. I didn't see much of Alastair. He was quite busy and spent most of each day away from the castle. Ordinarily I would have been upset by his absences, but now I was relieved, for, since the night of the party, I had felt uncomfortable in his presence, wanting to ask him many questions but curiously reluctant to confront him with my fears and suspicions.

The day after the party, I had come down with a bad cold. This, too, turned to my advantage, for any unusual moodiness on my part could be attributed to my illness. I had spent the previous few days in bed. Not in the tower room I shared with Alastair—that was too far from the main part of the castle—but in the small bedroom next to Ian and Mhari's. But now I had recovered enough to be downstairs, and I was spending my days on the couch in the living room with Bruce curled up beside me. He was content to stay with me all day, not minding that our daily walks had stopped. It was apparent he knew I was sick and was doing his part to make me well. I had to admit that I was rather enjoying my confinement, once the worst was over. I was constantly spoiled and petted. Mrs. Ross cooked delicacies to tempt my appetite, and Mhari was the perfect nurse, taking my temperature, reading to me, thinking of innumerable ways to make me comfortable. The only fly in this pleasant ointment was that my portrait sittings had to be postponed. I enjoyed Lewis's company and missed his cheerful chatter. Hearing that I was ill, he and Joan had dropped by one afternoon with a home-made remedy of their mother's guaranteed to banish every disease known to man. But that had been a week before, and I was sorely in need of a diversion.

That diversion came, as such things do, in a totally unexpected manner. I had slept late and was lying on the couch sipping my breakfast tea and feeding bits of toast to Bruce when Mhari came in with the morning's mail.

"Fiona, you're looking so much better; I can begin to see some color in your cheeks. You'll soon be up and about." Mhari was sorting through the letters as she spoke.

"Oh, I don't know. You've made it so pleasant, I may just go on being sick."

"Aye, it's nice to be lazy for a change. Oh, here's a letter for you, Fiona."

"Oh? Who could it be from?" I was puzzled, as I had already received my mother's weekly letter, Rosemary wrote infrequently, and Charles's communications always arrived encased in heavy manila envelopes. I took the letter and, slitting it quickly with the slim opener Mhari handed me, I scanned the brief type-written paragraph.

"It's from Charles. He's coming here, will arrive Friday. There are some papers I have to sign . . . the mails would be too slow . . . he's coming in person. He apologizes for imposing himself and hopes it's all right if he spends the night."

"Friday? That's tomorrow. Of course it's no trouble. Charles . . . Haversham? Is that right?"

"Yes, he's been in charge of . . . of Grimsby since I came here, but of course there are some things that need my approval." It was the first time I had discussed my connections with Grimsby Petroleum with Mhari, and I watched closely for her reaction. She betrayed nothing more than a polite interest. Inwardly, I breathed a sigh of relief.

"Isn't he the one who helped you when your first husband died?" I smiled. How like Mhari to focus on that aspect of my relationship with Charles! "It will be nice to have him here," she added. "I'll go right now and make sure the room is aired and ready."

Mhari left and I reread Charles's letter. It was the first "personal" letter he had written to me, but its tone was no different from the short notes attached to the forms and contracts he sent for my attention. ". . . and I would appreciate spending the night, if it is not too inconvenient." I sighed; that was so typical of Charles, so polite and formal. It was signed, "Yours truly, Charles Haversham." Again, very formal and polite. The letter was as impersonal as if it were written to a stranger. Charles and I, after all, had not parted on the best of terms. He had been too outraged by my marriage to Alastair—even going so far as to say he loved me himself. I had thought at the time it was a last-ditch effort to dissuade me, and now, having read this note, I was sure. Poor Charles, I laughed to myself, what would you have done if I had accepted?

Ian received the news of Charles's impending visit with aplomb, saying politely how nice it would be for me to see an old friend. Alastair's reaction, however, was more exercised.

"I can't believe he'd have the . . . the unmitigated gall to set foot in this house. I don't want him here!"

"It's hardly a social call, Alastair. I don't think he would come unless it was important to have my signature right away. It's only for one night."

"I don't like it. I don't like him, and I don't like what he stands for."

"You forget that what he 'stands for' is Grimsby Petroleum, which happens to be your wife's company."

"Nae, Fiona, you're different and always will be; *you're* not out to rob Scotland. But Haversham is out to get anything he can, by whatever means possible. You're not one to put yourself before what's right, but Haversham is. He considers himself above the law."

"What do you base that on?"

"I can read it in his face. We've been at many meetings together, and I've had long hours to study the kind of person he is."

"Well, I can't forget all that Charles has done for me: he was a good friend at a time when I was alone and a stranger in Scotland. And, Alastair, I'm sure you're wrong. Charles *is* ambitious, but whatever he does is what he thinks best for Grimsby. So please let him come, for my sake."

"All right, all right. But don't be expecting me to welcome that fellow with open arms."

Friday was warm and sunny—unusual for November—as though we were being granted a last reprieve before the single-minded harshness of the Highland winter swept down upon us. As I was feeling better, I decided to take advantage of the sunshine and take Bruce for a walk. We both needed a bit of exercise. Bruce had been showing signs of enjoying his lazy life as much as I was. I was playing catch with Bruce in the shelter of the courtyard when I noticed a car turning off the main road. I waited by the main entrance as the car sped quickly toward the castle. Whoever that was, I thought, he was driving too fast. The car screeched to a halt a few feet from where I stood and, much to my surprise, Charles emerged. I hadn't thought Charles was the daredevil type.

"Charles, it's so nice to see you again, even if it is business that brings you here. You must have gotten an early start; we weren't expecting you till teatime."

"No, but I made excellent time."

"I'm not surprised, if that was an indication of your speed. I'd be scared to death to ride with you!"

"Oh, there's nothing to worry about. I've had much experience with these Highland roads, and I'm an excellent driver."

I suggested that Charles join me in my walk, under the pretext of showing him the grounds. The truth was that I felt uncomfortable with him, and I thought I could talk more easily as we walked about the estate.

As usual, I headed toward the Hundred Steps. As we climbed, I explained that my favorite view of Lochinver Castle was from the plateau at the top of the steps. "I come here often; it's such a lovely spot, peaceful and secluded. I come here to think things over, and when I want to get away and be by myself."

"Fiona, have you been all right? You don't look all that well. You're rather pale." I was touched by this note of concern in Charles's voice.

"Of course I'm all right. I'm just getting over a very bad cold. Today's the first day I've been out in almost two weeks."

"You mustn't overdo. That's a long climb we just made."

"Now, don't worry. I come up here practically every day. Bruce and I could scale these steps in our sleep, couldn't we, fella?" As always when he heard his name, Bruce barked and scampered over to be petted. I scratched his ears, and Charles reached down to do the same; but Bruce backed away, snarling. I was surprised and explained it away by saying Bruce was shy with strangers. But that was not true. Bruce loved affection from anyone he knew to be a friend of mine.

We chatted for quite a while. Charles filled me in briefly on events in Inverness and I told him of my life at Lochinver, of the recent party and the new people I had met there. Something must have crept into my voice, for Charles immediately asked many questions about Ailis and Alastair's relationship with her. I wanted to confide in him, yet I had no basis for my fears and doubts and didn't want to give them undue importance. Nor did I want to give Charles the impression that I was unhappy. By this time, the wind had become quite brisk. I began to feel chilled and suggested we return to the castle.

We went slowly down the steps; Charles slipped several times. It had drained the day before and the stones were still quite treacherous in spots.

Mhari greeted us at the door and sternly lectured me on the dangers of venturing outside with a cold.

"But Mhari," I laughed. "I really feel fine."

"Aye, and tomorrow you'll have a fever. Mr. Haversham, I'm so pleased to meet you. I saw the car in the drive and assumed you had arrived, but I couldn't figure out where you had gone. I should have known Fiona would take you on one of her walks."

"Blame me, not Fiona. I insisted on a thorough tour. One has a wonderful view from the top of those steps."

"Och, Fiona, you would take him there. She goes up there every day. I would have thought there were enough stairs inside without wanting to climb more! Tea will be served in half an hour, so I'll show you to your room."

"I do hope you've not gone to any trouble on my account. I could stay in the village," Charles said graciously.

"Och! There's never a lack of rooms at Lochinver."

Charles was shown to a room in the west wing, and I continued to the tower room, where I had resumed sleeping. I was glad Charles had come. I had been made a little apprehensive by the formal and restrained tone of his letter, but now I felt sure we could once more be good friends. Charles had shown a genuine interest in my new life and appeared concerned for my well-being. I decided to wear the dark green dress Charles had always admired. Pulling my yellow shawl around my shoulders, I went downstairs, for once not minding the close confines and eeriness of the tower.

Apparently I had dawdled over getting dressed, for I found everyone in the living room already enjoying the lavish tea Mrs. Ross had prepared in honor of our guest. I was nervous as I entered the room. I hadn't seen Alastair all day, and I wasn't sure of his mood. But the conversation sounded pleasant, and I heard Mhari's happy giggle. I entered confident that things were going well.

"Fiona! Whaur hae ye been, lass? We couldna wait, we were tha' starved. Here, sit yersel' doon an' hae a hot cup o' tea. Perhap ye'd be likin' a tech o' somethin' wit' it, tae take the chill frae yer banes?'

My heart sank as I realized that Alastair's method of coping with Charles was to play the role of the Scottish laird to the hilt, a role sure to annoy Charles. Even though I looked reproachfully at Alastair, I couldn't keep from silently laughing. I bit my lips to prevent a smile, but Alastair sensed my amusement. His eyes twinkled mischievously as he embraced me roughly.

"Yer gran' friend frae the city mauna mind our rough Hieland ways. We've tried tae make him feel tac home i' this humble place." Alastair waved his arm expansively, endangering a vase that Mhari had placed on the table. At that I gave up and started to laugh. Throughout Alastair's speech, Ian had been studying the view intently, his shoulders shaking with silent mirth. Once I started to laugh, he and Mhari joined in, as did

Alastair. Even Charles smiled, though more from politeness than comprehension. I went and sat down by Charles on the couch, explaining it was just a family joke.

"You must forgive Alastair, Charles; he's not quite himself this evening." Mhari giggled again and I continued, "You see? I'm surrounded by crazy Scots!" We all laughed again, Charles joining in heartily this time. I was sure that Charles's visit would pass pleasantly, now that the ice was broken.

It was inevitable that, as the evening wore on, the routine topics of conversation would become exhausted and the subject of politics come up. Since politics meant the North Sea oil to Alastair, we were soon talking about Grimsby Petroleum. I tried to steer him away from such potentially dangerous territory, but Alastair would have none of it.

"Nae, Fiona, you wouldn't deny me the chance to get information firsthand."

"Yes, but . . ." I didn't like Alastair's tone; it was a shade obsequious. But Charles interrupted.

"I'd be glad to satisfy any curiosity you might have. You have a right to know, after all. You married into Grimsby, in a manner of speaking." Charles's voice had the same sarcastic edge to it as Alastair's.

The two men talked, and I was struck by the contrast they presented. Alastair was the larger of the two. His size was emphasized all the more by Charles's slim build and elegant dress. Charles was the more handsome, with his golden-blond hair and thick, well-groomed mustache, but there was a vitality in Alastair's dark rough face that Charles's would never have. One thing they did have in common was a violent temper, which they were now both struggling to keep under control. Charles had the advantage there; his impeccable English-gentleman manners were suited to hiding his true feelings. Charles was a snob, and I knew he secretly was aghast at finding himself engaged in conversation with a Scot, especially one wearing a kilt. Outwardly, however, he was politeness personified.

Mhari and Ian had excused themselves and gone to bed. I was feeling somewhat sleepy—my first day up since my cold had been a busy one—but I hesitated to leave Alastair and Charles alone. I struggled to concentrate on their talk.

". . . for the first time, Britain is emerging as a major oil nation," Charles was explaining. "And there's enough gas to quadruple the size of the British gas market. Production has lagged, but it should pick up in the next year or so, and by 1981 we'll be producing 2.4 million barrels—enough to be self-sufficient."

"You miss the whole point. Britain, Britain. Nonsense. The oil belongs to Scotland. You're condoning piracy."

"It's talk such as that that has held up production. Measures to aid drilling and laws that would eliminate red tape have been stalled in Parliament while you Scots debate endlessly whose oil it is. If it stays in the ocean's floor, it won't matter who owns it. It won't help anyone, sitting one hundred miles off the east coast."

"Perhaps if Scotland was realizing the profits, she would be more eager to co-operate. So far, the effect of the oil on Scotland has been negative. Aberdeen and Inverness and half a dozen other lovely towns have been taken over by the oil industry and Americanized. It's easier to get a hamburger than fish and chips . . . and the Scottish youth go South to find employment as they always have, and Scotland's development continues to be sacrificed for England's."

"But there are jobs being created and money is being spent." Charles's voice had the same measured tones a parent uses in explaining an obvious fact to his slightly slow child.

"Aye," Alastair replied bitterly. "Paltry leavings cast off carelessly. What we Scots want is to govern our own affairs, to control the oil and its profits, not to be ruled by a central government."

"Ah, yes. Devolution. You'd do well to look up the other meaning for that word in the dictionary: 'retrograde evolution.'" Alastair choked, but Charles continued without pausing. "And where will you get the money? The field we're working on now will cost over $1.53 billion to develop. Twenty billion dollars will have to be spent before 1981."

"I notice you speak of dollars, not pounds," Alastair said curtly. "Perhaps it's the foreigners who profit most of all?"

"If it weren't for the Americans, we wouldn't be able to get that oil as quickly as we are. It's a good partnership; they need our oil and we depend on their expertise. You Scots are all alike, totally unrealistic and crying for a moon that is hopelessly beyond your grasp."

"And you English have always been the same, thinking you're superior."

"There, there, old chap. Don't get excited. Besides, I think you've found your own way to effect control, eh?"

"Why, you pompous ass, you . . . how dare . . ."

"Alastair!" He had reached his boiling point and I had to stop him. "I think we should say good night before this collapses into a name-calling contest. Really, that can't solve anything. And I think we could all do with a good night's sleep."

"Yes, that's a good idea; I want to leave as early as possible. I had no idea it was so late. I apologize, Fiona, if we bored you. Good night." Charles kissed me on the cheek and nodded to Alastair, who sat glaring into the fire.

At last he stirred, and we went slowly up the stairs. When he was in one of these moods I knew better than to speak, and we continued up in silence. It was not until we were in bed that Alastair spoke.

"Fiona, I'm sorry I lost my temper, but I don't like the man. He refuses to listen. He's typical of them all. I get so frustrated trying to deal with the English; maybe we should blow them all up."

"Alastair!"

"Well, when one has to deal with people such as Haversham, I can understand my friends' impatience."

"Charles will be gone tomorrow. Try to forget him and get some sleep." Those were banal words, but I wanted to calm Alastair down.

Alastair had already arisen when I awoke the next morning. When I went downstairs, Mhari informed me he had left for the village. "He'll be gone until dinnertime, Fiona. There's some meeting he had to attend. Ian went, too."

"A political meeting?"

"I think so. They were talking about it when they left, but I didn't pay strict attention."

I was concerned. Alastair had been angry after his argument with Charles. I hoped it would not influence him at this meeting. There was no telling what he might agree to in his present mood.

I was sitting in the dining room finishing my breakfast when Charles came in. He had obviously been outside. His feet were wet and muddy.

"Oh. Good morning, Fiona. I've been walking around the estate. Let me go and change my shoes, and I'll get these proposals I want you to approve. I'm afraid I ventured a bit too near the loch."

Charles returned shortly and showed me the documents.

"You know, Charles, this recommendation that we increase the size of our Glasgow office could have been mailed. This is all routine."

"I know, Fiona; you must forgive me. I wanted an excuse to see you, to make sure you were all right. I said some, um, rather unpleasant things to you before your wedding and, well, we didn't exactly part friends. I wasn't sure how you felt, if you wanted to see me, so I invented this subterfuge. If you were still angry and upset with me, then the visit could be business only."

"Charles, how sweet—wanting to see me. You needn't have used the pretext of business. You should know you're always welcome." I was deeply touched. It must not have been easy for Charles to make that speech.

"Your husband doesn't share your feelings, Fiona. We had rather an unpleasant discussion last night, if you'll recall."

"The oil issue is one that Alastair feels quite strongly about, as you found out."

"We will never agree. Though, I must say this: I do hope you won't continue to allow yourself to be influenced by his radical views. Now I know where you get your pro-Scottish sympathies."

"We never discuss Grimsby; we've agreed not to." Alastair and I had made no such agreement, but it was true that we never discussed Grimsby Petroleum. "I will admit that I'm not unsympathetic to his cause. I'm sure a compromise would be beneficial to both sides."

"Fiona. Always the peacemaker. My dear, you really don't understand the situation, so I would not advise your becoming embroiled in it. It is all too personal for you."

"Really, Charles; don't be patronizing."

"I am just looking out for the best interests of Grimsby,

Fiona," Charles said stiffly as he returned the papers to his briefcase. "Something I hoped you were concerned with, too."

"Oh, Charles, don't get all stuffy. I do care about Grimsby and want what's best. Kiss and make up?"

Charles leaned down and I felt his mustache softly graze my cheek. "Fiona, you know I don't want to see you hurt. I hope you don't get caught in the middle." He paused as if to say more, but apparently he reconsidered. "Well, I must be off. I'll go upstairs and get my things."

Mhari and I saw him to the door, and we watched the car as it sped off through the gentle mist that had begun to fall. As the roads were wet, the curves would be slippery, and I mentioned to Mhari that I hoped Charles wouldn't drive too fast.

"Och, there's no need to worry. He's quite an accomplished driver and has done some racing on an amateur basis."

"How on earth do you know that?"

"He talked about it last night, before you joined us. Charles and Alastair had quite a discussion. They both have the same type of motorcycle. I thought it would never end. I was so glad when you came downstairs!"

"I never knew that about Charles. It seems out of character, somehow."

"Oh aye. The impeccable gentleman racing around on a huge machine. Do you suppose he has a tailored black-leather jacket? He really is beautifully dressed and quite gorgeous."

"I keep trying to picture Charles on a motorcycle. It really is impossible."

"Apparently he hasn't done much riding recently. Most of his racing was, och—six or seven years ago. That was before you knew him, wasn't it?"

"It was six years ago that we met, and I didn't know him very well. We didn't become friends till I came back to Scotland."

It continued to rain all day; the light drizzle gradually became a steady downpour. Rain has always had a depressing effect on me, and that day was no exception. I wandered morosely throughout the castle, but the stone walls were even grayer without the sun's brightness. The sound of the rain pelting against the windows completed the dreariness. I finally settled in front of the living room fire and tried to read a book, one of those heavy tomes I had always meant to read but never found the time. Needless to say, I soon fell fast asleep.

I must have slept for several hours. It was dark outside when Mhari woke me. Alastair and Ian had still not returned, but she suggested that we eat anyway. Dinner could be reheated when they returned. We were having coffee when they came in, drenched to the skin. It was still raining quite heavily.

"It's really turned into quite a storm. Some of the smaller roads are washed out. Thanks, Mhari, but we've already eaten. Ailis gave us supper."

"*Ailis?*" I quickly set down my cup; my hands had started to tremble, and I didn't want Alastair to notice.

"Aye, the meeting was held at Campbell's. Ian and I decided to take advantage of the supper she had prepared. We didn't want to drive back during the worst of the downpour, so we passed the time pleasantly, waiting for it to let up. Actually, the meeting was still going on, but we were afraid the roads would get worse. So we left."

"Everything important had been said." Ian sat down at the table and helped himself to some coffee and dessert. "Ah, Mrs. Ross has done it again. Another wonderful cake."

"Didn't you get enough to eat at the Campbells'?" Mhari asked as she brushed the damp hair off his forehead.

"Well, it was just glorified sandwiches. Besides, I find it hard to discuss politics and eat at the same time. That's one sure way to get indigestion, eh, Alastair?"

"I'd prefer not to discuss the evening, Ian."

"Didn't the meeting go well?"

"Let's say there was a difference of opinion. Mhari, cut me another piece, will you?" Ian's good mood contrasted sharply with Alastair's sullenness. "Alastair against the world. But I think an agreement was reached."

"Things certainly weren't helped by your announcement that Charles Haversham was a guest in my home."

"Sorry, it just came up in casual conversation. I thought you might have learned something about the oil situation that would be of interest to the others. The two of you talked to all hours last night, and from the sound of it it was a stimulating discussion."

"That man is a fool and I learned nothing that would be considered useful. And as for being a guest, he wouldn't have been allowed to set foot inside Lochinver if . . ."

"If it weren't for me? I'm terribly sorry, Alastair, to have caused you any embarrassment among your friends. Now, if you'll excuse me, I'll say good night before I bother you any further." I got up and turned from the table awkwardly, bumping my knee on one of the heavy oak chairs. I caught a glimpse of Mhari's and Ian's surprised expressions as I ran from the room.

I continued running until I reached the tower steps, where I paused to catch my breath. Alastair hadn't followed me. Apparently he had decided to let my anger subside. I stood in the stairway for some time, drawing deep breaths, not to recover from the exertion of racing up many steps, but from the shock of what I had said to Alastair. We had never fought, never even raised our voices to each other in anger, and I was stunned. This was no newlywed argument over meaningless trivia that Alastair and I could laugh about later. This went deeper, perhaps too deep. I felt as if something was casting a pall over my marriage, a pall as menacing as the shadows that flickered over the stones of the tower walls. As always when I was alone in the dark, I felt nervous, and I ran to my room as though those shadows were grabbing at my ankles.

Once in my room, I felt safe, but could my marriage be safe from whatever was pursuing it? My worst fears had been realized. In spite of our understanding and love for each other, Alastair's politics were conflicting with my connections with Grimsby Petroleum. He was torn between his friends and his wife. He was being accused of siding with the English oil companies. He had married the leading stockholder of Grimsby. Perhaps that could be explained, but now he had had Charles Haversham in his home. Charles Haversham, the director of Grimsby Petroleum. How did that look to Alastair's Scottish Nationalist friends? How could he explain Charles's presence at Lochinver? No one would believe that Alastair did not involve himself in his wife's affairs; that was unheard of. When a woman married, everything that she had, belonged to her husband. It was the husband who took care of business matters. If his friends did believe Alastair, then they would ridicule him.

It's all my fault, I thought. I shouldn't have allowed Charles to come here. But was I to cut myself off from my previous life, now that I was married? Give up what I had been, what I had worked for? No, I could not. Though I was not as actively involved in Grimsby, I couldn't turn my back on something that had been so important to Toby. True, he had been dead many years, but I felt I would betray him if I cut off my associations with the company he had nurtured. Besides, I enjoyed working for Grimsby and had missed that these past few months. No, I could sacrifice being directly involved, but I could not sever the connection. Sacrifice. I had not thought of "sacrifice" when I had married Alastair. There had been no sacrifice then. What I was gaining had been so much greater. Was I changing? No, I couldn't be—I loved Alastair too much.

Then the old question returned. Does Alastair love me?

When I awoke the next morning, the sun was pouring in through the window, creating lively patterns on the floor. I got up and pushed open the window, leaning out to enjoy the view. The fresh air was chilly, but the sun was warm and the ground looked fresh and green after the deluge of the day before. The world had that just-washed appearance.

I turned from the window reluctantly, but I was shivering in my nightgown, so I started to dress. I must have overslept, I decided, for Alastair was not in the room. He had probably come to bed after I fell asleep. I had been sleeping so soundly that I had not heard him then, nor when he arose. He probably wanted to avoid a confrontation, and so he had been especially quiet. Then the thought occurred to me that he might not have come to bed at all, but a quick check of his side of the bed reassured me that it had been slept in. At least we haven't come to that, I thought grimly.

"No, I don't know where Alastair is." Mhari was alone at the table when I entered the dining room. She reported that Ian was still in bed. He had come down with a cold.

"Oh, dear, I hope he didn't catch it from me."

"Don't feel guilty, Fiona. He was out all yesterday in the rain and didn't change when he came in last night."

"Did Alastair go out early?"

"Fairly early. I came down to fix Ian a cup of tea when Alastair was getting ready to go out. He barely nodded and sort of grunted a good morning. I haven't seen such a black look on his face in years. Didn't you two make it up?"

"No."

"Well, you soon will. You're too much in love with each other to let something bother you for long." Mhari reached over and patted my hand. "You do look rather low. Come on, cheer up."

"Oh, Mhari, I will. It's just . . ." I shook my head and couldn't finish for fear of bursting into tears.

"Och! Fiona! This is awful! I'm sorry, I didn't realize it was as serious as this. Do you want to talk about it?" Mhari sat beside me and put her arm around me. At any other time, this gesture would have made me laugh. Mhari's stomach made her awkward and prevented her from getting too close. She had to lean forward to get her arm over my shoulders.

I was tempted to blurt out everything. I had kept too many thoughts to myself for too long. But I knew Mhari would defend Alastair and would not believe he could do anything wrong. I did, however, confide my worries about what effect my connections with Grimsby Petroleum were having on Alastair's life.

As I had foreseen, talking with Mhari did not produce any real results, for she found it impossible to believe that Alastair might not love me or was resenting my working for Grimsby. But it was comforting to put into words the anxieties I had been feeling. It was also reassuring to be told not to worry, even if I didn't quite believe her. Yet Mhari was astute enough to see a little beyond what I was telling her.

". . . and I don't want you worrying about Ailis," she added. "It was coincidence that the meeting was held at her house yesterday."

"But I didn't say anything about her."

"You didn't have to. I saw your face when Alastair said they had been there. That must have contributed to your getting angry."

"Well, maybe. There's something about her; she always has this strange smile on her face when she looks at me, as though she knows something I don't. And . . . she is very beautiful."

"Aye, she is, but you're just as lovely, so don't let that bother you. As for her smiles, well, Ailis is a bit on the dramatic side

126

and enjoys making scenes. She may resent you . . . after all, Alastair married you after throwing her over . . . but I wouldn't take it too seriously. She's very involved in the Scottish Nationalist Party and is always going to meetings and demonstrating so it's natural that she and Alastair are together frequently. And she drags Graham around with her. Och! I wish she'd settle down and marry him."

"That's what Alastair said."

"Did he? There, you see? There's nothing to worry about."

Mhari then went upstairs to see if Ian needed anything, and I wandered around the great hall for a while. I felt better after talking to Mhari, but I still felt listless as I wondered where Alastair could have gone. I finally decided that what I needed was a good, long walk. Bruce eagerly responded to my whistle, and I changed into my boots, put on my coat, and went out.

The air was brisk and invigorating, and I felt my spirits revive as Bruce and I trudged through the fields. There was little warmth in the pale winter sun, so the ground was still quite wet, the earth squishing noisily where I stepped.

I didn't go immediately to my favorite spot, at the top of the Hundred Steps, for I thought that Alastair might be on the estate. I half hoped to run into him. I was no longer angry, just anxious to see him and to be held tightly in his strong arms, to feel secure in his love.

After a while, I decided that Alastair was not on the grounds. As it had been some time since I had walked so much, I felt tired and decided to rest. I made my way to the plateau not by climbing the steps as I usually did but by another, less taxing route.

I sat on a rock and basked in the sunshine while Bruce busied himself pursuing squirrels. It was a chase doomed to frustration, for they were too quick and would jabber indignantly from the swaying branches of the pine trees while Bruce barked hopelessly from the ground. Soon he was off after another squirrel, and the scene would be repeated. As I watched, I began to daydream—not of anything in particular, just pleasant thoughts, some memories, some visions of a rosy future when I would bring my children here to look down upon Lochinver. I must have fallen asleep, for when I sat up with a jerk, the shadows on the cliffs had begun to lengthen and the sun had lost what little warmth it had had. I whistled for Bruce but he didn't respond, and I spent some time searching for him. Finally he appeared, happy and covered with mud.

"Now we really will have to hurry, you little rascal, or we'll be late for tea." At the mention of food, Bruce barked happily and set off down the hill, jumping over the stone steps.

I followed him quickly down the path I knew so well. The stones were still damp after the rain, but I was wearing rubber-soled boots and didn't give them a thought. Bruce was well ahead of me and out of sight when, all of a sudden, I heard him barking excitedly. I stopped abruptly and looked up. As I paused, the stone that I had started to put my weight on moved and started to roll off the path, crashing onto the rocks below and then into the loch far below. Several other stones were jarred loose and they, too, fell crashing. Where, moments before, there had been a path of smooth stone steps, there was now a gaping hole. I watched the stones fall into the water, and I shuddered to think what might have happened to me if I hadn't stopped.

"Fiona!" I was standing dazed and had not seen Alastair on the path below me. Bruce was jumping about Alastair's feet. It was to greet Alastair that he had barked.

"Fiona! Are you all right?" I was still stunned, but I managed to wave and nod my head in reply. "Stay right where you are, I'm coming to get you. Don't move!"

I stood still while Alastair picked his way around the steps, not daring to step on them. Fortunately, Bruce had the good sense to remain where he was, his whiskers twitching with curiosity. After what seemed ages, Alastair clasped me tightly to him.

"Fiona, thank God you're safe. Nae, don't try to say anything; let me get you out of here." Alastair half led, half carried me past the gap in the steps. It wasn't until we were safely at the bottom that he relaxed his hold and quickly tightened it again as I was unsteady and almost fell.

"Are you sure you're not hurt?" I had never heard Alastair so concerned.

"Yes, I'm just a little shaky. The stones fell before I could walk on them. I heard Bruce bark and I stopped."

"Well, Bruce, you've earned your keep tonight."

"Yes, if I hadn't stopped, I would have . . ." I looked at the sharp cliffs and shuddered against Alastair's shoulder.

"Hush, lovely, hush. Don't think about that now. Let's get you home. A good brandy is what you need."

Mhari greeted us at the door, her face growing anxious at the sorry picture we presented. "What on earth has happened? Fiona, you look so pale; did you fall? Here, sit down. Let me get you some tea."

"Brandy, not tea, is what Fiona needs, Mhari. She had a narrow escape on the steps."

"What?"

"One of the stones was jarred loose and created a sort of avalanche down the cliffs. Luckily, Fiona stopped just in time. The heavy rain yesterday must have loosened the earth. The slightest pressure was enough to set it off."

"Och! Fiona, I'm so thankful you're safe," Mhari exclaimed as she handed me a glass.

"Yes, I'm all right now." The brandy was beginning to have a warming effect and I felt my strength return. "It was silly of me. I was tired from walking, and then I was in a hurry to get back and didn't watch where I was going. If I had been more attentive, I would have noticed."

"I don't think so, Fiona. You couldn't have told by looking at the stones whether or not they were unstable."

"Anyway, it was Bruce's barking that prevented me from stepping on them."

"Aye, he's quite the hero of the day." Alastair reached down and patted Bruce, who responded eagerly. "I think he should get an extra bone for dinner."

"I'll go get one from Mrs. Ross," Mhari said. "I don't think she'd allow him into the kitchen with those muddy feet."

Mhari left, and Alastair and I sat quietly on the couch, holding hands.

"How did you come to look for me?" I asked.

"When I came home, there was no one around. Mhari finally came downstairs and told me Ian was still in bed but that she hadn't seen you for a few hours. I realized Bruce was missing and figured you had taken him for a walk. I know you like to climb the Hundred Steps, so I looked for you there. I worried that the steps would be slippery after the rain, but I never would have suspected that they would come loose. I'll have to have them fixed. Meanwhile, Fiona, I want you to keep away from there and confine your walks with Bruce to safer territory. Och, Fiona, when I think of how close I came to losing you!"

"Alastair, I love you so much."

"I love you, too, and now I know how much."

"Alastair, I was pretty foolish last night and said some things that . . ."

"Nae, it was my fault. You were right to be angry, it did seem as though I was blaming you. I was just in a foul mood from that blasted meeting. I took it out on you, lovely; I'm sorry."

"I was afraid that . . ."

"That I was angry at you? Nonsense, that's impossible. A thousand Charles Havershams could overrun Lochinver, and I wouldn't be angry with you."

"I hardly think it will come to that."

We were laughing when Mhari returned with Bruce's reward. She had looked anxious, but she smiled happily when she saw us. She asked a silent question with her eyes and I nodded in reply. We both laughed, and Alastair looked puzzledly at us both.

"What is this, some female conspiracy?"

"No, I'm just happy to see the two of you have made it up. I couldn't stand it, you blacker than a cloud, Fiona moping about. I'm very pleased you've both come to your senses."

"Aye, Mhari and we promise never to do it again." Alastair bowed his head in mock apology.

We had a quiet supper that night, just the two of us in front of the fire. Mhari had taken a tray upstairs to Ian and was keeping him company. Alastair and I behaved like two newlyweds, holding hands and kissing; Bruce got most of our dinner.

After we had finished eating, we sat on the rug in front of the fire. Alastair lay with his head in my lap and we sipped brandy from the same glass.

"Fiona, I know this is the wrong thing to say at a time like this, especially after this afternoon." Alastair was rotating the large-bowled glass in his hands and the liquid gleamed gold-red in the fire's light. "But," he continued after a pause. "I've got to go away for a few days, to the east coast, to Aberdeen and Inverness. There are some important meetings of the Scottish Nationalist Party and I've been asked to speak. It was rather sudden; I would have told you last night, but . . ."

"Sssh. Last night is better forgotten."

"Aye. I do hate to leave you. I'd put it off if I could . . . well, it is rather important that I be there."

"Don't be silly; of course you have to go. I'm perfectly all right; there's certainly no need for you to stay here and hold my hand. When do you leave?"

"Tomorrow morning. Early. I'll be back before the weekend. I'd ask you to go, but I'm afraid it would be rather dreary; I'll be busy all the time."

"Nonsense. It's best I stay here. Mhari will have her hands full taking care of Ian, and she could use help. Besides, I must learn to be the good politician's wife and let you go off."

"There won't be many trips, and you'll join me on most. Especially if I run for Parliament. It never hurts to have a pretty wife by your side."

"Aha! That's why you married me. To win elections."

"Can you suggest another reason?"

"Oh, I might be able to think of a few."

"Hmmm Come on, milady, I've got to pack, and if I'm to be off early, I need to get some sleep."

It was still dark and quite chilly the next morning when we got up. I put on my fur-lined slippers and wrapped one of Alastair's robes about me and went downstairs to make us some breakfast while Alastair dressed. I had just finished making coffee when Mhari came in, yawning sleepily.

"Goodness, you're up early."

"You are, too. Is Ian all right?"

"Aye, he wants breakfast. A sure sign that he's well on the road to improvement."

"Alastair's off to some meetings on the east coast. He wants to get an early start."

"Och, that's right. He did say something about it Saturday night. Ian was going, too, but now he has this cold. He's probably happier being sick. This way he gets to be pampered!"

"Mornin', Mhari. Well, Fiona, that's a lovely outfit. It looks far better on you than on me."

"I have every intention of going back to bed after you leave. This is an ungodly hour to be up."

"You'll have your chance in a minute. I've just time for a quick cup of coffee."

Mhari went back upstairs while I sat and watched Alastair drink his coffee. Then he was off and I watched until the car had disappeared into the morning mist. It was going to be a gray and cloudy day, and I knew I would not be tempted to go for a long walk. Alastair had said he would have the steps repaired after his return. The narrow escape I had had the day before was now no more than a distant memory.

The days of Alastair's absence passed smoothly. Ian recovered from his cold and was soon up and about, though Mhari would not let him venture outside for a few days. I resumed my portrait sessions with Lewis. He repeated Joan and his invitation to tea, and I agreed to go that Wednesday.

As Alastair had taken the only car we owned, I walked the few miles to the village and arrived at the Demerests' just as Joan was returning from the one-room building that served the village as a schoolhouse. We spent a pleasant afternoon. Mrs. Demerest, Lewis and Joan's mother, was an elderly woman who walked with the aid of a cane and was obviously very proud of her son's talents. She insisted Lewis show me the studio his father had built and that he now used. There were some of the paintings I had seen at the show in Inverness and a great many more canvases and sketches scattered about. Lewis obviously spent a great deal of time working. I wandered about, admiring and commenting on several that I especially liked when suddenly one painting in the corner caught my eye. It was a rough sketch, a study for a future painting. I immediately recognized the Hundred Steps. They were painted fiercely; the tall, black pine trees filled the background. There was a figure coming down the steps, running, the head half turned as if looking at something in the distance, something that was not in the drawing. It was a girl; her long, dark hair flowed around her face.

"Why, it's me." I turned in surprise to an embarrassed Lewis.

"Aye, I guess it turned out that way. I've been painting you, so the person became you. I hope you don't mind."

"Lewis, of course not. I'm flattered."

"That spot is one of my favorites to paint. It must have been the power of suggestion that made me paint you in; you told me that you enjoyed walking there."

"I'm afraid my visits will have to be curtailed." I told him of my accident a few days before. Lewis was shocked and quite alarmed that I could have been seriously hurt.

'I never would have thought that could happen. I know the steps are old and worn, and I could understand if you had slipped, but they seemed so solid. It's practically impossible that they would fall away by themselves."

"It obviously wasn't impossible, for it happened. Let's not talk about it any more. It all turned out safely, and I intend to be more careful in the future."

Lewis drove me back to the castle, and I arrived as Mhari and Ian were finishing an early supper.

"Sorry, Fiona. I didn't know how long you'd be."

While Mhari set another place at the table, I went into the kitchen. Mrs. Ross was sitting at the small table next to the stove, reading the evening paper.

"Och, Mrs. MacLeod. I dinna hear ye come in. Let me get tha' fer ye, I was readin' aboot the explosion. It's scandalous!"

As she busied herself at the stove, I picked up the paper and read the headline. **BOMBINGS IN GLASGOW!** The bold capital letters ran across the page. The story said the offices of several oil companies, including the British National Oil Corporation and Grimsby, had been the scene of early-morning explosions the day before. There had been minimal damage and no one had been hurt. The IRA had been suspected, for they had been responsible for similar bombings in other industrial British cities, but a phone call to the police had established that it was the work of the Scottish Nationalist Party (SNP). The caller, who identified himself only as the Red Lion, had threatened further bombings if his non-negotiable demands were not met. I put the paper down. I didn't need to read any further. I knew what those demands were. I took my plate from Mrs. Ross, agreed that it was a "shockin' affair," and went back into the dining room.

"Did you see the paper?" I asked Ian and Mhari.

"Aye, isn't it terrible? Thank goodness no one was hurt."

"I wonder why Glasgow. Our, uh, Grimsby's offices there aren't very important. Actually, they're quite small."

"I suppose they had to start someplace and wanted to make their point while doing the least amount of damage, though it's a waste of time and energy." Ian sounded disgusted. "Now, if you ladies will excuse me, I'm still feeling a bit under the weather, so I'll retire early."

"Sorry, Fiona. Ian's upset about the SNP bombings. He thinks it should have been more large-scale, not just random attacks that don't accomplish anything." Mhari blushed, remembering that I worked for one of the bombers' targets.

"Would Ian justify some bombings?"

"In a way. He feels that a controlled effort could be quite successful and enable the SNP to gain their demands." Mhari spoke quickly, trying to end the discussion.

"Like the U. S. Air Force bombing Hanoi? That was a controlled effort that was successful, wasn't it?"

"Fiona! That sounds so awful. I know it's hard to explain nicely and I can't say it right, but Ian doesn't mean anything like that. Don't be angry, Fiona. I don't like it any more than you do."

"Is that what the meeting was about last Saturday, the bombings?" We were both uncomfortable, but I had to know.

"Uh—I really don't know. I don't understand politics, so I try to keep out of it. This was probably the work of a few radicals, not the whole Party. Don't be angry with Ian."

"Don't worry, Mhari, I'm not. Just at those who actually set the bombs off. It's so foolish, a terrible thing."

Mhari asked me about my visit to the Demerests', and we talked no more of the bombings. Later, however, while I tossed in my enormously empty bed with only concerned but confused Bruce for company, I thought again about the newspaper's headline and tried to force myself to believe that Mhari was right. It was the work of a few hot-headed radicals. But how I wished Alastair was home to—suddenly I wondered if Alastair knew about the bombings yet. Of course, I told myself, he would have read about it in the Aberdeen papers. But, with Alastair on my mind, I began to think about that Saturday-night meeting that had upset him so. Ian had said that they had all reached an agreement of sorts. Was that agreement the decision to go ahead with those Glasgow bombings? Or had that decision been made at the meeting Alastair had said he was going to in Inverness? Had Alastair been part of, or been forced to be an accomplice to, those hideous bombings? Then an even more chilling thought struck me, and I shivered despite the comforters weighing me down as much as my fears: Had Alastair really gone East, to Inverness and Aberdeen? Or had he, instead, gone South, to Glasgow? Were the bombings the sudden business that had come up, the business that couldn't be put off?

I fought that idea as hard as I could. I clenched my whole body and yelled, "No!" to the darkness that hung over me and, worst of all, to the dreadful darkness that seemed to be hanging over my marriage. Calm down, Fiona, I told myself. Time and time again Alastair has told you that he detests those in the SNP who talk violence. And yet, and yet, he has also said that he can understand how frustration makes good and decent men turn to all manner of terror. And that night of the meeting . . . hadn't Alastair been accused of being on the side of the oil companies merely because he was entertaining Charles in his home? Oh, Alastair, I thought, did they force you to show your questioned loyalty to the Party by going to Glasgow and . . . I couldn't finish that thought. It was too terrible to think even once. How I wished Alastair would come home right now and hold me in his arms and tell me everything was all right and that all my fears were wrong!

SIX

Christmas Presents

December. The grounds were covered with a light sprinkling of snow, and the winter winds buffeted the ramparts. The wind was a constant now, whistling through the long corridors and over-large rooms. The sounds it created were changeable. Sometimes I fancied I heard singing. Once, during a storm, I heard despairing moans as if the wind itself were protesting the harshness it had brought forth. I thought of the winds as the music of the Highlands, for it was not unlike the strange, half-mournful, half-joyous cries of the bagpipes that Alastair sometimes played as we sat huddled in front of the fire. At first I had found the pipes disturbing, but as I had grown used to the music I found beauty in the passionately strident notes. And so it was with the wind.

Although Alastair had had the Hundred Steps repaired, I seldom went that way any more on my walks with Bruce. We confined ourselves to the courtyard, sheltered on three sides by the castle. Once only did I venture to the top of the hill. There had been an usually heavy snowfall, and as the sun came out the gray northern light was brightened for an hour or so. With Bruce for company I climbed the steps cautiously. The snow had covered the spot where the stones had been replaced, yet I shuddered as I passed by. Once I had reached the top, however, I felt the climb had been worthwhile. Lochinver was even more beautiful in a blanket of snow, if that was possible. The powdery white clung to the gray walls, giving them a delicate appearance, so that the cut-granite stones seemed made of lace. The rays of sunshine were weak, yet they caused the snow to glisten and gave the windows a golden glow. It was a perfect scene, complete in its beauty—with the pine trees providing a gently moving green frame and the loch still as a striated sheet. I turned and saw in the distance the snow-covered heights of Ben More Assynt, a gentle giant of a mountain that brooded over Lochinver like a silent guardian.

"Fiona!" My name echoed, carried by the wind through the valley. I looked down, shading my eyes against the snow's glare. A figure was making its way up the steps so wrapped by scarves as to be almost unrecognizable, but I knew immediately this was Lewis, for that mop of gleaming red curls gave him away. I waved and waited for him to join me.

"Hi, Fiona." As Lewis spoke, his words were visible: minute white clouds appeared in the cold air. "I was doing some sketching and I saw you up here."

"I haven't been up here since . . . for several weeks, but I had to see how Lochinver looked in the snow."

"It is beautiful, but I think it's at its best in the spring, when everything is so alive."

"I'll look forward to that. Can you really be drawing in this weather?"

"Oh aye. Nothing daunts the artist," Lewis laughed. "See? The drawings are a little crude . . . I had to keep my gloves on, but I'll polish them up in the studio."

Lewis pulled out several sketches of the steps. I marveled how with a few quick lines he had captured their grace. There was none of the fierceness of the painting I had seen in his studio, the one that had shown me running down the steps.

"Lewis, they're lovely. You've really caught the feeling of this afternoon."

"I've finished the other painting. I had thought to make you a present of it, but perhaps you won't want it after . . . after what happened to you here."

"Nonsense, I'd be delighted. I still love coming here. No silly accident is going to change that."

"Fiona, that still bothers me. I just don't see how it could have happened. I came up here afterward, before Alastair had the stones replaced, and I tested the other steps—they were quite secure. It's odd that only those three could have fallen."

"There had been that heavy rainfall the night before. The earth was driven away—eroded."

"But, then, other stones would've been weakened, and they weren't; they're as safe as they've been for hundreds of years."

"Well, it happened, that's all." I was annoyed with Lewis. I wanted to forget about the incident, to forget the sick, frightened feeling I had experienced when I watched the steps fall and break apart on the cliffs. "And I'd prefer not to talk about it any more, Lewis. It was dreadful, and the sooner forgotten the better."

"I'm sorry, Fiona, I didn't mean to annoy you—I would never want to do that." Lewis had moved closer, putting his hand on my arm. "I'm just puzzled by the whole thing."

"Well, most freak accidents are a mystery. Now, why don't you come back to the castle with me and have some tea?" Lewis brightened at the suggestion, and together we made our way down the steps.

December brings Christmas, and in the weeks before the holiday Lochinver was humming with happy activity. Mhari and I decorated with greens: pine boughs draped the mantelpieces and holly filled the vases. Bright red berries and shiny green-and-white leaves brightened every room. We hung mistletoe in a strategic spot, dangling it from the chandelier in the main entrance, and Alastair made a great show of enticing everyone underneath it—even shy Maggie Stewart, who was so embarrassed she almost dropped the trays she was carrying into the great hall.

Everywhere there was the sort of pleasant secrecy that accompanies Christmas. Mhari spent many hours in her room doing something, and Alastair assumed mysterious airs and hinted so preposterously that I decided he had bought me a baby elephant. Even Ian dropped his serious mien and would appear at odd times carrying packages that would disappear magically if Mhari was there. A large box had arrived from my parents and stood waiting in an empty room. Alastair and Ian had chosen the tree, but it wouldn't be cut down until a few days before Christmas. We would decorate it on Christmas Eve; then, just before everyone went to bed, the presents would be placed under the tree to be discovered there on Christmas morning.

I, too, had secrets. I had finally learned to crochet, and every spare hour went into making a shawl for Mhari. On Mhari's suggestion I had ordered some books for Ian from Edinburgh, a handsomely bound set of Tennyson, his favorite poet. My other shopping was done: yarns for Mrs. Ross, heavy gloves for her husband, a history of Scotland for Maggie Stewart, and some fine sable brushes for Lewis. I had even bought some new toys for Bruce, though he would probably enjoy chewing the paper they were wrapped in more than the presents themselves. Alastair was the puzzler. This was our first Christmas together, and I wanted it to be special. I had several small packages for him, and I had filled a stocking full of funny presents, but I had yet to find that special gift. I had dropped hints to Alastair, trying to determine what he most wanted, but he soon realized what I was about and insisted that my presence was all he needed.

"When you married me, I became the happiest man in the world. There's nothing more I want," he had insisted. "But I could use a new toothbrush." I laughed; there was already one in his stocking. No, Alastair was no help, and I waited for inspiration to strike me.

There was another reason I was looking forward to my first Christmas at Lochinver. My friend Rosemary Beaton would be joining us. Her parents were traveling in the Middle East, a half-business, half-pleasure trip, and I had asked Rosemary to spend her holidays in the castle. She had eagerly accepted and was due to arrive the week before Christmas. I looked forward to seeing her, for I had enjoyed the summer we had spent touring the Highlands and been sorry when she had returned to school in London. She had never met Alastair, and I wanted them to become friends. Rosemary was bright and cheery, the perfect house guest at Christmas.

Rosemary arrived on what was probably the coldest day we

had had so far that winter. A great gust entered with her, and we both struggled to push the heavy door shut.

"Well, Fiona, you certainly have chosen to live in the wilderness. It took forever to drive from Inverness. At times I thought I'd go faster if I walked! These Highland roads!"

"Come in by the fire, where it's warm, and have something to drink. We do have brandy, even if we're far from civilization."

We sat and gossiped. Our letters had been infrequent, and we had a lot to catch up on. Rosemary thought my marriage to Alastair the epitome of romance and couldn't wait to meet him.

"It's like a fairy tale, Fiona. Marrying the tall, handsome prince and being carried off to a castle to live happily ever after." Then she added with a touch of bitterness, "I'm glad it happens for some people." Her affair with a fellow student had recently broken off, and she was still feeling the effects. I secretly thought that she was too young to mope for long and too lively not to find someone else quickly, but I refrained from stating the obvious and made the usual sounds of sympathy. "Oh, well, Fiona, my father was right as usual. It is maddening how parents are always right. You remember, that was why they wanted me in Inverness last summer, to keep me away from George. I must say, it would have been awfully dreary if you hadn't been there."

"The same for me. And here you are, so good came out of it, after all. Now, take the advice of an old married lady and don't fret. Come, I'll show you around."

I enjoyed taking Rosemary through the castle. It was as though I were seeing Lochinver for the first time myself, so great was her admiration. I assured her that Alastair would give her a more thorough tour, complete with the family history. We came into the room Lewis and I had been using for our portrait sessions, and Rosemary exclaimed over the half-finished painting.

"Oh, Fiona! How perfectly lovely! What fun, being painted!" I explained that it had been Alastair's idea, to have our portraits hung in the gallery. "This husband of yours really is a romantic, isn't he? He doesn't by chance have any younger brothers?"

"No," I laughed. "Just one sister."

"Too bad. You know, this painting is going to be rather special. There's a quality in it that's very interesting." Rosemary was getting her degree in art history and was knowledgeable in the subject of portraiture. "It's an excellent likeness, but it's something more. You look so beautiful . . . not that you're not gorgeous in person, Fiona," Rosemary broke off, laughing. "But the artist has seen something. He's made you fragile and vulnerable, not weak . . . definitely not that. Oh, I don't know . . . maybe it's your eyes. They're green mirrors. Who's the artist?"

"A young man here in the village, Lewis Demerest. He's fairly well known in these parts."

"Demerest . . . Demerest. Oh, yes. Didn't he have a show last summer in Inverness?" I nodded. "Well, then, no wonder. He's very good. I hope I have the chance to meet him while I'm here."

"Don't worry, you will. As a matter of fact, he'll be here tomorrow afternoon for our regular session. I'll ask him to stay for tea. I'm sure he'll enjoy talking to you about painting—I'm afraid I don't know very much, I just know what I like." I laughed, not at my feeble joke but at an idea that had just occurred to me. Lewis and Rosemary might very well get to like each other. He could be just the thing to take her mind off the late, lamented George. I laughed at myself; it must be true that married women like to matchmake; once they're settled, they like to see everyone else settled. Well, I thought, there's nothing wrong in planning a pleasant diversion to cheer up Rosemary. Besides, there would be the extra advantage of taking Lewis's mind off me. I had decided Alastair was probably right. Lewis did seem to be developing a boyish crush. The thought flattered me, and it was certainly harmless enough; but, no, it wouldn't hurt to have a young and pretty girl around when Lewis came to visit.

Rosemary fitted into our small household easily, and the remaining days before Christmas passed happily. Because of her knowledge of art, she was fascinated with Lochinver. This especially delighted Alastair, and he never tired of discussing the castle and the various aspects of its renovation with her.

Lewis came several times. As I had hoped, he and Rosemary became friends. They talked of art and compared their experiences as students in London.

"You two seem to get along very well," I couldn't help remarking one day after Lewis had left.

"Oh, yes. He's awfully nice. Hmmm, do I detect an ulterior motive behind those words?"

141

"Aweel, perhap a wee one," I replied with my best Scots burr. "No, really, I just hoped you'd enjoy talking to each other. Lewis hasn't been back in the village all that long. I don't think he knows many people, especially young people, and . . ."

"And I'm supposed to be recovering from a broken heart; I know. Well, he's a darling, but I don't think I'll have much of a chance with you around. He obviously adores you. He's always looking at you."

"Of course he looks at me. He's painting me."

"Uh-huh."

"Well . . . he's naturally fascinated by a mysterious, older woman."

"Whatever, I do think it's beastly unfair that the two most attractive men in the place are in love with you." She sighed, "Maybe mother's right; I should lose some weight. Anyway, I don't know if Lewis is in love with you or not, but he does seem to be slightly concerned about you."

"Concerned? Whatever for?"

"He mentioned an accident you had."

"Oh, honestly! I wish he'd drop that. I was climbing where it wasn't safe and some stones fell. Those steps I showed you the other day. It's true I might have been hurt, but I wasn't."

"Lewis seems to think it shouldn't have happened."

"Well, it did happen," I retorted. "Oh, I'm sorry, Rosemary; I didn't mean to snap at you. This isn't the first time Lewis has brought the subject up, and it's something I'd rather forget."

"He's just concerned, Fiona."

"But there's really nothing for him to be concerned about, is there? It was an accident, the steps have been repaired, and I fully intend to be careful from now on. End of discussion." But our conversation continued to prey on my mind. Why did Lewis's obsession with my accident upset me so? Was I afraid of what he was saying, that the stones couldn't have fallen by themselves, that—No! It was only natural that I should wish to forget such an unpleasant incident and to squelch any talk, no matter how well intentioned, that conjured up those frightening memories.

On Christmas Eve we had a small party at Lochinver. Lewis was there with his sister and mother, and so were several of our other friends from the village, including Graham and Ailis. I was not pleased to see Ailis, but she was on her best behavior and totally charming. The main event of the evening was decorating the Christmas tree. Over twenty feet high, its blue, bristly simplicity dominated the great hall. We decorated it with the homemade ornaments that had been in the MacLeod family for generations, and the result was truly splendid. We stood sipping mulled cider, and as Alastair placed an angel at the top of the tree, spontaneous cheers sounded. Soon it was time to go to the small village kirk for services. A light snowy sleet was falling, and though wet, it added the finishing glistening touch to the evening. After the simple candlelight procession was over and the traditional carols had been sung, we said good-by to our friends and headed back to the castle. There was great activity as we scurried about, getting our presents from their hiding places and placing them under the tree. We behaved like children, squealing at the sizes of some of the presents, poking and trying to guess what was inside. Finally, we all trooped upstairs to try to sleep despite the excitement.

Christmas morning was one of the most beautiful we enjoyed that winter. The sun was unusually bright and seemed to take the chill from the air. I awoke early and tickled Alastair's nose until he, too, woke up. We dressed quickly and went downstairs to pound on Mhari and Ian's door and then Rosemary's, and we were all sitting before the fire in no time, opening our presents. Ian took the role of master of ceremonies and passed out the gifts, making appropriate speeches. At last every present was unwrapped and we sat amid the gaily colored piles of paper and ribbons sipping coffee.

"What a wonderful day!" Mhari exclaimed contentedly. "I swear it's the best Christmas of my life."

"Mhari, you always say that," Ian teased gently.

"And it's always true. I hate it to end, though. It's a shame, but we've opened all the presents."

"Oh, no, we haven't, there's one more." Alastair and I spoke together and then laughed as we realized we had each saved a present for the other.

"Me first," Alastair announced and handed me a long, thin package. I opened it and saw it was a riding crop. I looked at him questioningly.

143

"Aye, you're wondering why. Well, within the month, you'll be the proud owner of a two-year-old mare. I would have liked to have her under the tree, but I couldn't manage it in time."

"A horse! How wonderful. Oh, Alastair, thank you! thank you! thank you!! I'm so excited."

"I knew you've always wanted one, and there was a show in Aberdeen last month when I was there. She's a pretty little mare and . . . Fiona, what's the matter? Why are you laughing?"

"You'll see in a moment. Here, open your present." I handed him a small package, which he opened quickly.

"What a lovely key ring, and it's engraved with the MacLeod crest. But what's this key? It's not one of mine."

"Yes, it is."

"I've never seen it before in my life."

"I think, if you take a look in the garage, you'll find that the key belongs to something of yours."

Alastair looked at me suspiciously but didn't say a word as we all went outside. There in the garage was a brand-new Triumph sports car, its bright yellow body gleaming, a TR7—the latest model available. I was proud of my accomplishment; it had taken some arranging, for it had had to be sent from London. It had been driven up the week before, and I had kept it at Lewis's, praying that no one would notice it—a bright yellow sports car was a rare item in Lochinver. Lewis had driven it over on Christmas Eve and it had sat in the garage waiting. I looked at Alastair, who was standing as if stunned, his mouth open.

"Do you like it?"

"Eh? Sorry, Fiona, I'm completely amazed. I never would have thought . . . it's a beautiful car, but you shouldn't have."

"Of course I should have. We could use more than one car, and I got to thinking, why not . . . this? I hope you like the color; now people will see you coming for miles."

"Aye, that they will." Alastair inspected the car.

"I had thought of having the seats upholstered in the Mac-Leod plaid, but I thought that might be a little ostentatious," I teased. "Though I could still . . ."

"No! I love it the way it is, and I love you for giving it to me."

"Now you know why I started laughing. We each gave the

other something to ride. Our minds were on the same wave length."

"Aweel, your mind waved to greater lengths, and there's a few more horses under that hood than will ever be in the stables." Then, seeing my expression, "Nae, Fiona, I was teasing. I've never had such a grand present in my life. I'm completely overwhelmed." He kissed me and asked, "What would you say to a ride?"

I accepted eagerly, and we roared off. The car was marvelous, just the vehicle to manage the steep Highland roads. We drove a few miles north, until we reached the Kylestrome Ferry, at Eddrachillis Bay. Alastair didn't want to entrust his new toy to the small ferryboat, so we parked on the hill and watched it go back and forth. It ran on no fixed schedule. When two cars came along, it would cross over and then wait for two more cars before returning. There was little traffic, so the boat made few trips. It was a lovely spot to stop. There were mountains around the bay, and the sharp cliffs beside the water resembled the fjords in Norway—or, rather, what I've always imagined them to look like. We strolled about, throwing stones into the water, which was too deep and too fast-moving to be frozen over. Soon it was time for lunch, and we raced back home even more quickly than we had come, Alastair praising the Triumph for its easy handling. As we neared the castle, he pulled over to the side of the road and suggested I drive.

"Oh, no, Alastair, I couldn't."

"You've driven British style before."

"Yes, but nothing quite like this."

"It's easy. Besides, you'll be driving it when I'm away. Can't let it sit idle."

"But I got this so you could drive it when you go on your trips. It's for you."

"Well, I don't know if . . . if it's the proper . . ."

"You *do* think it's extravagant and foolish. Oh, I should have gotten a Volkswagen."

"Nae, Fiona, I think nothing of the kind. I'll drive it to the moon if that will make you happy. I was thinking of when the weather is bad and a train or bus would be better. Now, come on, let's see if you know how to start this yellow monster."

145

Surprisingly enough, I did start the car quite smoothly. It was easy to handle, and I managed the rest of the drive quite well. I was reluctant to stop, enjoying it so much, but Alastair laughed and reminded me that soon I would have my very own means of transportation and to leave the car for him.

We were all quite busy that week after Christmas. There was a constant stream of visitors to Lochinver Castle, and we returned their calls; someone was always giving a party. These small gatherings were not "fashionable," but they were marked by generous, old-fashioned Scottish hospitality. Alastair and I were especially busy. Rosemary was returning to London, and we had decided on the spur of the moment to go with her and spend a week or so as a New Year's holiday. I was delighted. The only time I had been in London was when Toby had taken me to meet his mother; that had been unpleasant for us both and we had hurried away. I was looking forward to playing tourist, to shopping, to attending plays. Rosemary would not start classes for a few days, so she would have ample time to show me around. Alastair was planning to combine this trip with some business. He would have to go to London within the next month anyway, he reasoned, so why not now, when we could make this a real holiday?

We all drove down to Inverness one afternoon, Rosemary in her parent's car and Alastair and I in the Triumph. The next morning, we caught an early train down to Edinburgh, changing trains there for the 10:30 A.M. Flying Scotsman to King's Cross Station in London. The seven-hour trip was delightful, for I have always loved long train rides, and the changing landscape from the Borders by the sea, over the moors, through the Midlands, and into suburban London kept me well entertained.

Rosemary's flat was a charming apartment in the picturesque Bloomsbury section of London, decorated with odd pieces of furniture that Rosemary had discovered in secondhand, even third-hand stores. She was proud of her "finds" and revealed that the overstuffed armchair, her favorite piece of furniture, had been rescued from the sidewalk.

"And it was quite a job getting it up those stairs, but well worth the trouble. I covered it with new fabric and behold: a beautiful chair—free!"

The apartment had several rooms but only one bed, which Rosemary insisted Alastair and I use (though I had made reservations at the Ritz), saying her couch was more than comfortable and that she had to repay us for our generous hospitality.

Every day that we spent in London overflowed with activity. With Rosemary as guide, I saw every London landmark from the Tower to the Peter Pan statue in Kensington Gardens to the Elgin Marbles in the British Museum. We went on numerous shopping expeditions. Rosemary knew where the best deals on antiques could be find, and I made several purchases for the castle. I found a marvelous loveseat, a cherrywood desk that would be perfect for my "office," and a rocking chair for our bedroom. I even found some wallpaper that would add the finishing touch to the rooms in the north wing we were renovating, but not knowing their dimensions I had to wait until I returned to order it. We also shopped for clothes, but I bought only a few things. A "designer" wardrobe would have been ridiculously out of place at Lochinver, and Alastair preferred that I buy the more suitable sweaters and woolen goods in Scotland.

At night, we went to plays, to dinner, or to parties with Rosemary's student friends. I enjoyed these gatherings immensely. Perhaps I was vicariously reliving my student days, which had been cut short, but Alastair felt ill at ease. He enjoyed far more the performances of Covent Garden's new and controversial production of Wagner's *Ring* cycle. We spent most of our time together except for the few days Alastair spent with his political friends. He said little about them, and I didn't ask. I had no wish to involve myself too deeply in that part of Alastair's life. From his attitude, however, I gathered that he was pleased with the results of his meetings. This reassured me. There had been no further bombings, so I assumed Alastair and those like him had used their influence within the SNP to put an end to violent tactics. And I had forgotten, or at least learned to laugh at, my fears.

We were soon, too soon, on our way back to Inverness. We planned to spend a few days in our apartment there before returning to Lochinver. Alastair had more business to do, and I wanted to see Charles.

The January weather made Inverness quite cold. Bitter winds

blew constantly from the North Sea, and I longed for the more protected west coast. I laughed at myself for thinking that. Lochinver warm? I thought we would stay only a few days in Inverness, but Alastair's meetings were going to drag out and he was thinking of spending almost a week in the city. He had suggested that I drive up to Lochinver alone and that he would follow later. I discussed this plan with Charles over lunch.

"Is there anything more you'll need me for, Charles? Will it be necessary for me to stay any longer?"

"No, we've taken care of everything. What we've accomplished these past few days should see me through the next few months. You can return to your Highland paradise. It still *is* a paradise, I presume."

"Oh, yes. Especially now. It's lovely in the snow."

"Then, why the hesitation? Or has your Prince Charming begun to tarnish at the edges?"

"Charles!" I was shocked, but I had noticed a change in Charles's manner on this visit. I decided that he was still upset by the decision I had made that morning to do business with the Bank of Scotland exclusively. Charles had wanted Grimsby Petroleum to continue using the Bank of England, but I had insisted on making the change, feeling that it was unfair to send our monies out of the area where we earned them.

"Well, one can always hope. Seriously, Fiona, if anything does go wrong, I want you to know you can always come to me."

"That's very nice of you, but there's nothing wrong. It's just that Alastair has to stay on a few days longer and he suggested that I drive on home. I am a little nervous about driving all that way by myself, though. The Highland roads are not the best even in good weather, and now there's a lot of snow and ice. If anything happened to Alastair's new . . ."

"I think you're being silly, Fiona. Alastair must have confidence in your driving, or he would not have suggested it. Besides, it's not that far. You'll be home in no time."

"You're right. Rosemary drove up for Christmas, so if she can do it, I can. I guess I'll leave tomorrow morning, so I'll say goodby now. Call me if you have any problems with Grimsby."

As it turned out, I didn't have to make the drive by myself. Alastair finished up sooner than he had anticipated and so was able to leave with me. However, he did have some things to do that morning, and we were not on our way until late afternoon. It was already dark.

There were a few lights along the road. But the moon had risen and shone so brightly that the stars seemed dim beside it. It was a beautiful drive. The snow-covered fields were a soft silver, the mountains gray shadows in the distance. At any other time we would have gone slowly, enjoying the scenery, but we were both tired and eager to reach Lochinver Castle.

"Fiona, I'm going to pull over to the side of the road," Alastair said suddenly. We had been driving about an hour and had just turned off the main highway onto the two-lane road that ran north. There was nothing in Alastair's voice to alarm me, and I waited until he had slowed to a stop at the side of the road before I asked why.

"Because . . . we don't seem to have any brakes." Alastair switched on the light, and we both looked at the brake pedal, which was lying on the floor. Alastair moved it back into position with his foot, but it flopped and lay there, useless.

"How did it happen? It was all right a minute ago."

"Aye, it was. I felt it give when I slowed to turn on this road, then . . . nothing. It gave completely. Fortunately we're going uphill, so I could stop."

"What are we going to do?"

"There's a farmhouse not too far away. I can see its lights. I'll go there and call a garage. We're not too far from Inverlael, so perhaps we can get someone to come out. You'd best stay with the car. It'll be cold, but warmer than out there."

Alastair smiled reassuringly and kissed me. Then, taking the flashlight, he left and made his way toward the farmhouse. I watched until the flickering light of the torch disappeared, and then settled back into my seat, pulling my coat tighter around my neck.

It was freezing. I tried to amuse myself by studying the landscape, but that soon palled, so I closed my eyes. I felt as though I was the only person on that lonely road. No other car passed or came toward me. I began to feel slightly nervous and wished that Alastair would come back. Even if he hadn't found help, I wanted him there with me. All of a sudden, I heard noises out-

149

side and the thud of something bumping into the car. I screamed and shut my eyes tightly. When I mustered enough courage to open them again, I saw the dim shapes of a small group of sheep huddling for warmth on the side of the road. I sighed with relief and laughed at myself for being so silly—those stupid sheep, they're everywhere! I called them names, which made me feel better, and curled up once more. Finally Alastair came back.

"We're in luck, darlin'. I called and they're sending a truck to pull us in. It shouldn't be long now. Were you all right?"

"Yes, though some sheep bumped into the car and scared me. It seemed you were gone forever."

"More like fifteen minutes. But I'm here now."

The tow truck came along shortly, and soon we were on our way to the one garage in Inverlael. It turned out that the brake lining of the car had been worn through. It was a fairly simple matter to repair, taking the mechanic about an hour to fit a new lining; then we were once more on our way.

"What an odd thing to happen!" I didn't know much about cars, but it did seem to me that the brake lining shouldn't have worn out in a new car.

"I agree, but you would go and get this fancy vehicle. I'll have it checked again in Lochinver. Something could be wearing it down or something could have struck it. It's probably just one of those fluke things. At any rate, we're almost home. Now, don't worry and cheer up."

I don't think I have ever been so glad to see the lights of Lochinver winking through the darkness as I was that night. Mhari and Ian were there to greet us. Mhari, just eight months pregnant, resembled a plaid pillow, she was so wrapped up. They were properly sympathetic when they heard about the accident that caused our delay, Ian shaking his head over those "new fangled machines" while Mhari rushed off to get us something to eat. As we sat and warmed ourselves in front of the cheering fire, I once again felt the warmth and security Lochinver had always meant to me, and the memory of our misadventure on the road retreated.

I have always been amazed at how quickly one picks up the threads of one's life and settles into the daily routine after being away. Mhari's pregnancy was at last forcing her to slow down, although her decreased level of activity would have been more than enough to occupy a normal person. I was becoming more involved in the actual running of the castle. The furniture I had bought in London arrived, and it took many moves before I was satisfied with its placement. I had taken the measurements of several bedrooms, and the wallpaper would be arriving shortly. Among the patterns I had selected was a blue-and-gold design to be used in the nursery Mhari and I were preparing. It was a room adjoining Ian and Mhari's—small, yet large enough for the child to use for several years. Mhari had moved several pieces of furniture there. One piece in particular delighted me: an antique cradle that Mhari said had been used for generations of MacLeods. It was very imposing, almost too grand for a small baby, and I enjoyed picturing Alastair as he had lain in it.

The horse that Alastair had given me for Christmas arrived, and I was immediately delighted with her. She was a beautiful little mare, sleek and well formed. But it was the color of her coat that made her truly unusual. She was almost pure white, her tail gleaming silver in the sun's light and contrasting with the gently dappled gray of her haunches. It was her color that inspired her name, of course. When I was asked what I planned to call her, I had thought silently for several moments. All the usual names for white horses, such as Silver or Lightning, seemed inappropriate when applied to this dainty creature.

"Would you mind a suggestion?" Alastair asked, and I turned to him gratefully. "Why not Fionn? It's a variation of the Gaelic word for white. Perfect, don't you agree?"

"Yes. I was thinking along those lines myself. Fē-ŭn. I like the sound of it. It's graceful and feminine, so it suits her perfectly."

Bruce was not totally delighted with the arrival of Fionn, however. He regarded this new, large animal with alarm, barking as she approached him. Fionn did not shy away, though, but proceeded to look down at the furious terrier with mild interest. I picked Bruce up and carried him over to the mare so he could see he had nothing to fear. Fionn tossed her mane and nuzzled him. Bruce gave one excited yelp and, squirming out of my arms, took off toward the castle. At a safe distance he stopped and barked as if to assure us that he was really not frightened at all.

As the weather did not allow me to take Fionn for long rides about the estate, I confined my riding to the protected areas near the castle. There was a paddock near the stables, and I used that as an exercise yard, occasionally taking Fionn out onto the road. We soon grew used to each other, and the riding lessons I had had as a child came back to me. With Alastair's help, I fashioned a small jump, which we soon mastered, and I began to long for spring, when I could take Fionn out for long gallops.

"I'll have to paint you on your new horse," Lewis remarked one afternoon.

"I doubt if we could sit still long enough for a proper pose; Fionn's a lively animal," I laughed. "And then you'd have to paint Alastair with his car, to make a matched set."

"Nae, cars don't appeal to me. Though even I enjoyed driving that one. I heard you had a slight problem with it on your way up from Inverness last week."

"The brake lining failed. We were very lucky that we were able to get help quickly; spending the night on the road is not my idea of a fun evening."

"Aye, you were lucky."

"It turned out to be no more than a slight annoyance, causing us to be delayed a few hours. Just one of those things."

"Fiona, have you realized this is the second time?"

"The second what?" Lewis's expression puzzled me. It was so unlike him to be serious.

"The second time you used those words—about an accident that could have been very serious. The steps and now the brakes failing."

"Are you suggesting I'm accident-prone?"

"No, not really."

"Well, then, what?"

"I'm not really sure. I just think you ought to be very careful in future."

"Lewis, I appreciate your concern, but do stop talking about this or I'll begin to be paranoid. You brood too much about those stone steps. You even had Rosemary worried."

"That's what friends are for, to worry about you. How is Rosemary, anyway?"

I was relieved when Lewis said that, and even happier when

he asked for her address. That's just what he needs, I thought: Rosemary. Thinking of her will take his mind off me. I had decided that it was because of the mild crush Lewis had on me that he was so preoccupied with what happened to me. Otherwise, he wouldn't keep bringing up those two separate incidents and talking as though there could be a connection. That would be utterly impossible. Well, maybe I am accident-prone, I thought. I laughed at that. No, it was just coincidence, and Lewis's overactive imagination was seeing things that just weren't there.

SEVEN

The North Sea

We had been home only a few weeks when Alastair suggested we take another trip, this time to the oil fields in the North Sea. The idea appealed to me, but I was surprised by Alastair's proposing such a venture.

"I think it would be a good idea," he said. "After all, as principal stockholder, shouldn't you be aware of all aspects of your company?"

"Yes, I've wished I'd had the time to go again, but . . . why do *you* want to go?" I was now doubly surprised, for Alastair had never talked this directly about my involvement in Grimsby Petroleum.

"There's been talk that there may be a general election soon for Parliament. I fully intend to stand for one of the Scottish seats. It would be a great advantage if I have been out to the oil fields: I could speak more knowledgeably about the situation there, plead for better working conditions and so on."

"But now? It's the dead of winter!"

"The weather is always bad in the North Sea, and besides, if the election is to be held in the spring, I should go as soon as possible. It'll give me a chance to get the jump on my competition and to do a little campaigning among the workers. And," he added laughing, "if I go with Fiona Grimsby, I'm sure to have the best guided tour available—red carpet and all!"

"All right, I'll ask Charles Haversham to arrange it."

Alastair's reasons for going delighted me, for this would give me the opportunity to help him and, by helping him, I would be helping the Scottish Nationalist Party. My greatest fear since our marriage was that our interests would conflict with each other, but now the very fact that I worked for Grimsby Petroleum would benefit his cause. I felt this trip would bring us closer together and help to merge our differences. I dashed off eagerly to call Charles and make the necessary arrangements for our trip.

I was again surprised, for Charles Haversham immediately agreed to the idea. I had feared he might disapprove, especially as Alastair would be accompanying me. Naturally I kept secret Alastair's motives for going, but Charles was astute enough to realize that Alastair's reasons could be related to the Scottish Nationalist Party. Even so, Charles was enthusiastic.

"I'm delighted, Fiona; it'll give you a chance to inspect our newest rig, in the Beryl Field. I haven't had a chance to see it myself, though I've followed its progress closely. It's just now coming into full production. I wish I could go with you, but I'll be tied up here in Inverness the next several weeks; I may even have to go to London, so I'm glad Alastair will be escorting you. The weather will be bad, of course, and you'll see some gigantic waves, but you should be in no danger. I'll make all the arrangements and get back to you about the details. There will be some things I'll want you to take a look at." The rest of our conversation dealt with business.

"Fiona, I do wish you weren't going," Mhari said as she watched me pack for our trip. This was not the first time she had voiced her disapproval. At first, I had thought it was because she feared her baby might be born while we were away, although it was not due for several weeks—but such was not the case.

"It is so dangerous on those oil rigs," she continued. "One of the village boys, the MacDonnells' eldest son, was killed last year during a storm. One of those large waves hit the rig—he was on deck repairing a cable—and, well, they never found his body."

"Oh, Mhari, how tragic! But, I promise you, we will be careful.

It's only for two days and if there's any danger we'll stay safely inside. Besides, you know Alastair wouldn't have suggested this trip if he thought I'd come to any harm."

"No, but all the same . . ."

I stopped her from saying more. I was touched by Mhari's concern, but I refused to acknowledge her fears. I was too excited by the trip and too happy about what it would mean for me and Alastair to fret about something that had little chance of happening. Then I laughed. Of course, Mhari was just behaving naturally—women always worry more when they are pregnant.

Alastair and I arose early the next morning and drove to Inverness, where, having left our car in the station's large parking lot, we would catch the train to Aberdeen. The Triumph was in perfect working order, and the drive was as uneventful as it was pleasant. While we waited for the train, I called Charles, but his secretary said he had left for London the previous day. She confirmed the arrangements for our trip, saying that we would be met in Lerwick by Robert Douglas, one of Grimsby's public relations men. This news cheered me, for I had hired Robert Douglas the year before. He was one of the few Scots employed by Grimsby in an administrative capacity, and I was sure that he and Alastair would enjoy meeting each other.

Our train arrived in Aberdeen just an hour and a half before the boat for the Shetlands was scheduled to depart. This didn't leave us much time to see the "granite city," as Aberdeen is called, but Alastair insisted we visit one landmark: the "Auld Brig o' Balgownie," which spans the gorge at the mouth of the River Don. It is said to have been built by Robert the Bruce in the fourteenth century and is one of the oldest bridges still in use. When we boarded our boat, the *Caledonia*, it started to rain. As we slowly moved from the dock and steamed past the lighthouse at Girdle Ness, I looked back at the city and saw how Aberdeen had earned its other nickname, "The Silver City by the Sea." The soft rain had caused the blue-gray granite stones of the buildings to turn white, and the whole city was truly gleaming silver.

It was a long trip, lasting throughout the night. We had booked a stateroom, and as soon as we passed the lighthouse at Kinnairds Head, which marked the last land we would see until morning, I retired to our room. The quarters were close, but I found some relief there from the incessant rolling of the ship. The *Caledonia* was large, but I wasn't used to sea travel, and to my mind it reeled from the impact of each wave in the rough, January seas. Alastair fared better and spent much of the night in the ship's lounge drinking beer while I tossed in bed vainly pretending I was back in Lochinver Castle. The next morning, Alastair attacked his breakfast eagerly, while I barely managed a cup of tea and avoided looking through the portholes at the sea, which rose and fell regularly.

We arrived shortly after dawn at Lerwick, on Mainland, the largest of the nearly one hundred Shetland Islands. Once again, I was disappointed by our lack of time for sight-seeing. Lerwick is closer to Bergen, Norway, than it is to Edinburgh, and this shows in every aspect of the town—from its architecture to the pavings in its streets. The Shetlands are treeless, rocky islands with an austere, almost mesmerizing beauty, and I longed to explore them in order to visit the Bronze Age and Iron Age mounds that are still to be found. Alastair promised to bring me back in the summer, when—because of the island's proximity to the North Pole—nights are short and one long day blends into the next. At any rate, the regret I felt was soon swallowed up in my excitement.

Robert Douglas, a short and cheerful man, met us at Lerwick's tiny airport. It turned out that he and Alastair had met before. Apparently he, too, was a member of the Scottish Nationalist Party. I chuckled to myself, for if Charles knew that, he would certainly fire Robert on the spot and accuse me even more violently of allowing Alastair to influence my decisions.

We were to travel to the oil rig by helicopter. I blanched as we boarded, for I would have preferred to spend more time on solid ground. I steeled myself, however, for this was obviously to be a day for new experiences. The flight took several hours, and I was beginning to despair of seeing nothing but ocean when Robert touched my arm and pointed through the round window. (The helicopter's engines prevented all conversation.) There, in the east, was a vast structure rising above the darkening blue waters. As we drew nearer it seemed as if it were a small city, not an oil rig, we were visiting—so varied were its levels and components.

The helicopter set down on the pad at the top of the structure and we were met by Erik von Harz, the German-born chief engineer. We were to spend most of the day touring the structure while Mr. von Harz explained the more technical aspects of the giant oil rig.

BG-1, as Grimsby Petroleum's platform in the Beryl Field was called, was one of the new type of platforms developed in Norway for use in the North Sea called ConDeeps (Concrete Deep Water Structures). The platform was supported by three concrete cylinders, each over 460 feet long. Twenty wells were being drilled in two of the cylinders; the third was for utility purposes. There was also another concrete structure, which had capacity for storing one million barrels of oil. As a pipeline was uneconomical, the oil was loaded from the storage cells to tankers. Mr. von Harz said the platform's goal was 50,000 barrels a day by the summer and that they eventually hoped to reach 150,000 barrels a day, once the rig was in full production.

The platform, which measured 686 feet from the bottom of the drilling rig to its top, was built to withstand the 90-foot waves and the 130-mile-per-hour winds that are possible and not uncommon conditions in the North Sea. Eventually it would be manned by a crew of 120, though currently there were more than twice that number aboard completing construction. The crew was multinational, and I was surprised to see several women on deck, though in their heavy, dark, loose-fitting work uniforms and brightly colored hard hats it was hard to distinguish them from the men.

"Oh, aye, there's seven women working here now," Robert said in response to my query. "They do mostly maintenance jobs, such as scraping and painting, and there's two in the kitchens."

"But can they do the work?" I asked in amazement, watching as one woman slung a heavy cable over her shoulder and sauntered past us.

"Aye, they're husky, all right. Though we've had a few that have quit. We've found that the best female workers are those over thirty; they're more settled and not so flighty."

"Why do they come here?"

"A very good reason—money. They can make up to three or four times what they earn on the mainland."

"What are the working conditions like here?" Alastair asked.

"It's a hard life, Mr. MacLeod. We have staggered crews, working twelve-hour shifts. There's a complete change every two weeks. Every worker works two weeks and then gets two weeks off."

"Is there any recreation?"

"They're usually too tired to do much except eat when they come off a shift. There's card playing, the television, and that sort."

"What about safety precautions?" Alastair asked.

"Ah, now, there's a subject we care a great deal about. The platform can survive the worst conditions, including fourteen thousand tons of water pressure. To make doubly sure, there are regulations stating that rescue boats be permanently stationed off the rig." Robert pointed and we saw the ships bobbing on the waves one hundred feet below us. "The platform is equipped with gas- and heat-detection systems and, of course, there's one very important rule for the crew: no drinking. You can imagine what that does to a Scot," he laughed. "The first place they head for once they hit the mainland is a pub!"

Robert went on to say that there were many dangers inherent in operating a platform. "What we fear most is a blowout. That's a massive eruption of oil, which could occur if a high-pressure pocket is hit during drilling; the oil then spills wildly into the sea. There was one in the Gulf of Mexico that took twelve months to bring under control, and last year in the Persian Gulf one well released poisonous gases, and the platforms in the vicinity of the explosion had to be evacuated."

"These blowouts have occurred in all the major drilling areas," Mr. von Harz added. "And some of us feel it's luck only that's kept one from happening here."

"There are many things to worry about," Robert continued. "A tanker could collide with a platform, which is highly probable in bad weather, or a platform could collapse suddenly. But I can say that more effort has gone into preventing these accidents in the North Sea than in any other drilling site in the world. We have the most difficult conditions to work under, and so we have to be doubly prepared. If we can successfully drill for oil here, we can go anywhere. As a matter of fact, no one knew how treacherous the North Sea really is before the platforms were built out here. That's why we've started using these ConDeeps; they're the best. BG-1 is the ninth ConDeep to be installed in British waters; it took eight tugs to tow and position it here last spring."

"What about the effect on the environment?" asked Alastair.

"I'm afraid that the balance of nature is a luxury we can't afford. We have no choice. We have to get the oil from beneath the sea as quickly as possible. Taking the environment into consideration takes up valuable time, and with the weather delaying us and inflation pushing up costs, well . . ." Robert shrugged and then hastened to add apologetically, "Of course, it's deplorable, but it's the price one pays to become a self-sufficient oil nation."

Alastair scowled, and I knew he wasn't satisfied by Robert's answer. The conflicts between the fishermen and the oil companies were well known, and the damage done by the drilling to the fisheries on the east coast of Scotland was one of Alastair's main grievances against the oil companies.

That night, we ate in the cafeteria the crew used; it was good food, hearty and simple. Since it was the twenty-fourth of January, the date of "Robbie" Burns's birth, the traditional meal of cockaleekie soup (a combination of potatoes, leeks, chicken, and bannocks—biscuits made from oats and cheese) was served. That night, all of Scotland was sitting down to such a meal in honor of their beloved poet's memory, and the crew of the oil rig was no exception. To my dismay, the main dish was haggis. I managed to avoid eating it, though not without much good-natured hazing from the roustabouts seated next to me. Unfortunately for them, the other grand (and main) tradition could not be enjoyed that evening: toasting Burns's health far into the night with large quantities of whiskey. We talked to several of the workers and found they enjoyed their rugged life, even thrived on it. They told many stories, trying to outdo each other with harrowing tales of the dangers they had survived.

After such a long and festive dinner, I decided it would be especially invigorating to get some sharp sea air. Slipping on one of the heavy slickers Mr. von Harz had given us, I looked around for the hard hat I had been told to wear, but I couldn't find it. Anyway, I reasoned, I hardly need that ugly thing for the few moments I'll be on deck. As I headed for the heavy double doors, I waved to Alastair, but, as he was still deep in conversation with some of the workers, he barely nodded in reply; I decided to go outside alone.

The night air was chilling, so chilling that, even though I was securely wrapped in the heavy oilcloth slicker, it seemed as if I were unprotected from the icy blasts of the wind. The harsh gusts buffeted the narrow decks of the platform and I was forced to cling to the ice-cold railing to keep from being knocked down. The ocean spray stung my face, and, as it had started to rain, the deck had become very slippery. I wondered if a storm was rising. The weather was known to be capricious in the North Sea, often changing three or four times a day. I knew I should return to the safety and warmth of the cafeteria, but I was enjoying myself too much; the wild spectacle presented by Mother Nature and Neptune was too exciting to leave it so abruptly.

The winter wind was master here. The gray waves leaped and fell to its dictation: now forming a solid wall of water, now disappearing completely to leave a great, dark hole that was immediately filled in by more rushing waters. Black clouds streamed across the red-gray sky, growing fiercer, twisting and turning to the wind's sharp demands. Even the oil rig took a part; the hanging lamps on the tower above me danced in counter-tempo to the swaying of the massive iron ziggurat itself. It seemed as though several symphonies were being performed for my benefit and all simultaneously. That feeling was reinforced by the special effects the wind created: the humming as it swept the decks, the whistling as it penetrated the gaps in the structure, and the crashing of the waves as they fell over each other in their race toward BG-1.

As this harsh beauty swirled around me, I was happy—happier than I had felt for some time. This trip to the North Sea had been a successful one. Since I had been living at Lochinver, I had begun to feel remote from the oil business. True, I had kept in contact with Grimsby Petroleum. I dutifully read every report Charles sent me, and I spent several hours of each day in my office high in the castle's tower, but I was removed from the mainstream of activity, removed from the daily excitement inherent in the rushing search for oil. Now, once again, I felt as though I was playing a vital part in that search, as though I was making a contribution. I had learned a great deal during the day's tour. I had seen for myself how great the struggle was to extract the precious oil from a North Sea reluctant to permit any man or thing to survive for long.

My happiness was caused by more than that, however. I felt that I had truly contributed to Alastair's work. He, too, had learned a great deal about the oil drilling—information that could help him win a seat in the next Parliament, information that would aid his cause and help him to better understand my work at Grimsby Petroleum. I knew this trip had brought us closer together. Our interests were not in conflict, as I had once feared, but were working together. The fact that I was involved in Grimsby Petroleum had helped Alastair, not hindered him. Now, I thought triumphantly, Alastair can't regret his marriage to Fiona Grimsby; now his Scottish Nationalist friends can't accuse me of affecting his loyalties.

I turned and walked along the deck's edge, still holding onto the railing and taking cautious steps. In a few minutes I would go back inside, yet I wanted to prolong the feeling of exhilaration and joy. Suddenly I was struck from behind. I felt something hit the back of my head, and I went sprawling forward, skidding and scraping my knees on the deck's rough surface. I still grasped the railing, so I didn't slide too far, but the force of my fall caused me to pivot, and I struck my head again on the lower rung of the railing. I lay still for several minutes in that awkward position, gasping for breath as I struggled to clear my head.

"'Ere, miss, are ye all right?"

Someone was bending over and picking me up. With difficulty, I brought my eyes into focus, trying to identify the formless shape hovering above me. Finally I was able to identify it as one of the woman roustabouts, whose strength I had admired earlier.

"Did ye slip?" she shouted. At first her words were carried away by the wind and I tried to make out her mouthings, but at last she made herself heard above the wailing gusts. I nodded weakly, even though that slight effort sent rushes of dizziness through me. Then, although she was shorter than I, she picked me up and carried me back to the eating area, shielding me with her broad shoulders as we slipped and bumped against the structure's walls.

"The lady's had an accident," she announced as we entered the large room.

Everyone immediately crowded about us, and the doctor was sent for. Robert Douglas pushed a steaming mug of strong coffee at me, and as I tried to sip it, I looked for Alastair, but he was not in the room. Where could he be? I wondered, but my head was pounding too hard to think clearly, and it took all my concentration just to keep from falling off the hard chair I had been lowered onto.

The doctor arrived in a few minutes and quickly set about checking my injuries. Superficially I had no more than a few scrapes and bruises, but the doctor warned of the possibility that I could have sustained a concussion in the fall. He said he would radio to Lerwick and arrange to have a doctor examine me there the next afternoon. Alastair had come into the cafeteria with the doctor, and after I had been examined he carried me to the small room we had been assigned. The doctor gave me a mild sedative, and I fell asleep quickly—too quickly to think over the evening's mishap.

Too quickly to think, yes, but, that night, my dreams were filled with strange thoughts and images. I was falling down, down, down into a void, springing up before I touched the rocky bottom; I repeated this cycle over and over. I was once more on the Hundred Steps, but this time I fell with the stones. Then I was back on the rig, slipping off the platform as the railing I grasped turned to ice and melted from the warmth of my hand, giving way as I crashed into it. Where was Alastair? Why wasn't he here to help me? I called his name frantically each time I fell, and, each time, I heard a voice across the void: "I'm here, Fiona," but no hand reached out to save me. The voice was too far away, too far above me, and it began to laugh as I fell . . . fell . . . fell . . . If the voice was Alastair's, why didn't he help me? Why did he watch me fall? Why didn't Alastair save me?

The next morning, I felt much better, but Alastair told the

doctor what a restless night I had spent, so he ordered me to stay in bed until it was time for us to leave.

"I'm sure you're all right, but it's best not to take any chances," he insisted. "You're a very lucky young lady. That was a foolhardy thing to do, going outside like that without a hard hat to protect you."

"I looked for mine, but I couldn't find it. Besides, I didn't think anything would fall and hit me."

"Hit you? I thought you struck your head on the railing." The doctor came over and re-examined the back of my head closely. "I can only see one bruise, Mrs. MacLeod, and you said last night that you hit the railing as you fell."

"I did. But before that, I felt something hit me on the back of my neck."

"That must have been the force of the wind, Fiona," Alastair interjected sharply. "A sudden gust blew up and its force knocked you down."

"No, I don't think so . . ."

"You hit your head right after you fell. It happened so fast that you confused the two," Alastair insisted.

I was about to retort that he wasn't there, so how could he tell me what happened, when I decided Alastair was concerned about me. But I was certain that I was remembering correctly, and so I persisted. "Couldn't something have fallen from the platform above? Perhaps one of the crew dropped a piece of pipe? I thought I heard something."

"There was no one up there last night, and Von Harz said there was no damage reported. Besides, if something had fallen, it would have been lying there on the deck—and nothing was found."

"Did anyone go to look?" I asked stubbornly, refusing to give in.

"Now, Fiona," Alastair said gently. "It's only natural that you should be a little hazy about what happened last night. You had a bad nightmare last night about falling and you're getting that mixed up with what actually happened. You're still feeling the shock of your accident, isn't that right, Doctor?"

"Aye, that's right," the doctor agreed, silencing my protests with a stern look. "Now, I think you should rest, Mrs. MacLeod, and don't strain yourself by thinking any more about your accident. The important thing is that you be calm; that's the only way you'll get well."

I was far from satisfied, but I realized it was useless to continue. As the doctor spoke, the door opened and I looked up smiling, expecting to see Robert Douglas.

"Charles! You're in London, I mean, you're supposed to be. Excuse me, I'm still a little foggy."

"I was in London last night. When our office in Lerwick got the news about your accident, they contacted me and I flew up the first flight I could get. I would have been here sooner, but there was some delay in getting a helicopter. How are you?"

"I feel fine, but the doctor says I should rest."

"Aye, that's right, you should," the doctor agreed. "How are you, Haversham? You just flew in this morning? I thought I saw you around here yesterday."

"That's quite impossible, Dr. Fletcher."

"Aye, I suppose it is. Once someone has a hard hat and a slicker on, it's almost impossible to recognize him. Well, I'll leave you now, Mrs. MacLeod; you can talk to Mr. Haversham for a few minutes, but I want you to sleep before you take that helicopter ride."

Dr. Fletcher left, and after a few minutes Alastair left also, saying he wanted to talk to Robert Douglas. I knew that was just an excuse, that he really wanted to avoid talking to Charles. Charles was most solicitous and queried me in great detail about the accident. He looked exhausted; there were large hollows about his eyes, giving his face an unusually gaunt expression. Poor Charles, I thought; he must have stayed up all night trying to reach the oil rig as soon as possible. I was touched by his concern.

"You mean you were walking about the deck *alone?*"

"Yes, I wanted some exercise and fresh air."

"Alastair allowed you to do that?"

"There was no reason not to, Charles."

"Plenty of reason, as it turned out. I wouldn't have let you wander about by yourself. Douglas should have known better; I'll speak to him about it."

"For Heaven's sake, Charles. Robert had nothing to do with it;

he didn't even know I had gone out. I'm sure he would have stopped me if he had known."

"All right, if you say so. I feel so angry, because I feel as though I'm responsible. I encouraged you to come here; I should have made you wait until I could be here with you."

"I hardly was coming here alone."

"Yes, but Alastair doesn't know enough about oil rigs; I would have stopped you from . . ."

"Charles, stop it! It's nonsense to go on this way. It happened, and it's over, and I'm all right. It was just a freak accident." Freak accident; where had I heard that before? I struggled to remember, but the memory eluded me. "I'm feeling rather tired now, Charles, I'd like to rest before I have to leave."

Charles left, and I fell quickly and soundly asleep.

After what seemed a few moments, Alastair woke me, saying the helicopter was ready to take us to Lerwick. I was sorry to be leaving, for, in spite of what had happened, I had enjoyed our brief visit to the rig and would have liked to spend more time on it. Robert Douglas was accompanying us, and as he helped me into the helicopter I noticed he was unusually grave and quiet. I wondered if Charles had accused him of being lax in spite of my insistence that such was not the case. Charles was not going with us, because he had said he wanted to tour BG-1 now that he was aboard.

The doctor in Lerwick confirmed Dr. Fletcher's opinion that I was all right. After examining me and taking a few X rays, he said that I would be sore for a few days and that I should rest once I was back in Lochinver, but there was no concussion and I would suffer no lasting effects from my mishap. We took the boat to Aberdeen that night, arriving the next morning, then took the train to Inverness. It seemed impossible that we had made the same trip two days before, so much had happened in between. Alastair suggested we spend the night in our apartment in Inverness, as he wanted to make sure I didn't become over-tired. Though I assured him I was all right, he insisted on babying me, saying I deserved to be spoiled. I couldn't help but agree and thoroughly enjoyed being fussed over during our trip.

Mhari put me to bed at once upon our return to Lochinver, immediately calling in the village doctor. She seemed to derive great satisfaction from having her predictions of danger proved correct and scolded both Alastair and me for making the trip to the North Sea. There was nothing I could do but go to bed and fervently wish that Mhari's baby would arrive soon, so she could mother it instead of me.

EIGHT

Mhari's Misadventure

The last weekend in January, a week after our return from the North Sea, Alastair went on a business trip to Dublin. As usual, I stuck to my resolution of never asking too much—what Alastair thought I should know about the Scottish Nationalist Party, he would tell me. Nevertheless, I did worry about what he would be doing in Ireland. The IRA had been active that winter, setting off explosions in Manchester, Birmingham, and several other large industrial cities in England. Although the Scottish Nationalist bombings in Glasgow had not been repeated elsewhere, there had been several threats; on our trip we had seen posters in Inverness and Aberdeen to the effect that if the party's demands were not met, the "Red Lion" would strike again.

Could Alastair be going to Ireland to confer with the IRA? To suggest they work together against their common enemy, the English? That seemed unlikely, but I knew that some of Alastair's friends were partial toward violence—had they finally convinced him their way was the surest?

As I helped Alastair pack for his trip, I was quiet and moved slowly, sighing unconsciously as I folded his shirts.

"Fiona, why the long face? I'd like to flatter myself that you're going to miss me terribly, but it's more than that."

"Of course I'll miss you, I always do when you're not here. But I am a little worried about Ireland; there's been so much trouble lately. Alastair, do be careful."

"I'll be all right. A Scot is always safe in Ireland. Now, an Englishman . . . that's another story. Now, now, I promise you I won't be in any unpleasant situations and I won't be doing anything that would cause you worry."

"Promise?" I felt like a small child being reassured by her father that there wasn't a Big Bad Wolf despite all the things that were going bump in the night.

"Aye, Fiona, I promise."

"Then, I'll feel better, but do hurry back."

"It shouldn't take more than a week and I'll be sure to call you every couple of days." Alastair resumed packing and soon he was ready to leave.

I had considered accompanying Alastair, for I had been to Ireland only once, seven years before—waiting in Dublin for fog-bound plane connections to Edinburgh. The day had been a fey, gray one, and I had been gloomily exhausted by the transatlantic flight. The impression I had received was one of a dull, dark, and dreary old city on an equally sorry river, the Liffey, and I had always intended to disprove that quick impression with a longer visit. In the end, however, I had rejected the idea of going along, because I was still shaky from the oil-rig incident, and the thought of traveling again so soon intimidated me. Besides, Mhari had only a short time until her baby was due, and she had finally conceded that perhaps she would be doing—not trying to do—less. I knew that I should be at Lochinver to help her, running errands or whatever else seemed necessary.

A light mist was falling as Alastair left, and I didn't linger to watch him drive off. He left the Triumph at home, for he was traveling with others, and the TR7's cozy quarters were impractical. Moreover, he reasoned, the extra car would come in handy if Mhari had to be suddenly rushed to the doctor's.

Except for our growing excitement over the arrival of the baby, life continued to be normal at Lochinver. Lewis was nearly finished with my portrait, and soon it was to be framed. I had enjoyed choosing the frame and had settled for one that would complement, but not duplicate, the ones that elegantly dominated the gallery. I was sorry that the painting was done, since I knew I would miss the pleasant, long afternoons Lewis and I had spent together; yet I told myself in my most unsentimental voice that it would be best for Lewis to be separated from me for a while.

A few days after Alastair's departure, the wallpaper I had ordered arrived from London, and Ian and I immediately set to work papering the walls in the nursery. I had originally planned to hire someone to do the work. However, I had overlooked the sometimes bothersome fact that any seemingly unnecessary expenditure on Lochinver shocked Ian, so with the paper actually in our hands, and Ian looking at me with his best you-rich-Americans face, I had chuckled and agreed it would be fun to do it ourselves. Mhari perched on a straight-backed chair behind us in order to supervise the matching of the delicate blue-and-gold pattern, so when the phone rang unexpectedly around sundown she went to answer it, returning shortly to say it was for me.

"Fiona, it's Charles. I want to drive up tomorrow if it's all right. I need to talk to you and have you sign some papers; this time I do need them right away. I'm a little hesitant after my visit a few months ago; perhaps we should meet in the village?"

"No, Charles, it's all right. It happens that Alastair is away, so there won't be any confrontation."

"Oh, all right, then." Charles sounded relieved. "I should be up there around lunchtime. I'll be driving back tomorrow night, so there's no need to put me up."

"Charles, you're quite welcome to stay over."

"No, I have to be at a meeting in the morning, with those papers you'll have signed."

"See you tomorrow, then." As I replaced the receiver, I thought how sad it was that one of my oldest friends and my husband couldn't be brought together, that each one's presence was intolerable to the other. I could see no solution: they each hated what the other stood for, and therefore they hated each other. The best I could do was to keep them apart. I went back upstairs just in time to rescue Ian from an unruly roll of wallpaper.

170

Charles arrived the next day around one o'clock. I waved to him from the door as he put his car into the garage. It was sleeting, and Charles didn't want to leave his car standing in it all afternoon.

"I must say, Fiona," he said as he began shaking off his overcoat, "that vehicle in the garage sadly outclasses my humble machine. I would have thought Alastair would have taken it with him on his trip."

"It was more convenient to leave it here."

"Where is he?"

"In Dublin; some meetings. They were planning to go south by train, then take the ferry to Dublin from Wales—Holyhead, I think."

"Wouldn't it have been easier to fly?"

"Yes, but more expensive."

"Ah, yes, the thrifty Scot. Well, it must be nice to have the extra car; I imagine you're an expert at driving it by now."

"I've just driven it around here, trips to the village, things like that. Oh, that reminds me. I have to pick up something for Mhari tomorrow."

"But didn't you drive it back from Inverness?"

"No, Alastair was able to leave with me. And I was very glad he could; we had a bit of trouble on the way up. I don't know what I would have done if Alastair hadn't been there."

"What happened?"

"Something to do with the brake lining. It was a simple matter to fix, so it turned out all right. I do seem to have a knack for attracting mishaps," I laughed. "Maybe I'm accident-prone."

"What do you mean, Fiona?" Charles took my hands and was looking intently into my eyes.

"Nothing, really. You know those steps I like to climb? Well, some of them slid away just as I was stepping on them. It happened the day after you left. I wouldn't have thought of it, but a friend of mine mentioned the two things together. He seemed to think there could be a connection of sorts. It's all nonsense, really."

"Maybe this friend of yours is right. Most people don't have two misadventures within a few months, and now there's your fall on the oil rig."

"Really, Charles, not you, too."

"One shouldn't discount the possibility. Can you think of anyone who would want to harm you?"

"Charles! Think of what you're saying!" I was shocked. Pulling my hands away, I moved to the window.

"Sorry, Fiona, I didn't want to upset you. You're right, of course, the whole thing is coincidence. It's just my overactive imagination; forgive me?" I laughed, my good humor restored by Charles's penitence, though I never would have credited him with a fanciful imagination—he was always so practical and business-minded.

Charles then turned to the business that had brought him to Lochinver. The British Government was becoming more and more involved in the North Sea oil explorations. While they were dependent on the oil companies, especially the Americans, they did not want to be totally dependent, in case there should be another oil embargo of the kind imposed in 1973.

"The government is renegotiating the original licenses; that's what my meeting is about tomorrow morning. And they're suggesting new taxes that could take 70 per cent of our net revenues."

"Leaving us a 20 to 25 per cent return on our capital?"

"Yes, a large difference. Now, the government is considering various methods. Nationalization is out; that would set back production, and they've set 1981 as their goal for self-sufficiency. There's the possibility they may take up ownership in one of the British oil companies. Grimsby is under consideration along with several others. I've thought about it rather a lot, and I think it would be to our advantage, Fiona. We would have the opportunity to become a multinational oil company instead of remaining a small one. Grimsby could become a world-wide power, in the same league as Getty."

"Is it definite they will invest in Grimsby?"

"No, but I think our chances are good. Tomorrow I make the final presentation."

"I don't know, Charles. What would this mean in terms of operations? How much influence would they have?"

"It would be more on paper than anything else. We'd still be operating as a commercial concern, but the government would have its representatives on our board and be party to our operations. The worst that could happen would be for them to make us buy British."

"I hate the thought of losing any control. I like to think of Grimsby as Toby's company. This would make it so impersonal."

"It's not Toby's, Fiona. I don't mean to sound harsh, but you're letting your emotions run away with you. If Toby were alive he'd be the first to agree this will benefit Grimsby. So much has happened in the past six years, more than even Toby, with his faith in the North Sea oil, could have foreseen. Forget the past, forget Toby. He's gone and I'm running Grimsby, perhaps better than he could have done. Don't look at me that way, I'm not being disloyal; I think I have a better sense of business than he had. He was the dreamer, while I set about making sure his dreams worked. A good team, but now the dreams are realized, and going into partnership with the government is the direction in which to go. If not, Grimsby will continue to be a small operation and we'd probably have to sell out to someone eventually, most likely the Americans. I'd prefer to stay British, and I'm sure Toby would have."

"I still feel a little uncertain, Charles. Perhaps because I'm here and not in Inverness, I feel a little out of touch. It's not that I don't trust you, but I'd like to know more. I hate to plunge into something while being unsure of the results. When will all this be decided?"

"Not for a few months."

"Well, then. Go ahead with your presentations and your meeting. By the time a final decision is reached, I'll know more about it and we can decide then."

"I don't have your absolute approval, then?"

"You have my approval to make the presentations, but I don't want anything irrevocable done, not until I've had time to study the situation thoroughly. Don't be so despairing, Charles, I'm sure I'll agree with you that it's the best way. It's just not something I can decide overnight."

"Will you discuss this with Alastair?"

"I don't know. He doesn't involve himself with Grimsby."

"He's sure to be against it."

"I've learned never to try and predict what Alastair is going to

173

do or say. Are we finished? Good, I want to show you what I've accomplished in the few months since you've visited."

I took Charles around the castle, showing him my purchases and the rooms I was redecorating. He was impressed and commented on my good taste.

"These things must have cost a lot of money," he added.

"Yes. Yet, to my mind, it's money well spent. My goal is to restore Lochinver to the grandeur it once knew. Well, not really, but I would like it to be a showplace. Alastair loves it so much and I've come to love it, too."

"If it makes you happy, Fiona," and Charles just shrugged.

We went outside and I showed Fionn off to Charles; then we walked back to the castle and said good-by at the door.

"Fe, fi, fo, fum. I smell the blood of an Englishman."

Charles and I spun around and saw Alastair walking toward us, glaring at Charles.

"What's *he* doing here!" Alastair demanded fiercely.

"I had to see Fiona about a business matter and I was just leaving. And since you don't seem inclined to press me to stay, Mr. MacLeod, I'll be on my way. Good-by, Fiona, and do think over what we talked about."

Charles went off to the garage and Alastair stormed inside, leaving me standing on the stone steps outside. I quickly followed him into the great hall.

"Welcome back," I said, trying to smile. "You're back earlier than we expected. Did everything . . . ?"

"Aye, and my return seems to have been inconvenient for you. Why was Haversham here?"

"He had something to discuss with me. He'd just come up this morning and . . ."

"My return cut his visit short, eh? The minute my back is turned, *he* shows up."

"Alastair, it's not like that at all. What we had to discuss was rather important; he needed my approval right away."

"Up to his scheming tricks, is he?"

"That's foolish."

"Am I supposed to believe he didn't know I was away?" Alastair demanded angrily.

"Of course, he didn't. How would he? I hardly called him and

174

said: 'It's okay, Charles, the coast is clear, the big bad wolf is away.'"

"All right, darlin', all right. But I'd bet fifty pounds that Haversham knew I would be away. Was it all that important?"

"He needed my approval before a meeting tomorrow morning."

"All of a sudden? Or did he know about it beforehand?"

"It's something he's been thinking about for a while."

"Aha! I rest my case."

"Perhaps the meeting was called suddenly."

"I doubt it. No, I've said it before and I'll say it again: the man's a cunning schemer. What was so important that he drove up and back in one day?"

I told Alastair briefly about the reasons for Charles's visit and what my decision had been. He nodded.

"I agree with you, Fiona; it is best to wait until you know all the facts before making a decision. How did Haversham react?"

"He wasn't pleased. He's convinced that going into partnership with the government is the best thing for Grimsby."

"Hmmm. More likely, the best thing for Charles Haversham. Can't you see, Fiona? That's why he waited until the last minute to talk to you about it. He assumed you'd be overwhelmed by the prospect, too impressed to raise any objection. Then he stressed the need for an immediate decision on your part, trying to make sure you didn't have time to think it over. Fortunately, you were your usual cautious self."

"I do like to think about things. Charles is probably right that it would be a good move, but I want to know more. I feel so cut off here at Lochinver."

"Haversham was undoubtedly counting on that. That way, you would go along with his plans, assuming they were the best way. He was counting on your trusting him."

"Well, I do trust Charles. Whatever he does he does in the best interest of Grimsby Petroleum."

"In the best interest of himself, you mean."

"Alastair, why do you suspect Charles? He's done things for me, well, definitely above and beyond the call of duty. Charles got me through those terrible days when Toby was killed and was so helpful when I came back to Inverness. And, don't forget, he rushed out to the oil rig as soon as he heard I was hurt."

"Aye, that he did. But if Haversham does anything, you can be sure there's something in it for him. He was probably overjoyed when you went back to America after Grimsby died, leaving him in control."

"Alastair, really! It was the best thing I could do at the time; I was on the verge of having a nervous breakdown. And you can't say the company was any worse off. Actually, he built it up."

"While building himself up as well. Haversham thinks he's in control of Grimsby, and he has no right to. Now, this latest government thing, well, he's ready to set himself up as another . . . another John D. Rockefeller!"

"Alastair, I don't like what you're saying one bit. I admit that Charles tried to press me, but I'm sure it was just that he was so convinced that it will be beneficial to Grimsby. I just wish I knew more. I wish I weren't so isolated and far away from it all . . . so out of touch . . ."

"So stuck away in the wilderness?" Alastair's words were coated with acid. "I can remember a time, not so long ago, when that . . . that feeling of being so far away was not so unpleasant to you. When you didn't think of it as being isolated, because you would be here with me!"

"Oh, I didn't mean it the way it sounded, it's just that I'm so con . . ." I turned, but I found I was speaking to an empty room. Alastair had gone. I called his name and ran out after him, but a heavy thud told me that Alastair had gone outside.

I sat down on a chair in the cold entranceway and stared at the closed door. What I most feared had happened again. Alastair's and my loyalties had driven us apart, causing us to fight. This was more serious than our first argument, for we had questioned each other. By saying that I trusted Charles, I was in effect putting my friend before my husband. Now Alastair assumed I was regretting coming to Lochinver. That he had jumped to a silly conclusion made no difference; Alastair was an extremely proud man. My sentiments had hurt him deeply. I wished that Alastair were with me so I could tell him he was wrong, that I had never regretted for an instant marrying him, that I wouldn't trade one second of my life at Lochinver for years anywhere else. I knew that in time Alastair and I would forgive each other for what had been said, that we would love each other as much as ever. But, I wondered, could we ever really forget our differences?

The next day, as I was preparing to drive into the village, Mhari came into the hall and asked to run the errands instead.

"I don't think that would be wise," I replied. "After all, you should be careful."

"Och! I do wish that everyone would stop treating me as if I were a china doll. I feel perfectly fine and I'm dying to get out and *do* something. Driving isn't all that tiring. The doctor didn't say I couldn't drive. He just told me not to lift anything heavy. Ian said this morning it would be all right. He even asked me to pick up a tin of his favorite tobacco."

"Well, why don't you come with me? That way, you could get your outing."

"No. Fiona, you've been awfully good to me, doing all sorts of tasks, making me rest. I'm perfectly capable of driving the few miles to the village by myself. Now, admit it, it's a beautiful day. Wouldn't you rather be taking Fionn out for some exercise?"

I laughed and had to admit that Mhari was right.

"You see?" she said triumphantly. "Stop thinking of me, and do something that you'd rather do."

I finally agreed to let her go and walked with her out to the garage. Ian had left for a cattle auction in the family car, so Mhari had to drive the Triumph. Alastair had taught her how to drive it, so I wasn't worried on that account. I waved to her gaily as she drove off. Before I let her go I had made her promise to drive slowly and carefully.

I went upstairs to change into my riding clothes, thinking as I did so that I would have to get a real riding habit complete with jodhpurs and velvet hat if I was to do justice to Fionn's grace. The thought of buying new clothes had never failed to make me happy, and I whistled as I went back downstairs, clicking my heels on the stone steps in a rough imitation of a tap dancer. Alastair was in the hall sorting through the mail. He looked up in surprise as I entered.

"Fiona? What are you doing here?"

"What? Oh, I was just going riding."

177

"I thought you were going into the village. I saw the Triumph drive off."

"That was Mhari. She insisted on driving in herself to pick up those packages. She's been feeling a little pent up lately and wanted to get out by herself. Can't say that I blame her. We have been handling her with kid gloves, and she's not used to sitting around and being waited on constantly."

"*Mhari* drove the car?"

"Yes. I just said that." I stopped clicking my heels and looked at Alastair. His face had turned an ashen color, and the look in his eyes puzzled me. Perhaps he was still angry with me.

"You let her drive that car, in her condition?"

"Well, I didn't want to at first, but she was so insistent. She's very strong, even though she appears fragile, and she's certainly a better driver than I am. She won't take any chances. I'm sure there's nothing to worry about."

"Aye." Alastair shook his head. "But I won't be happy until she's returned safely. There's nothing we can do now, so go along and enjoy your ride, darlin'; I'll see you later."

Bruce followed me outside, but when Fionn whinnied as I entered the stables, he turned and ran back to the safety of the castle. Poor Bruce, I laughed, as Fionn nuzzled the pocket in which I carried the carrots I gave her as treats. She munched happily away as I saddled her, and looked hopefully around for more.

"No. You don't want to get fat and lazy, do you?" I asked and then chuckled at her crestfallen expression. Soon she was ready and I led her out into the paddock. As we rode around, I longed for warmer weather, when I could take her for real jaunts about the estate. I started to daydream of lazy summer afternoons, of how I would sail over the ground light as a feather on Fionn's supple back, Bruce—his fears conquered—scampering to keep up. My reveries came to an abrupt end as Fionn gave a bounce and then looked around reproachfully as if to say: "You weren't paying attention, you silly girl." I laughed and patted her neck. "You want to go for a real ride, too, don't you, girl?" I decided to take her out on the road; we could both do with a change of scene.

I had ridden a fair way down the road that led to the village and was turning back when a car went speeding past and then screeched to a halt. I had great difficulty in keeping Fionn under control and was cursing the driver of that car when I recognized Joan Demerest.

"Joan! Whatever are you doing, driving that fast? Fionn practically bolted, don't . . ."

"Och! Fiona, I'm so glad to see you. There's been a terrible accident. Mrs. Nicolson. The car. She went into a ditch. Lewis." Joan was so agitated she stumbled over her words.

"Joan, has something happened to Mhari?" I dismounted and took her by shoulders.

"There was an accident. Something happened and the car went off the road, just beyond the bridge. We didn't see the accident, we drove by just after. Lewis got her out of the car and is taking her to the doctor's. In the Stewarts' car. He sent me here, we figured you would need a ride into the village."

"Was Mhari hurt badly?"

"I—I don't know. She was unconscious. The car had turned over and she was wedged behind the steering wheel, so she wasn't flung out of the car. She did have a cut on her forehead."

"Joan, go on up to the castle and tell Alastair. I'll ride back, and then we can all go into the village together. And please don't drive so fast."

The girl nodded and got back into her car and drove off. I climbed on Fionn and urged her into a gallop, taking a short cut through the fields. Although I had acted calmly in front of Joan, I was far from feeling as confident as I had sounded. I was oblivious to my surroundings, with the words "It's my fault, it's my fault" sounding in my ears to the rhythm of Fionn's pounding feet.

I galloped furiously into the stable yard, leaping down before Fionn had stopped, and threw the reins to a surprised Thomas Ross.

"Mr. Ross, could you put Fionn away for me? Mrs. Nicolson's had an accident and we've got to go into the village." I barely thanked him and dashed into the castle. Alastair was standing in the hall listening to Joan repeat her story, and I ran over to him and clung to him tightly. He held me close and said we should go. As we left, a shaken Mrs. Ross promised to send Ian as soon as he returned from the auction.

Alastair drove the few miles to the village, as Joan was

179

exhausted and only too glad to relax. We didn't talk. We were too busy with our own, private thoughts. Soon we came to the small, one-lane bridge, and as we crossed over we saw the overturned Triumph. The village garage had already sent out a tow truck, and several men were attempting to right the vehicle. Alastair slowed the car as we passed, and I could see that it was not badly damaged. For the first time, I allowed myself to feel some hope for Mhari.

We pulled up in front of the doctor's office and went inside the large, stone building. Lewis was there, and after some confused exchanges we all sat avoiding each other's eyes. Finally Dr. MacKay came out and talked to us.

"Mrs. Nicolson is sleeping now, which is a good sign," he said without being asked. "She was not hurt that seriously by the accident itself—some minor contusions and bruised ribs. But I am concerned about the child."

Mhari's baby! In my anxiety over Mhari's life I had forgotten that she could live and still lose something almost as precious. I suddenly felt nauseous and sat down holding my pounding head in my hands, barely able to listen to what the doctor was saying.

". . . she was wedged in quite tightly behind the steering wheel. The intense pressure has induced labor pains, although the baby was not due yet. I haven't been able to determine if the fetus sustained any injuries, but I can tell you that it is alive. In addition, it will be a breech birth and even more risky, considering the internal bruising of the mother. However, I am fairly optimistic. Mrs. Nicolson is a strong and healthy individual. A colleague of mine, Dr. Farquarson, is on his way from Inverness and will be here in a few hours. I would prefer that Mrs. Nicolson be in the hospital there, but of course, in her present condition, there's no question of moving her."

"Could we see her, Doctor?" Alastair's face was grim.

"She's under heavy sedation, Mr. MacLeod, and may not recognize you. I must ask that only the immediate family go in. That means you and Mr. Nicolson. Has he arrived yet?"

Alastair followed the doctor inside, and Joan left to try to find Ian. Lewis and I were left waiting alone.

"Lewis." I barely recognized my own voice in the harsh croak that emitted from my throat. "Lewis, it's all my fault. Mhari's going to lose her baby and it's all my fault."

"Fiona, what are you talking about?" Lewis sat down beside me, taking my shoulders in a firm grip.

"I shouldn't have let her drive. I knew it was risky, but I let her go. She was so determined, but . . ."

"You couldn't have foreseen this. There was no reason not to let her drive a short distance."

"No. I shouldn't have let her. Oh, Lewis, if anything happens to that baby or to Mhari, I'll never forgive myself. And she is going to lose that baby, I know it!"

"Fiona, hush! For God's sake, you don't know what you're saying!" Lewis tried to quiet me and to stop the flow of incoherent words I was speaking, but failed. I was beside myself, sobbing, clutching Lewis's shirt, trying to make him understand that I was to blame.

Having heard my cries, Alastair came rushing into the room, followed closely by the doctor.

"Fiona, what's happened?" When I continued shrieking that I had killed Mhari, he sat down on the couch, pulling me to him, and cradled me tenderly. I had been holding Lewis's shirt so tightly that it ripped when Alastair pulled me away, and I continued to grasp the bits of white cloth in my clenched hands.

"I'm sorry, Alastair. Fiona started explaining that Mhari's accident was her fault, that she shouldn't have let her drive. Then she got hysterical."

"I'll give her something to calm her. It'll make her sleep." I heard the doctor's voice give instructions to his nurse and was only dimly aware of the sharp pick of the needle in my arm. Alastair continued to hold me paternally.

"There, it's beginning to take effect now. Perhaps it would be better if Mrs. MacLeod were taken home."

"Nooo." My protest was hardly more than a whimper. "I don't want to go, I want to stay here. Don't make me go home, Alastair, let me stay. Please. I want to stay. With you. Please." I was beginning to feel the drug, but I struggled to stay awake and plead with Alastair to let me remain.

"There, there, if you want to stay, you shall." He raised his head and spoke to the doctor in lowered tones. "Perhaps it would be better if she could remain, Dr. MacKay. Fiona would just get more excited and upset being at Lochinver, not knowing what was happening."

"Well, all right, then, but none of us will know anything for several hours yet."

"Just the same, it will help us all to be together now."

"Aye. Well, there's a couch in the other room. Mrs. MacLeod can rest there. This way."

When I awoke, several hours later, it was to a strange, darkened room. I sat up quickly and then fell back just as quickly, my head swimming. A hand pressed a wet cloth to my forehead, and, opening my eyes, I saw Alastair's concerned face.

"How are you feeling?"

"I . . . I'm not sure. A little dizzy, like I have a hangover."

"Aweel, that's from the good doctor's medicine, not from good honest whiskey, more's the pity. There, that's better, now how about a bigger smile? No, darlin', don't try to sit up. Just lie there; you'll feel better in a minute or two."

Then it all came rushing back. "Mhari! How is she? Is her . . . the baby? Has anything happened?"

"No, but Mhari is all right, so far. The contractions are closer together; the doctor thinks the baby will be born in the next few hours. Ian's in with her now; all we can do is wait."

"Oh, Alastair, I'm so sorry."

"No, Fiona, enough of that, now. I would have done the same. Mhari's got one devil of a stubborn streak and it's impossible not to let her have her way. Thank God for that stubbornness. She's determined to have that baby."

"Did you see her?"

"Just for a few moments. She was drugged, but she managed a smile and told us not to worry. She's got her share of the MacLeod spirit." As he spoke, there was a gleam of admiration in Alastair's eyes. "Now, some of that spirit should have rubbed off on you since you married me, so let's show some courage."

It was a long vigil that we kept that longest of nights. The details of that small office are permanently etched on my memory: the long, black-leather couch, the two straight chairs, the severe white walls with only two, old-fashioned pictures to break the monotony. One, a rural winter landscape in which a solitary figure could be seen making its way through the snowdrifts, was entitled "Making the Rounds." The other was a faded copy of a Norman Rockwell painting showing an old and paternal doctor taking the temperature of a small child while its mother looked on anxiously. There was an old rug covering the wide and uneven floor boards, its blue and red pattern the only bright colors in the room. It was an interesting design, consisting of interlocking flowers and strange animals that guarded the corners. There were several magazines scattered on the scratched table beside the couch, but, true to the profession, they were out of date and their covers were greasy and worn.

Joan had brought sandwiches and coffee to see us through the waiting, and the remains were on the table. Only Ian had shown any inclination to eat. Alastair had forced me to swallow half a sandwich, although he had only drunk coffee. I'm not sure why we all stayed. There was nothing that we could do, and the doctor would have sent word of any news, but we were compelled to remain—as if our presence would ensure Mhari's safety and the safety of her baby.

Ian spent most of the night by Mhari's side, but occasionly he emerged to say that nothing had changed or that the labor pains were closer together. Ian's face was haggard and gray, and his eyes showed the strain of waiting those many hours, but his voice maintained a vague cheerfulness. Alastair said nothing, only nodding at the remarks of others; he, too, seemed fascinated by the rug's design and paced it endlessly, following its contours.

It was about eight-thirty, the first lively rays of sun peeking through the heavy drapes, when the nurse came to the door and and asked for Ian, who was stretched out on the couch trying to rest. He looked around with a half-smile and followed her. I got up stiffly and went over to Alastair and took his hands between my own. He bent his head and brushed my hair absent-mindedly with his lips, all the while keeping his eyes on the rug. We stood there motionless, not saying a word.

Suddenly I heard a sound, faint, but definitely a sound. I looked up quickly at Alastair, but he gave no indication of having heard anything. I strained, concentrating on listening. Yes. There it was again, a small, hesitant noise. This time, Alastair heard it too, and he clutched my arm, scarcely daring to breathe.

Gradually the noise grew louder and stronger, finally erupting into the cries of a newborn baby announcing its entrance into our lives.

"Oh, Alastair, thank God, thank God!" I was unable to manage more than a whisper, and I started to tremble. Alastair led me over to the couch, and I sat down slowly and breathed deeply, the first real breaths I had drawn in hours. I felt as though a great burden had been lifted from me, allowing my heart to fill once more with hope.

"It's a girl, a . . . little girl!" Ian came stumbling into the room still wearing the white coat the nurse had given him to wear, a gauze mask dangling from one ear. "Mhari's going . . . she'll be fine!" As Ian sat down awkwardly on the couch, I could see that there were tears in his eyes. "She's going to be fine," he repeated as if to assure himself it was true. "The little girl . . . my daughter, my daughter!" He savored the new words. "Och, she's so small, so tiny, it seems a miracle she's alive. I never imagined a baby could be that little . . . or . . . that ugly!"

"Oh, Ian!" Alastair and I said together, and then all three of us laughed at Ian's reaction to his first glimpse of a newborn infant.

The doctor came in, exhaustion showing plainly in every movement he made. "I can see that Mr. Nicolson has told you the good news. Aye, it's a bonnie wee girl, and healthy, by the sound of things. Mrs. Nicolson is sleeping now; she pulled through fine. I don't mind telling you it was middling difficult for several hours, but Farquarson and I managed it together. We're not above feeling proud of ourselves; breech births can be tricky under the best of circumstances, and in this case, with the bruises and possible internal . . . aweel, enough of that; we were all aware of the dangers."

"When can we see her, Dr. MacKay?"

"I'd prefer it if no one disturbed her for a while, Mr. MacLeod. I want her to sleep; she needs the rest to build up her strength. I want to keep her here for a while, because of her other injuries. I want to keep her and the baby under observation."

"Is there any danger of . . ." I couldn't finish.

"No, Mrs. MacLeod, I'm not unduly concerned. Although the birth was premature, it was close enough to full term that there

184

shouldn't be any danger from that. All the same, it will be needing special care; she'll stay in the incubator Farquarson brought with him from Inverness Hospital. She appears healthy, but I want to make sure nothing develops. Her first few hours of life were fairly rough. Don't worry, in a few weeks both mother and baby will be home and you'll never know this all happened. Now the best thing is that you all go home and get some sleep. Doctor's orders. Mr. Nicolson, I'll call you when your wife wakes up. There's no reason why she shouldn't receive visitors."

We did leave then, glad to be out in the cool February sunshine. We drove slowly back to Lochinver, but it was not the slow and silent ride of the day before: I teased Ian mercilessly about his "ugly" daughter, while Alastair insisted that she must be a true Nicolson, for all the MacLeod babies were born beautiful. A relieved Mrs. Ross greeted us at the door; Alastair had called her from the doctor's, and happiness flooded her round face; Bruce barked continually as he ran about in circles to tell us that he, too, knew all about it. Mrs. Ross insisted on fixing us both breakfast and bustled about the kitchen humming "Blessed be, blessed be" to a nameless tune of her own making.

We recovered gradually in the days that followed, settling into a new routine. Ian spent most of the day in the village visiting Mhari; Alastair visited in the evenings. Mhari was still weak and the doctor had restricted her visitors. I was anxious to see Mhari, but the reports that Ian and Alastair gave of her progress were comforting and I knew that she would soon be home, happy and well.

I kept myself so busy that at night I would fall asleep almost immediately. Since Mhari's accident, I had several nightmares similar to the one I had dreamed on the oil rig after my fall, and Alastair had awakened me several times to stop my tossing. He asked me what I was dreaming about, but I was unable to tell him. These nightmares were vague, and I could only say that I had felt that something was pursuing me, trying to capture me. The fact that I couldn't put a name to this something made it terrifying. Alastair attributed this to the traumas of the past few weeks and the guilt I had felt about allowing Mhari to drive. He assured me that, once Mhari was home and I saw for myself that she and the baby were fine, my nightmares would stop. I agreed, but until that happened I decided to solve my problem by ex-

185

hausting myself during the day—thus ensuring a dreamless sleep.

There was still work to be done on the nursery, for we had not planned on its being used so soon. I set about doing it myself. In spite of everything Ian and Alastair could say, I still felt guilt over what had happened to Mhari. I constantly relived that awful day, asking myself endlessly why I had let Mhari drive. The Triumph was still in the garage being repaired, and, as far as I was concerned, it could remain there forever. I cursed the day that I had decided to buy that car for Alastair. It had become a metal monster seeking to devour those who drove it. That was silly, I scolded myself, but there had been two accidents in that car, both of which could have been fatal.

Dr. MacKay was true to his word, and in two weeks Mhari was home with her baby. Ian had gone to get her, and we met them at the door. It was touching to see how solicitous Ian was of Mhari, holding onto her and guiding her steps. I had never seen a more radiant face than Mhari's than when she stood with her husband's arm around her and with her new baby in her arms.

On a bright Sunday we all trooped into the kirk after services to witness the baby being christened Catriona, the Gaelic equivalent of Catherine. I found this to be a wonderful name that suited her well, for even though she was but a few weeks old, her gurgling laugh was musical. Thereafter, and much to Bruce's annoyance, Mhari and little Catriona occupied center stage at Lochinver. Mhari was still weak and needed to rest much of the day, so the greater part of caring for Catriona fell to Mrs. Ross, who couldn't have been more delighted. She never tired of reminding us that she had diapered and fed Mhari and what a pleasure it was to be doing the same for her "ain wee bairn."

"Mrs. Ross is a treasure," Mhari laughed one afternoon when Mrs. Ross had bundled Catriona off for her bath. "She's so happy to have a new baby in the house; it's her third generation of MacLeods."

"Please don't say that. Hearing it five times a day from Mrs. Ross is more than enough!"

"Aye, she does get carried away. It's very touching. All the

186

same," Mhari sighed, "I'll be glad when I can be up and about. I want to take care of Catriona myself. Och! It's so annoying to have to lie here all day!"

"Oh, Mhari, I'm so sorry that . . ."

"Now, Fiona . . . there, I've gone and upset you."

"Mhari, there's something I . . ."

"No. There's nothing you have to say. Alastair told me you think you could have prevented my misadventure, but you couldn't be more . . ."

"Misadventure?"

"Aye . . . why?"

"No reason . . . the word struck me as odd." Charles had used that very word in describing what had happened to me on the Hundred Steps and in the North Sea. How peculiar to hear it again!

"Well, that's what it was. I just misjudged my own strength. It was such a strange feeling; I felt the car going out of control, and yet, no matter how hard I held the wheel, it kept heading off the road. Oh, dear, I don't want to dwell on it, it's over and everything's all right. Now, I don't want to hear any more apologies for something you didn't do, Fiona, and no brooding. Please?"

"All right, I won't. I'll just be thankful it turned out as well as it did."

For Mhari's sake as well as my own piece of mind, I tried not to think of the accident any more. It was easier than I had thought; there was so much activity at Lochinver that I had little time to brood. Catriona kept us all busy, and there was a constant stream of curious well-wishers to the castle.

One afternoon, I was sitting in the living room reading when I heard a tapping on the door. I turned around and saw Lewis poking his head into the room.

"Lewis! What a pleasant surprise! If you've come to see Catriona, I'm afraid you'll have to wait a bit. This is nap time."

"No, my reason for coming was to see you, Fiona. Though, of course, I'll be delighted to see the baby. Are she and Mhari all right?

"Oh, yes, they're both fine, couldn't be better. You'd never know that . . . that anything happened."

"I'm so glad. Here, come out into the hall, I've brought you something." Taking me by the hand, Lewis led me into the hall and instructed me to close my eyes. There was a great rustling, and when Lewis told me to look, I opened my eyes and saw my portrait.

"I knew it would be ready today, and so I brought it myself. Mr. Ross helped me carry it inside."

"It looks so beautiful! That frame makes it seem so impressive! Oh, let's take it upstairs and hang it. There's a place all prepared, and that way I can surprise Alastair when he comes home."

The painting was large and fairly awkward, but with Mr. Ross's help we managed to get it up the stairs and position it on the wall next to the painting of Alastair's mother. We stood back to admire the effect.

"It's so strange to see myself there, with all the others. I feel, sort of, historical, as though I'm already gone and I'm one of my great-granddaughters looking up at an ancestor."

"Well, let's not hasten that day." Lewis's usually sunny disposition had disappeared and he seemed morbid. After Mr. Ross had left us, he added, "Fiona, the portrait was only an excuse; I actually want to have a serious talk with you."

"You hardly needed an excuse to come and see me," I said lightly.

"I wasn't sure that I could talk to you about it, and if I found I couldn't, well, then I would have had a valid reason for coming."

"Well, then, if it's as serious as all that, let's go downstairs and have some tea. That way, we can be comfortable while we talk."

I dashed ahead into the kitchen to ask Mrs. Ross to put on the kettle. Lewis was pacing in front of the fire when I returned.

"Ready in a minute. Now, tell me what's bothering you. Something *is* on your mind, isn't it?"

"I'm not sure how to go about this, Fiona. If I'm wrong, I'll have caused a lot of worry for nothing, and if I'm right . . . Och! I hope to God I'm not right. The whole thing is so wild. It couldn't happen, and yet . . . I'm sure that it has."

"What's happened? Oh, Lewis, do stop that and sit down. You're frightening me."

Lewis ignored me and continued worrying the rug as he

worried himself with his lip-biting. He seemed melodramatic, but I kept that to myself. Clearly, he meant well.

"Fiona, you told me that you were planning to drive the Triumph into Lochinver yourself the day Mhari was hurt and that at the last minute Mhari decided to drive instead."

"Yes, yes," I replied impatiently. "But why are you bringing this up?"

"Would anyone else have been likely to drive the car?"

"No. Ian always used the other car. Mhari hadn't driven for quite a while, because we hadn't let her. That's why she was so insistent about going herself; she'd been feeling . . ."

"Alastair drove the car, didn't he?"

"Oh, yes, but he'd been away all week. He'd just gotten back from Dublin the night before, so I had been the only one to drive it recently. That was why he had left the car, so we'd have an extra one if . . . Lewis, what are you getting at? Why all these questions? Oh . . . thank you, Mrs. Ross, just put the tray there, I'll pour."

Lewis waited until Mrs. Ross had gone. "Please, Fiona, be patient. I'm still thinking this through and I want you to follow closely. I want to be very sure there's no misunderstanding. Now, we've established that you were the only person who would have driven that car, in Alastair's absence, of course."

I nodded and sipped my tea, trying to smile to relax him.

"All right, all right. Fiona, I went to the garage and asked about the car. The man said the steering had been faulty, but he had corrected it and now it's as good as new save for some minor dents and scratches."

"I don't care if I never see it again. It's caused us nothing but trouble. Why I had to get such a fancy car . . . I should have bought something more sensible. The more complicated a car is the more that can go wrong with it."

"That's just it, Fiona. There was no reason for anything to go wrong with that car. The mechanic couldn't make sense of the accident. He couldn't understand why the steering wheel broke. That's not the way he put it, but I don't know anything about cars and can't explain what actually went wrong. But I do know this: What happened *shouldn't* have happened and *wouldn't* have happened under normal circumstances."

"Lewis, what . . . ?"

"The car was tampered with. That accident was no accident!"

"What? Who would want to hurt Mhari?"

"Not Mhari; *you*. You were the only one who would be driving the car. Mhari was hurt in your place. No one could have foreseen that she would be driving the car. Fiona, I'm certain, much as I've tried to fight it, someone wanted to harm you, perhaps kill you."

I couldn't believe what I had just heard; it was too fantastic, too unreal. I shut my eyes and breathed deeply several times, but, when I opened them again, Lewis was still standing in the same place, looking at me with the same look of anguish.

"Lewis, would you repeat that?"

"Someone is trying to kill you." Lewis spat the words as though they left a bad taste in his mouth.

"If this is your idea of a joke . . ." I began tartly.

"Fiona, Fiona. I wish it were a joke. But it's not. Can't you see? The car was 'fixed'!"

"How can you be sure? You said yourself you don't know anything about cars. How can you know? How, Lewis? You can't speculate such a thing on the basis of one incident that . . ."

"There hasn't been just one accident. This is the *fourth* time something has happened to you. You will admit it was God's work that you weren't driving the car that day."

"Yes, yes. Normally I would have."

"All right. Four narrow misses within months of each other. That can't be coincidence, Fiona, and don't try to tell me you're accident-prone again."

"Are you going to bring up those steps?"

"Aye. Listen, Fiona, for God's sake, will you listen to me? The earth was dug away in that one spot and nowhere else and . . ."

"Yes, yes, yes! What of it?"

"Just listen! There was the other time you and Alastair were driving up from Inverness and the brakes failed. That could have been serious. Suppose you had been going down a steep hill or had met another car on one of those blind curves." I shook my head frantically at the thought. "Aye, I thought you'd see my point, Fiona. You even said yourself that you've had nothing but trouble with the car. You put the two things together. The car could have been fixed then, too."

"In Inverness? But who?"

"I don't know and, in a way, I'm glad I don't know. Whoever did that knows a lot about automobiles, knows how to make it seem a natural accident . . . puzzling, but natural. Last, there's your fall on the oil rig a month ago. Didn't you say there was something strange about that?"

"I thought I was hit, but Alastair and the doctor said I was confusing that with hitting my head on the railing. When I insisted, they looked, but nothing was found that could have fallen."

"Or have been dropped on purpose. Afterward, whoever it was retrieved the object, making it seem a natural accident once again."

"But it was natural. It was slippery and windy and I went out without a protective helmet."

"Which you couldn't find. Fiona, Fiona, why don't you . . . ?"

"Lewis, if I were to agree that this is all possible, that they weren't accidents, I can't think of anyone who would want to . . . to harm me." I couldn't bring myself to speak the word "kill."

"I know, Fiona; that's what makes it wild. But, remember, you're not the average Scot, living a normal life in the Highlands."

"I'm an American."

"That's not what I meant and you know it. You're a very wealthy woman, Fiona, fantastically so. That in itself is enough to cause resentment. Secondly, there's the source of your income. You're connected with Grimsby Petroleum, one of the aggressive developers of oil up here. You're also married to one of the more vocal opponents of English control of the oil, so you're aware that Grimsby Petroleum is not likely to be popular. There hasn't been a more controversial issue in Scotland since the '45, and you're right in the middle of it, married to one side and working for the other. I'm overdramatizing, of course, but I wanted to make my point clear."

"Alastair and I have worked it out, Lewis. It's all right now." I tasted the lie as I spoke it.

191

"*You* may have worked it out, but what about others?"

"Others? Lewis, are you suggesting that this . . . this mystery person has political motives? That is silly! Getting rid of me wouldn't hurt Grimsby, it would hurt the Scottish cause. Charles Haversham would then be in complete control, and he's English through and through."

"The radicals in the Nationalist movement are hotheaded. Who's to say they've thought it through? Maybe it's just a warning. I'm not involved in the party, so I don't know what's going on. There were those bombings in Glasgow, and, once violence begins, anything can happen."

"But Alastair would know. He's very much against that sort of ugliness and tried to . . ."

"It could be a splinter group. Maybe they think you're influencing Alastair to go easy on the English. Or maybe they think if you were killed, Alastair would be goaded into action. Oh, I don't know. I'm just guessing, guessing . . . That's why I haven't told you before, I had no proof. But this last . . . well, I felt I had to say something."

"Do you think something else might . . ."

"Very likely; that's why something must be done!"

"But what can I do? If I drive, the car crashes. If I walk, the earth collapses. What's to do? Stay at home and wait for the sky to fall on me?" I wanted to laugh, but couldn't find even a chuckle in my heart.

"I know, I know, it seems outlandish. Seriously, though, I wouldn't go off too much by yourself. No long walks alone. No long drives alone. Maybe you should go away for a while, to Inverness or to London to visit Rosemary. She's suggested that."

"You've written to Rosemary about this?"

"Forgive me, Fiona, but I've had no one to talk this out with, and she agrees with my theory."

"Leaving Lochinver now is impossible. There's Mhari and the baby . . . but, but, I do promise to be careful and stay close to home."

"Good, good, and . . . Fiona, don't mention this to anyone. No one else."

"Not even Alastair? Surely he has a right to know his wife's life is in danger."

"Only if you must; he's excitable, you know, and . . ."

"You're right. It'll be our secret," I whispered.

Lewis smiled wanly at my air of conspiracy and departed, leaving me to ponder our conversation.

All the while, I had deliberately tried to keep the tone of my words light with Lewis, for I didn't want him to get even more carried away. In a strange way, it was flattering to be considered important enough for anyone to . . . no, I let that thought pass. Lewis had constructed an interesting, logical, even gothic explanation for what had happened to me at Lochinver, but in the end it was an irrational explanation. I would keep this from Alastair not from any conspirator's design but because I didn't want him to ridicule Lewis for being a dreamy fantasizer of horror stories.

I decided to go upstairs and take a bath before tea. I needed to relax after the afternoon. I left Bruce dozing by the fire and was halfway up the tower steps when I remembered something that Charles had said. When I had told him of my accidents, he, too, had cautioned me. He, too, had asked if I knew of anyone who wanted to harm me, and that was before Mhari's crash. What would he say now? I took a few more steps and paused again. Who would want to hurt me? I wondered. What if it wasn't some overzealous patriot but someone else, someone I knew! I gasped and leaned on the wall for support. The stones felt clammy and I quickly took my hand away, remembering where I was. I had never felt comfortable in that close stairwell, and as I looked around, it seemed that never had it been so dingy, with shadows flickering so ominously. I held my breath—was that or was that not a sound? I strained, trying to listen above the soft, moaning sounds the wind made as it caressed the tower. Yes! There definitely was something! I turned and ran wildly up the stairs, tripping in my haste to escape. I scrambled to my feet and didn't pause until I had reached the bedroom and shut the door behind me. I took a deep breath and went to lie down on the bed, stopping in mid-step. I had forgotten to lock the door! My hands were shaking and I fumbled with the heavy key. I heard a faint scratching sound and I started, dropping the key. I stood there, not daring to move; perhaps whoever it was would assume I had locked the door and go away. Then I heard another sound, which made me laugh at myself: it was Bruce, whimpering to get in. He had followed me up the stairs. I opened the door and he rushed into the room, barking his joy. I shut the door again and then scooped him up in my arms, hugging him until he squealed in protest.

"Oh, you little bundle of fur; I've never been so glad to see you." I released Bruce and he scampered to the other side of the room, returning with his favorite toy. I threw it for him, but my heart wasn't in the game, and we soon stopped. I lay down on the bed and Bruce jumped up beside me, licking my face. "Oh, Bruce," I said sadly. "Everything's become so complicated. What am I going to do?"

I lay on the bed for a long time, thinking over what Lewis had said. He seemed so sure that someone was planning to kill me. For all his boyishness, Lewis was not a frivolous person and would never say anything unless he was convinced. What was I going to do? Sit idly by and wait to see if the presumed murderer was more successful in his next attempt? Maybe Lewis and I could find out who it was, discover some sort of proof, and then go to the authorities. I felt suddenly sleepy and yawned. Yes, that was what we would do, find out who it was. I turned over, snuggling into the pillow, while Bruce readjusted himself next to me. But who, I thought dreamily, who on earth could it be? Someone I know; it has to be someone I know. Those were my last thoughts as I fell into an uneasy sleep.

As I slept, I dreamed. Not the nightmare that had haunted my nights until a few days before, but bits and pieces of reality. Snatches of conversations came and went, and though I tossed and turned trying to escape them, they made themselves heard.

". . . A stranger who is now the lady of the house . . . he's found himself a rich wife . . . one of the wealthiest women in Scotland . . . married her for her money," Ian said bitterly, and then Charles chimed in: ". . . Not that wild, Scottish madman . . . in love with you? Ha! He wants control of Grimsby . . . he wants your money." Then Alastair's voice, strong and clear: "I could cheerfully run down anyone who got in my way." "Alastair and Ailis were going to be married," Mhari whispered softly. I heard Lewis say, "You're a very wealthy woman, Fiona, be careful . . . don't tell anyone, not even Alastair," with Charles echoing: "Most people don't have two close calls . . . I was worried about you." Then Lewis again: "Someone wants to kill you. Be careful, be careful, be careful!"

The chorus of voices swelled, crashing upon me as breakers pound cliffs. Lewis's was over them all, tolling its warning. Through it all, I could hear Alastair calling my name. I twisted and turned, trying to escape, but I was held down and Alastair was getting closer . . . closer . . .

"Fiona! Wake up!"

I opened my eyes and realized with a start that I was in my own room and not, as it had seemed, high on a cliff listening to the sea below. And Alastair was there, shaking me, calling to me.

"Fiona, are you all right?"

I shook my head, trying to clear it. Words rang in my ears and I tried to understand them. "I guess I had another nightmare. I came up to rest before tea, but I'm afraid I don't feel very rested. I'll be all right now."

"I think you should see the doctor about these dreams. Maybe he can give you something."

"No! I'm sorry, I have an extreme fear about taking sleeping medicines. They'll go away soon."

"Well, I'm worried about them. They could be an aftereffect from that bump on your head. You should go for a checkup; aye, it wouldn't hurt . . . was Lewis here this afternoon?"

I looked up, startled, but Alastair seemed intent on nothing more than smoothing his beard. I nodded.

"Aye, I thought so. I saw your portrait hanging in the gallery. It's lovely, Fiona, but I must say I prefer the original."

"We . . . I wanted it up to . . . to surprise you."

"It's truly magnificent and outshines the other portraits in the gallery. Now, hurry up and change. High tea's about."

I remained half sitting on the bed with Bruce as Alastair bounded briskly down the stairs, whistling. I remained still for some time, staring at the open door. A new thought had entered my mind, sent there by my fey dreams. I had to face the very ugly and sickening possibility that the man I loved more than life itself could very well be intent on murdering me.

BOOK III

I Loved Him

My heart's in the Highlands, my heart is not here,
My heart's in the Highlands, a-chasing the deer;
A-chasing the wild deer, and following the roe,
My heart's in the Highlands wherever I go.

ROBERT BURNS

NINE

Flight!

I tried as best I could to behave routinely, despite my suspicions. I must have been fairly successful, for no one seemed to notice any change in my manner. Ian and Mhari were absorbed in their own happiness, as Catriona occupied most of their time. Alastair was more than usually busy with the estate in order to allow Ian more free time to be with his family, and there were also many political meetings that took him away from Lochinver.

These meetings were very involved, sometimes running far into the night, and Alastair would not return until I was already asleep. I wondered if it was the meetings themselves that fascinated him or the fact that Ailis Campbell was indubitably present. Was it to rendezvous with her that Alastair spent so much time away from home? Even if that was the case, I was slightly relieved. Alastair had always been able to read my thoughts, and he would have known something was wrong if he had been around more to watch me.

For the first few days after my nightmare-like revelation, I had told myself that the idea of Alastair trying to kill me was ridiculous. However, the more I brooded about it, the less fantastic that possibility became.

There was no one else it could be! I had jettisoned Lewis's theory of my accidents being caused by someone with political motives; that was too far-fetched, and, besides, anyone with any knowledge of Grimsby Petroleum would know that my death would not affect its operation. Then, try as I might, I could find no reason for anyone else to try to harm me. Ian might resent Alastair and might even more resent our marriage, but getting rid of me would not solve anything. Alastair would only marry again.

No, it had to be Alastair. Charles had been right: Alastair had married me for my money. The MacLeods were not poor, but Lochinver needed more money for proper maintenance and restoration than Alastair would ever have. Restoring the castle was something that Alastair wanted to do more than anything else. Lochinver was special to him, and he loved it above all else: enough to marry someone he didn't love in order to have money; enough to leave the girl he did love in order to have money; and now, enough to murder in order to have money. Once he had returned to Lochinver and seen Ailis, talked with her, spent time with her, touched her, he realized that he still loved her passionately. From then on, the thought of being married to me had become intolerable. It must have been then that he decided to get rid of me.

Alastair had moved the steps so I would fall, and yet he had been my rescuer. Fortunately for me, Bruce had seen him, and it was his barking that prevented me from going farther. Alastair had been there to ensure the success of my "accident."

He had been responsible for the car crash, too. After we had quarreled about Charles, he had tampered with the steering knowing that I would be driving the car the next day. No wonder he had been so upset when he learned that Mhari had gone instead. Alastair was the only one at Lochinver who knew anything about cars; he was the only one who could have done it.

Alastair had also caused my fall on the oil rig. Now I knew why he had insisted on making that trip during bad weather: it had not been to gather information for a political campaign, but to lure me into another situation in which another "accident" could be conveniently arranged. Alastair had taken my protective helmet, and he had thrown the object that struck me, retrieving it afterward. That explained why he hadn't been in the cafeteria when the female roustabout carried me there. That was why he had insisted I had not been hit, that I had struck my head when I fell.

The brake failure during our drive back from Inverness was not so easily explained, however, for Alastair had been with me. I had intended to drive back by myself, at Alastair's suggestion. Perhaps Alastair had had second thoughts and decided to go with me; or maybe it really had been an accident. But it had served to give Alastair the idea of arranging a crash.

Was it really true, then? I didn't want to believe it; I protested against it strongly. Yet, finally, I knew I had to face it.

I had to decide what to do, but no immediate solution seemed apparent. I wanted to be far away, but where would I go? I had come to love Lochinver and think of it as my only home. It seemed so horrible to feel I had to flee from it.

It would have been easier if I had had someone to talk to, but I had no one in whom I felt I could really confide. Mhari and Ian were out of the question, of course, for they would be scandalized and suspect that I was losing my mind.

Lewis was there for me to talk to, true, but our visits were infrequent. He had begun Alastair's portrait and, due to Alastair's odd schedule, it had been decided that all the work would be done at Lewis's studio when convenient. One afternoon, when Alastair was in Inverness, I strolled over to the Demerests' ostensibly for a visit. Once Lewis and I were alone, though, I couldn't help myself. I had to ask him!

"Lewis, have you ever considered that this mystery villain might be someone I know? Someone who's near to me?" The studio was badly heated and I shivered as I tried to find a seat among dirty rags and jars filled with brushes.

"Aye, I'm afraid that thought has occurred to me." Lewis uncovered the portrait of Alastair in order to show it to me.

I pulled my sweater tighter and asked, "What about Alastair? Isn't the husband always the first one the police suspect? Maybe he'll murder me for my money." I tried desperately to keep my voice carefree. If Lewis reacted badly, then I could pass it off as a poor joke.

201

However, Lewis halted what he was doing and stared at me. Now I knew he had been thinking the same thing. He regarded me with a sad certainty, and I wondered if he had suspected Alastair from the beginning and had just been reluctant to suggest it.

"Lewis, do you think it might be Alastair?"

"I don't know, Fiona, I honestly don't know. I'd hate to think such a thing of anyone I know and respect. I like Alastair very much, for himself and for what's he's doing for Scotland. I don't want to believe it, and yet . . ." Lewis stopped speaking and turned to the portrait, as if there was an answer in the face of the man he was painting. Curious, I went over and stood beside him. The face that looked back at us was a proud, brooding face with a suggestion of pain in the fierce gaze. I was struck again by Alastair's resemblance to his long-dead ancestor, Torquil. The same energy and sense of power were apparent in both portraits. As I stood looking into Alastair's face, I found myself mezmerized by those intense blue eyes. I told myself they were just blobs of oil daubed on canvas, yet I found it hard to face them. It was as if Alastair himself were there before me, defying me to name him as my enemy.

I turned away. I was close to tears anyway, and knew I would start to cry if I looked at the picture any more. Lewis threw a cloth over the portrait and came over to me. I looked back and saw only a gray and smudged sheet, but I could still feel Alastair's eyes boring into my heart.

"It's hard, Fiona, I know. You love him very much, don't you?" I nodded wordlessly, not daring to speak. Lewis put his arm around my shoulders. "I didn't want to believe it, either. But, as time went on . . . it was even harder when I started to paint him. It's such a strong, honest face, it's so hard to believe. However . . ."

"However, all the evidence points to Alastair," I finished.

We talked for quite a while, going over what we each knew and what we each suspected. In the end, we arrived at the same maddening answer, that Alastair was the one responsible for my accidents.

"What am I going to do?"

"I think the most important thing is to get you away from Lochinver," Lewis replied. "Why don't you stay here?"

"Lewis, that's very kind, but I could hardly do that. What reason would we give? It would be an unlikely thing for me to do."

"Aye, it would be rather awkward at that," Lewis admitted while turning a deep shade of red. "Anyway, it would be better for you to get completely away from Lochinver. The further away, the better," he added.

"Yes, but it still would be difficult to explain. I've never left except with Alastair."

"We'll think of something. In the meantime, don't do anything foolish."

"I won't," I promised, smiling through my tears. "And thank you, Lewis, thank you."

I left the Demerests' and walked slowly back to the castle. I was depressed, yet, contradictorily, I was relieved by what Lewis had said. His assertion that Alastair might be trying to kill me had confirmed my worst fears, that the man I loved hated me. I had been so worried about myself for thinking such a thing. How could any woman in her right mind suspect her husband of trying to kill her? Yet, since Lewis had agreed so easily with my thinking, it assured me that I wasn't just being paranoid, that there were substantial reasons for my suspicions. However, of the two possibilities, a sane victim or an insane victimizer, I would have preferred the latter. That was a problem that could be dealt with. I had no solution for the former.

As time passed, Mhari regenerated quickly, and very soon she was her usual, energetic self, bustling about the castle. Catriona blossomed, too, putting on healthy weight. Motherhood had changed Mhari profoundly. She was more serene now, not the slightly frenetic girl she had been when I first came to Lochinver. Being responsible for another human being, having that person totally dependent upon her, had given her a new disposition. She went about with a purposeful air that on her was charming and sweet.

There was such happiness at Lochinver in general that I began to think Mrs. Ross was right: homes with babies in them were happy homes. I found myself being lulled, almost forgetting at times that my life might be in danger. The only problem I had to deal with was Bruce's jealousy toward the new baby, who had usurped his place as the prize child of Lochinver. Yet, at night, I would lie sleepless beside Alastair and long for the time when I had felt secure in his love.

One gray morning, I was reading the local paper when an item caught my interest. The Queen was coming to Inverness to officiate in a ceremony. The royal visit was nothing new; it had been the talk of Lochinver, and the papers had been full of details about the royal family's trip. They would be going to Edinburgh and Glasgow and other points in the Lowlands, but now it seemed that she would be visiting an oil refinery just outside Inverness. It was a brand-new refinery, in operation for only a few months. I knew it well, for Charles had been one of those instrumental in its construction. The Queen's visit was to mark the official opening of the refinery. She would press a button signaling the official start of the flow of the North Sea oil into the refinery, although, in actuality, oil was already being processed there.

I daydreamed about the ceremony, imagining the excitement the little city must be feeling as it prepared for its royal guests. I hoped they'd take this opportunity to clean Inverness up a bit, for on my last visit I had been saddened anew at how dingy and littered the capital of the Highlands had become.

The morning's mail arrived, and I sifted idly through it, finding two letters addressed to me. One was from Rosemary, a short note scribbled in her hurried, almost indecipherable writing, saying that she planned to spend her Easter holiday with her parents in Inverness. She hoped to be able to visit Lochinver for a few days, she wrote, but she wasn't sure she would be able to manage it. I poured another cup of tea and concentrated on the particulars:

Mummy and Daddy are agog about the Queen's visit, as you can well imagine. There are all sorts of dreary receptions and teas being planned by the locals, and the folks seem to think my presence is required. I've insisted that I've seen the Queen before, but you know Mummy.

By the by, Lewis and I have established a fairly regular corre-
spondence, though you still hold first place in his heart, you
green-eyed femme fatale. Can't you go all fat and matronly so I
can have a chance?

I smiled as I folded her letter and put it back in the envelope.
Dear, irrepressible Rosemary, I thought. I was glad she and
Lewis were in touch, and I hoped a romance might develop. I
decided to write to the Beatons, asking if Rosemary could escape
Inverness for a few days.

The other letter was from Charles. It, too, was concerned with
the prospect of the royal visit:

. . . There's to be a large reception for the Queen, and quite a
few VIP's about. I'd very much like for you to attend, Fiona. You
should meet some of them and we could chat further about the
matter we discussed my last visit. Your presence would be ad-
vantageous at this time, and it would also mean a great deal to
Grimsby and to me. Now . . .

The rest of his letter contained details of the activities planned
and the list of people invited. Charles was right; there were
going to be some important people there: heads of the major oil
companies and members of the British Government were included. Charles must be thrilled, I thought, for he'd always
wanted to be special, to feel powerful, and now he'd be hob-
nobbing with these sorts. It would be fun to be there, and I'd
be sure of seeing Rosemary. Well, we'll see, I thought further,
setting down my cup.

Then it hit me! This was my excuse for getting away from
Lochinver. I had wanted a reason, and no better one than this
could be found. My position with Grimsby Petroleum required
that I be present at the refinery ceremony and at the functions
that accompanied it. And, of course, I would have to attend
meetings with Charles. I could stretch out the trip on the pretext
of visiting Rosemary. It was perfect, and I felt safer and stronger
than I had for some weeks. I immediately set about replying to
Charles, saying that I would be delighted to attend.

I sauntered upstairs and told Mhari of my plans. She was
thrilled. She displayed the typical British reverence for the royal
family and was impressed that I would actually meet the Queen.

"Och, Fiona, how exciting! You must be sure to remember every detail, what she was wearing . . ."

"It'll hardly be the height of fashion, from what I've seen of her pictures."

"Aye, she is a little dowdy, but *very* regal. And Prince Philip is quite handsome. I did see them once, when I was quite small. It was in Edinburgh. Daddy had taken us there for holiday, and it happened to coincide with a state visit to Holyrood House. I can remember sitting on my father's shoulders to see above the crowd. The children were with them. The Queen held Princess Anne in her lap, and I remember thinking: 'Why, she's just like me.' I played princess for weeks afterward, which quite annoyed Alastair. He kept insisting we were better, because we were descended from Scottish chieftains and that the Windsors sprang from a Prussian . . . uh, gigolo!"

"Talking about me behind my back again, eh, Mhari?" Alastair strode into the nursery, kissed me on the forehead, and went over to the cradle, proceeding to tickle Catriona until she gurgled with babyish delight.

"I was just telling Fiona about the time Daddy took us to see the royal family in Edinburgh. You remember? You had to jump up and down to see above the crowd, even though you were quite tall."

"That's right, I was thirteen. Aye, I was excited, though, of course, I pretended not to be. I'm surprised you recall it so well. You couldn't have been more than four or five. Your mind is amazing, dear sister of mine, what it does and does not remember."

"I do tend to remember the things we did with Daddy. There were so few."

"Aye. We didn't do much together. Well, what brought on this wave of nostalgia?"

"We were talking about the Queen's visiting Scotland. You didn't tell me, Alastair. Shame on you."

"Tell you what?" Alastair looked at her, slightly puzzled, and before I could stop her, Mhari continued:

"Tell me that you're going to see the Queen in Inverness. Fiona just told me. It's so exciting."

"Fiona told you . . . what?" Alastair straightened up and looked at me hard.

"That . . . you . . . well, Fiona said she was going to Inverness and the ceremony . . . and . . . and . . . oh dear. Have I spoiled your surprise, Fiona?" Mhari kept looking at us, twisting her head from side to side as though she were following a crucial tennis match.

"Meant or not, it is a surprise. Fiona, what is Mhari talking about? What trip to Inverness?" Alastair sat down and folded his arms, waiting for me to explain.

"There's no mystery, Alastair; the idea came to me ten minutes ago. I got a letter from Charles asking me to go. He thinks I should be there. There's the ceremony at the oil refinery and a reception; many important people will be there. Rosemary will be in Inverness visiting her parents and it will be a good opportunity to see her again. And, well, there are some meetings I should attend as Grimsby's . . ."

"And you expect me to accompany you to all these pressing affairs?" Alastair's voice cut sharply through my explanations.

"Well . . ." The thought that Alastair should want to go with me hadn't occurred to me, for I had been thinking only of getting away from Lochinver. My heart sank, yet I could hardly insist he stay behind. I fumbled for words, but fortunately Alastair saved me the trouble.

"You expect me to go and be polite to those English? To sit quietly and smile graciously while Haversham introduces us to his fellow pirates? That bunch of damned Southerns! I'd shake my fist in their faces before I'd shake their hands!"

"Alastair, please!" Mhari moved over to the cradle in order to rock it gently, for Catriona had begun whimpering. "Lower your voice, you're scaring her. Now, I'm sure that Fiona doesn't mean that you . . ."

"I don't care *what* she meant. I'm not going and I refuse to hear any more about it. And I forbid *you* to go, me darlin'!" That last was directed at me as Alastair abruptly left the room.

"Fiona, I'm sorry I was the cause of all that fuss. I didn't think about the oil-company people being there. I got carried away by the thought of your seeing the Queen. I'm sorry I was so thoughtless."

207

"It's not your fault. I should have warned you Alastair didn't know. It'll be all right."

"What are you going to do?"

"I'm going to Inverness to see the Queen," I laughed, paraphrasing the old nursery rhyme. I got up and left the nursery, leaving Mhari to stare after me openmouthed at the thought of my defying the laird of Lochinver Castle.

I found him sitting in the living room sucking his pipe and reading the paper amid a blue cloud of tobacco smoke.

"Alastair," I began.

"If you're going to bring up the subject of going to Inverness, you're wasting your time. There's nothing to discuss." Alastair rustled his paper emphatically and puffed harder.

"There's a great deal to discuss. I plan to go." Alastair lowered his paper, made a great fuss tapping out his pipe, and then glared at me. I found it hard to continue under his cold gaze, but I took a deep breath and went on rapidly.

"I feel that I should go and I intend to do so. I understand your feelings and you needn't come. I'll go by myself. It will be better that way, anyway."

"I told you I don't want you going, with or without me."

"I know you did, but I am going to Inverness."

"Even if I forbid it?"

"Husbands don't forbid wives to do things without reason any more. Elizabeth is the Queen, not Victoria."

"I have my reasons, and they're very good ones."

"Name me one." I was getting angry.

"I am not at liberty to explain. I wish I could, but I can't. You'll have to take my word for it that you shouldn't go; *that* should be enough."

"It isn't. And since you haven't given me any good reasons, I see no reason why I should change my plans."

"Blast, Fiona! Do as I say! I don't want you to get any more involved with the oil situation."

"I'm afraid it's a bit too late; I already am involved—I was involved before I met you. I don't think you're being fair, Alastair. I don't tell you what to do, I don't ask you to quit politics, so don't tell me not to be concerned with Grimsby Petroleum. I know you don't like Charles, and I'm sorry about that, as he's my

208

oldest friend. I do think you'd be more sensible and not let your personal feelings interfere."

"My feelings toward Haversham have nothing to do with my decision, though a bigger fool I've yet to meet. My feelings toward you have a great deal to . . ."

"I don't care. You're being unreasonable and tyrannical. I'm going and, short of locking me in my room, there's nothing you can do to stop me. I'm taking the afternoon bus."

"Fiona, for the last time . . ." Alastair thundered, but I was already at the door. "Well, go ahead, you little fool, but I won't be answerable for the consequences!"

I paused and stared at him. "You mean I might have another accident?" I said flatly and, with that, raced out of the room and went quickly up the stairs before Alastair could reply.

Once in my room, I packed swiftly. I needed only a few things. We had left clothes and miscellaneous items in the Inverness apartment. Since I had only a small bag to carry, I decided I could take Bruce for company, and I fetched his carrying case from the closet.

I lingered only to tell Mhari I was leaving and to ask her to make sure Mr. Ross fed and exercised Fionn in my absence. Mhari was worried, but I assured her everything would be all right and I would be back before she knew it. As I said that, I wondered if, indeed, I would be coming back to Lochinver. Descending the stairs, I dreaded meeting Alastair, but he was nowhere to be seen. Gathering up a puzzled Bruce, I called Lewis to ask him for a ride to the bus stop, and tramped outside to wait. After a short while he drove up to the castle, and soon we were gunning away from Lochinver. I forced myself not to look back, for I was afraid I would burst into tears.

"I'm glad you've decided to go to Inverness, Fiona. It's the best thing you could do."

"I hope it's the right thing. I feel as though I'm running away; I *am* running away." I told Lewis the circumstances of my departure and my fight with Alastair. "I have to face the possibility that I may never come back."

"You'll feel better, once you get off by yourself and have a chance to think things through. You haven't been able to do that, living at the castle."

"Yes, you're right. Inverness is the best and easiest place for me just now. Oh, and Rosemary will be there. It'll be good to see her again."

"Aye. She's a very nice girl and a good friend to you. Be sure to give her my best; I'm looking forward to seeing her again."

We arrived at the stop just in time for me to catch the bus. Lewis got out of the car with me and carried my bag over to the bus, saying good-by with a brotherly kiss.

"I'll be sure to deliver that kiss to Rosemary."

"In that case, here's another one—just for you," he replied, kissing me lightly on the lips. "Take care, Fiona, you're very special to . . . to . . . those who love you," he mumbled shyly.

I smiled bravely and then climbed into the bus. As it pulled away, I looked back and saw Lewis still standing by the side of the road, his hands stuffed deep in his pockets, his eyes narrowing as they followed the bus through the late-afternoon mist. Cozying back against my seat, I watched Bruce settle down in his case and make the best of things by napping. I tried to follow his excellent example, but I couldn't.

Suppose I was wrong about Alastair and he couldn't forgive me for leaving. No, I wasn't wrong, I wasn't. Someone *was* trying to kill me and that someone had to be Alastair. Everything pointed to that. I wondered what his reasons were for not wanting me to go to Inverness, for he had acted as though there was something preventing him from explaining. Don't be silly, I told myself, he just doesn't want you out of his sight. That's all. There was no good reason for me not to go; that's why he created the mystery.

I gazed through the large bus window and tried to concentrate on the landscape rolling by. There was little to hold my interest: barren fields with only the occasional small stone hut to break the monotony, smoke wafting from its large chimney. Strange how I had once found this wild land beautiful, for now I could see only its eeriness and felt as if I were traversing the terrain of another planet. This must be what the moon looks like, I thought, rough-textured ground with valleys dug by some careless child-god who had been given a shovel; he had tossed the dirt willy-nilly and mountains were born. Actually, I knew that the Highlands had been birthed even more demonically, for they were not shaped, like the Appalachian range back home, by a rising up, but instead were gouged out of a volcanic plateau by a ferocious glacier.

Yet even in my depressed state I could not dismiss this region as completely alien, and I could not call it ugly. There was figurative colors in the names of the towns where the bus stopped: Inchnadamph, Kincardine, Clachnahurry. There was literal color scattered about also: groups of gay daffodils nestled in brownish-green hollows beside narrow, ice-blue lochs, their sunbursts brightening this gray, fey land. Despite all my own and Britain's troubles, spring was coming.

I loved spring and had always anticipated the rebirth of the land eagerly; I had especially looked forward to my first spring at Lochinver: watching the foothills soften with gentle verdure, feeling the large raindrops warm against my face. I sighed and the landscape blurred. Would I ever see spring come to Lochinver? I forced myself to keep looking through the window and spotted a flock of sheep grazing on the hills. As the bus passed, they raised their heads, seeming to smile triumphantly as I went by. There was a look of self-satisfaction in their half-closed eyes and supercilious contentment in the way they slowly chewed. "We warned you," they bleated, "we didn't want you here. Now you're going, but we remain." I clasped my hands over my ears, trying to shut out the imaginary voices, but the rhythmic hum of the bus's wheels on the asphalt road echoed the message: warned you, warned you, warned you.

The bus pulled into Inverness past nightfall, and as I stood on Academy Street I felt lonely and more than a little scared. As the apartment was only three blocks away, I ignored the waiting taxis, releasing Bruce from his case and snapping on his leash with great difficulty, for he was too delighted at being freed to stand still. He strained at the leash, trying to go in every direction but the one I wanted. He had never been in a city before, and he was determined to investigate every smell.

We finally made it to the apartment, and as I stood on the bare stone landing unlocking the door, a wave of sadness swept over me. It was here that Alastair and I had spent our wedding night; it was here that . . . no, I mustn't remember. I clenched my teeth and went inside. The apartment was small and plainly furnished, yet every corner reminded me of Alastair. This won't do, I scolded myself. It had been several months since we had been there, and everything was covered with a thin layer of dust. Even though I was tired, I decided to clean right then and there; if I kept busy, then I wouldn't have time to think, and if I exhausted myself, I could sleep.

I was still tired the next morning. In the end, I had been unable to sleep, tossing and turning until the first streaks of red lightened the night sky. I had to force myself to get out of bed, for the apartment was very cold. A quick check of the icebox told me to go shopping, the cupboard was bare and—like old Mrs. Hubbard—I didn't have a bone for my dog.

I accomplished my errands on High Street quickly. I had forgotten how much colder the east coast was than the western coast of Scotland. Here, next to the North Sea, the cold winds blew harshly up from Loch Ness, creating wind tunnels in the narrow streets. I decided that I definitely did not like Inverness.

Back in the lonely apartment, I lit the electric fire and made some strong tea. I wondered if Alastair would call me, for this was the logical place for me to be. In a way, I did want him to call—it would prove that he did love me after all—yet I was terrified of speaking to him.

I phoned the Beatons, but Rosemary was not expected until the next day. I left a message and my number, finally managing to disentangle myself from my conversation with Rosemary's mother. Mrs. Beaton assumed that everyone she knew was as passionately interested in their acquaintances' behavior as she was. Since I had been away, she considered it her duty to bring me up to date on all the local gossip.

I then called Charles and, after being passed from secretary to secretary, I finally got through. He certainly is wellguarded, I thought impatiently, but that's the price one pays in a big corporation. I remembered the earlier days of Grimsby, when . . .

"Fiona, how nice! Where are you?"

"In Inverness. I came down last night."

"You didn't have to come down so soon, there's nothing scheduled for three or four days. I wrote you that."

"Yes, yes, I know, but . . . I'll explain when I see you."

"Do you plan to come into the office today?"

"Yes, of course I do." Why did Charles need to ask? Did he actually think I wouldn't?

"Good. Listen, we'll have lunch together. We can talk easier that way and I can fill you in on what has been happening here. I'll have one of my secretaries make a reservation. In half an hour? Good."

I replaced the receiver slowly. That brief conversation bothered me a little, for Charles sounded as though he had too much on his mind. When had we hired all those secretaries? Grimsby really had expanded rapidly, and I didn't feel entirely happy about it. I should have paid more attention to what's been going on, I thought guiltily. I've let Toby down. Grimsby has turned into an oil monster more terrifying than Nessie would ever be. I didn't blame Charles, he was only doing what he thought best, though he did seem to hunger for power. I shook my head; maybe that's the way it has to be: eat or get eaten.

The restaurant we went to was a new one and obviously popular with the oil-company executives. Charles seemed to know everyone, but I knew only a few faces.

Charles did most of the talking, waxing imperial as he always did when talking about Grimsby Petroleum. His eagerness touched me, and I reached out and took his hand.

". . . and that's where we stand, Fiona. The presentation went better than I had hoped, and although the decision won't be made until the first week in April, some of the council members have told me privately that we have a very good chance that . . . what's this? Holding hands in public? And you a married woman! What would your husband say?"

"Oh . . . Alastair . . ." I felt my eyes well up with tears and I quickly retrieved my hand, hoping to cover my eyes before Charles noticed. I failed.

"Fiona, what's wrong?"

"Nothing, just got something in my eye."

"Nonsense, you're unhappy. Here I've been talking a blue streak while you've been sitting there being miserable. Fiona, what is it? Is it Alastair?" I couldn't answer and continued to stare at my untouched pastry. "Some silly lover's quarrel, I warrant. It can't be all that serious."

I managed to raise my eyes to his. Though I could read concern there, they were cold and flat; their brown opacity showed my image, not Charles's thoughts. "Oh, Charles . . . I . . ." I tried to talk, but I choked instead.

"Something very serious has happened, hasn't it? This is no place to talk; come back to my flat. I'll call the office and tell them I won't be in the rest of the day. We'll solve this thing together."

I nodded and watched dumbly as he paid the check. He helped me into my coat and squired me purposefully along the crowded streets to his apartment. I suddenly realized that I had never seen where Charles lived. Apparently, I still had things to learn about Charles. How odd, I thought, you can think you know a person until you learn something new. I thought I knew Alastair, and yet I don't know him, for I never would have guessed him to be capable of . . . once again, I was unable to say the word.

Charles's apartment was neat and airy, surprisingly spacious for Inverness, but, then, he had rented it before Inverness started filling with half the greedy world. (Really, Fiona, I laughed at myself, you're beginning to think like Alastair. That will never do!) Charles had furnished it luxuriously with modern furniture classics that even my unpracticed eye recognized: two gleaming steel Wassily chairs in white leather faced each other across a glass-topped chrome table, and in one corner was a black leather Eames lounger and ottoman. I wandered around the living room while Charles mixed us some drinks, looking for some sign that it was Charles Haversham who lived there, but there were no personal effects, nothing to show that Charles had any life outside Grimsby Petroleum. Then, in a dark corner, I noticed a double picture frame. In one side was an old photograph of a lovely woman in her late twenties, her brunette hair arranged in a neat, page-boy style that had been fashionable in the 1940s. The other side contained two snapshots. One was a faded picture of a small farmhouse: a small, blond-haired boy stood holding the hand of the same dark woman in the other photograph. For an instant I thought the child was Toby. It was so like his boyhood pictures I had seen in his mother's London townhouse. No, I thought again, small blond boys often look alike. And then I realized that it was Charles and that the woman must be his mother. The other snapshot surprised me: it was of me! Charles had taken it one day last summer when we had gone on a picnic. I had forgotten that day, but as I looked at the picture of that laughing girl in her green dress, I remembered how I had teased Charles about Nessie. I had been falling in love with Alastair then, and life and love showed in my whole body. Had that picture really been taken less than a year ago? It seemed impossible, for that day felt so lost now and I felt so much older than that lover who had smiled for the camera.

Charles came over, handing me a strong whiskey and soda, and I returned the frame to its place on the table. Charles seemed slightly embarrassed by my discovery.

"Why on earth do you have this picture of me, Charles? I'm touched," I teased.

"Oh. Well, we had fun that day and that's always been my favorite dress."

"I think it's sweet. Is this your mother? She's very beautiful, though you don't take after her much, do you? Oh, dear, I'm sorry, I didn't mean that the way it sounded. I just meant you're so fair."

"Yes."

"You have her eyes, though, large and brown. You must resemble your father."

"Yes. I do."

"Do you have a photograph of him?" Charles's terse replies were puzzling.

"No. No . . . I . . . he, uh, he left before I was born. He deserted my mother." Charles seemed to be bordering on rage, and I found myself shrinking from it. "My mother raised me the best she could on her own, but it wasn't easy and her strength wasn't up to it. That's the house we lived in, in Kent. Her name was Joan and we made a great game of pretending she was Joan of Kent and I her Black Prince." His voice hardened. "She died when I was ten and I was kindly, so kindly, taken by the state to live in foster homes."

"Didn't she have any family?"

"I suppose so. She never mentioned them. I think they disapproved of her marriage, and she was too proud to ask for help."

"I'm so sorry; I had no idea. Your mother would be very proud of you if she could see you now."

"Yes, I'm sure she would." Charles had a terrifying bitterness on his lips, but there was a triumphant gleam in his eyes as he looked at the picture. "In a way, everything I've done has been for her. Look here, let's not talk about my problems, that's all boring ancient history. Now, come here and sit down. I want you to tell me what's troubling you."

After several hesitant starts, I poured out the whole story, from the misadventure on the Hundred Steps to my talks with Lewis. Charles sat calmly and blankly throughout my recital, never prodding or pushing me to be more specific or less fantastic. As a result, I told him more than I had intended. As I talked, I thought again of how lucky I was in having Charles for a friend. He had been a source of much-needed strength when Toby died, and now, once more, I was turning to him for relief from a weight that was crushing me.

I finished, but Charles continued to sit silently staring into his glass. I, too, remained silent, waiting for his advice.

"Well . . . I certainly appreciate your telling me all this, Fiona; it can't have been easy for you. Here, I think we could both use a new drink." I watched him as he went to the other side of the room. I was emotionally drained and the whiskey seemed to revive me.

"There. Better now?"

"Yes, thank you. And thank you for listening to all that. I really do feel so much better."

"I should think so. No wonder you were upset. Oh, my poor Fiona, what a horrible, horrible story!"

"Then, you do believe me? You don't think I'm being silly or, or . . . mad?"

"To the contrary. I think you're being rational for the first time in many months. Dear Fiona, it's never pleasant to be in a position to say 'I told you so,' but I *did* warn you about this marriage."

"I know you did, Charles, and I should have listened to you. But I'm afraid it's very late for it to make any difference and, as the saying goes, I've got to 'pay the piper.'"

"I'm here to help in any way I can."

"I know that and I'm more than grateful, Charles. How could I have been so wrong? I was so . . . *certain* that Alastair loved me. Even now, I have trouble believing that he could be capable of . . ."

"Of murder. You've got to say it, Fiona, and you've got to believe it, totally. You wanted so hard to believe he loved you, you convinced yourself. Now you've got to face up to the truth! Oh, I can understand how it happened. You were alone in a foreign land and MacLeod was exotic . . . exciting, I suppose. I'll give him that. A colorful character, and he made everyone seem pale by comparison, including me."

"Oh, Charles, you know that I told you . . ."

"I know, I know and I'm sorry. This isn't the appropriate moment." Charles reached over and brushed my hair off my forehead. "What we should be talking about is what you're going to do."

"I'm afraid I haven't gone beyond getting out of Lochinver. I must say I do feel better, having left."

"But that's just a temporary solution, Fiona. You probably won't want to hear this, but have you thought of divorce?"

"Divorce?"

"Yes, divorce."

"But, but . . . how could I? I mean . . . divorce."

"Look, Fiona. Be honest with yourself. You can't stay married to a man who wants to destroy you."

"But . . . well, I have to think about it."

"Of course you do, dear. Listen, why don't you go away for a while, after all the fuss about the Queen's visit is over. Maybe you should go back to America. Visit your parents. Give yourself a decent chance to make up your mind without being influenced by the past."

"Running away won't help matters. I did that after Toby died. I was no more than a hurt child then. No, I've made a life here; Scotland is more my home than America now. There comes a time in one's life when you can't keep running home to mother."

"You should be very thankful you have a mother to run home to."

"Oh, I'm sorry. I wasn't thinking. But . . . but you know what I meant. No, whatever happens, I'm going to stay here. Besides, it's time I should get involved with Grimsby again. It's gotten so that I'm sure you could use some help. I've been selfish, Charles, retreating into a castle world and letting you do all the work."

"There's no need . . . I mean, if you want to. Of course! You're right. You should start a new life, and that's as good a way as any. I do think you should consider taking a vacation, anyway. You'll need rest, especially after next week."

"I will, but just a short one. Now I really should be getting back to my flat. Bruce isn't used to being left alone."

"Why don't we have dinner together?"

"Oh, thank you, Charles, but I'm beat. Going to bed early is all I want to do."

"Tomorrow, then. I'll get your wrap and walk you home."

It was chilly, and I was glad of Charles as a support against the wind. He accompanied me to the door and stood there with his hands crammed in his pockets as I opened the door and Bruce came rushing out. He made a dash for Charles's ankle, and I think he would have bitten him if I hadn't grabbed and held him. I apologized to Charles, explaining that Bruce was probably upset by being left in strange surroundings. I didn't put him down until Charles had gone, but he rushed immediately to the door again and continued barking until Charles's steps could no longer be heard on the stone stairs. Then he came over to me, prideful at having scared off the intruder.

"You rascal, what was all that about?" I asked, picking Bruce up again and shaking him gently. Then I remembered that Bruce had snapped at Charles once before, at Lochinver, when there hadn't been the excuse of his feeling uneasy in a strange place. "You don't like Charles, do you, Bruce? I'm afraid you're going to have to; you'll be seeing him again. I'll have to teach you better manners; no more spoiling for you." At that threat, Bruce proceeded to act so adorably that I started to laugh. "You always know how to get what you want, don't you? An admirable quality, which few of us have. Oh, Bruce, I'm so glad you're here with me. I don't think I could bear it otherwise. But you'll have to learn to be polite to Charles."

The evening dragged. I fixed myself some supper, but I only picked at it halfheartedly, and in the end Bruce got most of it. I still felt drained of my energy and decided I would go to bed early. But, once there, I lay awake. I thumbed through an old copy of *Vogue* I had found, scarcely looking at the glossy pages. I was tired but discontent, full of nervous energy. I felt lonely, afraid and very uncertain about my future.

The next morning, I was jarred awake by the persistent, harsh double ring of the telephone. I was sleeping late, for Charles had suggested I take a few days to relax. I reached blindly for the receiver, knocking the phone to the floor in the process.

"Good heavens, Fiona. What on earth was that?"

"Hmmm? Oh, I just knocked the phone over . . . Rosemary!"

"Oh, dear, did I wake you? My . . . aren't we lazy? I just got in. Took a sleeper overnight to Edinburgh and came up this morning. Listen, I want to see you."

"Well, yes, Rosemary, I want to see you, too."

"Now."

"This very minute?"

"Fiona, Lewis called me yesterday . . ."

"Oh."

". . . and I want to talk with you. I'll be there in a few minutes; I'll pick up some breakfast on the way."

Rosemary was true to her word and arrived directly, carrying a large bag of groceries as she brushed past me into the kitchen.

"Just as I thought, nothing to eat. No wonder you're so thin. Now, give me a few minutes and . . . where's your coffeepot?" Rosemary was a study in efficiency, and soon we were sitting down to a delicious breakfast while she began to explain herself.

Knowing Rosemary would be in Inverness, Lewis had called her, telling her that I had left Lochinver and the reasons why. She was full of questions and, between sips of coffee, I told her the story.

". . . And Charles has suggested that I get a divorce. I suppose he's right, but somehow . . . well, I have to think about that. I don't want to divorce Alastair, I love him. I guess I can't admit the truth to myself. Even though I know . . . I just can't believe that Alastair . . ."

"Would want to hurt you? I can understand that; as a matter of fact, I find it hard to believe myself."

"Why do you say that?"

"I don't know. It certainly appears that Alastair is the one, but

. . . I've met Alastair, Fiona. I've seen him with you, and I'd
have sworn he was madly in love with you."

"Yes," I agreed ruefully. "He's a colorful actor."

"So it would seem. I was fooled. Listen, don't do anything
drastic until we've absolute proof."

"What kind of proof—my death?"

"Fiona, really! I meant divorce. If you filed, that would let
Alastair know you're on to him, and he might do something. I
think you're safer if he doesn't know you suspect anything."

"I hadn't thought of that."

"Good. Let's just leave it that you two had a fight and you're
here for a while. If Alastair calls you, act as though you're still
angry. And if he's the man I think he is, he won't chase after you.
That is, if his suspicions aren't roused. Besides, I think 'Wick' has
an ulterior motive in wanting you to be divorced."

"'Wick?' Oh, Charles. I forgot." I smiled, remembering our expedition last summer to the castle that turned out to be a trash
dump. "But what do you mean?"

"How can you be so blind? That man's in love with you! And I
don't know how you do it. All the dashing men in Scotland in
love with you. Not that I'd want old Wick—the cold, cunning
type has never grabbed me."

"No, no, Rosemary, you've got it all wrong about Wi—
Charles." I told her what I had found out about Charles's childhood.

"Really? Kent? Well, I still don't like him one bit. Oops! I've
got to run. I promised to meet Mummy for lunch."

"*Lunch?*"

"I just won't eat very much. That'll make her happy. She's always after me to slim. 'Ta, Fiona, I'll call you later. Listen, why
don't you come and stay with us? . . . I'll ask Mummy, no, no,
it's no trouble . . . They like dogs, too . . . Good, that's settled.
I'll come by and pick you up this afternoon."

Rosemary let herself out and I cleaned up the kitchen. The
idea of staying at the Beatons' did cheer me and I hummed some
nonsensical version of "Loch Lomond."

Rosemary picked me up that evening and we drove to her parents' vine-covered stone cottage on the outskirts of Inverness. It
felt wonderful to be out of the constant bustle of downtown In-

verness, and it was comforting to be with friends. The Beatons were sweet, though Mrs. Beaton (when she wasn't caught up in Inverness' social life) tended to worry overmuch about her only child, while Mr. Beaton invariably talked about the oil business. Actually I found his monologues helpful, for they made a good refresher course, and I was soon completely caught up on business events of the past few months. And Rosemary was delighted to have me there, saying, as she made up the other bed in her room, that it was like having a sister.

The next few days were hectic and I found myself too busy to brood about Alastair. I spent the days at Grimsby Petroleum, the evenings at the inevitable dinner party arranged by Mrs. Beaton. I knew that Rosemary was in touch with Lewis, but she told me little of their conversations—just that he had told Mhari where I was and what I was doing. She would occasionally drop mysterious clues, hinting that they were searching for "evidence." I knew she enjoyed the detective game, and I didn't try to stop her, although I doubted there was anything to discover.

The main topic of conversation in Inverness was the Queen's visit, and the discussion at dinner always turned to that subject. One night, with Charles present, Mrs. Beaton was chatting about her dress for the reception when Charles interrupted with some startling news.

"You've heard about the bomb threat, of course."

"Bombs, what bombs?" Mrs. Beaton forgot her wardrobe and gaped.

"It was in the paper today; there's been a phone call from the 'Red Lion' saying there'll be a bomb planted at the ceremony site. They've threatened to blow up the oil refinery and everyone who is there, including the Queen."

"Who has? Why, that's impossible."

"It's those Scottish Nationalist radicals." Charles looked at me intently. "The same ones that blew up our offices in Glasgow. They've given a long list of demands they want met. It's outrageous, of course. These Scots have always behaved like gangsters and they'll never change."

"Charles! The people who want to bomb *are* gangsters, but they are hardly representative of the Scottish Nationalist Party." I would have continued, but Mrs. Beaton interrupted.

"Really, Fiona, you're taking *their* side. Anyone would think you were a Scot yourself the way . . ."

"Mummy!" Rosemary's sharp warning stopped her.

"What? Oh, yes. Sorry. Uh, well, Charles, do you think the Queen will cancel her visit?"

"Dear, that's hardly likely," Mr. Beaton joined in. "Can't give in, you know. Can't let 'em think they've got the upper hand. We mustn't encourage the scoundrels."

"Yes, I think you're right," Charles said. "Well to the point. Killers. But the Queen will still come. Of course, there will be very strict security and the refinery will be gone over with a fine-tooth comb before anyone is allowed to set foot in the place. Some of the activities may be curtailed, but the ceremony will go on as scheduled."

"Oh, I think it's dreadful. First the Irish, now the Scots. Oh, dear, and everything was going to be so nice." Mrs. Beaton looked crestfallen, shaking her head.

Charles was, of course, absolutely correct; the Queen's visit was not canceled. There was very tight security and a curfew was imposed on Sinclair's, the meeting place for Scottish Nationalists. The police were more visible, ready to stop and question anyone who looked suspicious. More bomb threats were made, shortening the official visit. The Queen was to make a momentary appearance at the ceremony and then leave. There would still be a reception, but without the royal guests, to Mrs. Beaton's despair.

The afternoon of the ceremony, I was alone in the house, waiting for Charles to escort me to the refinery. The Beatons had already left, for they were attending a private luncheon. Dressing slowly, deliberating over what I should wear, I thought of the tartan sash Alastair had given me, but decided that was out of the question. Finally, I slipped on a long dress in my favorite green, fastening the brooch with the MacLeod crest to its shoulder just as the phone rang. I picked up my shoes and ran downstairs with Bruce scampering behind me.

"Ye mauna go tae the refinery gin ye ken wha' gude f' ye," a voice with an especially thick burr hissed through the receiver.

"Hello? What? Who is this?"

"The Red Lion, an' ye heard wha' I said. Ye mauna go."

The caller clicked off and I stood staring into the silent receiver. What was this? A bad joke? The voice had seemed familiar, though it was too muffled and the call too brief for me to be sure. Then the front doorbell rang and I jumped, but I couldn't move and remained where I was staring at the door knob. The bell sounded again and then I saw the door knob being turned slowly . . .

"Fiona, why didn't you answer the door? Are you ready? We should be there in a few minutes."

"Charles! I'm so glad you're here. I don't think I can go."

"Nonsense. You're all dressed. Of course you'll go. People will notice if you're not there."

"There was a phone call just before you arrived, warning me not to go to the refinery."

"Do you know who it was?"

"He said he was the 'Red Lion.' Whoever it was spoke with a thick burr. I think the voice was disguised."

"Well, then, you see? It was some radical. I'm sure half the people in town received that call; you mustn't take it personally. Now, come on or we shall be late."

"I am silly to let it bother me. It's just that the voice seemed so familiar. I'm sure if the man had talked longer, I could have identified him."

"Possibly you have heard the voice before. Didn't MacLeod have some of his friends to the castle? It's probably one of them."

Charles must be right, I thought as we drove to the ceremony. The caller could have been the person . . . Peter Mac-Some-thing-or-Other . . . whom I had overheard castigating Alastair for not wanting to take drastic measures against the English oil companies. Yes, he was the type of person to make prank phone calls. But, still, I was not convinced, for I didn't know Peter's voice well enough to recognize it from a few words. I let it go, for we were arriving at the heavily guarded refinery.

The buildings and grounds had been meticulously searched every day for a week, and no bombs had been detected. Yet there were the sort of dogs used for sniffing explosives standing to one side of the maintenance plant, and I saw three men with metal detectors as we drove by.

Once inside, there was a great crush of people, and as we made our way through them—stopping to chat politely with those we knew—I felt stifled by the tension that hung over all. No one mentioned the threats of violence, but they were hard to forget, with guards at all the doors and windows.

The Queen and her party arrived and—with the guards at attention and drums rolling—she pushed the button that signified the start of the constant flow of oil from the North Sea into the refinery. The photographers' cameras flashed, and then it was over and the reception line was formed. What a lot of fuss for nothing! I thought as I stood in line waiting to shake the royal couple's hands. A look at Charles told me I was alone in this opinion, for he was effusive as we went through the line, clapping people heartily on the back. Finally we reached the Queen and my hand was met with a dry, firm grip. She seemed to smile sincerely as we exchanged a few pleasantries about what a happy day this was for the Free World. Does she really enjoy doing this kind of thing, I wondered, or does she find it as tiresome as I do? Regardless, I made a mental note of her salmon-colored coat and matching large-brimmed hat so I could fulfill Mhari's request.

I moved off to the side of the decorated large room and began chatting with Rosemary. Charles excused himself and walked over to converse with some members of the government. The Queen and Prince Philip made a quiet, polite exit using a side passageway, but the reception continued with the same zest. After a while Charles came over, looking very dignified and taken with himself, and asked me to join him.

"Fiona, I really think you should meet these people, it could be very advantageous."

"Oh, Charles, do let's leave business alone for one day," I replied, laughing.

"It's business that brings us here, and these are the people who could make the difference in achieving that government contract. If you don't greet them, it will look to be a snub. They won't do business with a company that couldn't care less."

"Pooh. A cocktail party can't mean all that much. Besides, I won't desert Rosemary."

"No, dear, you run along." Rosemary smiled sweetly. "We

mustn't upset Mr. Haversham's plans. Anyway, I want to sample some more hors d'oeuvres!" Charles glared at her as he whisked me off.

Finally, it was time to leave and we went readily to collect our coats. I had developed a bad headache from all the talk and wanted nothing more than to lie down for several hours. But that was a vain hope, for Mrs. Beaton was hosting a large dinner party that night. Charles took my arm and we were moving toward the door with the others when a noisy commotion outside seized my attention.

There was a very large crowd yelling and waving placards directly across the road from the buildings. The police had formed a human barricade, but they were having great difficulty containing the crush. One of the signs read, RICH SCOTS OR POOR BRITONS? and I heard chants of "It's Scotland's Oil." Clearly, they were Scottish Nationalists and they probably thought that it was the Queen who was departing. When they finally realized that she had already gone, their shouts grew louder and uglier as they surged toward us. I was terrified by their savagery and clung to Charles, who pushed ahead, displaying neither anger nor fear. Suddenly someone threw a rock. That seemed to be a signal, for other rocks were thrown and even the placards were hurled. One large rock struck me on the shoulder and, startled, I stared into what was now an out-of-control mob. We were in the midst of a political riot. I could look for only a second, for Charles pulled me to my feet and with a superhuman effort got me into the car and then got the car moving recklessly away.

"I'm glad to be out of there; those madmen! What good can come from displays like that! Are you all right, Fiona?"

"I'm not hurt, scared more than anything else. Just get me home, please. I want to lie down." I rested my pounding head against the seat and held my hands together, trying to prevent their trembling. I was badly shaken. I couldn't be sure, but as I had looked at the angry protesters I had caught a brief glimpse of a woman with dark red hair. She had disappeared into the crowd, but I had recognized her. And the more I thought about it, the more positive I became: Ailis Campbell.

My shoulder was not seriously damaged, but I did use it as an excuse to lie low for the next few days. I stayed in the house, not

225

wanting to go anywhere. Charles called frequently, wanting to visit, but I asked Mrs. Beaton to say I was still too shaken to receive visitors. Mrs. Beaton was a more than willing ally, for she had been even more distressed by the incident than I, and insisted on treating me as if I had been permanently crippled by the bruise. I submitted to her ministrations, for I needed the time to think. Rosemary was planning to return to London shortly, and I knew I would have to come to some sort of decision.

I couldn't go on staying at the Beatons' indefinitely, yet I didn't want to go back to Lochinver; I knew I wasn't ready to face Alastair. The apartment seemed best for a while, and Bruce and I moved back in the day Rosemary left for London.

I couldn't forget the hateful scene at the refinery. I had read about it the following day in the papers; some of the demonstrators had been arrested, but I had not seen Ailis's name among them. Perhaps I had been mistaken in thinking I saw her, but I thought not: I would know that face and hair anywhere. And, if Ailis was in Inverness, I was sure that Alastair must have been there, too.

Then a thought occurred to me that alarmed me even further. Something Alastair had said kept haunting me: "I won't be answerable for the consequences if you go to Inverness."

At the time, I had thought he had said that as a last-ditch attempt to keep me at Lochinver Castle. Now I wondered if Alastair had been serious. Had the rock that hit me been the result of a wild throw, or had it been aimed? Had the person throwing it meant to harm me? Did he hope the rock would hit me in the head?

He . . . why did I assume it was a he? I had seen Ailis at that moment; had she been the one to throw the rock? Had she recognized me? She would have known that I would be at the ceremony; was she waiting for me to appear? Had she held the rock ready in her hand, ready to throw the minute she saw me?

Even if that was not the case, I had to face the possibility that this might very well have been another attempt on my life.

TEN

Charles Haversham

I found that I missed Rosemary desperately after she had returned to London, for I was left without a close friend in whom I could confide. I tried talking about Alastair to Charles, but that was nearly impossible. Charles was quick to condemn Alastair as a scoundrel who had married me only for Grimsby Petroleum's money. While I could understand his viewpoint, I really needed someone who could argue both sides dispassionately, someone who could try to make some sense out of what was happening to me.

Charles seized upon only one subject whenever we were together: he wanted me to divorce Alastair. Whenever he mentioned it, I tried to change the subject, but he would always return to it with the persistence of a pack of hounds closing in on a cornered fox. The thought of divorcing Alastair still abhorred me. If I did file, it would be as though I were admitting what was still so hard to believe, that is, that Alastair was trying to kill me. Moreover, Rosemary had made good sense when she had reasoned that Alastair would suspect that I knew he had caused my "accidents" if I started divorce proceedings. Finally, there was the very real possibility that he would oppose the divorce. If he had married me for the money, as Charles insisted, then he would fight to keep it.

I tried to tell all this to Charles, but he brushed my speculations aside as though they were the sort of irrelevances a victim might propose in order to avoid facing the sad truth that she had been used.

"Fiona, Fiona, when will you open your beautiful eyes? You have to admit to yourself that your marriage to MacLeod was a disaster. That's nothing to be ashamed of and, thankfully, it's nothing that can't be corrected. Look, I know this isn't easy. You were an impressionable young widow and lonely in a strange land. MacLeod is not unattractive and he swept you off your feet with his bullying ways. He tricked you so much that you convinced yourself that you were in love. Why can't you admit that to yourself?"

"Charles, it wasn't like that. I *was* in love with Alastair, . . . I'm still in love with him."

"How well did you know him when you married him?"

"Not terribly well, but enough to . . ."

"And you were wrong, weren't you? He set out to marry you. It was premeditated. He set the trap and you . . ."

"I know it certainly seems that way."

"For God's sake, Fiona! I know you. You're a sensible, intelligent woman. Stop letting your emotions run your life. Don't let your imagined love blind you to this awful truth!"

"Oh, Charles."

"Fiona, you know I wouldn't be telling you this if I didn't want to help you. I care for you, very much. I can't let this happen to you, and I can't let you go on this way. Do you want to go back to Lochinver Castle?"

"No, not yet."

"When? A month, two months? Time isn't going to change anything. It's not much of a marriage you're trying to hold on to. You here in Inverness frightened for your life, and MacLeod lurking about the Highlands."

"Oh, you're right, you're right, you're right. I admit I'm hoping for a miracle."

"Fiona, listen to me. You remember I asked you to marry me once. I know . . . I know you dismissed it as an attempt on my part to dissuade you from marrying MacLeod. Part of it was that, it's true. But a large part of it was sincere. I do love you, Fiona, and I still do. Maybe even more now."

"But . . ."

Charles put his hands to my lips. "No. I mean what I say. I certainly don't expect you to come to a decision this very minute. You're too upset and overwrought by what you've been through. But promise me one thing. That you'll think it over. Take all the time you need. I can wait. I know you think of me as a friend and maybe you'll always think of me that way. But I do love you, Fiona, and I'd be a good husband to you and take good care of you. That can sometimes be more valuable than love, and, in time, perhaps you would come to love me a little.

"I won't push you, Fiona, but I do want you to consider very carefully what I've said. You deserve a chance for some happiness."

I promised to think about it, and Charles left. I sighed, and whistled for Bruce, who always hid in the bedroom while Charles visited my apartment.

"You wouldn't be very happy if I married Charles, would you, boy?" As always, when he heard Charles's name mentioned, Bruce growled, drawing his mouth back in a slight snarl. "Well, I don't know if I would be all that happy, either. But I promised him I'd think it, and I will. Poor Charles! He deserves that, at least."

I did think briefly about marrying Charles, for the possibility was not a completely unattractive one. Charles had always been a good friend to me, and I knew that he would continue to take care of me, doing his best to make me happy. I didn't love him, that was true, but what did that matter? I had been deeply in love with Alastair and what had that achieved? I was miserable and scared. If I did divorce and then marry Charles, I would be safe, for Alastair would have no reason to kill me. He would gain nothing then.

Then I thought of Grimsby Petroleum. Our marriage would also benefit the company, for one person would be in control.

Had that occurred to Charles? Was he thinking of this as a business proposition, a merger of sorts? Well, what if he is? I asked myself angrily. It wouldn't be the first time Grimsby Petroleum had influenced my life, and Charles did care for me over and above the company. Even Rosemary, who didn't like Charles, had supposed that he was in love with me.

No, there was something else I had to face. The days were gone when I could be married just for myself and not for what I owned or what I was worth. I had to face the fact that I was a very wealthy woman, and no man would ever be able to forget that, no matter how much he loved me.

Well, then, I thought, the answer is not to marry. Ever again. That way, I'll be, if not happy, at least secure from treasure hunters.

That seemed the best decision, for I was leery of placing complete control of Grimsby Petroleum into Charles's seemingly all-too-eager hands. There were so many things we didn't agree on, and I worried that he might be overly ambitious. He seemed always to be in such a hurry, almost as if he were trying to prove something to someone. Well, I reasoned, considering his background, that's only natural. He's had to work hard for everything he has, and he's probably compensating for his early troubles. Then I laughed bitterly. There you go, Fiona, playing analyst when you aren't able to make sense of even your own life!

Rosemary had written regularly since her return to school, and I knew this new development was a result of her concern at my being alone. Her letters weren't long, often no more than scrawled notes, but I was glad to get them and always replied immediately. Occasionally there was also a letter from Lewis. He reported on the village gossip and gave me news of Mhari and Catriona; yet he never mentioned Alastair, and I never asked him to in my replies. Once, I received a large envelope from Mhari that included letters that had arrived for me at the castle and a note from her saying they were all fine. But though it had been more than a month since I had left Lochinver Castle, I heard no word from Alastair.

I wrote Rosemary about Charles's proposal, saying only that I had agreed to consider it carefully. She wrote back immediately, and, though I knew she didn't like Charles, I was amazed by her vituperativeness.

Fiona, under no circumstances should you marry him! That would be the worst thing you could do! Don't even consider it for a second. I know you're upset and want to escape from the nightmare you're going through, but this is hardly the answer. Please, please, please don't marry that man. If you get desperate, come down here.

More later. Love, Rosemary.

I was touched by this, for it proved what a good friend she was. Perhaps it would be a good idea to go and stay with her for a while in order to get away from all the influences, past and present, that haunted me. I sat down to write her, assuring her that I had no intentions of marrying Charles and to say that I should be glad to visit in a month or so.

When I had finally collected myself enough to tell Charles of my decision never to marry again, he had showed little reaction, saying only that if I ever changed my mind he would be nearby. He asked again about my plans to divorce Alastair, but I replied that I wasn't emotionally ready to take so final a step. For once, he seemed to accept that. I decided he probably thought that, once I was ready to file for a divorce, I would be ready to marry again. The idea of Charles waiting for me made me feel a little guilty, for I knew I would never change my mind; but I realized that he had little time for a life outside of Grimsby and had no desire to search actively for a wife. Waiting for Fiona undoubtedly provided satisfaction for him, for it required no extra output of energy and left all of his time free for the business.

Speaking of which, ever since the ill-fated ceremony at the oil refinery, Charles and I had repeatedly disagreed over Grimsby's affairs. He resented what he considered my pro-Scottish decisions, and I was still hesitant over accepting the British Government's proposal. The more I learned about it the less I liked it. Of course, Charles badgered me every day about it; yet, since I refused to give my approval, he could do nothing. I owned 51 per cent of Grimsby's stock, and this entitled me to the final decision. No matter how much Charles might object, he had to accede to my wishes.

Spring was everywhere in the Highland air with each fresh morning, though the often misty afternoons and definitely chilly evenings combined with the winds that still swept down from the North Sea to make spring's warmth more a state of mind than a state of comfort. In spite of this, however, the sun moved ineluctably farther north in the sky, and the daffodils and forsythias colored the roadsides as the pastel green of determined new leaves helped to soften Inverness' endemic gray harshness. Since Toby's death I had been ambivalent about the coming of spring, for it was then that he had been killed by the motorcyclist. And if that memory wasn't bad enough, I wistfully thought how beautiful Lochinver Castle must now be. I had so looked forward to the spring there, when I could have helped Mhari with her large garden and ridden Fionn through the lush fields.

However, I tried to put such thoughts away and to concentrate on the new life I must lead from now on. I became very involved in Grimsby and spent long, hectic hours at the office. In a way, it was similar to how I had felt when I had returned to Scotland from America determined to pick up the pieces of my life and to make them meaningful. Then my motivation had been Toby's untimely death. I had wanted to work for the company he had reveled in and nourished. Now I was my own motivation. I was going to have a fulfilling life, and I was going to do without anyone else's help.

One rainy morning while I was getting ready to leave for the office, the morning mail arrived. I quickly glanced through the letters and noticed one from Rosemary. It was markedly thick, which surprised me, for most of her letters barely filled a page. I knew I wouldn't have time to read it before I left, so I stuffed it into my purse as I ran out the door.

Once in my office, I had a few minutes before the morning's meeting, and I decided to read Rosemary's letter while I drank the cup of coffee my secretary always had ready for me. I don't think that any one letter has affected me as deeply as that one did, and my coffee grew cold while I read it quickly through once and then just as quickly reread it to make absolutely certain I was not going mad.

Dear Fiona,

What I'm going to tell you is quite shocking and you probably won't believe it, but I assure you that everything checks out. I wouldn't be writing you about this if I weren't positive in my own mind. I would have called, but I'm quite sure it isn't safe.

You know that I've never liked Haversham, though I'll admit that had always been based on instinct. You've insisted that he has his good points, but while I wanted to believe you, I've never been able to trust him.

Your story about his childhood intrigued me, for it was possible that he could have been affected by it. His ambitions could result from being poor, and it is quite possible that he is a decent sort on the inside while maintaining the façade of the ruthless businessman. At any rate, I was intrigued and decided to learn more about his past.

I was spurred into action by your letter announcing his proposal, for if you were actually considering marrying him (and it seemed likely at the time, thank God you've decided not to), I thought you should know all about him. And I considered it my duty as your best friend to find out.

I shan't bore you with details, but by using Daddy's name, I managed to get a look at your company's employee records. I looked Charles up. He was born in Kent on 29 October, 1941. I must say, I wasn't surprised to find out he's a Scorpio. I have a friend who's studied astrology, and she says they're the ones who are quiet on the surface, but watch out for what is going on inside. And that explains why I've never liked him; I'm a Leo and we don't get along with Scorpio men.

Anyway, the records mentioned his mother, Joan Haversham, but there was no mention of a father. That would make sense, for if he had deserted her before the baby was born, she would be hardly likely to put his name on record. Still, it puzzled me a little bit, and the possibility that she hadn't been married occurred to me. That would explain his attitudes even more, for illegitimate children are often ridiculed and looked down on.

Forgive me if I seem to be taking a roundabout method, Fiona, but I want to be sure you understand how I found these things out. It's very important there should be no misunderstanding.

I decided to go to Kent, to the town where Charles was born. I was there yesterday and spent quite a bit of time where Charles was born. I was right; he was illegitimate. His birth was recorded there, but there was nothing of a wedding, and Haversham is the name of his mother's parents.

Well, that much was settled, but I still wanted to find out more. Then, as luck would have it, I struck up a conversation with the woman who runs the office. She's a sweet old lady and I took a chance that she might remember the Havershams.

She did, though she took her time telling me the story. It seems that there was once an army camp stationed on the outskirts of the village, and Joan Haversham had had an affair with one of the officers, a lieutenant. Apparently he had led her down the old garden path and made her all sorts of promises, but when she became pregnant and her father went to confront the man, it turned out he was already married. The old story, and one that happened quite frequently during wartime, I'm afraid. So the poor girl was turned out into the cold by her unfeeling parents and forced to make a life as best she could for herself and her baby.

Then I asked about the father, hoping that the old lady, a Mrs. Boswell, would know his name. Unfortunately, she didn't. She remembered only that the lieutenant was a "gentleman" and that he was "uncommon handsome."

However, Mrs. Boswell did remember Charles as a little boy. He was something of an outcast, and the other children teased him constantly about not having a father. But Charles would insist that he did have a father, who lived in London and who was an extremely wealthy man. His father was a lord, Charles would brag, and one day he would come and take Charles to live with him, and then Charles would be wealthy, too. Of course, nobody in the town believed him, and he was laughed at even more. By the way, I told Mrs. Boswell what Charles is doing now, and she was quite taken aback. As I left, she was shaking her head and muttering to herself that it was true, after all.

That phrase stuck in my head, and last night I got to thinking. What if it were true? Charles's mother could very well have told him who his father was. Maybe Charles went to his father and blackmailed him for money, or used that connection to get where he is now. Then it hit me! Suppose, just suppose, that Charles's father was Tobias Grimsby II, Toby's father. That could explain how he got started working for the Grimsby Corporation in the first place. As a matter of fact, it explains an awful lot about Charles.

All the time, he was working for his half brother, his younger brother. Toby must never have known, for surely he would have told you. Haversham has kept quiet all these years. He must have had a very good reason, for no one would hold it against him; his birth wasn't his fault, after all. No, Haversham has kept quiet all these years for purposes of his own. I told you he deserved to be called "Wick."

I think Charles has taken great pleasure in working for Grimsby Petroleum. He's been in virtual control of the company for the past six years, which has been what he's always wanted. It's been a way of getting back at his father, so to speak. How he must have loathed working for his younger brother! and how glad he must have been when Toby died! You conveniently went back to America and he continued being in charge, doing things the way he wanted. But then you came back. That was bad enough, but then you married Alastair, who threatened everything that Charles had worked for. There was the danger that he could lose control of Grimsby.

Charles must be responsible for the attempts on your life. Haven't you noticed that everything that happened to you took place right after he was at Lochinver? The steps, Mhari's crash . . . you've said that he arrived on the oil rig the morning after your fall, but who's to say he wasn't there all along?

They didn't work, so he tried another tactic: marriage. That way, he'd be sure not to lose Grimsby. But, Fiona, you've said no, and I'm very much afraid that he might try something again.

I realize that I have no concrete evidence for my theory, but after thinking it all out, I'm sure. And I fully intend to get proof that Charles's father and Sir Tobias were one and the same.

But I'm writing to you now, because you must leave Inverness immediately. The best thing is to come to London; you'll be safe here.

I can't stress this enough; your life is in danger from Charles. I'm expecting you. Be careful.

Love, Rosemary

P.S. Remember, don't call me!

I was stunned. As I read the letter again, I realized that most of what Rosemary had written made sense, if one accepted her basic premise. Charles had had the opportunity to cause my "accidents." He knew quite a bit about cars, so it would have been child's play for him to tamper with the Triumph and to do it well enough so that no one would suspect.

Something else was now explained by Rosemary's theory. The strong resemblance between Charles and Toby now made sense. The few times I had commented on it, Charles had seemed shocked, demanding to know what I meant by such a statement. I had not paid much attention then, but now it could mean that Charles had been afraid that I knew or might suspect that he and Toby were brothers. If it were true, it seemed strange that he would have kept it a secret, for Toby had told me how much he had wanted a brother when he was small. (That was one of the things that had brought us closer together. We both were only children and had known the loneliness, and the joys, that could mean.) Toby had liked Charles and would have been delighted if he had known. I remembered how he had talked about Charles, saying what a good businessman he was and of his loyalty to the company. I had looked forward to meeting Charles, though the circumstances of our meeting were not what I would have chosen. I had not met Charles until after Toby's death.

And, yes, it could be possible that Charles was Toby's older brother, for Toby had told me what a rake his father was and that he had always had other women.

Fiona! What are you doing? I screamed at myself. Rosemary has no proof, she said so herself. No, I couldn't believe that Charles had tried to kill me, any more than I had wanted to believe that Alastair had done those things. First it had been my

236

husband. Now it was a man I had considered one of my best friends. Both possibilities seemed equally unacceptable.

I felt confused and angry. Angry at the thought that I must suspect those I loved best, and angry at Rosemary for her theory about Charles. And what did she mean, saying it wasn't safe to use the phone? Was I now supposed to believe that Charles monitored my calls? Really, Rosemary, I thought disgustedly; my phone tapped, indeed!

My thoughts were broken by the telephone's ring. I started at the sharp buzz, and hesitated before answering, but it was only my secretary reminding me that the morning's meeting was starting. I hurriedly folded the letter and stuffed it back into my purse; then I rushed off to the conference room.

That day passed painfully. The hours seemed filled and empty all at once. At last it ended, and I rushed, almost ran, from the office. Charles frequently asked me to dine with him, and this was one night I just couldn't face him. Once at home, I went to bed early, too overcome by Rosemary's accusations to think clearly. I soon fell fast asleep with Bruce curled up in his accustomed place at my feet.

However, I slept only a few hours, waking well before dawn. For the first time in several weeks I had been plagued by nightmares. The last, the familiar one of being atop a cliff, had frightened me so much that I woke to the sound of my own screams. Only to find Bruce licking my face, not Alastair kissing me back to security as had happened other, happier, mornings.

Perhaps it was this that made me so despondent that early morning. So early that there was no sun and the gray mists greeted my rising. I felt alone, more alone than I had ever felt before. The man whom I loved was miles away, my friends . . . ah, yes, my friends. My *friends* advised me—not for the sake of helping me, but to further their own ends. Charles, who hated Alastair, was all too willing to name him a murderer. Rosemary, who had never liked Charles, was now trying to accuse *him* of being a murderer! And what would Mhari say if I asked her opinion? . . . that Lewis was the villain who had sabotaged the Hundred Steps instead of painting them?

I turned all this over and over in my mind as I, half asleep and half hysterical, turned over and over in my bed. The two thoughts that emerged clearest were that Rosemary was a silly alarmist and that Rosemary was the sole cause for my apprehension. Once I had finally cleared the sleep from my eyes for the last time, I saw that it was just five-thirty. Out of sheer maliciousness, I decided to call Rosemary and tell her what I thought of her maidenly maunderings. She answered on the seventh ring.

"What? Fiona . . . no, no! Don't s . . ."

"Oh, really, Rosemary. That phone-tap nonsense is . . ."

"No! Fiona, it's not; it's true." Rosemary was squealing now and, rather than convince me of her sincerity, it served instead to make me really angry.

"Listen here, Miss Detective. There's no reason to write me a letter saying that Charles . . ."

"Shut up, Fiona! I'm right. I know I'm right and if you would just listen to me, I've . . ."

"I will not listen to you. How dare you accuse . . ."

"Oh, Fiona! . . ." Click.

She had hung up on me. Furious, I started to dial back, but couldn't make my finger work fast enough, so that I botched it badly on the first, second, and third tries. I slammed the receiver down. I had told her off, anyway. And felt the better for it. It was about time I stopped letting other people, for their own queer reasons, tell me what to do and what to think.

Pushing myself out of bed and growling at Bruce, who sleepily protested the ungodly hour by rolling over on his back and whimpering, I trudged into the kitchen to put on the kettle. I was still angry enough to grab some chocolate cookies from the icebox and swallow them down with hardly a solid chew. Using my strongest tea, I managed to calm myself down so that within an hour I was in the shower and humming some half-remembered Scottish tune while I arranged my plans for the day.

Then I did the oddest thing. At seven o'clock on the dot, my dress half on, I grabbed the phone and dialed the train station. I can't imagine now what I could have been thinking. Perhaps, in my cranky sleepiness, I had somehow managed to ingest part of Rosemary's warning and therefore had done exactly what she had wanted me to do . . . , get out of Inverness. But as soon as I heard "Inverness Station Information," my real self reasserted herself and I slammed down the phone. Damn Rosemary, I

238

thought. She had made me betray Charles, even if I had only dialed a way out and not actually arranged anything. I kicked at my desk, atop which her letter still lay as I stormed out the door to my office.

"Good morning, Fiona. You look lovely today. What brings you to the office so early?"

It was Charles. I found him sitting pensively in the outer offices looking as dapper and wide awake as if it were noon instead of 8 A.M. The only thing out of the ordinary was that he was wearing an attractive leather jacket over his vest, and not his usual suit jacket.

"Oh, hello, Charles. I wanted to get a good start on some work I should've finished yesterday." There I was, lying just as if I believed Rosemary. I smiled as warmly as I could at him and gestured toward my office.

"Really? On such a gorgeous day? I was thinking about taking it off and just . . . relaxing." He sounded tired and just a little sad. My heart went out to him, and I realized that in all these months of thinking about myself I had selfishly forgotten that Charles was trying to hold me together while at the same time keep Grimsby prospering. I flushed with embarrassment.

"Is that so odd? That hard-working Charles should want to . . . in that quaint American phrase . . . goof off?"

"No, Charles, of course it's not odd. You should have a vacation. I can hold down the fort while you . . ." I looked at him and saw Toby. Somehow, with this inexplicable show of weakness, Charles had transformed himself into a real human being who very much reminded me of that beautiful Englishman I had once loved and married . . . and lost. If this was a new Charles, I liked him very much. Alastair and Rosemary had never really understood Charles Haversham, and maybe they never could. He was that special kind of man that took a lot of getting used to.

Charles got up and walked over to me, smiling shyly. "No, Fiona, just the day. That's all I need. And it's such a fine day for a drive . . . would you, would you like to . . ."

"Go with you?" I finished his awkward invitation for him.

"Just the two of us?" he continued.

"Oh, Charles, I've so much . . ." I let that go and thought

239

again. This was my chance to make up for almost believing Rosemary. "Yes, Charles. I would like that."

"Thank you. By the way, do you like my new jacket?"

"Oh, Charles!" I laughed. Charles had actually come close to preening. "You go on and get the car. I'll be right down."

"Fine. But there's no need to let them know where we're off to. They might want to reach us."

"Of course. But where are we going?"

"I thought north. Along the coast. I thought we might take a look at a new site for a refinery."

"I thought you wanted to take the day off!"

"Well . . . we are."

"Yes, and if everyone took days off like you do, then there'd be no need to ever take a day on." I shook my head. "Okay . . . but then you must promise to buy me an outrageous lunch somewhere very far from oil fields."

He promised and quickly left while I plopped my briefcase on my desk and made sure I wasn't expecting any calls that day that couldn't wait. Absent-mindedly, almost as a reflex, I scribbled a note to my secretary that I was off to some new refinery site and then I dashed out to meet Charles.

As we left the city and rolled along the highway north, I managed to relax. I was enjoying the view. The sun was shining strongly, and the wind-tossed sea sparkled, each wave holding a thousand dancing jewels.

"You are glad to get away for a day, aren't you, Fiona? I must say, though, you're awfully quiet."

"What? Oh, I was just enjoying the scenery. *And* trying very hard not to notice how fast we are going. Honestly, Charles, if you don't slow down on these curves we'll find ourselves in the sea!"

"There's nothing to worry about. There aren't any cars on the road and I'm enjoying having it all to myself. But, if you insist . . ." and Charles slowed the car, to my relief.

"Charles, I don't remember any talk about a new refinery."

"Just north of Wick. There's nothing settled yet; it will depend on our going partners with the government."

"Charles, you know how I feel about that."

"All right. Just sit back and enjoy our holiday. That reminds me; we're low on petrol. There's a station, I'll stop there. I also want to get out of this. It's warmer than I thought."

We stopped, and while the attendant was fueling the car, Charles took off his new jacket, threw it over the seat, and went inside the building. I sat still for a while and then, noticing how carelessly Charles had tossed his coat, I started folding it neatly on the back seat. As I did, some papers fell out of the pocket. I started to replace them, then stopped. One lay face up. On it was typed 5:30 A.M. and then Rosemary's London phone number.

Oh, God, Rosemary had been right! Charles had been monitoring the phone! And now he knew that I . . . Did that mean that Rosemary was also right about . . . ? My hand shook as I stuffed the papers back into his pocket, and, for a moment, I considered getting out of the car and running. But that was ridiculous. I could hardly run all the way back to Inverness, and Charles would certainly catch me before I took two steps. I had no time to think further, for Charles came back to the car and we were once more speeding north.

"Here, I got us some candy bars. I'm afraid there's no really good place to lunch up here, but I'll make it up to you by taking you out to dinner tonight. Fiona, you look a little pale. Anything wrong?"

"I do feel a little faint; perhaps I'm coming down with something. I have been working too hard. Could we turn around and go back?"

"Are you joking? This is our day off. Getting out and walking around in the fresh air is the thing for you. Your problem is that you've been cooped up. Now, eat your candy bar; it'll give you energy."

I munched absent-mindedly and continued to look out to sea, but there was only fear out there now.

"Here we are. Let's get out and I'll show you around. It certainly doesn't look like much now, does it?"

Charles was right. It didn't look like much. It was a desolate area; a few brave clumps of grass forced their way between the rocks, here and there were scattered remains of an unruly civilization—broken bits of beer bottles peppered the ground. Charles explained the advantages of the site. It was removed from everything and no buildings had to be torn down or interfered with. I didn't pay much attention to him, and I wandered over to a grassy plateau. I sat down on a sun-warmed rock and watched the restless blue-black sea pound the rocks far below.

Charles came up behind me, putting his hands on my shoulders. "Fiona, I must confess I had another reason for bringing you here."

"Oh? What was that?" I strove to keep my voice carefree, not daring to turn and look into Charles's face.

Charles remained silent for some moments. When I finally looked up at him, he, too, was staring into the sea. "It is beautiful here, isn't it, Fiona? That's why I wanted to come here, because it's so beautiful. Fiona," he said, turning me so I faced him. "Fiona, I'm going to ask you again to marry me."

"Charles . . ." I began.

"It would be the best thing, for us and for Grimsby Petroleum."

Charles's proposal had caught me off guard, and I replied unthinkingly. "Charles, I told you how I felt. If I can't be married to Alastair, I don't want to be married to anyone. Besides, I'm not sure it would be the best thing for Grimsby; we don't agree on many things, and I can't let you have complete control. . . ." I broke off as the look on Charles's face made me realize the folly of my speech.

"Fiona, I'm asking you for the last time." Charles's grip tightened on my shoulders and I flinched involuntarily, taking a step backward. "Say you'll marry me." Charles's voice had taken on a menacing tone. I took another step backward, pushing him away.

"For the last time, Fiona."

I looked from side to side, realizing just how desolate the area was, just how close I was to the cliffs that dropped straight into the sea. I made a move toward the car, but Charles caught me in his arms, holding me so tightly that I had to bite my lips to keep from crying out.

"You can't get away, and there's no one to help you. We're quite alone." I looked into his face and saw a Charles I didn't know—his mouth twisting into a horrible, sneering laugh, his usually calm eyes glinting with a strange expression I couldn't identify.

"If you won't marry me, then . . ." Charles's words trailed off. I struggled, but to no avail. Charles's grip on me tightened, if that was possible.

"I can't let you go, Fiona. I can't let you get away from here. I know about your call to Rosemary this morning, and I can just imagine what was in that letter she wrote."

"Ch-Charles, you can't think that I . . . that I believe the things she said about you." I lied desperately, ready to say anything. Then, with a sinking heart, I realized that I had just given away Rosemary's accusation of Charles. And now I knew, knew too late, that Rosemary had been right.

"Oh, Fiona. You believe her. It shows in every line of your lovely little face. It won't work, Fiona; you've never been a very good liar. Your face shows your emotions too plainly."

"But, we're good friends, we . . ."

"I was Toby's friend, too. Look what that got him."

"What?"

"Toby's dead and now you will be, too."

"But . . . but Toby . . ."

"I killed Toby, Fiona. My sweet, dear baby brother, though he never knew it. That fool, so idealistic—it was *my* brains that made Grimsby Petroleum. I saw my chance and I took it. I outdid myself that night, getting back to Inverness with time to spare."

"*You* killed Toby?"

"It was a hit and run, all right, but *I* was riding the motorcycle. I had hoped that when you learned your precious Alastair owned the same make, you might think he had done it, but you never made the connection. That might have convinced you to divorce him and marry me. Though, you believed him capable of killing you. It's been so easy, Fiona. You've been so easy."

"Charles, please. This is madness."

"It was a shock to learn that Toby had married you," Charles continued. "I hadn't suspected that. His mother had always kept a tight rein on him, disapproving of all the girls he went out with, breaking off his romances. But it was easy enough to send you back to America, and I didn't consider you a serious threat. Even when you came back, I didn't worry too much. Then you married MacLeod. I saw everything I had worked for slipping

243

away. You were bound to be influenced by that wild Scot. No, you were definitely a thorn in my side and I had to do something."

"Does running Grimsby mean that much to you?" I hardly knew what I was saying, but I wanted to keep him talking. It was my only chance.

"Mean that much? Oh, Fiona!" Charles again laughed in that strange, high-pitched voice. "It means everything. Tobias Grimsby ruined my mother. He promised to marry her and then when she was in trouble, he turned his back on her, leaving her stranded. In all those years he never helped her, never sent her money, never thought about her. He didn't even care to learn if she had had a boy or a girl.

"She hated him and she taught me to hate him. Once, after she died, I went to see him. I ran away from the foster home I was in and traveled all the way to London to his office. You know what he said when I told him who I was? He laughed. He laughed! 'If I supported all my bastards, I'd be a poor man indeed.' He gave me a fiver and shoved me out the door, but I tore the note in half and threw it back in his face. I didn't want his charity, I wanted him to acknowledge me as his son.

"I swore I'd get my revenge. And I have. I killed his son and heir. I'm in control of his company now. *I* run it. Charles Haversham, whom he threw out. Oh, I wish he were still alive, I'd laugh in his face!"

"Oh, Charles, I'm so sorry . . ."

"And you! You, a woman, thwarting my plans. Fiona, I am sorry for this, I do like you, perhaps I even love you in a way. It's a pity you wouldn't marry me. I would have been a good husband."

"Maybe . . ."

"No. It's too late. You'd run to the authorities the first chance you got. No, I don't want to kill you, but it must be done."

"Charles, I wouldn't tell, I promise." I pleaded wildly, willing to say anything if only . . .

"No, Fiona, it's too late. I never really wanted to kill you. I was just trying to scare you. I hoped that you'd believe Alastair was responsible. And you did, you came running to me, but you couldn't take that final step: you couldn't divorce Alastair and marry me. I decided then that I would have to get rid of you; you were getting in the way of my plans. My plans to make Grimsby Petroleum powerful. Poor, dear, silly Fiona."

"Charles, wait. You'll be caught. People will know you've killed me."

"No, they won't. Poor Fiona. She was so upset. She was certain her husband was trying to kill her. She had nothing left to live for. She jumped off a cliff; it was very tragic."

"Rosemary knows! And Lewis . . ."

"I'll find and burn her letter, Fiona; no one will know she wrote it. Rosemary may be suspicious, but she knows how unhappy you were, so she'll go through life feeling guilty, thinking it was her news about me that made you do it. I'm quite safe, Fiona; no one knows we're here. I'm clever, Fiona; I've made sure."

I started to scream and struggle wildly. It was hopeless. There was no one who could hear me or help me. Charles and I were totally alone. I continued to scream louder, shrieking until I thought my throat would break with the effort. I fought, trying to scratch, to bite, pushing with all my strength. But it was no use. I began to weaken and felt myself being pushed backward, one step at a time. My nightmare of the past few months had come true: I could hear the sea pounding, beating upon the slimy rocks below. The noise the waves made filled my ears, drowning out all other sounds, even my own screams.

Then I felt myself being lifted from the ground. I was tired, too tired to fight any more. I relaxed in Charles's arms, unwilling to struggle further. Then I felt an impact as though there was some giant force pushing us, and I felt myself falling . . . falling . . . I made myself faint before I hit the sharp rocks below.

Conclusion

I lay where I had fallen, not daring to move. My eyelids were too heavy to lift, and I relaxed on the cold, hard ground as best I could, waiting for my strength to return. At first, I didn't know where I was, but as I began to hear more clearly, the sound of the crashing waves told me I was still on the cliff where . . . There were many other sounds that I didn't recognize echoing in brisk counterpoint to the rhythmic sea. I forced my eyes open for a second. Strange shapes and flashing lights flickered, but the images were blurred meaninglessly. I retreated thankfully into the darkness.

The shouts grew louder. It's all a dream, I told myself, a nightmare of noise. Soon I will awaken and then . . . and then what? The voices grew louder, clearer . . . I could begin to hear words. And then I knew it truly was a dream, for I could hear Alastair's calling above the rest.

"Here she is! Over here! Bring blankets!"

I felt someone near me, felt myself being lifted, but, try as I could, I could not open my eyes.

"Fiona! Are you all right? Fiona! God! Please be all right!

Fiona!" Alastair was holding me tightly to his chest and I could sense the warmth of his body. I wanted to speak in order to reassure him that I was not hurt. I wanted to tell him how very much I loved him, but it was as if I were surrounded by a fog too thick to penetrate.

Now there were other voices.

"She's alive . . . wrap her in the blankets . . . she must be warm . . . suffering from shock . . . careful!"

Someone scooped me up effortlessly. I felt warm now, and I burrowed deeper into my cozy cocoon. Now I was lying on something flat and softer than where I had been before. Now there was another noise, a loud roar steady and constant and not nearly as pleasant as the sea sound. Alastair was still there, for I could feel his arm encircling me. He was tense. The hand holding mine was clenched and restless. I had to tell him I was all right; I couldn't let him worry so. I summoned all my strength and screamed, opening my mouth as wide as I could. But all I could muster was a whisper so frail that surely he could not have heard.

"Fiona? What is it?" He *had* heard and was bending closer to my face.

"Alastair." I breathed his name.

"I'm here, Fiona. You're safe. Don't try to talk."

"No . . . no. There's so much . . . I have . . . to . . ."

"Nae, darlin'. Later. You can tell me later. All that matters now is that you're all right and that I'm here to take care of you."

I lay back, smiling as Alastair kissed me gently on my forehead. Yes, everything was going to be all right.

I spent the next two days in Inverness Hospital. I had not been seriously injured, but I was suffering from shock, and I was a while in mending.

Alastair was at my side as much as he was allowed to be. We spent all the visitors' hours just holding hands and smiling foolishly at each other. I didn't ask how he had come to rescue me. His presence was explanation enough. On the second afternoon, when I tried to tell Alastair what had happened, he tried to silence me.

"We'll talk about that later, Fiona, when you're stronger. I'm under doctor's orders not to upset you. You'll be telling us soon enough, but, for now, concentrate on getting well."

"But I *am* well, Alastair. I'm just a little tired. But there is one thing I have to know. Alastair, where is Charles?"

Alastair was silent for a few moments, keeping his eyes fixed on the floor. Finally, he looked at me steadily and said quietly, "He's dead, Fiona."

Gradually, painfully, our mutual stories were told and the pieces of the puzzle fell together.

As I had expected, Alastair's pride had prevented him from following me immediately to Inverness. He had been hurt and angered by my insisting on making the trip. Part of that anger had been directed at himself, for he knew he was being unrealistic to expect me to obey him unquestioningly and to accept his statement that he couldn't divulge his reasons for not wanting me to go. That MacLeod stubbornness had prevented Alastair from admitting this aloud to himself and to me, and so he had sat and fumed at Lochinver Castle.

Alastair had known there would be a demonstration at the oil refinery. It had been planned well in advance of the ceremony. He had done his best to prevent it from taking place, but his protests went unheard. He knew that if I went to Inverness, I would be present at the official opening of the refinery and possibly in great danger if there was trouble. Quite naturally, he didn't want me to go. But he had remained silent about the impending demonstration out of loyalty to his fellow Scottish Nationalists.

Alastair had wondered about my behavior in the weeks before I left. At first, he had ascribed it to my feeling guilty about Mhari's accident, thinking that I was still blaming myself for letting her drive that day. But as time had passed, Alastair had realized that it went deeper than that, for I had continued to be withdrawn even after Mhari and Catriona were home and everything was well.

It was then that it had occurred to him that Mhari's was not the first accident and that other things had happened to me. He had realized that I should have been in the Triumph that afternoon instead of Mhari. At first, these had been vague doubts, for Alastair found it hard to believe that the incidents could be connected. That would mean, he had reasoned, that someone wished to harm me—a fact equally hard to believe. However, these doubts became a certainty when Alastair went to talk with Lewis.

Knowing that Lewis and I had become good friends, Alastair had gone to see him in order to determine if Lewis knew why I had left Lochinver. Lewis had been hesitant to talk, for he didn't know how much he could or should tell Alastair. However, he soon realized that the sorrowful and confused man before him was anxious about me out of love and not hate. Then Lewis told him the whole story, tactfully omitting all those obviously now wrong suspicions about Alastair. Lewis explained that I had become panic-stricken and resigned to leaving Lochinver Castle.

Alastair had been worried about my safety then, but still his pride prevented him from coming after me. He felt that I was wrong to leave him, and that I should have turned to him for comfort instead of Lewis. He was angry, and his anxiety increased that anger. However, he instructed Lewis to give him any news of me that he might receive.

Believing that Charles had had my phone tapped, Rosemary had called Lewis immediately after our early-morning conversation. She had been hysterical. Much of what she said had been unintelligible, but Lewis had understood enough to realize that I was in mortal danger at that very moment. He had raced to the castle to fetch Alastair, and they had set out for Inverness within the half hour.

After a mad drive, they had reached the city and gone straight to the apartment, only to find a lonely and morose Bruce. Then they had gone to Grimsby's offices, but I was not there either. No one had seen me all morning. They couldn't find my secretary. Fortunately Alastair saw the note I had left for her on my desk. Realizing what Charles probably intended to do, Alastair had rushed after us, hoping to reach me before it was too late. Lewis went to summon the police.

Alastair had stopped at several petrol stations, finally finding the one where Charles had refueled. The attendants had remembered us, and they told Alastair that a coatless Englishman had said something about sight-seeing. That information had worried Alastair, for it meant that we could be going all the way to John

O' Groats, where there were any number of side roads and lonely passes. However, Alastair had at least obtained a description of Charles's car, and continued to search diligently.

Alastair, driving the Triumph, made excellent time. He soon reached Wick, and was considering going on when he saw a side road. Alastair decided to risk everything and explore it. Reaching the plateau, he had espied Charles's car parked behind some rocks. He got out and looked around, but we were nowhere to be seen. Suddenly he heard my screams and ran toward the cliff.

The rest of Alastair's story was briefly told, but every word was horrible to hear. He had reached us just as Charles was attempting to push me over the cliff. Alastair had lunged at us, tackling Charles about the waist. That had been the impact I had felt. That had been the force that had sent me hurtling. And I had rolled along the cliff edge, fainting for the first time in my life. Alastair then tried to pull Charles away from the cliff edge and wrestle him to the ground, but it had been no use. Charles had fought him wildly with the strength only the mad possess. Finally, as he grabbed for Alastair, his foot slipped and he plunged off the cliff into the sea. His body dashed upon those waiting rocks. Charles met the death he had planned for me.

Lewis and the police had arrived in time to see Charles fall, but not in time to prevent it. They had tried to recover his body, but it was swept out to sea.

I shuddered as Alastair told me this, for I could picture myself falling. I could feel the sharp, piercing blows as I struck the rocks.

"I didn't want to kill him, Fiona, I tried to hold him back, to knock him out, but it was almost as if he wanted . . ."

"No, Alastair. It had to happen that way. Poor Charles!"

"'Poor Charles'? After all that happened?"

"I know. But I still can remember what a good friend he was. Alastair, he had this obsession about Grimsby. He had to control the company, to get back at his father. And that obsession blinded him to all else. It made him insane."

"You must try to forget what's happened. We must both put this behind us."

"Oh, Alastair, can you ever forgive me?"

"Forgive you, darlin'? For what?"

"For running away from you, for not trusting you, for . . . for not loving you enough."

Alastair laughed and drew me close. "Fiona, if you loved me any more than you do you would burst. We've both made mistakes. I've kept things from you, too. I should have told you more about the Scottish Nationalist Party, and not left you to guess and wonder what I was doing."

"I wondered about Ailis, too," I admitted, blushing. "I was afraid you might still be in love with her."

"Aye, she's lovely. And it was tempting, especially when you started behaving peculiarly." Then, seeing my shocked expression, Alastair threw his head back and roared, pleased that he had succeeded in teasing me. Then he kissed me and said, "We're lucky, Fiona, for we've got a chance to start a new life together. A new life in which we will love and share completely."

Alastair was right. I, too, felt as though we were starting over. I realized that although I had loved Alastair passionately, I had not really known his soul. That was why it had been so easy for me to believe him capable of trying to kill me, though part of me had refused to believe that and had fought against it. Still, I had been unable to talk to Alastair about my fears and suspicions. He had been my lover, and not my friend.

In the days that followed, we talked as we had never talked before, and I knew that I would never keep anything from him again. We would, in Alastair's words, love and share completely.

And that is the way it has been ever since.

We are back in Lochinver now, and I am watching the summer transform it into a magical place. The land is growing, and I am growing with it.

I sold my interests in Grimsby Petroleum, not to the British Government, as Charles had wanted, but to a group of Scottish businessmen. Whatever happens with the North Sea oil, if the profits to be realized are large or small, there will now be Scots participating fully in the explorations. It was a painful decision, but necessary. I had to cut off all ties with Grimsby—with its constant reminders of Charles and Toby—if I am to be truly happy in the life I have chosen.

Alastair has refused any money from the sale of the stock, saying that Lochinver must pay its own way, and he is working very hard with Ian to make that happen. Instead, I am investing the money in small Scottish businesses, helping in my own way to revitalize the Highlands, which have been too long a depressed area.

These days are busy days. Alastair is standing for Parliament in the next general election, and I am working and in his campaign. One of my busiest co-workers is Ailis Campbell, or I should say Ailis MacKenzie, for she and Graham were finally married in the spring. I don't know if I shall ever really like Ailis, for I shall always be a little jealous, but I admire her for her devotion to the Scottish Nationalist cause.

Rosemary has hinted that there may soon be another wedding. She is a frequent visitor at Lochinver Castle, yet she spends more time with Lewis than with us. I am delighted, for it is to those two people that I owe my life.

Occasionally, I think of the past and of Toby and of Charles. I can still remember Charles as a friend, in spite of all that happened. I refuse to believe that Charles was truly a cold-blooded murderer and that he really wanted to kill me. In the end, I believe, he was driven to a murderous frenzy by his great need to possess Grimsby Petroleum.

I do not brood upon the past. It is part of me, and I have learned from it. The past is the foundation on which I build my present and my future. Here, here at Lochinver Castle. Mistress of my fate.

S9